PANDEMIC

BY ROBIN COOK

ROBIN COOK

PANDEMIC

MACMILLAN

First published 2018 by G. P. Putnam's Sons,
an imprint of Penguin Random House LLC, New York

First published in the UK 2018 by Macmillan
an imprint of Pan Macmillan
20 New Wharf Road, London N1 9RR
Associated companies throughout the world
www.panmacmillan.com

ISBN 978-1-5098-9293-8

1 3 5 7 9 8 6 4 2

A CIP catalogue record for this book is available from the British Library.

Printed and bound by CPI Group (UK) Ltd, Croydon, CR0 4YY

Visit **www.panmacmillan.com** to read more about all our books
and to buy them. You will also find features, author interviews and
news of any author events, and you can sign up for e-newsletters
so that you're always first to hear about our new releases.

*This book is dedicated to the mystical clairvoyance
that some gifted scientists have, which allows them to look
at data available to all and see diamonds in the rough,
resulting in a scientific quantum leap forward.
Such is the case with Jennifer A. Doudna
and Emmanuelle Marie Charpentier,
who are responsible for the gene-editing technology
CRISPR/CAS9 and its evolving permutations.*

PANDEMIC

On the warm summer day of August 17, 2012, the newly released issue of *Science* magazine contained an article about bacterial immunity with a title so esoteric that late-night talk-show hosts could have used it in their monologues to make fun of scientific gobbledygook. But the article's publication has turned out to be an enormously important biological watershed event, despite the modest prediction offered in its concluding sentence that the mechanisms described therein "could offer considerable potential for gene targeting and genome applications."*

Seldom has there been such an understatement, as the potential has already become a virtual explosion of applications. The *Science* article was the first to introduce the world to a biologically active chimeric molecule called CRISPR/CAS9, which had been engineered from a bacterial immune system that had evolved to counter viral invaders. This extraordinary molecule made up of three easily produced and inexpensive bacterial components can be custom-tailored to seek out and alter genes in plants or animals. All at once, even a high school student armed with

---

* "A Programmable Dual-RNA-Guided DNA Endonuclease in Adaptive Bacterial Immunity" by Martin Jinek, Krzysztof Chylinski, Ines Fondara, Michael Hauer, Jennifer Doudna, and Emmanuelle Charpentier, *Science*, vol. 337, pages 816–21.

readily available low-cost reagents and a little instruction could learn to modify the genetic makeup of living cells, which can pass on the changes to daughter cells. With CRISPR/CAS9, any gene whose sequence is known can be removed, replaced, turned on, or turned off, and all this can be done in the equivalent of someone's garage. It is that easy. Heretofore, such a capability existed only in the futuristic dreams of academic molecular biologists with huge, expensive laboratories at their disposal. In other words, rather suddenly, CRISPR/CAS9 has emerged as an enormously powerful, democratized gene-editing mechanism capable of rewriting the fabric of life, including human life. There is no doubt that this capability will revolutionize medicine, agriculture, and animal husbandry.

But there is a dark side. The ease and availability of this versatile and powerful tool that puts the power of the creator in the hands of so many unregulated players beget as much peril as promise. With so many potential actors involved, the situation is even more worrisome than it was in nuclear physics following the splitting of the atom, because in that instance few people had access to the necessary raw materials and equipment to experiment on their own. With CRISPR/CAS9 the question becomes whether future experimenters, be they world-renowned biologists, well-funded entrepreneurs, or high school students, will be more moved by ethical concerns or by the opportunity to maximize their own individual advantage or by whim, with little or no concern for the consequences to the planet and to all of humanity. *Pandemic* is the story of such danger.

PART 1
WEDNESDAY, APRIL 7, 1:45 P.M.

Twenty-eight-year-old David Zhao took the cloverleaf exit off Interstate 80 onto New Jersey 661, heading south toward a small town called Dover tucked away in the relatively rural northwestern part of the state. He knew the route well, as he had traversed it hundreds upon hundreds of times over the previous five years. With relatively light midday Wednesday traffic it had been a quick trip, accomplished in a little more than an hour. As per usual, he'd picked up the interstate right after crossing the George Washington Bridge. He'd come from the Columbia University Medical Center in upper Manhattan, where he was a Ph.D. student in genetics and bioinformatics at Columbia University's Department of Systems Biology.

David was driving alone, as he usually did when he went to Dover. Also as per usual, it was a command performance by his imperious father, Wei, who, if truth be told, was somewhat of an embarrassment for David. Like a lot of successful Chinese businessmen, Wei had been given the opportunity to ride the crest of the economic miracle that modern

China represented. But now that he'd become a billionaire, he wanted out of the People's Republic of China, as he had come to much prefer the more laissez-faire business environment of the United States. To David, such attitude smacked of treason and offended his sense of pride in his country's extraordinary progress and uninterrupted history.

David's given name was Daquan, but when he was sent by his father to the United States nine years ago to study biotechnology and microbiology at MIT, he needed a Westernized name, as Zhao Daquan wasn't going to suffice, especially in the normal Chinese order of family name first. He needed an American name so as not to confuse people or stand out, as he knew how much discrimination played a role in American society. To solve the problem, he Googled popular boys' names in the United States. Since *David* started with the same two letters as *Daquan* and also had two syllables, the choice was simple. Although it took some time to adjust to the new name, now that he had, he liked it well enough. Still, he was looking forward to reverting to Zhao Daquan when he returned to China. His game plan was to move back there when he finished his Ph.D. the following year and eventually run his father's Chinese biotech and pharmaceutical companies, provided they were still there. David's biggest fear was that his father might succeed in moving the totality of his operations out of the People's Republic.

On the secondary road, David made himself slow down. He knew he had a heavy foot, especially when it came to the new car that his father had given him for his last birthday, a matte-black Lexus LC 500 coupe. David liked the car but wasn't thrilled with it. He had specifically told his father that he wanted a Lamborghini like another Chinese graduate-student friend of his had been given, but in typical fashion, his father had ignored the request. It was similar to how the decision had been made for David to come to the United States for college. David had expressly said that he preferred to stay in Shanghai and attend the Shanghai Jiao Tong University, where his father had gotten his graduate degree in biotechnology. But his father had ignored David's feelings. David doubted that his father ever realized that David might have a different point of view on any subject. In that sense, his father was very old-school, demanding unquestioning filial piety.

Turning off NJ 661, David slowed down even more. He'd already gotten more than his share of speeding tickets in New Jersey, so many that his father had threatened to take away his car. That was the last thing that David wanted, as he enjoyed driving. It was his escape. He was now on a rural road surrounded by fields that were just beginning to turn green, interspersed with stands of leafless forest. Within a few miles the first part of his father's considerable entrepreneurial domain came into view. Dover Valley Hospital was an impressively modern private hospital currently nearing completion after a total renovation. In its previous incarnation, it had been a small, aging community-hospital-cum-nursing-home that David's father had purchased out of bankruptcy. Once Wei owned the property, he began pouring capital into it, to the surprise and delight of the surrounding towns.

David motored past the nearly finished hospital that he knew now had state-of-the-art operating rooms, among its other modern assets. David was well aware that it was his father's intention to turn the institution into a world-class cancer treatment, gene therapy, in vitro fertilization, and transplant center, all to capitalize on the incredible financial opportunities being opened up by CRISPR/CAS9 technology.

Next to the Dover Valley Hospital, another modern architectural complex loomed. This was his father's GeneRx company, which was the American equivalent of his similarly named company in Shanghai. Here were the brains of the American operation manned by a large workforce of mostly Chinese biotech engineers and technicians that David's father had imported, including a considerable bevy of interns coming from all the major biotechnology programs at China's many universities. Surrounding the spacious complex was a high chain-link, razor-wire-topped fence that angled off into the surrounding forest from both sides of a security booth that stood in the middle of the access road, partially hidden by tall evergreens.

Generally, David would merely drive to the gate and expect it to be raised by the duty officer, but since his car was relatively new, he pulled up to the security booth and lowered the window. He was immediately greeted by one of the guards, who addressed him in Mandarin, welcoming him back to GeneRx.

"Are you heading to the main building?" the guard asked.

"No," David said. "I'm going to the Farm for a performance."

The guard laughed, saying it was going to be well attended. He then raised the gate.

Passing the entrance to the multistoried parking lot, David drove around the right side of the main building and into a wooded area. After a few twists and turns, the road opened up into another clearing and another parking area. Beyond it was another matching three-story structure composed of three wings in the form of *T*'s with hip roofs that stuck off the back. There was a sign on the front that read FARM INSTITUTE, but David knew that no one called it that. It was known merely as the Farm.

David knew he was a little late, so he quickly found parking and jogged up to the front entrance. Five minutes later he was in the central wing, changing into clean clothing and donning a mask and surgical cap. He was heading into a sterile area that had air flow going only out, similar to a patient isolation room in a hospital. When he was fully decked out and after being checked by a technician to be certain he was adequately covered, David pushed through swinging doors and entered the sterile area. This was the part of the Farm that housed the cloned and sterile pigs whose genomes had been modified by CRISPR/CAS9. There were multiple other areas for various other types of animals, including goats, sheep, cows, monkeys, dogs, mice, rats, and ferrets. The Farm Institute represented a new direction of "farmaceuticals," with large-molecule, protein-based biopharmaceuticals being manufactured by animals rather than by chemical processes or fermentation vats.

After descending a perfectly white hallway to a door marked INSEM-INATION ROOM, David pushed inside. The square room with a central depressed area was occupied by a large, mostly white pig in heat; a tall individual David could tell was the Farm's head veterinarian; and a handful of his assistants, who were restraining the sow. Grouped around the periphery were some twenty people. David recognized only two, as everyone was in the same getup as he was, their identities obscured beneath face masks, caps, and gowns. The two people he recognized were his father, Wei Zhao, and his father's man Friday, Kang-Dae Ryang. It was easy to recognize his father because of his unique silhouette. For one thing, his father was tall and commanding, at six feet five inches. David himself wasn't too far behind, at six-three. But his father's build was what really stood out, particularly the breadth of his shoulders and the waist that was still remarkably narrow, despite his advancing years. When Wei Zhao was a university student in the seventies, he picked a unique hero, Arnold Schwarzenegger, and became a bodybuilder. Although it had started as a fad, it morphed into a lifelong addiction, and he was still currently doing it in his sixties, albeit in a much-reduced fashion. Kang-Dae's appearance was the exact opposite, thanks to his pencil-thin frame. His gown appeared as if it were hanging on a wire clothes hanger, and his eyes had a beady look that brought to mind a bird of prey.

David made it a point to sidle up to his father to make sure that his presence had been noted. It had, but he could immediately tell Wei wasn't happy that David was later than he had been told to arrive. David had done it on purpose, as he derived a modicum of pleasure from his passive-aggressive behavior.

The veterinarian, who was wearing a headlamp, straightened and motioned to Wei with the syringe he was holding that all was ready. A speculum had been inserted by one of his assistants, so presumably the cervical os was visible.

Wei cleared his throat and spoke first in Mandarin and then in English for all to hear. "Welcome, everyone! We're represented by the whole team, including the CRISPR/CAS9 molecular biologists, the stem-cell experts, the geneticists, the embryologists, and the veterinarians. We're all here to witness this 'one small step for man and one giant leap for mankind.'"

There was a little forced laughter at the reference to the United States' landing on the moon. "As you all know, GeneRx is in great need of an additional revenue stream now that my financing plans for our American operations have been interrupted by Xi Jinping, the Politburo, and the People's Bank of China, all conspiring to generally restrict capital outflow. I am convinced that what we are doing here today will minimize that problem by helping GeneRx be first out of the gate, so we can corner crucial patents and reap the benefits. As you all know, today we are implanting ten cloned bespoke embryos, and we only need one to succeed to ensure our success. Next week we will do the second implantation to answer our crucial question as to which is better: a chimeric pig or a transgenic pig. Thanks to CRISPR/CAS9, we have a choice. Thank you all for pushing ahead so diligently to make this day happen. This will be the first immunologically custom-designed pig. I'm totally confident it will soon lead to hundreds and ultimately thousands of such creations."

After concluding his brief remarks, Wei stepped down into the "pit" to observe firsthand the insemination. Kang-Dae stayed where he was, and David moved next to him. David eyed the man out of the corner of his vision, keeping Wei in sight. He didn't want his father seeing them talking together. In David's estimation, Kang-Dae couldn't have weighed more than eighty pounds, or a bit more than thirty-six kilograms. David attributed the man's rawboned frame to his having grown up in North Korea and been starved as a child. Although he had managed to defect to China thirty-eight years ago, he'd never gained the weight he would have had he not been severely malnourished when young. David had known Kang-Dae for as long as he could remember, as Kang-Dae had been sent by the Communist Party to work for Wei in Wei's very first biotech company, where he proved to be a tireless and totally dedicated worker. He'd even taught himself biology and biotech. Devoid of a family, he ended up living in a tiny room in Wei's home despite Wei's knowing he was essentially a spy. As a consequence of proximity, David and Kang-Dae had become close and remained so, particularly after they both unexpectedly and somewhat unhappily ended up in the United States. There, in New Jersey, they learned that they shared a wish for Wei's American enterprise to fail so they could all return to China.

Leaning toward the Korean man and speaking sotto voce, David said: "Did you do what I suggested?"

"Yes," Kang-Dae said. He was a man of few words.

"Once or several times?" David asked. As Wei's trusted aide, Kang-Dae had unparalleled access to the entire complex. He still lived at Wei's nearby private estate. He was more like an appendage than an aide.

"Three times, like you suggested," Kang-Dae said. "I put it in the drinking water. Will it work?"

"There's no way to know for sure," David said. "This whole project is breaking new ground for all of us. But it was definitely toxic to human kidney cells in tissue culture, so if I had to guess, I'd say it is going to work very well—maybe too well!"

PART 2
SEVEN MONTHS LATER . . .
MONDAY, NOVEMBER 5, 9:10 A.M.

"Wait! Hold on!" Carol called out. She'd just entered the subway station at 45th Street in Sunset Park, Brooklyn, to see that the R train was already there. To her shock, it had arrived early, something New Yorkers did not expect the subway to do. Holding on tightly to her new miniature Gucci backpack, Carol started to run. It wasn't easy, for reasons that had less to do with her attire, which was one of her favorite dresses and relatively high heels, than with her physical stamina. Any running was a feat that, until recently, she hadn't been able to accomplish for more than a year. As she ran, she frantically waved her free hand in the hopes of catching the conductor's attention to keep the doors ajar.

As out of shape as she was, the effort was Herculean for Carol, and as she leaped onto the train she was seriously out of breath. She could also feel her heart pounding in her chest, which gave her a touch of concern, but she trusted it would soon subside, and it quickly did. Over the last month she'd been religious in her trips to the gym and was now up to twenty minutes every other day on the treadmill, which she considered fantastic progress. If someone had predicted four months ago that she'd be doing that much exercise at this point in her life, she would have considered them certifiably crazy. Yet, needless to say, she was thrilled. In many ways, being able to run again was like being reborn.

No sooner had Carol gotten on the subway than the doors slid closed, and the train lurched forward in the direction of Manhattan. To keep her balance, Carol grabbed one of the upright poles that ran from floor to ceiling and glanced around for an appropriate seat. Since it was only the sixth stop from the train's origin at 95th Street in Bay Ridge, and since it was now 9:11 and hence mostly after the morning rush hour, there were plenty of openings. But as an experienced subway rider, she knew that certain seats were better than others. Being hassled on the subway was not an infrequent event, and a bit of attention to detail was worth the effort. She quickly spied an auspicious spot only ten feet away.

As soon as the train reached its desired speed, Carol made her way to the seat she had her eye on. There were no immediate neighbors. The closest people, each an empty seat away, were an elderly, well-dressed African American man and an attractive white woman who Carol guessed was close to her own age of twenty-eight. The slender woman impressed Carol with her style and the quality of her casual but elegant clothes. She had a haircut not too dissimilar from Carol's, with a dark-brown-base undercut that was mostly covered by a bleached-blond combover. It made Carol wonder if they went to the same hairdresser. As Carol sat down she exchanged a quick glance and smile with the woman. It was a part of New York that Carol loved. You never knew who you might see. Life here was so much more interesting than it was in the boonies of New Jersey where she'd grown up. There people became set in their ways as teenagers and never tried anything new and exciting.

Making herself comfortable, as she had a long subway ride ahead of her, Carol pulled her iPhone out of her backpack to go over the disturbing texts she'd been exchanging of late with Helen, the woman she had expected to marry if and when Carol's serious health problems had been put behind them. The sad irony was that the health problems were almost resolved, whereas the relationship had been challenged and had taken a turn for the worse, so much so that Carol had recently moved from their shared apartment in Borough Park, Brooklyn, to her own studio in Sunset Park. It had all happened rather suddenly. Almost three months ago, while Carol had been in the hospital for her life-saving operation, Helen had invited a dear old high school boyfriend, John Carver, to stay with her, as he happened to be in New York and was in need of an apartment. She'd been looking for emotional support, someone to comfort her while she battled the fear that Carol might die, but then the unexpected had happened.

Between the trying emotional circumstances and their close proximity, Helen and John's old romantic relationship reawakened. When it had become clear that Carol was going to live, Helen had hoped she would be understanding and would embrace John as a permanent third party in their relationship.

Although Carol was initially dismayed and shocked, her desperate need for love and acceptance after the stress of her hospitalization and near death inspired her to give the unconventional arrangement a good try over several months. But it wasn't for her. At age thirteen she'd come to accept her sexual preference and adjusted, and she had just become more certain as the years had gone by.

Rereading all the texts and reexperiencing the emotion they represented didn't help Carol's mind-set. It also made her look at the tattoo she had got together with Helen six months ago. It was hard for her to ignore, since it was on the under surface of her right forearm. The image was of a puzzle piece next to a matching image of the puzzle piece's supposed origin. Both were drawn in perspective to make them look all the more real, and the base of the origin was done in a rainbow of colors. Helen's name was on the puzzle piece, as Carol's was on Helen's tattoo. Carol had always loved the tattoo and had been proud of it until now, but her current goal on this trip was to return to the tattoo parlor in Midtown Manhattan where they had gotten the ink and have something done to erase the painful reminder of all that had gone wrong between them. Carol didn't know what the options might be but assumed the tattoo artist would have some ideas. Besides, the trip gave her something to do, as she still had not gone back to her career in advertising. That wasn't going to happen for another month. It had been a deal she'd made with her doctor.

As Carol's train made its way north through Brooklyn, people boarded at each of the many stations, with far fewer people getting off. By the time they were approaching the tunnel to Manhattan, the train was almost as packed as if it were rush hour. It was then that Carol got the first disturbing symptom—a shudder-inducing chill, as if a blast of arctic air had wafted through the subway car. It came on so suddenly that Carol instinctively looked around to see if other people had experienced it, but it was immediately apparent that it had come from within her own body. Her first instinct was to feel her pulse. With relief, she determined it was entirely normal. For a moment she held her breath, wondering if the unpleasant sensation would return. It didn't, at least not at first.

Instead she felt a sense of weakness come over her, as if she might have trouble standing up if she tried.

Still holding her mobile phone, Carol checked to see if she had a strong signal. She did, and she contemplated calling her doctor out in New Jersey. But she hesitated, wondering exactly what she would say. Sudden weakness hardly seemed like an appropriate symptom to tell a doctor. It was much too vague. She was certain he would tell her to call back if it didn't go away or if the chill returned. She decided to wait as she raised her internal antennae to seek out any abnormal sensations. She looked around at the faces she could see. No one was paying her any heed, as everyone was pressed together cheek to jowl.

As the train entered Manhattan, Carol began to relax a degree. There was still the sense of weakness, but it hadn't worsened, and although she got several more chills, they were nothing like the first. They were just enough to let her know she had probably developed a slight fever. When the train stopped at Canal Street, she thought about getting off but was afraid to try to stand up. If she were to fall, it would be much too embarrassing. She felt the same at Prince Street, and then things went downhill. She began to experience difficulty getting her breath, which worsened quickly. By Union Square station, where there was to be a mass exit and mass boarding, she was beginning to feel desperate. She needed air, but her legs seemed not to want to respond.

As the train's doors opened, her phone slipped from her grasp and fell to the floor. In the blink of an eye it was snapped up by a scruffy sort who had been eyeing Carol's behavior. The second he had the phone he melted into the people departing the packed car. Carol tried to call out that she needed help, but no words emerged as she attempted to breathe. A bit of froth appeared at the corners of her mouth. Pulling her legs under her, she marshaled her remaining strength and tried to stand, but as soon as she pushed off the seat, she collapsed, falling against the legs of the people standing immediately adjacent to the bench seat she had been sitting on. People tried to move to give her more room, but there was no place to go. One person tried to arrest her fall but couldn't, as Carol was like a dead weight. Mercifully, she lost consciousness as she slumped like a rag doll, partially propped up against the legs of fellow riders.

As quickly as her phone had disappeared, it was now time for her Gucci backpack to follow suit. Several of the other passengers tried to grab the offending individual, who also departed before the doors closed, but their attention was quickly redirected at Carol, who was twitching uncontrollably and turning blue. It was obvious to everyone that she was desperately ill and struggling for air. Nine-one-one was dialed on multiple phones. As the train lurched forward, another knowledgeable passenger notified the conductor. She came pushing through the crowd as she communicated the bad news to the engineer. As the conductor reached Carol, the intercom sprang to life to announce that a sick passenger was on the train and the train would be stopping at the upcoming 23rd Street station for an indeterminate amount of time. There were a few audible groans. It was a problem that happened far too often on the NYC subway system, inconveniencing thousands upon thousands of passengers who were not sick.

The gravity of Carol's condition was immediately apparent to the conductor, who was confused as to what she should do. With almost no first-aid training other than CPR, which didn't seem to be indicated, since Carol had a pulse and was breathing, she felt helpless. It was quickly apparent to everyone present that there was no good Samaritan with medical training available. Meanwhile, up in the first car, the engineer alerted the rail control center to the emergency and was assured an EMT team was being dispatched to the station.

Once the train was at 23rd Street, it took more than twenty minutes for masked EMT workers to arrive. Many riders had departed the train by then, seeking other transportation, and so the paramedics had a relatively clear path to Carol. What they found was a livid patient with an undetectable heart rate and blood pressure who was barely breathing, if at all, and had lost control of her bladder. After putting a mask on the patient and attaching her to an oxygen source, they quickly lifted her onto a gurney. They then whisked her off the train, up to the street, and into the waiting ambulance.

With the siren blaring, they rapidly weaved their way across town to pull up to the ER unloading dock at Bellevue Hospital. As they unloaded her from the ambulance, a triage nurse corroborated that there was no heartbeat. One of the EMTs leaped up onto the gurney as the others rapidly propelled it into the depths of the Emergency Department and ultimately into one of the trauma rooms, calling out a cardiac arrest in the process. This unleashed a resuscitation team poised for such an emergency, which included a medical resident, a nurse practitioner, and a resident in anesthesia. With the history of breathing difficulty obtained from fellow subway passengers, the patient was intubated and given positive pressure. The assisted respiration required a shocking amount of pressure, suggesting the lungs were possibly consolidated, meaning ventilation was impossible.

With no heartbeat and no ventilation, Carol was declared dead on arrival at 10:23 and covered with a sheet. The only trouble was that no one knew her name was Carol. When the ER clerk called the NYC Medical Examiner's Office, she gave the deceased the temporary moniker of Jane Doe, explaining that there was no identification and the patient was unaccompanied. At that point, Carol's gurney was unceremoniously parked in a corner to await the medical examiner's van. Under the white sheet, she was still dressed in her finery, and the endotracheal tube still protruded from her mouth.

1

By 10:30 in the morning all eight autopsy tables at New York City's Office of the Chief Medical Examiner, known colloquially as the OCME, were in use, as the team tried to catch up with demand. Over the weekend there had been a backup of ten bodies that had not been considered forensic emergencies and had been left for Monday morning. Besides those ten, six new cases had come in between late Sunday afternoon and early that morning. Table #1, the table farthest from the stainless-steel sinks, had seen the most action. This was the table favored by Dr. Jack Stapleton. Since he was almost always the first doctor in the "pit" in the morning, he got to choose his station, and he always told Vinnie Ammendola, the mortuary tech with whom he usually teamed, to nab it. Situated at the periphery, it was a little bit separate from the main commotion in the autopsy room when all the tables were in use. At that time Jack was already starting his third case. Most of the other tables were still on their first.

"So!" Jack said, straightening up. He had just carefully shaved away the blood-soaked, matted hair from the right side of the victim's head.

He had been very careful not to distort the wound he wished to expose. What was now obvious was a completely circular dark-red-to-black lesion an inch or two above the woman's right ear, surrounded by a narrow circular abrasion. The patient was on her back, with her head rotated to the left and propped up on a wooden block. She was naked and so pale she could have been mistaken for a wax-museum model.

"Is the entrance wound round or oval?" Jack liked a didactic style and frequently used it even when other people weren't listening, as often happened when he was working with Vinnie. Vinnie had a habit of zoning out on occasion. But this morning Jack had an attentive audience. Lieutenant Detective Lou Soldano, an old friend of Jack and Jack's wife, Laurie, had shown up. Over the years Lou had come to truly appreciate the enormous benefits forensic pathology could provide to law enforcement, particularly when it came to homicide investigation, which was his specialty. Whenever there was a case that Lou thought could be helped by forensics, he made it a point to observe the autopsy. Although there hadn't been any such cases for a number of months, that morning there had been three.

"I'd say circular," Lou said. Lou was standing across from Jack on the patient's left side. Also on that side was Vinnie. Next to Jack was a second mortuary tech, Carlos Sanchez, who had been newly hired by the OCME and was now at the very beginning of his orientation and training. As one of the more experienced techs, Vinnie generally broke in newbies by having them work closely with him. Jack was accustomed to the routine and usually didn't mind, provided it didn't slow him down too much. Jack was one of those people who didn't like to waste time and had little patience for incompetence. So far, he wasn't all that impressed with Carlos. It wasn't anything specific, more an attitude thing, as if the man wasn't all that interested.

"I agree," Jack said. "Vinnie?"

"Circular," Vinnie said, rolling his eyes. Vinnie and Jack had worked with each other so many times over so many years that they could anticipate each other. Vinnie knew that the tone of voice Jack had used strongly suggested he was about to start a "teaching" session, which invariably meant the autopsy would end up taking considerably longer than otherwise, keeping Vinnie away from the coffee break he always took after the third case was over. Vinnie was a coffee addict and his last cup had been just after seven that morning.

"Mr. Sanchez?" Jack asked, ignoring Vinnie's mild acting out.

"Huh?" Carlos blurted.

Jack turned to look into the eyes of the new hire, just visible through the man's plastic face shield. "Are we keeping you from some other, more interesting engagement, Mr. Sanchez?" he asked sarcastically, but then let it go. He turned back to Lou. "It is definitely circular, meaning the bullet entered perpendicular to the plane of the skull. More apropos, it is certainly not what is described as stellate or jagged. Now, do you see any stippling around the periphery of the wound?" The little red dots in the skin that sometimes surrounded gunshot wounds resulted from gunpowder residue emerging from a gun barrel along with the bullet.

"I don't see that much except on the ear," Lou said, trying to be optimistic.

"There is a bit on the ear and also some on the neck," Jack said, pointing. "Obviously the full head of hair absorbed most of it."

"I don't think I'm going to like where you're going with all this," Lou said. The victim was the wife of one of Lou's detective colleagues who also worked out of the NYPD's Homicide Division.

Jack nodded. There was no doubt that Lou had become quite forensically knowledgeable over the years of their friendship. "There's more. Let's use a wooden dowel to align this entrance wound above the right ear with the exit wound below the left mandible."

Vinnie handed Jack the wooden rod he had leaned against the autopsy table. Grasping it at both ends, Jack held it so that it rested on the crown of the patient's head but lined up with the two wounds.

Lou reluctantly agreed. "I'm getting the picture: The pathway of the bullet is definitely downward."

"I'm sorry to be the bearer of bad news," Jack offered, hearing the disappointment in his friend's voice. "Unfortunately, what we see here is not a contact wound. My guess at this point would be that the gun barrel had to have been about two feet away and maybe as much as thirty inches. And the trajectory was definitely oriented caudally. Are you aware of the statistics about this?"

"Not exactly," Lou said. "But I know it's not what I was hoping. Jesus, I've known this guy for more than twenty years. I've even had dinner in their home out in Queens a dozen times, especially after I got divorced. They had their problems, like all couples. But hell! They have two grown kids."

"Ninety percent or more of small-arms suicides are contact wounds, meaning the barrel of the gun is up against the skull when discharged. In only about five percent of suicides is the bullet path downward, and an even smaller percentage where it's directed from the back to the front, both of which we see here."

"So you don't think this was a suicide?" Lou asked, almost plaintively.

Jack shook his head.

"Can we get on with this freakin' autopsy," Vinnie complained.

Jack flashed a dirty look at his favorite mortuary tech. Vinnie ignored it. "I'm having caffeine withdrawal."

"Was there a suicide note?" Jack asked, returning his attention to Lou.

"Clutched in her left hand," Lou said with a nod. "One of Walter's service automatics was in her right hand. She was lying on their bed on her back. It was a mess."

"And he had called you?" Jack said.

"Yeah," Lou said. "We'd been together most of the evening after being called out on that first autopsy we did. Walter found her dead when he got home, or so he said. I was the one who put in the nine-one-one call as I was leaving my apartment on my way over to see him. I got there before anyone else, and the man was beside himself. It was god-awful. Not that I haven't seen worse."

"Well, we'll have to see how it plays out," Jack said. "Maybe there was a third party involved. But I certainly will not be signing this out as a suicide. I'm definitely thinking homicide. But let's do the autopsy and go from there."

"Hallelujah," Vinnie said, making a rapid sign of the cross in the air in appreciation.

"Let's not be blasphemous," Jack chided sardonically.

"You should talk," Vinnie scoffed. More than anyone at the OCME, Vinnie knew just how irreverent Jack Stapleton could be. Jack was not a religious man after his first wife and two young daughters had been killed in a commuter plane crash. He couldn't imagine a Christian God would let such a terrible thing happen.

The postmortem went quickly. Other than a number of uterine fibroids, the woman's general health had been excellent and there was no pathology. The part of the autopsy that took the longest came after Vinnie had shown Carlos how to remove the skull cap. With appropriate exposure, Jack had carefully followed the bullet's transit through the brain, where it had wreaked complete havoc. While Jack was busy, Vinnie exposed the underside of the skull cap to photograph the beveled edges of the inner aspect of the entrance wound.

When Jack's third autopsy was complete, he left Vinnie and Carlos to clean up and return the cadaver to the walk-in cooler. Although Lou usually departed as soon as the main part of the autopsy was over, on this occasion he stayed until the bitter end. Jack sensed he was reluctant to head back to his lonely apartment in SoHo. The implication was that he needed to talk more about the disturbing autopsy results, even though he was plainly exhausted from having been up all night.

After changing out of their autopsy gear, Jack took Lou up to the so-called lunchroom on the second floor, which wasn't much with its blue-painted concrete-block walls, cheap molded-plastic furniture, and handful of vending machines. For a modern medical examiner's office with a staff of highly trained, world-class forensic pathologists, it was pathetic. But there was a light at the end of the tunnel. A brand-new high-rise NYC medical examiner's building had been constructed on 26th Street, four blocks south of the sad, existing six-story structure that had been built almost a century ago at 30th Street and First Avenue. Most of the Manhattan office's hundreds of employees had already moved to the palatial new location. Those who had yet to go were the toxicologists and the entire bevy of MEs. The problem was that the new building did not have an autopsy room. A new state-of-the-art autopsy facility was still in the planning stages, to be built as a separate structure next to the new high-rise. Until it was operational, Jack and his colleagues had to remain in the old, outdated structure.

"Knowing the choices, what can I get you?" Jack asked. He regarded his friend of almost twenty years. As his name clearly suggested, Lou was distinctly southern Italian, with thick, reasonably long, mostly dark hair and equally dark eyes and decidedly olive skin. A handsome, heavy-featured man of medium height and musculature, with a girth that suggested too much pasta and not enough exercise. As usual, he was wearing a dark blue suit that didn't appear to have been pressed in the previous year. His rumpled white dress shirt was open at the collar and his gravy-stained silk tie was loosened and appeared never to have been untied, but rather slipped over the head at the end of each and every day.

The comparison with Jack was stark, especially when the two were standing right next to each other as they were now. Jack's hair was a light brown, cut moderately short, with a blush of gray over his temples. His eyes were the color of maple syrup and his complexion suggested he had a slight tan even when he hadn't been in the sun for months. At six feet two inches tall, with an athletic build from bike riding and street basketball, he seemed to tower over Lou, whose habit was to hunch over as if his head were far too heavy.

"I don't know," Lou admitted. He was having trouble making up his mind.

"How about a water," Jack suggested. He knew the last thing Lou needed was more coffee. What he really needed was sleep.

"Yeah, water's fine," Lou said.

Jack got two waters and sat down across from Lou.

"You'll let me know what toxicology shows on the second case," Lou said.

"Absolutely," Jack said. "As soon as I know." All three cases that Lou had come in to watch that morning involved the NYC Police Department. The one Lou was currently referring to was a "death in custody" case. During the autopsy Jack had been able to show Lou that the prisoner's hyoid bone had been fractured, which was a clear demonstration that a lethal choke hold had been used. It had happened during an arrest. The question now was whether the force was justified or whether it was excessive. The neighborhood where it had happened was up in arms and wanted answers.

Lou was also awaiting final word on the first case he had watched Jack handle that morning. It, too, was an arrest that had gone bad, resulting in a shootout with the victim holed up in his car, where he was hit four times. Several bystanders claimed that the victim had yelled "enough" and had stopped firing, yet still the police shot him. Once again it was a potential PR nightmare for the police department, and a tragedy if it proved to be true. To get answers, Jack had painstakingly tracked all four bullets in the man's body and now wanted to re-create the scene in the special laboratory in the new high-rise building to figure out exactly what had happened and when.

"It's been an interesting morning," Jack said. "I'm especially sorry that I couldn't be more help for your buddy. Probably the case is going to turn on the suicide note and whether it's authentic. Divorce isn't fun, but it is a lot better than homicide, if that's what the case turns out to be."

"Enough about me and my problems," Lou said with a wave of dismissal. "What's up at the Stapleton-Montgomery household these days?

I haven't talked to you or Laur for ages." Lou had met Laurie Montgomery, Jack's wife, before Jack had been hired by the NYC OCME. Lou and Laurie had even briefly dated until they both sensed it wasn't to be and became fast friends instead. When Jack came on the scene, Lou had been his advocate. *Laur* had been the name one of Lou's daughters had used when she'd first met Laurie, and, thinking it cute, Lou had adopted it as well.

"Please," Jack said. "Let's not go there."

"Uh-oh." Lou leaned forward over the table. "Knowing you as I do, I don't like the sound of this. What's up?"

"I don't know if I want to get into it," Jack told him.

"If you don't talk to me, who are you going to talk to?" Lou arched a brow. "I love both you guys."

Jack nodded. Lou was right. He was the only person Jack could talk to about what was going on. The question was whether he wanted to talk at all. Ever since the plane crash that annihilated his first family more than twenty-five years ago, Jack had more difficulty than the typical male in talking about emotional issues. When problems arose, he much preferred to work harder and play harder, which meant more hours at the OCME and more hours playing evening basketball. But even he knew such a strategy had the major drawback of not contributing to a possible solution. It was like sweeping dust under a rug or sticking your head in the sand.

"Whatever it is, it has to get solved," Lou said. "Listen. You and Laurie are my last holdout for belief in the possibility of marital bliss, especially with this new possible homicide disaster with my buddy Walter. One of the reasons I haven't been in touch with you two over the last month or so is that I have met a new woman, and I'm actually toying with the idea of tying the knot once again."

"Congratulations, my friend." Jack's tone didn't hold a lot of enthusiasm.

"I hear the reservation in your voice," Lou said. "Come on! Talk to me. Does it have something to do with Laur's becoming the chief here at the OCME?"

Two months ago, Dr. Harold Bingham, the chief medical examiner, had passed away following a heart attack, and an ad hoc NYC search committee had recommended that Dr. Laurie Montgomery take over the reins. The offer had surprised both Jack and Laurie, but particularly Jack, especially after Laurie had accepted. Jack had always hated what he called the bureaucratic bull crap that was a necessary adjunct to being a medical examiner, having little patience for kowtowing to powers-that-be in any form or fashion. It had taken years for the OCME to establish a degree of political independence, particularly from the police or the people who controlled the police, so as to become an unbiased voice for the dead. The importance of such independence was obvious from the three autopsies Jack had done that very morning. All too often in the distant past, the mayor or the police commissioner would tell the medical examiner what he was to find on his autopsies. Jack prided himself on his ability not to let the opinions of others influence him. But with his wife as chief and the line between his personal and professional lives suddenly blurring, his hard-won impartiality had taken on a whole new complication.

"I can tell you this," Jack said. "I was shocked when she took the job. Between you and me, she's not having all that much fun. Not only is she now beholden to some degree to her bosses, meaning the mayor and the Commissioner of Health, she rarely gets to do what she does and likes best—namely, forensic pathology. Those two politicos have her running ragged just to maintain funding. She doesn't like confrontation, nor is she good at it, thanks to her autocratic cardiac surgeon father, who tortured her when she was a teenager."

"So is she bringing home her frustrations and taking them out on you?" Lou asked.

"Well, you know Laurie. Whenever she does something, she does it one hundred and ten percent. She's the boss now both here and at home."

"I'm sorry to hear it," Lou said. "Have you tried to talk with her about it all?"

Suddenly Jack put down his water with such force on the table that Lou started, spilling some of his own. Jack then threw up his hands and shook his head in disbelief. "I don't believe myself," he admitted. "I don't know why I'm even saying all this."

"I think it's pretty obvious," Lou said. "It's bothering the hell out of you. I can tell."

"No, it's not," Jack snapped. "Oh, it's bothering me some, especially when Laurie has been trying to dictate how much basketball I should be playing or telling me I shouldn't be riding my new Trek road bike to and from work. But her bringing her CEO problems home isn't the issue that's driving me up the wall. Laurie is a big girl, and I'm a big boy. It's Emma who's turned me into a basket case."

"Oh, no," Lou said. "What's with Emma?" It had been a while since he'd seen Jack and Laurie's daughter, who'd just turned three.

"Two weeks ago our pediatrician tentatively diagnosed her with autism."

"Good God," Lou said.

"We've known something has not been right, but we didn't want to hear it was autism. She'd been doing fine with her babbling and relating to us and JJ but then started going backward."

"I hate to admit to my ignorance, but I'm not all that sure what autism is. I've heard about it, but I don't know anyone whose kids have it."

"You're not alone," Jack said. "It's mysterious. It can cause difficulties for the kid in terms of social interaction and communication. It's not even a specific diagnosis, as far as I'm concerned. It's a spectrum thing, with some kids seriously afflicted and others not so much. Even the so-called experts have no idea of the specific underlying pathology."

"What causes it?"

"There again, nobody really knows." Jack shook his head. "They talk about environmental factors, genes, and epigenetic factors. It could be some mysterious combination of all three."

"What the hell are 'epigenetic factors'? You doctors love to make us normal people feel like idiots."

"Sorry," Jack said. "Epigenetic factors refer to inheritable characteristics that don't depend on the DNA sequence of a gene."

"Sorry I asked," Lou said. "Is there any treatment for autism?"

"Not really. There's a range of behavioral interventions and special-education programs that have some promise but not a lot of evidence-based results. The uncertainty of it all is what's driving me bananas."

"How is Laur taking it?"

"In some ways she's doing better than I, in that she's taken it on as an intellectual challenge, willing to read everything and anything as the way to deal with it. I'm the opposite. I get almost immediately fed up with the vagueness and wordiness of it all and want to rail against the gods. It's my surgical personality. But the downside for Laurie is her feeling of guilt. She keeps beating herself up about not having taken a maternity leave sooner, thinking that all the weird chemicals we're exposed to around here could have played a role."

"Has that been proven to cause it?"

"No, of course not," Jack said.

"Then she shouldn't blame herself," Lou pointed out.

"Yeah, well, you tell her that," Jack said. "I've been saying the same thing until I'm blue in the face. Besides, I have my own struggles with guilt."

"How can it be your fault?"

"I'm a total jinx on kids," Jack said. "You know my daughters from my first marriage were killed in a plane crash, but did you know they were on the plane to begin with because they were on the way back from visiting me when I was training in Chicago? And look at JJ. The poor kid had neuroblastoma as a baby. I wouldn't want to be my kid."

"I never thought of you as superstitious," Lou said.

"I didn't, either," Jack said. "But it's hard to argue with the facts."

"Talking about JJ, how is he doing?"

"Terrific," Jack said. "He's the bright light in all this."

"How old is he now?"

"Eight and a half," Jack said. "He's in the third grade. No sign of a recurrence of his tumor, and you should see him dribble a basketball. The kid's a natural."

"Does he get along with Emma?"

"He does. He has the patience of a saint despite Emma's retrogression. I wish Laurie's mother, Dorothy, was half as cooperative and understanding."

"What's with Laur's mother? Is she making things worse?"

"Inestimably worse. If it weren't for her having invited herself to move in during this trying time, I might not be such a wreck. And it's not just me. She's driving our live-in nanny just as crazy. You remember Caitlin O'Connell, don't you? We were lucky to find her after JJ's kidnapping."

"That, I'll never forget. Seems like yesterday."

"Well, she confided in me that she's thinking of moving out if Dorothy stays. I've tried to talk to Laurie about it, but Laurie has always had trouble dealing with her parents, her father especially, but her mother, too."

"What's the mother doing that's so bad?"

"She's the one who's been critical of Laurie not taking a maternity leave as soon as she knew she was pregnant, and she won't drop it. Plus, she's a conspiracy theorist of sorts and continues to insist that Laurie and I are to blame for letting Emma get the MMR vaccine."

"Wait a minute," Lou said. "Now, that's something I have heard about. Don't they think the MMR vaccine causes autism? Did I read that someplace?"

"That was years ago, when there was a medical-journal article that said so," Jack snapped. "But the study was totally disproved as bogus, and the medical journal that published the article retracted it. Simply put:

Vaccines in general and MMR in particular do not cause autism, period, end of story."

"Okay, okay," Lou said soothingly. "I didn't know."

"Well, sorry to jump on you," Jack said. "But Dorothy's attitude about this drives me up the wall. And to think she's been married to a doctor for most of her life but prefers to listen to her paranoid, conspiracy-minded bridge friends. And, worst of all, she will not shut up about it. Nor will she shut up about autism and neuroblastoma not being in the Montgomery family, meaning both have to be from my family. Well, as far as I know, neither have been in my family, either. Anyway, I'm being driven to distraction. I even asked Warren if I could sleep on his couch." Warren was one of the neighborhood basketball players with whom Jack had become fast friends.

"I'm sorry about all this, my friend," Lou said. "Do you want me to try to talk with Laur and see if I can help?"

"I appreciate your heart being in the right place," Jack said. "But I think you bringing it up will only make things worse. As I said, Laurie has trouble dealing with her parents. It's just going to have to play itself out—provided Caitlin doesn't act on her threat, because there is no way Dorothy can take care of Emma on her own. As for me, I have to find something here at work to occupy my mind. I had to do the same when JJ got sick. Luckily, back then I got all steamed up about the dangers of alternative medicine with the chiropractor who killed a young woman with a stupid neck adjustment. I need something like that now."

"I'll see if I can rustle up some confusing homicides to tax your skills," Lou suggested, chuckling. "Like the floater that ended up taking you to Africa."

"There you go," Jack said with a smile. "That would be perfect." He remembered the case very well, along with the trip to Equatorial Guinea. It seemed like yesterday, even though it was going on twenty years ago.

The sudden ringing of Jack's mobile phone startled both men. Jack had his ringtone on *Alarm* to make sure he'd hear it when he'd ridden his bike to work that morning and hadn't returned it to its usual setting. It sounded like a fire truck racing through traffic and was particularly loud as it echoed off the snack room's cinder-block walls. Jack snapped the phone up, stopped the racket, and looked at the caller ID. It was Dr. Jennifer Hernandez, this week's on-call medical examiner.

The on-call role rotated among the more junior doctors and included backing up the pathology residents on night call, coming in to the OCME earlier than everyone else to schedule the autopsies involving the cases that had landed during the night, and handling any queries during the day that required a response from a medical examiner. It was busywork for the most part, and Jack had been glad when his seniority exempted him. When calls did come in, they usually were from the in-house MLIs, or medical-legal investigators, whose job was to get the details of all cases referred to the medical examiner. These were all deaths that occurred in an unusual, unexpected, or suspicious manner, including suicide, accident, criminal violence, in custody (like the cases Jack had processed that morning), or merely suddenly when the victim was in apparent good health. The MLIs were very experienced and rarely contacted the on-call medical examiner.

"Do you mind if I take this?" Jack asked, gesturing with his mobile phone in his hand.

"Be my guest," Lou said graciously. "You're working. I'm just a free-loader."

Guessing it probably related to an MLI question and therefore might be a harbinger of an interesting case, Jack was eager. "Maybe this is what the doctor ordered," he said.

2

MONDAY, 11:45 A.M.

"I'm up on the second floor in the formal dining room, Dr. Hernandez," Jack said into the phone. "I'm here with a group of visiting nuns. Come on up!" He was using the speakerphone while he adjusted the ringtone to a more normal setting.

Lou chuckled. That kind of impious exaggeration sounded more like the irreverent Jack Stapleton he knew and loved. Maybe Jack wasn't as bad off as he'd been suggesting.

A minute later a youthful-looking woman approached who reminded Lou of Laurie, with the care she obviously expended on her general appearance. She was wearing a fresh, highly starched white doctor's coat, which was the opposite of the rumpled and soiled ones the veteran MEs generally wore. Beneath it was a bright red dress that, in Lou's estimation, wouldn't have been out of place at a cocktail party. Her features, coloring, and tightly gathered hair suggested a Hispanic genealogy.

Jack performed the introductions, describing Lou as a dear old friend of both his and Laurie's. Then Jack explained that Jennifer was the granddaughter of the woman who'd been Laurie's nanny from when Laurie was pint-size all the way up to her teenage years.

"Jennifer even came to the OCME under Laurie's tutelage and spent a week here as a high school student," Jack said. "I was told she was quite a pistol back then and needed some direction, which Laurie supplied."

"I'm afraid I was on the wild side," Jennifer agreed. "My poor grandmother Maria, who raised me, didn't know what to do with me and turned to Laurie in desperation. But my coming here ended up being a life-changing experience. It got me so interested in academics and forensics that I went to medical school and did the whole nine yards. And here I am."

"And there's even more to the story," Jack said. "It was because of Jennifer that Laurie and I ended up taking that trip to India about ten years ago. So she has expanded our lives as well."

"I remember that trip," Lou said. "It was about medical tourism."

"That it was," Jennifer agreed. "Unfortunately for my grandmother."

"It was a disaster for Maria," Jack said in agreement. "So, Jennifer. What's up? How come you're looking for me?"

"I got a call from Bart Arnold, the MLI supervisor," Jennifer said. "A problematic case is on its way in to the OCME from the Bellevue emergency room. He'd heard about the call-in and was concerned enough to head over there himself. He called me from the ER to say that he thinks it might be a contagious case, and he specifically asked me to ask if you would get involved. He told me something I didn't know. You are known around here as the 'contagion guru.'"

"What the hell does that mean?" Lou asked. He visibly cringed. He was a world-class germaphobe, and anything to do with pestilence gave him the creeps.

"During my first year here at the OCME I made a couple surprisingly accurate diagnostic calls on a number of fatal contagious cases that were being artificially spread."

"You mean someone was doing it on purpose?" Lou questioned. "Like bioterrorism?"

"You got it," Jack said. "But we nipped it in the bud. It could have been bad."

"Bart wants to know if you'll give him a call," Jennifer told him.

"Sounds like my kind of case," Jack said. "I'll do better than call him. I'll run down to 421 and see him in person." 421 was how everyone at the OCME referred to the new high-rise building on 26th Street. The old building that still housed the morgue and the medical examiners was referred to as 520, its First Avenue address.

"Then I'll let him know you're coming," Jennifer said. She nodded to Jack, told Lou it had been a pleasure to meet him, and then left.

"Doctors are getting younger and prettier all the time," Lou said once she'd gone. "Makes me feel like an old fart. But be that as it may, I'm outta here. Thanks for the morning entertainment, and let me know the final dispensation on the three cases we did ASAP."

"It goes without saying." Jack stood. "Come on. I'll walk you to your car on my way down to 421."

After closing the door to Lou's unmarked Chevy Impala, Jack waved him goodbye as the car backed up from the OCME unloading dock and pulled out onto 30th Street. Besides the OCME vans, Lou's car was the only vehicle permitted to park there, and to ensure it wasn't towed away, Lou always made certain to leave his laminated NYPD detective card in full view on the dash.

The moment Lou's car disappeared, Jack returned to 520's interior to retrieve his bike, which he'd parked near the autopsy room. Even though it was only four blocks south to the 421 high-rise, he couldn't pass up the opportunity for even a short burst of speed and a bit of fresh air. Unfortunately, it wasn't really fresh air, since the OCME was situated on the East Side of Manhattan and therefore constantly bathed in the considerable car, truck, and bus fumes carried along on the island's prevailing westerlies. Hopping on the bike, Jack pedaled east and then south along the edge of Franklin Delano Roosevelt Drive with his not-so-clean doctor's coat flapping in the wind. Despite the cool temperature, he was wearing only blue scrubs underneath. The trip was over practically before it had started. Jack carried his bike in through the building's loading bay, parked it next to a security booth, and took the elevators up to the fifth floor.

The fifth floor was the busiest in the entire building. Not only did it house the medical-legal investigative team, but Communications as well, where all calls came in to the OCME day and night. It was also the arrival area, where all specimens came into the building for analysis from the autopsy room and from off campus. That included everything from run-of-the-mill histology, bones, and teeth to the most sophisticated DNA tests. The only samples that didn't come into the fifth floor of 421 were toxicology specimens, since Toxicology was the only major department of the OCME besides the morgue itself that had yet to move from the 520 building.

The MLI Department occupied the area immediately beyond the glass doors defining the elevator lobby. It was an open office, comprising rows of desks with their backs pushed up against one another. Bart Arnold's desk was in a central location, so he had a bird's-eye view of his team.

Bart had been with the OCME since way before Jack's arrival, back when the department had been a shadow of its current self, with a mere handful of employees. In those days the investigators were called physician assistants and sat in tiny individual shoulder-height cubicles behind the telephone operators' switchboard. Now the department was large enough to field its own softball team at the spring picnic.

Bart himself was a heavyset man with just a handful of curly grayish hair that extended from just a little over each ear in a ring around the back of his head. He was an intelligent, quick-witted individual with a remarkably calm personality. He needed his patience. His team was quite variegated in temperament, age, and gender, and the MLI role had to be maintained 24/7, holidays notwithstanding. Like Jack, he was wearing a white coat a little worse for wear over scrubs. As a hands-on supervisor, Bart was known to make frequent trips out of the office to investigate troublesome deaths, particularly at local hospitals. He was known in his field and had been influential in getting forensic pathology to adapt *therapeutic complication* as the new term for hospital deaths. This was the label used when the death was unexpected, as with a patient undergoing a normally safe procedure. It had replaced the more vague *accidental death*.

"My gosh!" Bart said, getting to his feet when he caught sight of Jack approaching. As an old-school employee, he had more respect for the professional staff than some of his younger colleagues did. "I didn't mean for you to have to come over here, Dr. Stapleton. I was just hoping for a call."

"No problem," Jack said. "Please sit." Jack snagged a stool on wheels, pulled it over, and sat across from Bart. "Whatcha got? Dr. Hernandez said you were concerned about a possible contagious case."

"That's right," Bart said. "My intuition is telling me this is no ordinary case. The call came in not too long ago. Let me tell you what I learned. The patient was on the R train from Brooklyn and the engineer let MTA operations know about a sick passenger. The EMTs who picked her up from the Twenty-third Street station knew she was in extremis, so they had to move quickly and couldn't get much history. But it seems that the victim, who's a twenty- to thirtysomething woman, had been fine while on the train, which of course makes sense. She wouldn't have gotten on the train if she felt really crappy, especially getting all dolled up the way she was. Whatever befell her came on like gangbusters, with apparent breathing difficulty, making her turn a bit blue, although it wasn't anything she choked on. My guess is an overwhelming case of pneumonia, because when they tried to ventilate her, they couldn't. The only thing I noticed when I looked at her was some froth in the corners of her mouth, around the endotracheal tube."

"Could it have been some sort of overdose?" Jack asked.

"I truly don't think so," Bart said. "In my considerable experience, this is not the way an overdose presents itself. I think it's a case of sudden and overwhelming viral or bacterial pneumonia. This woman was on the move and very well dressed. She could have been on her way to lunch at the Ritz, the way she was decked out."

"You know what this is reminding me of?" Jack asked, sitting up straighter.

"A scary-ass illness," Bart said. "Something like Ebola."

"Actually, I was thinking of something more pedestrian but ultimately even scarier," Jack said, allowing the first hints of excitement to trickle into his voice. He didn't want to get his hopes up, but suddenly this was all sounding to him like something the "doctor might order" to take his mind off Emma, autism, and his mother-in-law's invasion. "Back in the disastrous flu pandemic of 1918 that killed upward of one hundred million people, there were stories of asymptomatic people getting on the subway in Brooklyn and being dead from viral pneumonia by the time they got to Manhattan. Whether such stories were apocryphal or not no one knows for sure, but I think they were true because of the virulence of that particular flu strain. What is believed now is that they died from their own immune systems going wild in what is called a cytokine storm."

"I've heard the same stories," Bart said. "It's why I jumped on this when the call came in."

"Did you advise the Bellevue people to do anything with the body for safety concerns?" Jack asked.

"I certainly did," Bart said. "I advised them to put the corpse in a body bag and treat the outside with hypochlorite and to do the same thing to the ER room. I even called the EMT station and told them to follow suit with the ambulance, but they had already done it."

"Good call," Jack said. "I would have advised the same thing. Where do you think the body is now?"

"It should already be in the cooler at 520. I sent one of our vans right away. If it's not there yet, it will be shortly. Bellevue was eager to have it out of the emergency room, for obvious reasons."

Jack stood up quickly. The stool he'd been sitting on scooted off to collide noisily with a nearby desk. Jack grimaced and apologized to the surprised occupant. Jack was eager to get cracking. Being in a position as a medical examiner to possibly head off an influenza pandemic had a huge, mind-numbing appeal. Last year's flu had been bad. This year's could be catastrophic if this sudden death turned out to be the index case.

"Thanks for cluing me in," Jack said. "This could be really important."

"I thought as much," Bart said. "Let me know what you find out. I'll be interested to learn."

"I'll keep you posted," Jack promised.

"Oh, there is one problem I didn't mention." Bart rose from his own seat. "There's no identification. My guess is that when she collapsed, whatever she was carrying, be it a purse or a phone or both, was taken."

"You said she was well dressed," Jack said. "Getting an ID shouldn't be much of a hurdle. Someone will undoubtedly miss her sooner rather than later and call Missing Persons when she doesn't show up where she lives or works."

"That would be my guess," Bart agreed.

"ID is going to be important if it is a contagious case, as we suspect," Jack said. "Social history and contacts might turn out to be crucial."

"I know. I'll check back with the ER just to make sure they didn't misplace a purse or a phone. It wouldn't be the first time. If I find out anything, I'll let you know."

Jack flashed Bart a thumbs-up before making a beeline for the elevators. He hit the down button repeatedly in the vain hope of encouraging an elevator to come more quickly. His heart was racing. Coming across an index case for a possible influenza pandemic was heady stuff. Best of all, it might keep him busy and occupied for a week.

3

Jack dialed his mobile phone before he was even out of the 421 elevator, but he waited until the doors opened and he got a decent signal before he put the call through. He wanted to talk to Vinnie ASAP. Vinnie's irritated voice came on the line after two rings. Over the years, Vinnie had gotten wise to Jack's demanding nature, as Jack performed far more autopsies than any of the other doctors, by a long shot. When Vinnie saw it was Jack calling, it usually meant yet another trip back to the pit, no matter the time of day. If it was after three P.M., he avoided answering at all.

"A case should have come in recently," Jack began, unable to keep the excitement from his tone.

"Aren't we lucky," Vinnie said. He'd also acquired a strong predilection for serious sarcasm from Jack. "Should I clap or cheer?"

"I'd like you to take your sorry ass into the cooler and let me know if it's there yet," Jack said. "It will be in a body bag and labeled JANE DOE or something similar. I'll hold on."

Jack arrived at his bike and waited. He smiled at the guard in the tiny booth that overlooked the entire loading area. The guard glanced at him askance, as if he'd never seen a doctor in a white coat using a bike in the city, even though with Bellevue and NYU Hospital in the immediate area there were doctors galore.

Maybe Jack's impatience stemmed from his exhilaration after meeting with Bart, but it seemed to take Vinnie an age to accomplish such an easy task. Finally, he came back on the line.

"It's here, zipped up tight. Don't tell me you are thinking of us doing it today. It's after twelve, and we've already done three cases. Why not spread the wealth?"

"This one has the makings of being an interesting case," Jack said. "We might even become heroes. Who knows? It is a potentially contagious problem involving a woman who died on the subway."

"Shit! Double whammy," Vinnie complained. "You know how I hate contagion cases. Can't you find another sap to torture? Why me?"

"I wouldn't want to deny you the pleasure, and we are a team, my friend," Jack said. It was true, to an extent. They had worked so often together that they often anticipated each other's actions. "I want to do the case in the decomposed room, for safety's sake." The decomposed room was a separate, relatively small autopsy room usually reserved for decomposing corpses, to limit the smell of putrefaction. It had its own self-contained ventilation system with high-efficiency particulate filters and odor absorbers.

"What did I do to deserve this?" Vinnie questioned rhetorically, then sighed. "Well, the upside is that Carlos Sanchez will get a serious introduction to what being a mortuary tech is all about. Does this mean we'll be in moon suits?"

"For sure," Jack said. *Moon suit* was the in-house term for a one-piece isolation getup made of Tyvek that featured a hood and a self-contained HEPA filter with a battery-driven ventilation pack. Like spacesuits, they were cumbersome and difficult to work in. They were also hot and generally uncomfortable. Needless to say, they weren't the most popular item of apparel at OCME.

"Weigh and X-ray the body in the body bag," Jack added. "And don't take the body out until I get over there and we're ready to start. We can do the photographing and fingerprinting after the autopsy is under way."

"Where are you?"

"I'm at 421, but I'm on my way back to 520. I'll be there in minutes, so let's get the show on the road."

Hefting his bike up on his shoulder, Jack carried it down the half-flight of stairs from the receiving dock to the street level. Once on the bike, he pedaled up to First Avenue and turned north. He had to go only four blocks, so he made the best of it by accelerating to almost the speed of the traffic. By the time he turned into the receiving dock at the 30th Street building, he was breathing heavily from the exertion. It gave him a bit of a high, as if he'd had a cup of espresso.

When he passed the decomposed room, he glanced in through the small central wire-meshed window. The light wasn't even on yet, meaning Vinnie needed more time to get set up. After storing his bike near the Hart Island coffins used for the unidentified dead, Jack made a quick trip up to the front office on the first floor. With the concern he felt about the potential ramifications of the upcoming case, he thought it best to at least let Laurie know there was a potential extraordinarily hot-button issue on the horizon. If it turned out the woman had died of a particularly lethal new strain of influenza, the involved city agencies in the Department of Health needed to know right away. Notifying them appropriately would be Laurie's responsibility.

"Hello, Cheryl," Jack said in a chipper tone. Cheryl Sanford was the administrative secretary to the chief medical examiner, meaning she now reported to Laurie. For the whole time Jack had been a member of the OCME staff, she had been secretary to Dr. Harold Bingham, and Jack had had many interactions with her, as he'd been called to Bingham's office more times than he liked to admit. Jack's attitude toward rules was best described as selective. He thought rules were suggestions, and if they got in the way of his work, he often ignored them. Although he'd been proven to be inordinately effective as a medical examiner, his methods often got him in trouble with the front office, ergo many visits to the couch beside Cheryl's desk while waiting to be reprimanded by the big boss. On one of those visits, Jack had learned that Cheryl was also a neighbor, living only a block away from Jack. At the same time, Jack had also learned that she was raising a teenage grandson who played basketball. Jack ended up getting the boy involved in the basketball games across from the Stapletons' house in the public playground Jack had paid to have refurbished.

With his excitement brimming Jack didn't stop to chat but rather headed directly for Laurie's closed office door. Cheryl called out sharply enough to stop him in his tracks. "I wouldn't go in there!" she warned, under no uncertain terms. "Dr. Montgomery is on a conference call with the mayor and members of the City Council and will be for some time. Can I give her a message?"

For a second Jack debated whether he should just push right in despite the warning.

"It has been a heated phone call," Cheryl added.

"Okay," Jack said. He realized he was jumping the gun in his enthusiasm, and Laurie had already asked him not to barge in as he had on one occasion a month ago. "Fair enough. Tell her I'm doing a post on an important case she should know about and that when I'm finished I'll pop up and fill her in."

"Should I tell her anything specific, like what kind of post it is?"

"No, it's probably better if you don't," Jack said. The more he thought about the situation, the more he understood he'd need concrete laboratory confirmation of a new influenza strain if any official whistles were to be blown. Such news could cause a panic in the city, depending on who happened to get the info and what they did with it. Jack even felt a bit embarrassed he'd not given enough thought to what he had planned to do. As he walked out of the front office he felt distinctly thankful that Cheryl had saved him from himself.

In the public waiting area, Jack asked the receptionist, Marlene, to buzz him into the family ID area, where relatives gathered when they were required to identify their deceased family members. He was looking for Rebecca Marshall, one of the clerks trained to deal with bereaved families. He found her finishing up with a couple who had to identify one of their teenage sons, who had overdosed just that morning. Such tragic scenes were a daily occurrence not only in NYC but all across the country.

As soon as she was free, Jack took her aside. She was in late middle age and had a kind face and tightly curled silver-gray hair. "What can I do for you, Doctor?" Rebecca asked. She was one of those employees who was always eager to help, which was why Jack often sought her out.

"A case came in within the last hour," Jack said. "The death of a relatively young woman on the subway. I haven't seen the victim myself, but I spoke with Bart Arnold, who has. There was no ID. Have you heard about this case yet?"

"I haven't," Rebecca said.

"Bart said the woman was well dressed, so I imagine she'll be missed rather soon. Would you keep an eye out for any information or inquiries? Making an ID as soon as possible is going to be important on many levels."

"I'll certainly keep a lookout," Rebecca assured him. "And I'll pass the word to the rest of the team. I'll let Hank Monroe and Sergeant Murphy know as well, although they might have both already been given a heads-up. One way or the other, they can get things moving on their end as well."

"I'd appreciate it," Jack said.

Hurrying back downstairs, Jack looked into the decomposed room once again. Now the light was on and a black body bag was stretched out on the single autopsy table. Next to it was a separate metal stand with various instruments, specimen containers, preservatives, labels, syringes, evidence custody tags, and all sorts of other stuff needed for the autopsy. Jack was encouraged, but there was no Vinnie Ammendola or Carlos

Sanchez. Guessing they were in the locker room donning moon suits, Jack hurried in himself.

When Jack arrived, Carlos was completely encased in one of the OCME's level-A hazmat suits. Because of the glare of the overhead fluorescent lights off the helmet's curved plastic face mask, Jack couldn't see the man's face, but he could sense that Carlos was terrified. He was standing motionless, with his arms stuck out to the sides at an angle from his body. Jack had to smile.

"He doesn't like this," Vinnie explained with a laugh as he stuck his legs into his suit and then pulled the back up over his shoulders.

"That's apparent," Jack said. He got his suit off its peg and unplugged the ventilation battery pack from the charger. "Relax, Carlos! The suit is designed to protect you, not hurt you."

"There's going to be dangerous bacteria in there?" Carlos couldn't seem to control the quaver in his voice.

"We're more worried about dangerous viruses," Jack said.

"You mean like Ebola?" Carlos asked.

"Something like Ebola," Jack agreed. "Viruses are viruses. What I'm thinking we might be dealing with is influenza. You've certainly heard of the flu virus."

"Of course I've heard of it, but it's nothing compared to the likes of Ebola," Carlos said.

"I wouldn't be quite so cocky," Jack said. "Influenza has killed infinitely more people than Ebola. Let's put it this way: If this case is a new lethal strain of influenza, it could be as bad as or worse than if it were Ebola, because flu spreads much more rapidly than Ebola. Haven't you ever heard of the 1918 flu pandemic? It killed more people than World War One and World War Two combined."

"I don't like the sound of this," Carlos said. "Has anyone died here at OCME doing autopsies like this? I didn't think this job was dangerous, just gross."

"Oh, yeah, we've had a ton of deaths," Jack said as he stuck his feet down into the legs of his suit. "We lose mortuary techs maybe once a month. That's why you got hired."

"Jesus, Dr. Stapleton!" Vinnie complained. "Don't tell him that. You're going to scare the shit out of him. We've never lost a mortuary tech, Carlos. He's pulling your leg."

"Listen, Carlos," Jack said. "The reason you're in this godawful torture contraption is to protect you. You'll be fine. Just don't stick a knife blade or a needle through the suit while we are doing the case. At the end, be sure to do exactly what we tell you to disinfect."

"This is not what I expected this job would be like." For a grown man, Carlos had an uncommon knack for imitating a whiny child.

"You'll be fine," Jack repeated. He hadn't meant to scare the novice as much as he apparently had. At the same time, Jack didn't particularly care. He wasn't convinced Carlos was going to be a permanent addition to the team. There had been a handful of not-so-positive quirks about the man's behavior that morning that didn't sit right with Jack. One way or the other, he planned on saying something to Twyla Robinson, the chief of staff.

Once Jack was fully suited and his HEPA ventilation fan was turned on, he led the way out of the locker room, down the hall, and into the decomposed room. He could tell that Carlos was still seriously spooked, but Jack decided to let the guy stew. Jack was eager to get going.

In his typical efficient fashion, Vinnie had already put up on the view box the X-ray that he and Carlos had taken of the body through the body bag. Jack switched on the light. X-raying the body was routine for MEs. The X-ray was a way of making sure that things like bullets or broken-off knife blades weren't missed, which had happened in the distant past. Jack certainly didn't expect anything like that on this case. Still, he entertained a minor possibility of coming across something like an old fracture. Such a finding could possibly assist in making or confirming the patient's identification. But to his surprise, Jack was immediately presented with a totally unexpected and significant discovery.

"Good grief." He stared at the image. "Do either of you bums know what we're looking at?"

"Looks like a bunch of twisted wires," Vinnie said.

"Yeah, wires," Carlos echoed.

"They are most definitely wires," Jack said. "Wire closures wrapped around the woman's sternum, holding it together."

"Did she have surgery?" Vinnie asked.

"Without a doubt," Jack said. "And if I had to guess, I'd say she had open-heart surgery. Most likely valvular surgery on either her mitral valve or her aortic valve."

"Could that account for her death?" Vinnie asked.

"By all means," Jack said. He tried to keep the disappointment out of his voice. If a sudden rupture or, more probable yet, a rapidly progressive inefficiency of a cardiac valve was the cause of the woman's demise, then there wouldn't be any ongoing issue. He wouldn't be looking at a possible contagious case that could potentially threaten the city and occupy his mind by keeping him busy for days on end.

"Well, that would be good," Vinnie said. "Right?"

"Of course," Jack said. If Vinnie noted his lack of enthusiasm, he kept it to himself. "Let's get to it."

"If it is a heart problem, then we didn't need to put on these god-damn miniature hothouses," Vinnie said. All three men were already beginning to sweat.

They moved over to the autopsy table, with Jack on the patient's right and Vinnie and Carlos on the left.

"Here's how I want to proceed," Jack began. "We're still going to consider this a potential contagious case until proven otherwise. So we'll unzip the body bag and fold it to the sides over the edge of the table. If the case does turn out to be contagious, we can merely fold the body bag back when we are done and treat the outside with hypochlorite. Agreed?"

"Okay," Vinnie said. "But personally, I think the wire closures change everything."

"Maybe," Jack reluctantly conceded.

With all three men lending a hand, it took only a few minutes for the fully clothed body to be exposed.

"I think Bart was right with his assessment," Jack said. "He thought she was about thirty, which looks spot-on to me. He also described her as well dressed, like she was going on a lunch date. He also thought she looked a tad cyanotic. Agreed?"

"Agreed," said Vinnie, who then explained *cyanotic* to Carlos.

Meanwhile, Jack looked at the label of the coat that had been tucked into the body bag separately. It was from Bergdorf Goodman. Jack was hardly a clothes horse, but he knew when he was looking at something expensive. He then noticed the woman's unique hairstyle and how it was carefully undercut along the left side of her head, with dark roots. On the top of the head and on the right side the hair was moderately long and professionally bleached to an attractive blond. The condition of the hair suggested a lot of professional attention. She was also wearing a Cartier watch, diamond stud earrings, and a narrow ring encrusted with pavé diamonds.

Jack took some scissors and handed a pair to Vinnie. "Let's cut her out of her clothes and leave them in place for now."

"Fair enough," Vinnie said. He handed the scissors to Carlos and then instructed him in how to cut the clothes along the seams. Carlos worked on the woman's left side, while Jack took the right. They started on the arms.

As Jack cut the right arm of the woman's blouse from the wrist up to the armpit, he immediately saw the tattoo on the inner surface of the forearm and stopped cutting. "This should be helpful in terms of ID," he said, twisting the arm into a supine position to expose the tattoo in its entirety. "Look at this! Isn't this unique. It's a tattoo of a puzzle piece in perspective. And this colorful portion of the tattoo is where the piece is supposed to have come from. I'm not a tattoo fan, but this is very clever."

"You've never seen anything like that?" Vinnie questioned in an amazed and disparaging tone. "You're more out to lunch than I thought."

"You've seen something like this before?"

"Sure. Rainbow colors are often a symbol of gay pride. Pretty common these days to see tattoos that feature them." He slanted a look at Jack. "Look on Pinterest if you don't believe me." He knew full well Jack had no idea what Pinterest was. "And you see the name *Helen* on the puzzle piece? I'd guess this woman was a lesbian and Helen was her partner."

"Well, we live and learn," Jack said. "I suppose that means we'll be hearing from Helen in the not-too-distant future."

When the woman's chest was exposed, Jack halted the cutting again to inspect the impressive pink scar that ran down the midline. "Well," he said, "this median sternotomy is certainly going to help with the ID issue. I'd say this scar is only about three months old. She must have had open-heart surgery just this past summer, and it would be my guess that she had it here in the city."

"Can we move along with this autopsy," Vinnie complained. "I don't want to be here all day."

Jack didn't say anything but went back to cutting the clothes and peeling them back. While Jack was finishing, Vinnie took off the jewelry and put it all aside. It would be disinfected and carefully notated, to be available for the next of kin.

When the body was completely exposed, Jack checked to make sure the endotracheal tube was in the trachea and then removed it. Then he did an extensive and careful external exam. Except for two more tattoos, which included a stylized palm tree in the small of her back and what seemed to be a small Chinese character on the inside of her right ankle, there was no other pathology or markings. Jack took photos of all the tattoos.

At that point, Jack began the internal portion of the autopsy. To proceed he used his favored modified Y incision that went from the point of the shoulders to the clavicular notch, and then down to the pubis through the surgical scar. He needed wire clippers to cut the wires holding the sternum together.

Once the body was flayed open, Jack's first point of attack was the abdomen. Although the liver appeared to be entirely normal, he did see some very mild evidence of inflammation, with a small amount of extravasation of blood involving the gallbladder, the spleen, and the kidneys. The findings served to key off in his mind a distant association with hantavirus, even though he knew instinctively that hantavirus couldn't be involved. Hantavirus pulmonary syndrome was extraordinarily rare, especially at that time of year in New York City. But the thought did raise again in his mind the idea of contagion.

Jack's next job was to run the intestines, examining and palpating every inch while in situ. He found nothing abnormal. Then, while Vinnie and Carlos took the freed intestines over to the sink to wash them out, Jack turned his attention to the thorax. It was here that he thought he'd find some answers.

He decided to take the lungs and the heart out en bloc so he could examine them together, and the first hint of significant pathology was their weight. As Jack carried the mass of tissue, which also included the severed great vessels, over to a side table, he could tell they weighed maybe twice what he expected. What he assumed was that the swollen lungs were filled with edema fluid, and he was right. But it wasn't only edema. Making a few slices into the lung, which burst open as if under pressure, and looking at the cross-sections, he could tell there was a significant amount of inflammation, with some bleeding and a lot of exudate, or what the general public might call pus. It was plainly obvious that the woman had died of massive pulmonary inflammation, which Jack now knew could not have been caused by a catastrophic problem with a heart valve. A suddenly failing heart valve would have filled the lungs with frank blood, not blood-tinged exudate. Consequently, Jack was back to the idea that a contagious disease might have killed this woman, and if that was the case, it had to be a particularly aggressive virus, maybe even similar to the strain of influenza that had killed a hundred million or more back in 1918. As he came back to this line of thinking, the expression

"Be careful what you wish for" passed through his mind. Although he sorely needed a diversion from his problems at home, he certainly didn't want it to be at the expense of a large number of innocent people. A new lethal influenza pandemic would wreak havoc in the city and around the world.

Taking a pair of scissors, Jack began cutting into the pericardium to expose the heart nestled between the two lungs. Usually this was an easy job, but not in this case, as there was considerable scar tissue, additional evidence that the woman had had heart surgery. As he slowly exposed the organ, he was in for another shock. The patient certainly had had open-heart surgery, but it wasn't surgery on one of her valves, as he had assumed. To his surprise, Jack could see that the patient had had a total heart transplant.

"Vinnie, get over here and look at this!" Jack shouted.

Both Vinnie and Carlos rushed over to the table where Jack was working.

"Check this out," Jack said, using the dissecting scissors as a pointer. "Look at these suture lines in the great veins and arteries. What you are looking at is a relatively recent total heart transplant, and it's the newest bicaval transplant technique. I'm impressed. Back in the early days they used to attach the atria, but no longer."

"So it wasn't a heart valve problem that killed her," Vinnie mused.

"I doubt it," Jack said. "But it will be easy to prove one way or the other. Let me open the heart." Cutting into the heart muscle, Jack exposed the interior chambers and spread the edges. "Obviously it wasn't the valves. Check them out. They're all perfect."

"Could it have been sudden organ rejection that killed her?" Vinnie asked as he straightened up to let Carlos look. Vinnie had recalled a case that he and Jack had handled where the patient had had a massive and sudden rejection of a liver transplant.

"That's a good question," Jack said. This line of thought was one of the reasons he liked working with Vinnie. Despite Vinnie's frequent grousing about working too hard, he occasionally contributed something significant to the conversation. Jack hadn't yet thought of a rejection process being involved. With that in mind, Jack carefully examined the heart. When he was done, he shook his head. "It's certainly not rejection of the heart. There's no sign of inflammation whatsoever in the organ, nor in the pericardium."

Vinnie explained to Carlos that the pericardium was the tissue that covered the heart.

"The pathology is all in the lungs," Jack said. He then showed the two men the cut surface of the interior of the lungs. "The lungs are completely full of fluid and exudate. I'm back to the influenza idea."

"It looks like she fucking drowned," Carlos said.

Jack gritted his teeth. He was old-school in respect to foul language. He knew that the younger generation thought of it totally differently, but that didn't mean he would stand for it in a professional setting. "Listen, Carlos," Jack snapped. He took an intimidating step in Carlos's direction. "Tone the language down when you are around me. You get what I'm saying?"

"Sorry," Carlos said. He backed up and rolled his eyes for Vinnie's benefit.

Jack let it go.

"How would influenza kill so fast?" Vinnie asked, to defuse the situation. He was well aware of Jack's sensitivities. "This patient might have gone from the first symptom to death within an hour. How could that happen?"

"Another good question," Jack said. "Back in 1918 they had absolutely no idea. What we now know is that it's a process called cytokine storm. It's when the body's immune system senses the virus antigens and then goes berserk, releasing a bevy of extraordinarily damaging hormonelike proteins."

"What are you saying?" Vinnie questioned. "Are you talking about a kind of cellular hari-kari?"

"That's a colorful way to put it," Jack said. "But yes. It's the person's own immune system that suddenly cranks out these cytokines that irreversibly damage the lungs. The virus just sets it all in motion, so to speak."

"Holy f—" Vinnie started to say but caught himself.

"I want samples of the lung fluid for culture," Jack said, pretending he hadn't heard. There was a definite urgency in his voice. "And I want samples from the main bronchi. Then I want all the usual samples. Let's get this show on the road!"

"Now you're talking," Vinnie said. Since Vinnie's employment responsibilities had him coming in before seven to smooth the transition from the night crew to the day shift, he was supposed to leave at three. Too often Jack kept him busy well beyond then. And Jack's sudden ardor hinted that this was going to be one of those days.

4

Because of the possible contagious nature of the case, when the autopsy was complete Jack stayed around to be sure everything was handled according to protocol, including decontaminating the outside of the body bag, all the specimen samples, the jewelry containers, and the outsides of the moon suits. He thought it was too much responsibility to leave with Vinnie, especially with Vinnie having to deal with the newbie, Carlos, meaning Vinnie was figuratively working with one hand tied behind his back.

Since Jack was again considering the serious possibility of a new influenza strain, he returned to the front office. He still thought it best to clue Laurie in to the situation so that she could begin to formulate a plan for how to alert the appropriate city agencies if Jack's worst fears were substantiated. But Jack was thwarted on this second attempt just as he had been on his first. As soon as he appeared, Cheryl informed him that Laurie was still on the same conference call.

"It's about the budget," Cheryl explained in a forced whisper.

Jack couldn't help but feel sorry for Laurie. He was impressed she was finding the patience and the stamina to stay on the phone, as he knew he'd find it impossible. Jack had trouble remaining on phone calls for anything over a few minutes. Apparently, Laurie had been on for hours.

After again telling Cheryl he'd be back, Jack decided to see that the specimens he'd taken during the autopsy got delivered to their appropriate laboratory destinations. The toxicology samples were easy, since it just required him taking them up to the sixth floor. All the other samples were a bit more difficult, since the other laboratories had been moved to the new building. To get them there required using the OCME van drivers when they weren't out picking up bodies. To make it even more complicated, microbiology testing wasn't done at the 421 OCME high-rise, but rather in a large building directly across First Avenue called the Public Health Laboratory, which was a separate city agency.

Since Jack wanted answers ASAP, particularly as to whether a dangerous respiratory virus was involved, he decided to do the deliveries himself. In order to have a specific destination, meaning a real person, for the virus cultures, he used his mobile phone to call the Virology Department of the Public Health Laboratory. After speaking with several secretaries, he finally managed to get through to one of the virologists. Her name was Dr. Aretha Jefferson.

"I'm one of the medical examiners," Jack explained, after introducing himself.

"I've heard of you," Aretha said, to Jack's surprise. And then, to his further surprise, she added, "I understand you play basketball at the playground on West 106th Street. Are you that Jack Stapleton?"

"I am," Jack said. "I didn't know I was quite so famous. How did you hear about me?"

"I live on the Upper West Side," Aretha explained. "I played basketball at UConn as an undergrad and kept it up through grad school. I have been looking for a game since I took this job in the city. I was planning on trying to get in touch with you to ask if there was any chance of my coming by your playground some evening."

"It's not my playground," Jack said. New York never ceased to amaze him. It was a huge city, yet in some ways it felt like a small town.

"That's not what I heard," Aretha said with a laugh. "Anyway, I'd like to meet you and your friends, in hopes of getting into a game or two."

"I'd be happy to meet you," Jack said. "And maybe we can exchange favors. The reason I'm calling is that I have some lung and bronchial specimens, as well as serum and cerebrospinal fluid from an autopsy I just did, that I need to be tested. The woman died of a respiratory problem. I'm concerned about a possibly virulent influenza and would like to run a rapid screen test as well as a more detailed analysis ASAP. Can you help me?"

"Certainly," Aretha said. "That's what we're here for. Have them sent over. We'll take care of them."

"Thank you," Jack said. "Actually, I'd like to bring them over myself and deal with you directly. Would you mind? You see, the sooner I get an answer, the better. I'm concerned it might be a new strain and I don't want these samples to disappear down a bureaucratic rabbit hole."

"No problem," Aretha said. "When would you like to do this?"

"Would now be okay?" Jack said. He knew he was being overly pushy, but he thought the situation demanded it. It seemed particularly opportune that he could potentially do her a favor as well. Between city agencies things always worked better when there was a personal relationship and a give-and-take.

"Why not," Aretha said. "It will give me a chance to meet you in person. Are you familiar with the Public Health Laboratory building?"

"I'm not," Jack admitted.

"The easiest way would be for you to come in the back entrance off Twenty-sixth Street and take the service elevator directly up to the third floor. That's where our level-three lab is located, where the testing will be done. I can meet you there."

"Perfect," Jack said. "I'm on my way."

Initially Jack debated using his bike again for the quick high it invariably gave him, but decided against it. He worried there wouldn't be a safe place for it when he went into the Public Health Laboratory unless he brought along his ponderous collection of chains and locks. Instead he merely ducked directly out of 520 onto First Avenue with a shoulder bag full of specimens and jogged the four blocks down to 26th Street. Although there was ancient-appearing scaffolding erected around the massive Public Health Laboratory building, Jack was able to find the service entrance with comparative ease. As he rode up in the battered service elevator, he guessed the building was from approximately the same era as the old OCME structure.

As the elevator doors opened, Jack was greeted by a tall, youthful, and athletic-appearing African American woman with bright eyes and an equally bright smile. Her hair was meticulously done in cornrows with colorful beads. She introduced herself with infectious alacrity and pumped Jack's hand. Without hesitation she took the samples Jack had taken out of his shoulder bag and handed over her business card.

"I put my mobile number on the back," Aretha said. "How about you give me yours?"

Jack took out one of his business cards and added the number. He handed it to Aretha.

"I'll run rapid tests for the usual culprits," she told him. "That will certainly include the standard influenza strains, SARS, MERS, and even the new bird flu, plus the usual run-of-the-mill respiratory villains. I should have some results in a few hours."

"I'll appreciate a call as soon as you have the results," Jack said. He couldn't have been more encouraged and pleased. "Could you test for hantavirus, too? I know the chances are probably zero, but there was some inflammation in the gallbladder, spleen, and kidneys, like what is seen with hantavirus."

"I'll run all the rapid tests," Aretha promised. "It's actually auto-mated. If there's a known virus present with a decent titer, meaning there's enough of it, it will pop up. And if it killed the woman, it's got to be a decent titer, especially since you got it directly from the lungs. Now, with that decided, is there any chance you'll be playing basketball tonight?"

"I'm not sure," Jack said. He was impressed with Aretha's tenacity. "Sorry, but my daughter is having some health issues. I'll have to see. But I could call some of the other guys and set it up for you, whether I come out or not."

"I think I'll wait until you are available," Aretha said. "I'm an old hand at street b-ball and know the politics can be dicey."

"You're right in general," Jack said. "But our court is neighborly and everyone is pretty laid-back. And there is no gender issue, if that's your concern. There was a few years ago, but that's not the case now. Skill is the determining factor for both sexes, which shouldn't be a problem if you played college ball for UConn. But if you're reluctant to show up on your own, I'll give you a call if I can get out there tonight. I could definitely use a run."

"I'll keep my fingers crossed," Aretha said. "Meanwhile, I'll get to work on your samples. I'll also inoculate some cell cultures just to let you know over the next couple days if any viruses are present. That might be helpful if the rapid tests are negative."

"I appreciate your help," Jack said. "This could be important, especially if it is a new influenza strain."

After promising to get together at some point at the playground across from Jack's house, Jack returned to the street. From the Public Health Laboratory, he merely had to cross First Avenue and skirt a small park to get to 421. In less than five minutes he was back on the fifth floor, sitting across from Bart Arnold.

"This case you turned me on to is getting progressively more interesting," Jack said. "I just finished the autopsy. Thanks for cluing me in."

"What did you find?" Bart asked. He leaned forward, all ears.

"First of all, the woman had had a recent heart transplant," Jack said.

"No!" Bart said. He laughed briefly in disbelief and shook his head.

"There's always surprises in this job. Who would have guessed to look at her. And is that what you think killed her: something going haywire with the transplant?"

"No, the transplant couldn't have looked any better than it did. It appeared like the heart of an athlete, with absolutely no signs of inflammation or rejection whatsoever. All the pathology was in the lungs, which showed a huge amount of inflammation from what I'm guessing was a cytokine storm secondary to a viral pneumonia, possibly influenza."

"Having had a recent heart transplant, she must have been on high-dose immunotherapy," Bart said.

"No doubt," Jack said. "I'm sure Toxicology will confirm that."

"But if she were on high-dose immunotherapy, wouldn't that preclude her having a cytokine storm? Wouldn't immunotherapy block a cytokine storm or at least keep it in check?"

As soon as Bart said the words, Jack knew he was absolutely right. All heart transplant patients took high doses of immunotherapy to block rejection, which probably would have blocked the immune response that triggered a cytokine storm. Jack had let his excitement get the better of him. All at once he was back to square one.

"Did I rain on your parade?" Bart asked, looking a smidgen guilty at the change in Jack's expression.

"I suppose, to a degree," Jack said, trying to reorganize his thinking. "Well, we'll have to wait and see what Toxicology will tell us. And what we learn from Virology. I just left lung and bronchial samples over at the Public Health Laboratory. We should have some preliminary results in a few hours. Meanwhile, have you had any luck getting any more information on the patient? It's going to be important to have a social history if there's a need for any quarantining and prophylactic antivirals. Did the Bellevue ER come up with a purse or a phone or anything?"

"Nada," Bart said. "I even called them to check. And there haven't been any calls coming in through Communications looking for a young, well-dressed, attractive female. But that is not unusual. It's only been hours. I'm confident somebody is going to be missing this woman as the day drags on."

"It's probably going to be someone named Helen," Jack said. He went on to describe the tattoo on the woman's forearm and what he had learned from Vinnie. He told Bart that photos of the tattoos were available in the digital record.

"I'll let Communications know," Bart said. "Every bit helps."

"If another case similar to this comes in, I want to be notified immediately," Jack said. "Day or night."

"I'll let the entire MLI team know," Bart promised.

"I'm going to go up and talk with Hank Monroe in ID and Sergeant Murphy and see if they've had any luck," Jack said.

"Personally, I wouldn't bother," Bart advised. "I'm sure they haven't done anything. It's too soon. No one gets concerned until at least eight hours go by, or even twenty-four."

"Maybe you're right." As frustrating as it was to acknowledge, there was little else for Jack to do at the moment.

"I know I am," Bart said. "I've been working this side of the OCME for more years than I care to admit. But let me help you in other ways. What's clanking around in your shoulder bag, samples from the autopsy you just did? If so, I can see that they get to the right people."

"Good guess." Jack pushed the shoulder bag across the desk to Bart. "There's a bunch of tissue samples for histology, but, more important, there's also samples for the DNA and serology people to do their thing. Since it was a heart transplant, I want them to run the same DNA analysis on the heart, so we'll know how good a match it was. That would be important if rejection played any role whatsoever. I mean, there was no sign of any inflammation in the heart, so the woman's body couldn't have been rejecting it unless the inflammation is microscopic, which we'll see on the histology sections. But maybe the heart was somehow rejecting the body."

"Graft-versus-host disease? We had several cases of that in the past," Bart said.

"It's a long shot in this case," Jack admitted. "Graft-versus-host disease is more apt to be seen with bone-marrow transplants, not solid organ transplants. But there's something about this case that's bothering me. My intuition is trying to sound an alarm, although I have no idea what it might be. But over the years I've learned not to ignore it."

"Well, I'll do what I can," Bart said. "We don't want to ignore your intuition. I'll see to it that all the right people get these samples and they get right on it."

"Thanks, Bart." Jack stood and stretched. Then he headed back to the elevators.

5

It was now deep into rush hour, and the traffic heading north on First Avenue was bumper-to-bumper and moving slowly. With the sun soon to set and evening approaching, red taillights appearing like rubies extended off into the far distance. Although Jack usually entered 520 via the 30th Street freight dock into the basement morgue level, on this occasion he mounted the front steps and went in through the front door. His goal was the front office. Once again, he was going to try to speak with Laurie.

As he entered the outer waiting area presided over by Marlene stationed behind her high-topped desk, Jack caught sight of Rebecca Marshall sitting with a youthful couple on one of the aged couches. Changing direction, Jack approached her.

Sensing Jack's presence, Rebecca looked up. When she caught sight of Jack she excused herself from the couple she was talking with and stood.

"I don't mean to interrupt," Jack said sotto voce. "Has anything been learned about the subway victim?"

"Nothing at all," Rebecca said. "I've spoken with Communications and told them to call me directly if there is any word. I've not heard anything. If I do, I'll let you know first thing."

"Thanks," Jack said. "I'll be leaving soon, but I'll have my mobile with me, and I'd like to be informed if any information becomes available, even after hours."

"Okay. I'll let my evening replacement know," Rebecca said. "And I'll do the same with Communications. We expect something to happen at any time now. Surely the woman will be missed at the end of the day."

"I appreciate your help." Jack turned and traversed the waiting room. As he passed Marlene he smiled at her. Smiling back, she buzzed him into the main part of the building.

On this occasion Cheryl had a different response as Jack entered the outer office. "She's finally off the phone," she said. "It was a marathon."

Laurie's office door was still closed. For a second, Jack debated whether to knock or just walk in. He decided to err on the conservative side. He knocked. A moment later he heard Laurie call out for him to come in.

Laurie was sitting behind her massive mahogany desk, the same desk that Bingham had used, but now in a slightly different location. These days it faced the high windows that offered light but no real view, as there was an NYU Hospital building only a few feet away. The room itself had a totally different feel from its appearance in the Bingham era. It had been painted a light color and the heavy, dark bookcases and ponderous library table had been removed, along with several dark paintings of brooding old men. In their place were white bookshelves and a blond library table. There were also some brightly colored draperies, a matching couch against the wall under the windows, and a coordinated rug. Jack had helped Laurie paint the room and pick out the furniture at IKEA. Anticipating how long approval from the city would have taken, they had used their own funds.

But the biggest difference was the room's new occupant. Instead of a rheumy, balding, overweight septuagenarian male in a dark rumpled suit, the chief was now an attractive middle-aged but youthful-looking woman in a stylish blue dress. Befitting the new bright, cheerful decor, Laurie's sculpted features and shoulder-length brunette hair with auburn highlights were a conspicuously welcome change.

As soon as Laurie saw Jack enter, she stood and came around the weighty desk with her arms extended. They met halfway. For a long moment they hugged. Jack was impressed with the intensity she expressed. He hugged her back with equal force.

Finally, with a deep exhale, Laurie let her arms fall to her sides. "What an afternoon!" she said, and then added, "What a day! I can't tell you how long I've been on the phone. You wouldn't believe it."

"I have an idea," Jack told her. "This was my third attempt at a drop-in visit. Cheryl has turned me away twice."

"I'm sorry," Laurie said. "It couldn't be helped. The City Council wants to cut the OCME budget by fifteen percent. Can you imagine?"

"I can," Jack said. "I can hear various uninformed City Council members pontificating that they would rather spend money on the living than on the dead."

"Luckily the mayor is on our side. I don't know what I'd do if he wasn't." Laurie leaned her backside up against the desk and attempted to relax by folding her arms across her chest. "How has your day been? I'm jealous that you still get to do forensic pathology. I miss it more than I thought I would. Taking on a few handpicked teaching cases on Thursdays with the residents doesn't compare."

"It's been a challenging day," Jack conceded. "I did have an especially interesting case this afternoon, which is why I'm here."

"I thought you came in just to give me moral support," she teased.

"Well, that, too," Jack said diplomatically. "But really, listen to this. A twenty- to thirty-year-old well-dressed and bejeweled woman was brought into Bellevue moribund and quickly pronounced dead on arrival. She'd boarded the R train someplace in Brooklyn in apparent good health, started having respiratory problems due to the pneumonia she rapidly developed, and had to be evacuated in dire straits by EMS when she got to Manhattan. Does that story ring any bells?"

"It certainly does," Laurie said. "It sounds like the great flu pandemic of 1918."

"That was my first thought as well," Jack said. "We've all heard the stories of that scary time. That's why I jumped on the case and posted it right away. My fear was that it could be the index case of a really bad seasonal flu strain, maybe as bad as or even worse than 1918."

"Did you take precautions?" Laurie asked. She stared at Jack. Her face had paled at the dire implications of what Jack was saying.

"Most definitely," Jack said. "I wasn't going to take any chances. I had Vinnie set the case up in the decomposed room with the HEPA ventilation turned on."

"Did you wear isolation suits?" Laurie questioned. She was well aware Jack was not a fan and had had a couple of run-ins with Dr. Bingham over not wearing them when Bingham thought they were called for. If anybody knew that Jack had a mind of his own, it was his wife.

"We did," Jack assured her. "I have too much respect for influenza from sore experience." Jack was referring to a flu outbreak that had been artificially spread nearly twenty years ago. He had almost singlehandedly aborted it, but not before contracting it himself.

"So what did you find? Did it look like influenza?"

"Yes and no," Jack said. "The lungs did appear as if it could have been a primary influenza pneumonia, complicated by a cytokine storm. They were completely full of fluid and exudate."

"I've never seen a cytokine storm," Laurie said. She was getting increasingly concerned.

"Nor have I, to be honest," Jack said. "I've just read about it and seen slides. Anyway, it seemed grossly consistent with the descriptions I've come across, but obviously we don't have any slides yet. But there was a major surprise in the case. The patient had had a total heart transplant not more than three or four months ago."

"Really?" Laurie frowned as she tried to fit this surprising new information into the picture she was forming of the case. It wasn't easy. "So what was your conclusion?"

"I haven't come to any conclusion," Jack said. "Everything is pending, including multiple rapid respiratory virus screens. I literally ran the samples over to the Public Health Laboratory myself and gave them to a specific individual who is going to get back to me ASAP."

"Good gravy," Laurie said.

Jack smiled behind a concealing hand. He wasn't a fan of foul language, as he'd let Carlos know that afternoon, but he certainly would have come up with a more appropriate expletive than *good gravy*. In the face of such a potentially important case, with time of the essence, it was comically virtuous.

"There's another complication," Jack said. "We don't have any identification yet. There was no phone or purse with the body. As for the body itself, we're in luck. There were a number of tattoos, so if and when we get a loved one or a friend to call in, we can be sure of an identification, even over the phone. Making an identification and reconstructing her social connections will be critical if quarantining and/or prophylactic treatment is to be done. It could involve everyone on the subway car she was riding and their contacts. What I'm thinking is that maybe you should start putting all the major health entities on notice, possibly even including the NYC Emergency Management and the CDC."

"But there is no diagnosis yet," Laurie said. "When do you expect to hear from your contact at the Public Health Laboratory?"

"Within a few hours," Jack said. He briefly thought about telling Laurie that the virologist coincidentally lived in their neighborhood and was interested in joining the local street basketball game. But remembering Laurie's current feelings about his own playing, he decided against it. He didn't want to prompt another lecture.

"Then we wait," Laurie said firmly. "I don't want to say anything to anyone until we have a confirmed diagnosis. I'd also like to have an ID. Which MLI is on the case?"

"Bart Arnold," Jack said.

"Good. He's got the experience to deal with something as potentially disruptive as this."

"I think you should at least let the Commissioner of Health know," Jack said. "Some of the preliminary plans they've drawn up for this kind of eventuality could be put in motion. If it is a new, particularly lethal strain of influenza, which it would have to be for her to develop a cytokine storm in the face of the immunosuppressant medication she undoubtedly was taking, time will be critical. Getting enough antivirals alone into the city might be a serious challenge in itself, so best to start immediately."

"But that's just the point." Laurie raised a brow. "There has been so much worry and planning put into dealing with a possible lethal influenza pandemic like the one in 1918 that the mere suggestion one is in the making will cause a veritable panic. And if a panic starts it will be very difficult to stop, and it could bring the city to a standstill and cost hundreds of millions of dollars. What I'm saying is that putting out word at this point will do more harm than good."

"Yet getting a jump on the situation could save lives," Jack persisted.

"Jack, I am not going to alert anyone until there's a firm diagnosis," Laurie said sternly. "I'm the chief medical examiner and that is my decision. Period!"

Taken aback by Laurie's sudden vehemence, Jack merely stared at his wife. It was painfully obvious that she was exerting executive privilege and ending the discussion as if he were a mere low-level employee. The disagreement, if there had been one, was over. Jack couldn't believe it.

"And let me be clear," Laurie continued. "I don't want you going over my head on this issue. I know you did that to Dr. Bingham on at least one occasion. I won't be happy if you do it to me. We will wait for laboratory confirmation before we terrorize the city and the Department of Health.

And that goes for the CDC, too. Do not call the CDC! Having their epidemiology officers nosing around here would have the same result."

Jack studied her in silence for a moment. "Are you ordering me as my commanding officer or as my wife?"

"That kind of question doesn't even deserve an answer," Laurie said. "When I accepted this job, I accepted the responsibility it entails, which you and I talked about ad nauseam. We both entered this new phase with our eyes open. I expect you to support me both as an OCME employee and as my husband."

"I thought I was already doing both," Jack said while fighting against his rising irritation.

"I'm afraid I need a lot of support," Laurie confessed, her tone softening. "I'm handling it, but it's all so much more stressful than I imagined. At a minimum, I'm counting on you not to make things more difficult. And I'm sensing you are getting . . . how should I say it? . . . overly invested in this subway death, which could be problematic."

"How could I not?" Jack questioned.

"I know you, Jack Stapleton," Laurie said. "I distinctly remember back when we learned about JJ's tumor you went overboard on a chiropractic case that almost got you fired. Now we are facing a struggle with Emma. I'm worried that you might be latching on to this current case in the same way."

Jack could feel his irritation continue to mount. It was demeaning to realize he was so obvious. What she was saying was true. He needed a diversion.

"So I'd like to also ask you to allow Bart Arnold and the other experienced MLIs we have to do their job. Don't go running out into the field yourself, provoking people and causing trouble on this case. When you're motivated and come across incompetence, which we both know there's a lot of out there, you are not the most diplomatic person in the world. If you cause trouble now, it will only make my job more difficult, especially since you are my husband."

"You've done some serious 'running out into the field' yourself," Jack snapped. Both he and Laurie had trained at programs that encouraged the medical examiners to go out into the field as an adjunct to their investigations into the manner and cause of death. Since the NYC OCME had a different philosophy, relying on the MLIs to do the fieldwork, he and Laurie had run afoul of the previous chief on several occasions.

"When we were training," Laurie said, "neither one of us had the kind of MLI support that we have here."

"Okay, I'll try to behave myself," Jack said tersely. "Are you coming home soon?" He wanted to change the subject before he said something he might regret. In his reincarnation as a furiously independent person born out of the demise of his first family in the air crash, he didn't like to be bossed around. At the moment he felt he was being bossed around big-time.

"I wish," Laurie said. She relaxed a degree. "After being on the phone most of the afternoon, I've got a ton of things to attend to before I can leave. Also, I have to prepare for tomorrow's conference call about the new morgue building alongside 421. Budget problems are nonstop. They're going to be the death of me."

"I cannot for the life of me understand how you can put up with all the bureaucratic bullshit," Jack said. "All right, I'll see you at home. I'll be leaving in a few minutes." He headed for the door.

"And I wish you wouldn't ride that bike," Laurie called after him. "I need you healthy on multiple fronts."

Don't go there, Jack thought but didn't say. He'd been given enough orders, thank you very much. Instead of responding verbally, he just waved over his shoulder, indicating he'd heard but was going to ignore the suggestion.

Back in his office, he grabbed his leather bomber jacket, which he wore on his bike rides to and from work at that time of the year. But before he descended to the morgue level to get the bike, he put in a call to Bart Arnold.

"I don't suppose you've heard anything," Jack said when he had the man on the line.

"Nothing yet," Bart said. "But we are expecting something imminently. This is the time of day people are expected to arrive home from work, or from wherever the day took them. I'm confident we'll be hearing in the next hour or so. Have you heard anything from Virology?"

"Not a word," Jack said. "Listen, be sure to let the evening and the night MLI team know that I would like a call the moment an ID is made. Also, I definitely want to be notified if there is another similar death, wherever it might take place. It doesn't have to be on a subway car. It just has to be a sudden respiratory death or one from a known case of influenza."

"I understand completely," Bart said. "I'll make absolutely sure everyone knows."

After hanging up, Jack kept his hand resting on his phone as he debated calling Aretha Jefferson. Ultimately, he decided against it. He didn't want to disturb her when she might be in the middle of doing the tests he wanted. More important, she'd promised to call him as soon as she had any results. Instead, he took out his mobile and changed the ringtone to *Alarm* so he'd be sure to hear it from deep within his jacket pocket while on the bike.

6

By far the best part of Jack's day was the ride home on his Trek road bike. It was the lightest and best-designed bike he'd ever had, and he could easily get his speed up to more than twenty miles per hour. Especially when there was traffic, which there always was in New York City in the late afternoon, he was much faster than any motor vehicle. From the 520 OCME building he could make it all the way up to the southeast corner of Central Park in less than twenty minutes, just as he did that evening.

The Central Park portion of his ride was always the pinnacle. Since the park was crowded with numerous homeward-bound pedestrians filling the walkways, Jack had to stay on the East Drive all the way around until it started heading south and changed its name to West Drive. With no motor traffic allowed on the road, it was a pleasant and safe route. There were lots of other bike riders, joggers, and in-line skaters. Jack enjoyed racing with a few of the other, more serious bikers. At the very end of his journey he allowed himself to ride on a short section of sidewalk, even though he knew it was verboten. The sidewalk brought him out onto Central Park West right at the corner of his block, West 106th Street.

By the time Jack got to his house, night had completely fallen. Across the street in the small neighborhood park, the floodlights he'd paid to have installed were ablaze and a basketball game was already under way. There were also still quite a few children in the sandboxes and on the swings. The park was a big draw.

Jack cycled over to the chain-link fence that surrounded the park and leaned against it. With a bit of effort, he was able to make out who was playing. His two closest basketball buddies, Warren Wilson and Flash Thomas, were nowhere to be seen. Jack wasn't surprised. Like him, they didn't usually appear until after seven because of work responsibilities. Both were employed by an African American–owned and –operated moving company. Jack wondered if they would show up tonight. With their jobs, it was hit or miss. If he knew for sure they would appear, Jack thought about trying to get out there himself. He could use a run, as he'd mentioned to the virologist, although he felt a little guilty about not spending the time with the children, particularly given the new situation with Emma.

After re-crossing the street, Jack carried his bike up the stoop and stored it in the utility room that he'd designed specifically for bikes and other sports equipment, just inside the front door. As Jack hung his bike up by the front tire, he noticed several of JJ's lacrosse sticks sprawled on the floor. He picked them up and hung them on their designated hooks. Jack loved to take JJ into Central Park to toss a lacrosse ball back and forth. JJ had picked up the knack with surprising ease.

Jack and Laurie had renovated the town house soon after they married. They had taken the top three floors for their private residence and designed six rental units for the other three. It had turned out to be a perfect setup, as they had plenty of room, and the income from the other apartments covered most of the expenses, even some of the mortgage. The trick was getting good tenants. Currently things were going swimmingly in that realm.

As Jack mounted the stairs he wondered what he would be facing.

Unfortunately, he had a pretty good idea, but tried not to dwell on it. Once inside the apartment, he stopped to listen. He could hear several televisions. The closest was coming from behind the closed door to the guest room some twenty feet away. He could hear it was tuned to the evening news, and it was not a positive sign, as it indicated that Dorothy Montgomery, Laurie's mother, was still in residence. That morning Jack had taken the risk of suggesting to her that maybe she'd enjoy spending a relaxing week or so back at her Park Avenue abode. Laurie had been in the shower at the time, and the suggestion wasn't something he had discussed with her in advance. The idea had just occurred to him out of the blue as he was getting ready to leave while listening to Dorothy criticize the breakfast Caitlin had made for the children. The longer Dorothy had stayed, and it was now going on a week, the more apparent it had become that she felt Caitlin didn't do anything right. Jack certainly hadn't counted on Dorothy taking him up on his suggestion, and now that he heard the guest room TV he was sure she hadn't.

The second TV was obviously coming from the kitchen/family room on the floor above. Jack mounted the stairs and found Caitlin, JJ, and Emma. It was a deceptively pleasant domestic scene. Caitlin was cleaning up from having made the kids' dinner. JJ was watching cartoons, and Emma was in her playpen. Jack said hello to Caitlin, who merely rolled her eyes in response when he asked whether everything was copacetic. Jack then high-fived JJ before turning his attention to Emma.

Emma was sitting in the center of the playpen. She did not make eye contact with Jack, even though Jack tried to position himself in her line of vision. Nor was she making any noise whatsoever, even though three or four months ago she would have been babbling incessantly. More disturbing still, she was rolling her head in her newly developed repetitive fashion. In the playpen was a collection of cute beanbag toys in the form of African animals, including a hippo, an elephant, a lion, a buffalo, a giraffe, a rhino, a gnu, and even a crocodile. Curiously, as she had done in the past, she had carefully arranged them in a straight line, nose to tail.

Reaching into the playpen, Jack stroked her arm and then her head in hopes of eliciting some response. There was none. For the next five minutes he just watched her. The entire time she ignored him and merely continued to roll her head silently. Finally, Jack reached again into the playpen and took the rhino out of its position, moving it half a foot to the side. Since he had done something similar in the past, he knew what to expect. Without a sound or any apparent emotion, Emma picked up the rhino beanbag and simply returned it to its position in line. Then she went back to her rhythmic head rolling.

What is going on in your little brain? Jack silently wondered. As a medical student, he'd studied embryology and neuroanatomy. He knew something about the process of brain development. But looking at his own daughter, he realized dejectedly how little was actually known about the process. All at once he was consumed by the same feeling he'd had when JJ had been diagnosed with a brain tumor. It was a feeling of utter helplessness.

Struggling against his own depressive thoughts, Jack looked up at JJ. Seeing the boy's face and appreciating the intensity he was displaying while watching the cartoon on TV helped Jack regain some sense of composure. When JJ's face suddenly lit up with laughter, Jack found himself smiling. Purposefully, he avoided looking back at Emma. Instead, he straightened and walked over to JJ. Grabbing a chair, he pulled it over to the table where JJ was sitting. He sat down and gazed at his son.

After a few minutes JJ became aware of his father's attention and looked up at him questioningly. "What's wrong, Dad?" JJ asked when he saw his father's expression. JJ's face had clouded over with the suddenness of a summer storm. This swift reaction made Jack realize how much he was unwittingly reflecting his response to Emma's lack of reaction. Jack's heart melted, and he reached out and enveloped his son in an appreciative hug.

"Stop it, Dad!" JJ said, pushing Jack away. "I'm watching *Curious George*. What's with you?"

Jack sat back, suppressing a burst of affectionate laughter at his son's disdain. It was so wonderfully and reassuringly typical and in such sharp contrast with Emma's behavior. Although he continued to watch JJ out of the corner of his eye, he gave some attention to the *Curious George* cartoon. His intention was to get into an ethical discussion about whatever issue the current cartoon was about. Jack had watched a number of them with JJ, and they had stimulated some fun conversations in the past. Unfortunately, it was not to be. Dorothy came up the stairs.

On previous days, Dorothy had always followed the network news with *PBS NewsHour.* On this evening it seemed that the network news had sufficed. She said a pleasant hello to Jack and said that she had heard him come in. She asked for Laurie. Jack told her that her daughter was working late and would be home shortly. Her response was to say that she would never understand why her daughter had chosen to take on the responsibility of being chief, much less become a medical examiner in the first place, not with so many other, much more acceptable specialties available.

Dorothy was a tall, thin, and intense woman with small, delicate features. Thanks to several facelifts in her seventies, her skin was stretched tightly over her high cheekbones. Her silver hair was so carefully coiffed with hairspray that it looked more like a helmet than a bouffant. Even in the face of a stiff breeze, nothing moved. She'd been married to Sheldon Montgomery, a highly successful Park Avenue cardiac surgeon, since she'd graduated from Vassar College. As such, she had been a fixture in New York City society and had been a prodigious fund-raiser for numerous medical charities. For a number of reasons, including a keen intelligence, she was a highly opinionated woman who was accustomed to getting her way.

"JJ! What did we decide about those cartoons?" Dorothy asked. Her voice was high-pitched and penetrating.

"I had to turn them off at seven."

"Well?" Dorothy questioned rhetorically.

Dutifully, JJ slid off his seat, using the remote to turn off the TV in the process.

"And what did you agree to do after the TV was turned off?"

"Play with Emma," JJ said.

"Good boy," Dorothy said. She took a chair and sat at the table with Jack. She was dressed in a long, dark robe clasped high on the neck, which reminded Jack of what movie stars wore in old 1930s movies. On her feet were equally dark mules, each with a tuft of white fur on the toes.

Jack watched with awe and surprise as JJ climbed over the playpen railing. What surprised him was that Emma reacted. It wasn't overwhelming, but she definitely was aware of JJ's presence, in contrast to when Jack was stroking her. He watched JJ move the beanbag animals into various different gatherings while maintaining an uninterrupted monologue. Emma didn't answer vocally or look at him, but she was engaged on some level despite continuing her head rolling. Each time JJ indicated he was finished, she would proceed to return the beanbags to her original line, with each animal in its original position.

"It's important for her to interact," Dorothy said, as if Jack needed to be told.

For the next fifteen minutes the three adults watched the children. Caitlin had come to the table after finishing her cleanup duties. Jack was content and even allowed himself to be mildly encouraged. But the tranquility didn't last, as Dorothy had other ideas.

"I managed to get ahold of an old friend of ours today, Dr. Hermann Cross," Dorothy said innocently enough. "Have you heard of him?"

"I don't think I have," Jack said. His guard went up. Whenever Dorothy started a conversation with a question, it invariably went downhill.

"I'm surprised," Dorothy said. "He's a very famous and knowledgeable doctor who has written a lot of books. He's CEO of a large hospital corporation and very wealthy. He was in Sheldon's medical school class. Significantly, he knows a thing or two about autism."

"Oh," Jack said noncommittally. He'd yet to have a civil conversation with Dorothy about autism. From downstairs he heard the apartment door close. He felt a bit of relief. Laurie was home.

"I called him, and he was nice enough to take my call, as busy as he is," Dorothy continued. "I asked him specifically his opinion about autism and the MMR vaccine. Do you want to know what he said?"

"Probably not." Now he was sure he didn't want to have this conversation.

"Now, that might be the most unenlightened comment I have heard in a long time," Dorothy said derisively.

"Thank you for the compliment," Jack said. "But you and I have already had this conversation about the MMR vaccine and its totally debunked association with autism."

"Not according to Dr. Cross, I'll have you know," Dorothy asserted. "He thinks there's a definite association and did not have his kids vaccinated. You just don't want to face facts and accept responsibility."

"Is this Dr. Cross a medical specialist of some sort?" Jack asked. He couldn't believe that a doctor could still be laboring under such a misconception, considering all the information that had been in the medical journals about the issue.

"Of course he's a specialist," Dorothy said. "He trained here at Columbia in psychiatry, and psychiatrists are well versed in the issue of autism."

"Well, apparently not this psychiatrist. Clearly, he's a businessman rather than a doctor, and I hope, for his investors' sake, he is a better businessman than doctor. If he's still laboring under the misconception about vaccines causing autism, I'd have to say that he's a miserable doctor."

"How dare you say such a thing," Dorothy sputtered.

"Hello, everyone," Laurie called out as she came up the stairs. "Hi, Mom! Hi, Jack! Hi, Caitlin!" She went directly over to the playpen and said hello to the children. For the moment they both ignored her as JJ arranged the beanbag animals into a small pyramid.

"JJ, I'm so proud of you for playing with your sister," Laurie said. She watched as Emma rearranged the animals back to her liking. "Was this your idea all by yourself?"

"No, Grandma made me," JJ admitted. "She said I couldn't watch cartoons unless I agreed to play with Emma."

"Well, I'm glad you listened," Laurie said with a laugh. She tousled JJ's blond hair, briefly rubbed Emma's back, then turned her attention to her mother and Jack, who were staring darts at each other.

"Jack, dear. Could I have a word with you?" Laurie said with a forced smile.

Jack stood up, and without answering followed Laurie down the hall and into their shared study. It had two big windows facing 106th Street. He glanced out and saw that the crowd had significantly increased on the basketball court.

Turning back into the room, Jack could tell Laurie's demeanor had changed from her initial apparent cheerfulness. She was now livid. "How dare you be disrespectful to my mother in our house. After the day that I've had, I have to come home to behavior like this? I truly don't understand. What do you gain by baiting her like you were doing when I came up the stairs? Hermann Cross is one of my parents' oldest and dearest friends."

"I think you misread who was baiting whom," Jack snapped back.

"Enough!" Laurie threw her hands up in the air in exasperation. "She's an eighty-three-year-old woman struggling to cope with her only granddaughter recently being diagnosed with autism. What do you expect?"

"I expect peace in my own house. I might not be eighty-three, but I'm struggling myself and she is not helping."

"Oh, give me strength!" Laurie said, raising her eyes skyward.

"Your mother is out of control," Jack said. "And I am not the only one who thinks this. Caitlin is fit to be tied as well. She even told me that she's thinking of leaving. I don't need to tell you where we would be if that were to happen."

"She's never said anything to me," Laurie said.

"Of course not," Jack said. "She's afraid to say anything."

"I'll talk with her," Laurie said.

"It would be better if you talked with your mother. Even if she is having trouble adjusting to what's going on, she shouldn't be camped out here indefinitely like this. To be truthful, she's also driving me crazy. If she tells me again that there is no autism in the Montgomery genealogy, meaning of course it must have come from the Stapleton side, I'm going to scream."

"I can't ask her to leave," Laurie said. "I just can't do it. You know I've had difficulty dealing with my parents for what seems like my entire life."

Jack was well aware. The problem originated from a Montgomery family tragedy. Laurie's brother, who Laurie worshiped, had confided in her that he was experimenting with speedball when she was at the impressionable age of thirteen and he a freshman at Yale. By accident over Thanksgiving break, Laurie had found a syringe in his Dopp kit that he'd pilfered from his father's medical bag. As a condition of revealing his secret, which he described as a passing fad, he'd forced her to promise not to tell their parents. To get her to agree, he threatened never to talk to her again if she told. Four weeks later, during Christmas vacation, he'd accidentally overdosed and their parents found out that Laurie knew he had been using. In their intense grief over losing their beloved firstborn, they blamed Laurie totally for his death without taking into consideration the emotional toll on her psyche. From that moment on Laurie had had trouble standing up to her parents, as doing so always awakened the pain of losing her brother and the sense of responsibility that came with it.

"I understand your problem," Jack said. "But we have a conundrum here. At this point, if Caitlin were to leave, I truly don't know what we would do."

"God!" Laurie ran her fingers through her hair. "I don't need this added stress right now."

"If you want me to tell Dorothy to go, I can do it," Jack said. "I'll be my normal diplomatic self."

"No, I don't want that," Laurie said. "All right, I'll give the idea of making a suggestion to her some serious thought."

"Okay," Jack said. "You do that. Meanwhile, I'm going to go out and play some basketball and blow off some steam."

"Oh, please!" Laurie said, her irritation returning. "Must you? We'd also be in serious difficulty if you were to mess up your good knee or the one that has already been operated on. It's selfish of you not to consider what it would do to the family if you get injured, Jack. I don't want you playing stupid pickup street basketball. It's childish and not worth the risk."

With a certain amount of disbelief, Jack stared at Laurie. His response to this new demand and put-down of his favorite pastime was similar to how he had felt back in her office when she mentioned she didn't like his bike riding and wanted him to stop. He had always thought that she understood his need for strenuous physical activity. It was his way of dealing with the demons that had been unleashed with the death of his first family.

"I'm sorry you feel that way," Jack said. He controlled his anger with some difficulty. "But I feel differently, and I'm going out to play basketball." That said, he turned around and headed for the stairs leading up to their bedroom to change into his gear.

7

Jack always enjoyed a sense of anticipation prior to getting into a neigh-borly game of b-ball, but tonight it was particularly satisfying. After the interactions with Emma, with Dorothy, and finally with Laurie, he needed to clear his mind, and in his estimation, there was no better way than a good run. People who didn't play the sport had no idea. Jack was convinced that in the hour and a half that he generally played, every muscle he had, and a few he didn't know he had, got called upon. And then there was the unique sense of satisfaction after making a basket. Jack always knew if his shot was going in the moment the ball left his hand. And when it did go in, there was a kind of thrill that was almost erotic. At one point in the past, soon after he and Laurie had started see-ing each other on a personal level, Jack had tried to explain it all to her, but he'd quickly given up. It had been obvious that she didn't believe him and thought he was romanticizing the experience.

Emerging onto his stoop, Jack looked over at the playground. As late as it was, he was concerned about how long it might take him to get into the game. It was a complicated system. The games were to eleven, with each basket counting one point. The winning team stayed on the court, and the next challenging team was selected by the individual who had established the right to play next. As a decent player, Jack was frequently chosen, particularly by Warren Wilson, who was the best player.

It was at that moment that Jack's mobile phone rang. Since he had again forgotten to take the ringtone off *Alarm*, the fire truck noise made him jump until he realized what it was. He pulled the phone out to look at the screen. He was afraid it was going to be Laurie, continuing her lecture. But it wasn't Laurie. To Jack's relief, it was the virologist, Dr. Aretha Jefferson. Jack quickly answered.

"Hello, Dr. Stapleton," Aretha said cheerfully. "I hope I'm not catching you at a bad moment, but I wanted to check and see if you were going to be playing ball tonight."

"As a matter of fact, I am," Jack said. "You caught me on my way over to the playground."

"Wonderful," Aretha said. "What do you think of my coming by this evening?"

Jack went up on his tiptoes and scanned the crowd over at the court. "It looks like a rather popular night, so it might take some time to get in a game. I'm sure you know the usual street rules."

"I do indeed," Aretha assured him. "I'm willing to be patient."

"Then come on over," Jack said. "I'll introduce you around. I'm sure when they hear you played college ball at UConn you'll get in a game at some point."

"Thank you," Aretha said. "See you in ten minutes or so. I'm already in my kicks."

Sensing that the woman was about to hang up, Jack added, "What's the scoop with the viral samples?" He was surprised she'd not mentioned the test results.

"Let's just say it's interesting," Aretha said. "I'll explain it more when I see you." She disconnected.

As Jack crossed the street he pondered Aretha's word choice. *Interesting* was hardly the description he'd expected. What he gathered was that she wasn't finished, even though some four hours had passed. That in itself was unusual, or so he thought. The problem was that he wasn't as conversant with rapid tests for viruses as he should have been. With the accelerated advance of molecular biology, the laboratory testing capabilities were in a constant state of change.

It was definitely crowded when Jack arrived courtside. But he was in luck. Warren Wilson had gotten out earlier than usual and had secured "winners" for the very next game. And hoping Jack might appear, he had left one of his slots open. Jack was more than happy to accept, especially since the other players on the pickup team included Flash, David, and last, Spit, whose sobriquet was based on one of his less endearing habits.

As they waited for the current game to be over, Warren asked how things were going at home, since two days ago Jack had asked if he could sleep on Warren's couch if things ever got intolerable with the in-law. "So-so," Jack said, but didn't elaborate.

Aretha Jefferson showed up before Jack got into the game so that he could introduce her to a number of the regular players, but particularly to Warren and Flash. They were the two most important male personalities in the neighborhood and on the playground. Aretha's outfit and ability to talk the talk suggested she was an accomplished player, and she was well received, including by the three relatively new female players who consistently showed up. With the males it was a help that Aretha had a killer body, the female equivalent to Warren's, whose physique put all the other men to shame. Jack was confident she'd get into a game. From then on, her general acceptance for future participation would be up to her skill level.

As the current game neared completion and Jack prepared to get out on the court, Aretha pulled him aside. "I'm sure you're wondering why I didn't call you this afternoon as I promised. I wanted to wait until I had more information. I ran all the rapid tests for viruses on your samples right away after you dropped them off. All of the tests were negative for virus, and that included all the usual culprits, as well as the new guys on the block like MERS, SARS, and bird flu."

"I don't believe it," Jack said. He let out a breath that sounded like a balloon deflating. Once again, the subway death was thwarting and surprising him. "Are you sure it wasn't influenza?"

"I know you suspected it would be," Aretha said. "So I didn't call you with the first round of results. Instead, I ran the tests again, which required a bit of overtime. But it was the same outcome. To be specific, it looks like it's not influenza. I'm sorry."

"Okay, it's not influenza," Jack said reluctantly. "So it's not a typical viral pathogen. But do you think a virus could still be involved?" The more he'd thought about the possibility of a weird graft-versus-host rejection phenomena, the less probable he considered it. It just didn't happen with a solid organ like a heart. There weren't enough immune cells. It had to be an infectious process.

"Of course an unknown virus could be involved. I suppose it is not totally out of the question that it could also be a totally new strain of influenza. The rapid tests are very specific. That's the reason I inoculated the tissue cultures I mentioned. I'll be watching them over the next twenty-four to forty-eight hours. If there is a virus, there will be a cytotoxic reaction. Cells will die. I'll let you know the moment I see anything suggestive."

"If it shows a virus is present, how do you figure out which one it is?"

"We have some tricks," Aretha assured him. "I'll fill you in if and when we get to that point."

"Thank you, Aretha," Jack said. "I really appreciate your personal attention to this."

"You are most welcome, Dr. Stapleton. And thank you for introducing me around here on the playground. I'm sure I am going to enjoy the experience. And now let's see what you've got. Word is that you aren't bad for a white boy, so good luck in your upcoming game." She laughed and fist-bumped with Jack before he trotted out onto the court.

8

Jack's eyes popped open, and despite it being pitch black in the room and outside the window, he knew instantly that any more sleep was out of the question. His mind was in turmoil with a mélange of Emma, Dorothy, and the subway-death conundrum. Being careful not to awaken Laurie, he slipped out of bed and tiptoed into the bathroom. Since Laurie was the opposite of the morning person that Jack was, they had designed their bedroom such that Jack could go from the bathroom directly into their dressing room without having to return to the bedroom.

It didn't take long for Jack to shave, shower, and dress. It was a little after five when he soundlessly descended the stairs to the kitchen/family room. At this point he wasn't worried about disturbing Laurie. Nor was he concerned about waking the kids or Caitlin. It was Dorothy he was terrified of rousing. He knew she was a poor sleeper and would occasionally wander around in the dark like a specter. He was relieved when he didn't see her. Already on two occasions he'd had to face her early in the morning when he'd made himself coffee and a bit of breakfast. Fearing it would happen again, Jack skipped the breakfast idea and continued down the second flight. The closer he got to the guest room door, the more catlike he became. Exiting the apartment, he closed the door as quietly as he could. With the final loud click, he winced and then descended the rest of the stairs quickly, worried that she might call out his name.

By the time Jack got his bike out of the storeroom, he found himself irritated all over again about Dorothy's continued presence. He was not confident in the slightest that Laurie would do anything about it, despite their discussion the previous evening. They had talked again after his b-ball playing. All he could hope for was that she'd have a real talk with Caitlin, because the only thing Jack was absolutely certain about was that they could not afford to lose the nanny at this point. Maybe once Emma's diagnosis was firmly established, as there was some disagreement, and a plan of action conceived and started, they might be in a better position. There was just too much up in the air at the moment.

Once he was on the bike, particularly when he reached the park and the wind was whistling in his helmet, Jack began to calm down. Instinctively he knew he had to leave the home problems at home, since they were not something his surgical personality could fix. He was also enough of a realist to fully comprehend that he could not metamorphose into a house husband. The requirements were simply beyond his current ken. Instead, he had to concentrate on the frustrating subway death, and as he shot along West Drive with a handful of other cyclists, he began to plan his day.

As Jack continued to pedal furiously, he found himself smiling. He could tell that his presence irritated the other bikers, who were all very serious. They were all decked out in biker's gear, with special shoes and skintight shorts and tops in wildly bright colors, with European advertisements plastered on the arms and bodices. In contrast, Jack wore a leather bomber jacket with unstylish jeans and tennis shoes. But what annoyed them was that Jack was keeping up with them, despite his lack of appropriate apparel, and even pushing them to greater effort, especially on the uphill sections.

Jack exited the park at its southeast corner, cycling past the recently regilded statue of William Tecumseh Sherman. From there he rode over to Second Avenue before turning again to the south. Although Jack used to challenge taxis with an apparent death wish, he'd matured enough over the years not to do that anymore. Though he still weaved in and out of the traffic, allowing him to travel considerably faster than the cars, buses, and trucks, he no longer tempted fate. He even found it relaxing enough that he had a chance to think about his day. What he decided was to take a "paper day," meaning he would not do any autopsies. Since he did many more autopsies than all the other MEs and rarely asked for a paper day, he knew it would not be a problem. His plan was to concentrate on the subway death. What he didn't know was that by doing so, he would be facing more surprises.

Since it was so early and he was famished, Jack stopped at a bagel shop between 39th and 38th Streets and had a bagel smeared with cream cheese and piled with lox and sliced red onions. By the time he got down to the area where the two OCME buildings were located, it was still just after six A.M. Knowing that neither Vinnie nor Dr. Jennifer Hernandez, the current on-duty ME, would be available at 520, meaning there would be no fresh coffee and Jack wouldn't be able to request his paper day, he continued all the way down to the 421 high-rise. He'd not heard from any MLI, despite having asked Bart to be sure he got called when the subway death case had been identified. But he wasn't surprised. Requests that required word of mouth often got messed up.

The building seemed deserted as Jack rode up in an empty elevator. The only person Jack had seen was the security guard at the front desk, who'd looked at Jack with surprise when Jack had gone through the turnstile. When Jack got off on the notoriously busy fifth floor, he didn't see a soul. It took a bit of effort to find Janice Jaeger, the lone night-shift medical-legal investigator, in the canteen along with the night-shift Communications person.

"Dr. Stapleton!" Janice called out with surprise when she caught sight of Jack. "What on earth are you doing here so early?"

"Couldn't sleep," Jack quipped. Professionally, he knew Janice very well. She was one of the most skilled and reliable MLIs. She and Jack had worked many cases together, and Jack knew that he could always count on her to do an extremely thorough job.

Guiltily, the woman from Communications got up as Jack sat down. She returned to her station.

"Busy night?" Jack asked.

"No, it's been very light," Janice said. "What's up?"

"I wanted to talk about a case I processed yesterday afternoon," Jack explained.

"Is this the subway death?" Janice asked, with no other provocation.

"Exactly," Jack said. "I was supposed to be called when she was identified."

"So I heard," Janice said. "When I came on duty, the evening people told me."

"Don't tell me there's still no ID."

"Apparently not."

"That's incredible," Jack said. "Bart was so sure there'd be a call. It was a young woman, well dressed. She even had a coat from Bergdorf's that I'd probably have to take out a mortgage to buy."

Janice laughed and then shrugged. "What can I say. Maybe she's from out of town and here on her own."

"I suppose," Jack said, even though his intuition was telling him something else. How many people from out of town rode the R train from Brooklyn? The answer was zilch, in his estimation.

"I'm sorry I couldn't have been more help. If a call had come in, I was prepared to do some footwork for you. But there was nothing."

Jack ran a hand through his hair, frustrated. He wondered how the hell he was going to use the case as a diversion from his own domestic problems if he couldn't learn anything about it.

"What did she die of?"

"Some sort of an acute pulmonary problem," Jack said. "My first fear was it was a new lethal strain of influenza, reminiscent of the infamous influenza pandemic of 1918. And it looked like it could be influenza grossly, but it wasn't. The samples all tested negative."

"A call will most likely come in today," Janice said encouragingly.

"What time does Bart usually get here?"

"Early. He's always the first day person to arrive. He's usually here between six forty-five and seven o'clock. Should I ask him to give you a call?"

"It's not necessary unless there's an ID," Jack said. "I'll be back over here to talk with Sergeant Murphy and Hank Monroe at some point. We've got a body in the cooler who is certainly not a homeless person. It's their job to figure out who the hell it is. I'll stop in to see Bart at that point."

Jack left 421 and rode his bike up to 520. By the time he had it stored in its usual location it was going on seven. Since he knew there was one person who made it a point to come in early every morning to avoid traffic, Jack headed up to the sixth floor. The person he wanted to see was John DeVries, toxicologist extraordinaire. There had been a time when Jack had first joined the staff that John DeVries, the Toxicology head, had been a major problem for him. The man was a bear to get along with, and he took forever to produce the data that was sorely needed in so many of Jack's cases. The explanation for both problems was simple. Toxicology was crammed into a space that was far too small—the director's private office literally had been a broom closet—and the department's budget was totally inadequate for the key role it was expected to play.

But then the tragedy of 9/11 occurred. Because of the enormous increase in workload that the OCME shouldered, its overall budget was increased proportionately and the new high-rise building was funded. The result was that John DeVries ended up with two complete floors of the old OCME building and a spacious private office that got sunlight, and his budget was quadrupled. The effect on his personality had been nothing short of miraculous. Overnight he changed from an unpleasant curmudgeon to one of the nicest, most agreeable members of the OCME staff. It was now a pleasure to deal with him. The previous day, when Jack had gone up to his lab with the serum samples from the subway death to ask for a screen on immunosuppressant drugs, John had cheerfully told him without being asked that he'd run the screen overnight and that Jack could stop by in the morning.

"My, my! Aren't we the early bird," John joked with raised eyebrows when Jack walked into his office. "I don't think I've ever seen you here this early."

"For good reason," Jack said. "I've never seen myself here this early."

John chuckled. "Are you looking for the results of the screen for the sample you brought up yesterday?"

"As a matter of fact, I am."

"Well, it was negative," John said. "I just looked at it a few minutes ago."

Jack's mouth slowly dropped open. "You're kidding? Please tell me you are kidding."

"Why would I kid about such a thing?" John asked.

"How accurate is this screen?"

"It's very accurate, with high sensitivity," John said. "Does this surprise you? Was the patient supposedly on immunosuppression?"

"She'd had a cardiac transplant a few months ago," Jack said with exasperation, as if John was trying to prank him. "Every heart transplant patient is given high doses of immunosuppression."

"Not this one," John said. "Sorry!"

"It's not your fault," Jack said. "I apologize for overreacting. It's just that I'm finding this case really frustrating. It's like it's mocking me."

"One thing did come up positive on the screen," John said. "Are you interested?"

"Of course."

"Cannabis. Most likely recreational cannabis. It was just a screen, but if you'd like a level, I could use gas chromatography."

"I don't think that's necessary," Jack said. "A bit of marijuana certainly didn't contribute to her dying on the R train."

"I'm sure not. But if you change your mind, let me know."

With yet another surprise about the subway death needling him, Jack left Toxicology and took the elevator down to the first floor. He thought it was possible that Vinnie and Jennifer might have arrived. He was right on both counts. Unfortunately, things didn't go as he expected with Jennifer Hernandez. Despite Janice's quiet night, a rash of cases that didn't need her services had come in overnight, and two of the MEs had already called in sick. As inexperienced as Jennifer was in how to handle such a situation, Jack could tell she felt overwhelmed.

To help out, Jack immediately volunteered to take two fentanyl/heroin overdose cases. As a general rule, overdoses were the least popular autopsies to do, since there had been so many. But Jack knew they wouldn't take long, as he and the other MEs had them down to a science. He sent Vinnie down to the pit along with his sidekick, Carlos, to get ready while Jack had a coffee and made suggestions to Jennifer on how to divide up the rest of the autopsies. So much for the paper day he had planned on, but he didn't mind. Without an ID on the subway case, his hands were tied.

9

With Vinnie's help, Jack finished both the routine overdose cases in just a smidgen over an hour and a half. Carlos didn't help, but he didn't seriously hinder the process, either. As far as Jack was concerned, whether the new guy was going to work out was still up in the air. Jack still felt he had an attitude problem besides a foul mouth.

The only difference between the autopsies was that the second had some signs of head trauma, which Jack interpreted as most likely caused by terminal seizure activity. Both patients were male and in their early twenties. From a forensic point of view, both showed the usual and characteristic pulmonary edema. From his experience with some fifty similar autopsies, Jack guessed the culprit was most likely a combination of fentanyl and heroin, with the fentanyl coming from China. Whatever it was, John DeVries and his miraculous toxicology machines would have the last word. Jack felt a certain detachment from the tragedy the cases represented, even though the young men were otherwise perfectly healthy and in the prime of their lives. For all the MEs, including Jack, repetition bred a kind of stoic acceptance.

After finishing the second case, Jack checked his phone for messages. He'd half expected there would be a text or a voicemail from Bart. But it wasn't to be. Jack changed back into his street clothes, as he had no intention of doing any more autopsies, no matter what came in through the door. He was now committed to making some sense of the subway death and somehow getting enough facts to get himself really involved. He had no idea what to make of the newest surprise that the patient had no immunosuppressant drugs in her system. In one sense it favored a rejection phenomenon, but that did not compute with there being absolutely no sign of inflammation in the heart. Consequently, Jack was back to favoring the infectious idea. With that in mind, he put in a call to Aretha Jefferson as he climbed the stairs to his office.

"Dr. Stapleton," Aretha said brightly, the moment she picked up.

"Let's skip the formality. Jack is fine. After last night we should be on a first-name basis!"

"Fair enough," Aretha said. "Thank you again for introducing me to your friends and getting me into the game. It was really fun."

"You impressed the lot of them," Jack said. "Ultimately, you didn't need my help in the slightest." Aretha had proved herself to be personable as well as a gifted player. Jack was certain from then on she would be in high demand whenever she showed up at the playground.

"I disagree," Aretha said. "From experience, I know something about the sociology of street basketball. Anyway, I'm sure you aren't calling about last night's game. You want to know what's up with your samples, am I right?"

"If you don't mind, I'd love it."

"Here's what I can say at this point. There is a suggestion of cytotoxicity with one of the inoculated tissue samples. It's the one with human kidney cells. I used a variety of different tissue cultures, as viruses can be choosy. The reason I didn't call you is that it's not absolutely definitive. Not yet. But in my mind, it is mighty suggestive. I should know more by this afternoon. If it turns out to be true cytotoxicity, it would be considered a rapid reaction, meaning the virus has to be quite pathogenic or in a very high titer or both."

"I wish you could just out-and-out tell me." Jack was aware the comment sounded perilously close to a complaint.

"Sorry," Aretha said. "Working with viruses is a tricky but fascinating business, which is why I ended up majoring in the field. People mistakenly think viruses are primitive, but they're not. Not by a long shot. They have been evolving for millions upon millions of years."

"I'm glad you're a fan," Jack said. "But for me, at the moment, I see them as the enemy. What I need to know is whether a virus killed this woman. And if it did, what kind of virus it is and whether it's planning on killing a whole bunch more people."

"I'm on your side," Aretha said. "I'll be checking these tissue cultures on a regular basis. As soon as I know something, I'll call. If there is a virus, the next step will be to try to identify it. Let's touch base this afternoon."

"Much appreciated," Jack said.

"Will you be playing tonight?"

"That I can't say. Depends on what's happening on the home front."

"I hope your daughter is doing okay."

"That remains to be seen," Jack said noncommittally before ending the call.

Jack had reached his office with plans to work on his many outstanding cases, but the conversation with Aretha had reenergized him. Hearing that some cytopathic effects were potentially showing up in less than twenty-four hours in tissue cultures of human cells certainly increased the chances that a lethal virus was loose in the city. It might not be influenza, but influenza wasn't the only bad guy in the viral hall of horrors.

Grabbing his leather jacket, as the weather was a bit cooler, Jack went back down to the basement level and got his Trek. Just as he had done the day before, he took the short ride down to 26th Street. When he arrived, he went directly up to the fifth floor.

"You look all charged up," Bart Arnold said, the moment Jack appeared.

"I am," Jack admitted. He mentioned the possible evidence a virus was involved with the subway death, even though all the rapid viral tests had been negative. "I also learned something else surprising, if not shocking. John DeVries in Toxicology ran a screen overnight for immunosuppressants. The woman had none on board. Zero!"

"How can that be if she recently had a heart transplant? I mean, you are sure she had a heart transplant, aren't you?"

For a few beats Jack just stared at Bart, expecting the man to laugh. It seemed absurd for him to pose this question at all, let alone to one of New York's most seasoned MEs. With some difficulty Jack suppressed the urge to make one of his cuttingly sarcastic responses. Without immediately responding, he got one of the stools on wheels from a neighboring desk, as he had on his last visit, and sat down.

"I'm going to assume that was a rhetorical question," Jack said. "Let's cut to the chase. Did Janice mention that I popped in here on my way in to work today? I was so sure it was an oversight that I hadn't been called during the evening. Instead I learned there hadn't been any calls about a missing, attractive, elegantly dressed woman. In particular, no calls from an apparent partner or wife named Helen."

"Janice did tell me," Bart said. "And she told me the time. You certainly were early."

"What's happened since I visited? Have there been any calls into Communications about the case that could lead to an identification?"

"I'm afraid not," Bart said.

"That's disappointing, to say the least. So what are you doing to solve this situation?" Jack couldn't keep the touch of sarcasm from his tone. He knew they were doing nothing. "You said that no one gets concerned until at least eight hours or even twenty-four hours go by. Well, for your edification, we are rapidly closing in on the twenty-four-hour marker. We need an identification! Especially if it turns out to involve some sort of a lethal virus, containment is going to be the number one priority. To do containment, an ID is absolutely essential. Have you spoken with Sergeant Murphy or Hank Monroe?" Sergeant Murphy was a New York City police officer attached to the NYPD Missing Persons Squad of the Detective Bureau. Hank Monroe was the director of the relatively new Identification Department. Prior to the 9/11 catastrophe, there hadn't been such a department; but after 9/11, when identification had been an operational nightmare, it was deemed essential.

"Not yet," Bart admitted.

"How about with the DNA people? Have you spoken with them this morning? Any results yet?"

"No, I haven't spoken with them. It is much too early for any results. Same with histology and serology."

"Call up everybody potentially involved and light a fire under them!" Jack said. He stood. "Meanwhile, I'm going to go up and talk with Sergeant Murphy and Hank Monroe myself. Something needs to be done around here."

Without waiting for a response, Jack headed over to the elevators. He knew he was being unfair, as ID was not officially in the purview of the MLI. But Jack felt this case was an exception. As far as he was concerned, the whole OCME team should have been on it as a priority right from the start.

Sergeant Murphy, or Murph, as he was known, had been assigned to the OCME seemingly for forever. He was past retirement age but seemed ageless, and no one pressed the issue. He loved his work, and everyone loved him. Previously he had the tiniest office in the entire organization, even smaller than the Toxicology director's. It was located on the first floor in the old 520 First Avenue building, directly behind Communications, and had been designed to be a small storage closet. But like a lot of OCME staff, Sergeant Murphy had been moved to the new high-rise when it opened and had been given a real office with not only a window but one with a fantastic view. He shared the space with two other PD officers who were also members of the NYPD Missing Persons Squad. These other officers, in contrast to Murph, were rotated on a three-month schedule.

Since Jack had gotten to know Sergeant Murphy over the years and thought of him as a friend, he sought him out first. The red-faced, silver-haired Irishman was at his new, comparatively large desk, kibitzing with his two youthful officemates. As usual, he had a mug of coffee in his hand. When Jack walked in, his already smiling face lit up further. He introduced Jack to the younger men. All three were in uniform.

"I have to talk to you about a body that came in yesterday," Jack said, wasting no time with small talk.

"Let me guess," Murph interrupted. "You want to talk about the Bellevue case that originated from the Twenty-third Street subway station."

"That's the one," Jack said, encouraged. "We have no ID, and making one could be extremely important. Unfortunately, Communications hasn't gotten any calls about a missing, youthful, well-dressed woman, which is very strange. Do you have any information at all?"

"No ID," Murph said. "The patrolman at the Bellevue emergency room copied me on his report sent to the Missing Persons Squad at One Police Plaza. It's standard operating procedure in this kind of case that I get notified. My understanding is that there was no ID when the patient was taken off the R train at the Twenty-third Street subway station. I have the report someplace." Sergeant Murphy opened a side drawer of his desk and began fumbling through a disorganized bunch of papers.

"Do you know if the Missing Persons Squad has made any headway on making an ID?" Jack asked.

"Not to my knowledge," Murph said as he pulled a paper free, "or I would have heard." He quickly read over the paper. "Okay, the case was assigned to a missing-persons case detective at the Thirteenth Precinct by the name of Pauli Cosenza. He's the one in charge. He also copied me with his report. Do you want his telephone number?"

"Please!" Jack said. "Have you spoken with him?"

"Nope," Murph said. "There would have been no reason. It's much too early in the case. It's not even been twenty-four hours." Sergeant Murphy took out a Post-it Note, jotted down a number, and handed the note to Jack. "But I have spoken with him in the past. Between you and me, he's not what I would call a ball of fire."

Jack took the slip of paper and made sure he could recognize the numbers. Sergeant Murphy's handwriting was notorious for illegibility. Jack tucked it into his wallet to be sure not to misplace it.

"You know what I find most amazing about this case," Murph said, "is how similar it is to one that Dr. Montgomery had five or six years ago. That patient had no ID when the body was picked up from the Fifty-ninth Street IND subway platform. It, too, involved a relatively young, well-dressed victim that no one called about. Of course, that one turned out to be very different in that it was a homicide and the victim was a Japanese male. But do you remember the case I'm talking about, Dr. Stapleton?"

"I do," Jack said. "You're right. I'd forgotten about that." Suddenly all the details flooded back into Jack's consciousness. There were definite similarities. Most interesting of all, thinking about the case reminded Jack of how creative Laurie had been in her investigations, which he'd made fun of at the time, but which now gave him a few ideas he'd not thought about. With such thoughts in mind, he asked Sergeant Murphy if he would do him a favor.

"Of course, Doc," Murph said. "Name it."

"I'd like you to find out the name and phone number of the Transit Police Officer involved in having the patient picked up from the Twenty-third Street station. There had to be one involved to coordinate with the EMTs."

"I'm sure there was," Murph said. "Shouldn't be a problem. I'll put one of these young guys on it right away."

Jack thanked Sergeant Murphy for Pauli Cosenza's number and for reminding him about Laurie's case, which he admitted might come in handy. After they assured each other that if one learned anything significant about the mystery woman's ID they would let the other know, Jack left the PD Missing Persons office. His destination was the newly expanded Anthropology Department, which happened to be on the same floor. Prior to 9/11, OCME Anthropology had been a single individual. Now it was an entire team and part of the Identification Department that included forensic dentistry. Within minutes, Jack was in the director's office, standing alongside a long Formica-topped table on which various groupings of human bones were laid out anatomically, each representing a different deceased human being.

"What can I do for you?" Hank Monroe said. He was a heavyset man sporting a long white coat, similar in silhouette to Bart Arnold but with a full head of hair. Also, his facial features were strikingly different. Whereas Bart's were appropriately rounded, Hank's were all full of sharp angles. It was as if the body and the face belonged to two different people. Jack had met the man on numerous occasions but didn't know him well. They hadn't worked many cases together and had offices in different buildings. The new OCME organization was not as collegial as the old was.

"Have you heard about the subway death case that came in yesterday?" Jack asked. When Hank said he had heard a bit from Rebecca Marshall but not much, Jack gave a rapid synopsis of the case, emphasizing the woman's youth, expensive clothes, Cartier watch, diamond earrings, tattoos, and the startling fact she'd had a relatively recent heart transplant.

"This is not the kind of case we usually get involved in," Hank said. He gestured toward the piles of bleached bones. "They've usually been dead for some time or are victims of mass disasters like 9/11."

"I understand," Jack said. "But we need an ID, and we need it now. I'm concerned it's a contagion case and possibly an index case of a potential outbreak. If there is a chance to control it, the effort has to start immediately. I need all the help I can get. Strangely enough, I'm having an equally difficult time isolating what I believe is a virus."

"Sorry to hear about your struggles," Hank said. "But let me tell you this: It is almost unheard of for a case of this kind to go unreported by a family member, a friend, or a coworker. Invariably it happens within hours, especially in this day and age, with our mobile phones keeping us in constant touch with each other."

"I'm well aware, but there has been nothing, and it is now approaching the twenty-four-hour limit."

"That's phenomenal," Hank said. He pursed his lips and shook his head. "In this business we all know if someone doesn't come forward within the first twenty-four-hour period, the chances of making an ID begin to fall precipitously. Not too many people know this fact, but it's true, even in this era of DNA technology."

"That doesn't sound encouraging," Jack said.

"It's not," Hank agreed. "But let's think positively. Do you think the patient having had a heart transplant might be of assistance?"

"Certainly," Jack said. "But how much, I don't know. There are a number of centers here in the metropolitan area that do them, and there must be hundreds of cases done each year. On top of that, there's no way to know whether she had her procedure here in the city or not."

"Okay, I understand," Hank said. "Here's what I can do. I can get my department actively involved and see if we can help. Meanwhile, the DNA people will be doing their magic, which will allow us to tap into the FBI's CODIS system and NamUs, the National Missing and Unidentified Persons System. The only other thing I can do is get in touch with my contacts at the NYPD Missing Persons Squad at One Police Plaza and try to goad them into action. Sometimes they need a bit of coaxing."

10

With the Post-it Note Sergeant Murphy had given him pressed against his monitor screen to be in full view, Jack called Detective Pauli Cosenza at the Thirteenth Precinct. Jack had returned from the high-rise building and was back in his office. From having had to call police stations around the city as well as other city bureaucratic offices on many previous cases, Jack knew he would have to be patient. In anticipation, he had his feet up on the corner of his desk and was sipping a fresh mug of coffee as the call went through.

Using a pen, he absently made a mark on a scratch pad with each ring. As he did so, he vaguely wondered what Detective Cosenza might tell him. Jack was hoping for the best, as Cosenza was most likely the only member of the NYPD Missing Persons Squad specifically tasked with making an identification on the subway death. From experience, Jack was not particularly optimistic that he'd learn much. After twenty rings, he became even less hopeful, realizing there was a chance no one would answer the extension he was calling. After thirty rings, he began to consider calling the main number of the Thirteenth Precinct and asking for the detective, although from sore experience he knew that wasn't necessarily better and was maybe worse.

After thirty-six rings, just when his patience was at an end, the phone was answered. And to Jack's astonishment it was the detective himself rather than someone else lower on the totem pole.

For a brief moment Jack was flustered and tripped over his words as they spilled out too quickly. Having the phone answered just when he was about to hang up made him fear that if he didn't speak fast enough the man might disconnect. Making an effort to slow down, Jack introduced himself, giving his name and position as a medical examiner at the OCME. He then told the detective that he had autopsied a youthful, unidentified woman the previous day who'd become sick on the R train and then had been declared dead at the Bellevue Hospital emergency room.

"I know the case," Pauli said. His voice was flat and unemotional, as if he was bored to tears.

"Excellent!" Jack said. He remembered Sergeant Murphy saying the man wasn't a ball of fire, so Jack purposefully tried to sound enthusiastic and upbeat. "I was told the case had been assigned to you."

Hoping the man would pick up on the thread of conversation, Jack purposefully paused. Unfortunately, there was nothing but silence on the other end of the line. "Hello?" Jack questioned after a few beats. He feared they'd been disconnected.

"Hello yourself," Pauli said.

"Am I wrong?" Jack questioned. "Was the case assigned to you or not?"

"It was assigned to me," Pauli said.

"Okay, good. What's happened so far? The OCME has not received any inquiries from family, coworkers, or friends. We still do not have an identification, and it's important that we get one."

"What do you mean, 'What's happened so far'?" Pauli questioned. "I got the report from the responding officer at the Bellevue ER and forwarded it down to One Police Plaza Missing Persons like I'm supposed to do. I also copied it to the OCME PD liaison, whatshisface."

"You mean Sergeant Murphy?" Jack questioned.

"That's the guy," Pauli said.

"Okay," Jack repeated. "What has Missing Persons done?"

"Not much, would be my guess, beyond adding the case to the list of missing persons. Just to give you an idea, we get around thirty-five missing-persons reports every day, three hundred sixty-five days a year. The Squad has a backup of almost thirteen thousand cases."

"And what have you done as the assigned detective during this critical first twenty-four-hour period on this particular case?" Jack asked, struggling to keep sarcasm out of his voice. It was already clear to him that Pauli was giving him the classic runaround. The so-called assigned detective was just sitting at his desk doing nothing instead of investigating anything.

There was a short silence until Pauli said, "Look, Doc, I sent the material where I'm supposed to send it. Since then I've been waiting."

"Waiting for what?" Jack questioned with obvious incredulity.

"I wait for more information. So far there's almost zilch, you know what I'm saying? I got a sketchy description from a patrol officer and that's it. I wait for prints, photos, and whatever you guys get from the autopsy in terms of descriptions of scars, tattoos, broken bones, you name it. When I get prints I run them locally, and if no hits are found, we run them on the state level up to federal. But I have to warn you. On a case like this with a snappily dressed broad, we rarely get hits. It's up to family to come forward. Beyond all that, we wait for DNA info so we can run CODIS and NamUs. And to give you an idea of what I'm up against, I have a hundred and seven other missing-persons cases besides this one sitting here on my desk."

Struggling to be civil, as it would be counterproductive to alienate the detective, Jack thanked him for his time. Jack then gave his mobile number on the outside possibility that Pauli might learn something that could be helpful in making an ID. Jack promised to do the same before ringing off.

After hanging up, Jack rocked back in his desk chair, stared up at the ceiling, and fumed for a few minutes to regain his composure. Even though he was a civil servant himself, he'd always found dealing with bureaucrats and government employees in general to be emotionally challenging, and Detective Cosenza was no exception. Jack had the sense that the man did as little work as humanly possible and merely shuffled papers around on his desk. But to make certain he had all the information, Jack called Sergeant Murphy to make sure the detective received what was now available—namely, the digital body photos, tattoo photos, and fingerprints.

When his mind was clearer and his emotions under control, Jack struggled to remember the name of Laurie's friend who was a supervisor at PSAC, the NYC Public Safety Answering Center. He and Laurie had talked about the woman a few months ago because Laurie had learned she'd been moved to the new, fortresslike 911 PSAC II building in the Bronx. Previously she'd worked at PSAC I in Brooklyn. Jack remembered the woman as having been a big help to Laurie when Laurie had investigated the case involving the unidentified Japanese homicide victim. Jack thought she might be able to help him in a similar fashion, if he could only remember her name. He thought briefly about calling down to the front office and asking Laurie, but quickly changed his mind. Laurie would want to know why he wanted the number, and after their words yesterday afternoon and last night, Jack preferred she didn't know what he was up to. Despite Laurie's orders to the contrary, Jack was hoping the subway death would lead to some serious fieldwork.

The raucous ring of his office phone snapped Jack's attention back to the immediate present. It was Sergeant Murphy.

"I got the responding transit patrolman's name, badge number, and mobile phone," Murph said. "You have a pencil and paper handy, or do you want me to text it?"

"I have pencil and paper," Jack said. "Go for it."

"His name is Dominic Golacki. Obviously, a nice Irish boy," Murph joked. The sergeant had a renowned sense of humor. He spelled the name for Jack and then gave the badge and mobile numbers. "I was told he's Polish."

Jack was about to dial the number when he suddenly remembered the name of the 911 supervisor. It was Cynthia Bellows. Although Jack had the Brooklyn 911 call center phone number in his contacts, he didn't have the new Bronx one. To get it, he called Sergeant Murphy back. A few minutes later he was talking to the operator of PSAC, and he asked to be put through to Cynthia's line.

Half expecting he'd have to leave a number for a callback, Jack was pleased when he found himself on the line with the woman directly. He explained who he was, and, most important, that he was Dr. Laurie Montgomery's husband, and then told the woman that Laurie had been promoted to be the chief medical examiner of New York City. Cynthia had not heard and was thrilled.

"I'm calling for a favor," Jack said after the pleasantries. "I remember you did this for Laurie on at least one occasion. What I need is the name and mobile number of a nine-one-one caller. It happened just yesterday, and it came in from an R subway train. The call was to report a sick passenger."

"Do you have the time of the call?" Cynthia asked. "We average around one hundred eighty EMS calls per hour."

"I don't have the exact time," Jack admitted. "But I could find out the exact time the transit police were notified. Would that help?"

"Do you have an approximate time?"

"Yes. It was around ten A.M."

"That might be good enough," Cynthia said. "I'll see what I can do. Give me a number and I'll get back to you."

After giving Cynthia Bellows his mobile number, Jack hung up his office phone. As soon as he did so, he chided himself for not asking Cynthia when approximately he might hear back from her. Probably due to his dislike of talking on the phone, he wasn't good at it. Like a typical

Luddite, he much preferred face-to-face interaction, although emails were becoming a close second and he was learning to appreciate texting.

Looking at Dominic Golacki's mobile number, Jack thought about him being his next call. But he hesitated. Laurie had benefited greatly from the help of the transit police's Special Investigation Unit, as they had provided her with the videotapes of the 59th Street IND subway station. It was from the videotapes that she had determined her case's death had been a homicide, which broke open the case. Jack knew that subways now had continuous video recordings inside the trains, and, remembering Laurie's successes, he thought about getting them. His idea was to watch the tapes and determine who had stolen the subway death's phone and purse, which she undoubtedly had, in hopes of apprehending the individual and making an ID. But the more Jack thought about the idea, the less reasonable it seemed. Even if he got an image of the thief or thieves, the chances of finding them were slim at best. Besides, it would all take too much time, and time was of the essence.

In a minor fit of exasperation, Jack balled up the paper with Golacki's number, and then shot it like a basketball into his wastebasket, which he'd placed on top of his file cabinet for exactly that purpose. Jack was tired of the telephone and tired of the subway death case thwarting him at every turn. Then, as if to mock him, his mobile rang with the firetruck alarm that he had again forgotten to change.

"I found it," Cynthia Bellows said without preamble when Jack answered. "You were very close on the time. The first call came in at 10:02 A.M. There were two others, but those people were informed that EMS had already been alerted. I have the caller's name and mobile number if you are still interested."

"Absolutely," Jack said. It seemed like a minor success. The name was Tess Eggan. "Thank you muchly."

"You are most welcome," Cynthia said. "And give my best to Laurie and congratulate her for me on her promotion."

"Will do, and thanks," Jack said, even though he knew he was lying.

He wasn't going to tell Laurie that he'd been speaking with Cynthia. It would raise too many questions. Jack knew he was being at least partially childish, but he didn't care.

As soon as he had disconnected from Cynthia, Jack put in a call to Ms. Eggan. As he expected, assuming the woman would be working, he had to leave a voice message. In it he carefully described himself as a senior medical examiner at the Office of the Chief Medical Examiner who wanted to talk with her briefly about her 911 call the previous day. He then left his mobile number. Just to be absolutely sure she got the number, he also texted it along with the main OCME number, in case she wanted to check if he was who he said he was.

With that done, Jack again rocked back in his chair and stared up at the ceiling. He wished there was more he could do, but for the moment he couldn't think of anything. At the same time, he knew he shouldn't be spending so much effort on the ID issue, since it was other people's job, but he couldn't help himself. He needed the diversion, as evidenced by his mind switching back almost immediately to Emma and, ultimately, to Dorothy. Was Emma's diagnosis for certain or was it going to remain up in the air? Autism was not an easy diagnosis because it wasn't a single disease with a telltale biomarker that could be confirmed in a medical laboratory. It was an impression, and via her pediatrician, Emma was still being evaluated. As far as Dorothy was concerned, Jack wondered if Laurie was going to have the strength to deal with the issue before Caitlin was driven to distraction and abandoned them.

"Hello! Dr. Stapleton!" a voice called out simultaneously with a knock on Jack's partially open office door.

Jack rocked forward with a thump and found himself looking up into the face of a woman who looked more like a teenager than a college graduate. He vaguely recognized her as one of the newest medical-legal investigators. With the OCME physically split between two buildings, there wasn't the familiarity that had previously existed among the departments, something Jack missed.

"Mr. Bart Arnold wanted me to run these slides over and give them to you in person," the MLI said. She extended a microscope slide tray toward Jack, and then, with a toss of her head and its attached ponytail, she was gone.

Jack blinked. It had all happened so quickly, and had he not been holding the slide tray, he might have thought the brief encounter had been more in his mind than in reality. Looking at the slides themselves, Jack immediately understood why Bart had had them hand-delivered. They were the Jane Doe slides. Apparently, Bart had managed to motivate the Histology Department to exceptional efficiency. In Jack's mind, getting mounted and stained histology slides in less than twenty-four hours might qualify for *Guinness World Records*. Jack knew that he had been a bit hard on the MLI supervisor, but maybe it was paying off.

Using the wheels on his desk chair, Jack moved over to his microscope and turned on the light source. The first slides he looked at were of the lungs. Even using low power, the amount of inflammation of the lung tissue was obvious. It was also apparent there was no real consolidation, as death had intervened before it could occur. Going to higher magnification, Jack could appreciate the hyperacute inflammatory cell infiltration of macrophages, granulocytes, immune dendritic cells, and natural killer cells that filled the lung's alveolar spaces and septa. There was significant destruction. From Jack's perspective, it was like looking at the aftermath of a horrendous microscopic battle that characterized a cytokine storm. If it was a virus, it was an impressively lethal one that made the immune system go into hyperdrive.

Next, Jack picked out the slides of the heart and was about to place the first under the microscope's objective when his mobile phone scared him yet again, as he still hadn't changed the ringtone back to something reasonable. Snapping up the phone, he answered curtly.

"Is this Dr. Stapleton?" a high, nasal-sounding voice asked.

"It is," Jack said as he adjusted the ringtone.

"My name is Tess Eggan," the woman said. "You left a voice message for me to call you back about my nine-one-one call yesterday."

"Oh, yes, of course," Jack said, mildly flustered. He'd been so entranced by the microscopic inflammatory carnage that he'd forgotten.

"Since you're a medical examiner, I suppose that doesn't bode well for the woman I called about."

"It doesn't," Jack agreed. "Unfortunately, the woman was moribund by the time she was taken from the train and was essentially dead on arrival at the Bellevue Hospital emergency."

"What a tragedy," Tess said. "She was young. She looked about my age and very attractive. She even had a hairstyle somewhat similar to mine. Early on, I almost spoke with her. I was tempted."

"Are you saying you were on the train with her for a while?"

"I was," Tess said. "I live in Bay Ridge, where the R originates. She got on soon after, in Sunset Park. It was either the fifth or sixth stop, meaning Fifty-third Street or Forty-fifth Street. I don't remember exactly."

"Had you ever seen her before on the train?" Jack asked. He was encouraged.

"I never have. And I would have remembered."

"Did she act as if she was well when she boarded?"

"Completely. At that point the train wasn't yet crowded. I was hoping she'd sit next to me, but she didn't. She sat in a seat nearby, but not next to anyone."

"Was she carrying anything?"

"Yes. She had a small, stylish backpack."

"How about a phone?"

"Yes. I saw her use her phone soon after she boarded."

"When she was brought in to Bellevue, she had no backpack and no phone," Jack said. "And that is the core of the problem. We have no identification. No family members, or coworkers, or friends have reported her missing."

"That's terrible," Tess said. "I can't imagine why no one would call about her. And about her backpack and phone: Someone must have stolen them."

"We are equally confused why no one has called."

"What did she die of?"

"That's still to be determined," Jack said. He was tempted to ask Tess if she felt any kind of symptoms whatsoever, but he didn't. He didn't want to alarm her, and since he had her phone number, he knew he could alert her if it developed that it was necessary. Instead, he asked, "Do you know when she began to get sick?"

"I don't," Tess said. "I started to read my book, which is how I spend my time on the subway. And the train got crowded, as it usually does. The next thing I knew was that she was gasping for breath. I think it was around the time we had reached the East River. But I'm not sure. Then I saw her collapse on the floor at the Union Square station. That was when I called nine-one-one."

"Thank you for your help," Jack said. Tess had certainly confirmed his fear that the victim had gotten on the train feeling quite normal, only to be on death's door by the time she got into Manhattan. Jack thought again of the stories he'd heard about the 1918 influenza pandemic. He found the similarity disturbing.

"If I think of anything else, I'll call back," Tess said graciously. "It is such a sad story."

Jack disconnected the call and for a moment thought about what he had learned, which wasn't much. Possibly the victim lived in Sunset Park, Brooklyn, although there was no way to be certain. He wondered if there was any chance that some flyers describing the deceased and placed at both the 53rd Street and 45th Street subway stations would result in any calls. He doubted it. The trouble with the idea was that it would take too long just to figure out which city agency would execute it. Besides, his intuition told him it would have a low chance of success. Instead, Jack found himself back to thinking about the victim's heart transplant. Since that history put her in a very special, small group, he thought there was a good chance it could solve the identity issue. He just didn't know how exactly to use the information and do it quickly.

While his mind played with that idea, he returned to looking at the histology slides. The next slides he was interested in examining were those of the heart. Although there had been no signs of inflammation grossly, he wondered what he was going to see microscopically. The case was full of surprises.

Using low magnification, Jack scanned the first slide. It looked entirely normal, almost too normal, considering the woman had essentially drowned in her own body fluids. Switching to high power, he was able to confirm that there was absolutely no inflammation whatsoever. Now he had proof the woman did not suffer from organ rejection, although he still thought there was an outside chance her death could have been caused by a bizarre form of graft-versus-host disease, even though scientifically it made no sense to him.

The rest of the heart slides were as normal as the first, including sections through the sutured portions of the aorta, the pulmonary arteries and veins, and the large veins of the body. Everything had healed superbly with no inflammation. From everything Jack could see, it had been a perfectly performed heart transplant, and the patient should have lived a relatively normal life-span.

Turning next to the organs where he had seen some suggestion of mild inflammation during the autopsy, Jack found consistent microscopic evidence of the same. That included the kidneys, the spleen, and the gallbladder. Again, it suggested to him a viral illness, but a nonspecific one, and the amount of inflammation wasn't enough to cause the woman any symptoms, much less her death.

The rest of the slides were pretty much normal. When he was finished, Jack returned them all to the slide tray, keeping them organized by organ systems. He put the slide tray on the corner of his desk with the idea of showing the lung slides to his former officemate,

Dr. Chet McGovern. Jack and Chet frequently shared interesting cases. Jack wanted to know if Chet had ever seen what Jack was planning on calling a cytokine storm and whether he had any idea of what could have caused it.

Returning to the ID conundrum and that the victim had had a recent heart transplant, Jack Googled heart transplant centers in the New York metropolitan area. He was surprised and daunted by how many there were, including NYU Langone Medical Center, which was situated right next door to the OCME. Since the two institutions had a formal connection, with NYU Pathology residents rotating through the OCME for their forensic pathology, Jack called the heart transplant referral line for some general information.

After being transferred a number of times, causing significant delay, Jack finally found himself talking to Nancy Bergmeyer, a certified nurse practitioner who functioned as a transplant nurse coordinator and as director of the program. Jack immediately sensed from her commanding voice that she was a no-nonsense, well-informed individual. After making sure the woman had a few minutes available, he launched into an explanation of why he was calling: "Yesterday, I autopsied a female in her late twenties or early thirties who died of a very rapidly developing pulmonary disease. My worry is that it might have been infectious. The problem is, we have no ID, and we really need one quickly." He went on to say that he'd determined the woman had had a heart transplant three or four months earlier, which made him wonder if that fact could help make an identification.

"It's possible," Nancy said. "But it probably won't be as easy as you might believe, and it likely would take more time than you might imagine. In this day and age of strict adherence to HIPAA rules protecting medical records, we can't offer anything to someone like yourself or even law enforcement on a fishing expedition. It's a catch-22 in that you are looking for a name, but we can't give you anything unless we have authorization, meaning a warrant or a subpoena, and to get a warrant or a subpoena a name is needed. And what you are talking about involves a lot of patients. To give you an idea of the number, somewhere around fifteen to twenty percent of the heart transplant recipients are in the age bracket of your patient."

"Yikes! This is what I was afraid of," Jack admitted. "How many heart transplants are done in the metropolitan area in a year?"

"I'd say two to three hundred," Nancy said. "There would be more if it wasn't limited by the supply of organs."

Jack whistled under his breath. It was obvious the transplant club had more members than he had bargained for, magnifying the difficulties. "Let me ask you this: Post-transplant care is pretty intense, correct?"

"Absolutely. For the first month we see them every week at a minimum, with cardiac biopsies as needed. Up until three months, every other week at a minimum. After three months, maybe every other month. Of course, the patients are seen more often if problems develop, like acute rejection or arrhythmias or high blood pressure."

"So post-transplant patients generally remain near their transplant center," Jack said. He was thinking that if the subway death patient lived in Sunset Park she probably had had her surgery in the metro area.

"I'd say that was the case. At least, that has been our experience."

"At autopsy this patient's heart looked perfect. There was no sign of any inflammation whatsoever. From what you are saying, she might not be scheduled to be seen for a month or two."

"That would be an appropriate assumption. If what you're thinking is that it might take some time before she is missed in terms of her post-op appointments, you are probably correct."

Suddenly Jack remembered the surprising toxicology result. "One other thing of note: Toxicology determined she had no immunosuppressant drugs on board. Is that surprising?"

"It is more than surprising," Nancy said with obvious incredulity. "I think you should run the tests again. She had to be on immunosuppressants to avoid acute rejection. It's standard procedure."

"What if the heart happened to be a particularly good match?"

"It would have to be from an identical twin," Nancy said with equal skepticism. "And if that had happened here in NYC, it would have made the headlines or even the front page of the *Daily News*! Maybe with a kidney, but not a heart, for obvious reasons. She had to have been on immunosuppressants. Even if it had been a decent match. No question."

Jack thanked Nancy for her time.

"No problem," Nancy said. "Do you want my mobile number, in case you have any other questions?"

"I would," Jack said. He wrote it down on his scratch pad and then rang off.

"Damn!" Jack shouted at no one, and he slapped the surface of his desk with an open palm hard enough to make his keyboard jump. He felt frustrated. But then, out of the blue, an idea popped into his head: *What about the tattoos?*

11

Like most people, Jack thought of himself as having a reasonable amount of self-knowledge. A realist, he knew that some of his personality traits were not ideal, like his limited patience with lazy, self-indulgent people—a designation he unfortunately gave to most of the people he had to deal with. But there was one trait he prided himself on that had stood him in good stead, and that was determination. When he got something in his craw, such as this subway death case, he didn't give up easily.

Turning on his monitor, Jack brought up the digital images of the three tattoos on the woman's body. He looked at each carefully and was again impressed by the puzzle piece. Vinnie had said something about Pinterest, so that seemed like a good place to start. He was somewhat hesitant to sign up, not knowing if he'd be bombarded with unwanted emails, but he took the risk. Once he was on the site, he searched for "puzzle piece tattoo." He was surprised by the variety available, including permutations of the one on the woman's arm. Then he searched for "puzzle piece tattoo rainbow" and found the exact image, complete with the rainbow colors in the puzzle piece's base, just as Vinnie had said.

He then Googled palm tree tattoos and discovered they were also extremely popular, even more so than the puzzle piece. He was interested to find that they appropriately stood for beach life, summer, and relaxation. Researching for the meaning of the Chinese character, he learned it meant "love." He then read a long Wikipedia article about tattoos and how their popularity had grown in mainstream culture.

Jack sat back in his chair and thought about what he'd read and about tattoos in a general sense. He'd never understood why someone would be tempted to permanently mar his or her body with ink, what with the risks of infection or just a subsequent change of heart. But having seen the profusion of images on Pinterest, some of which, like the puzzle piece, were quite clever, he thought of the activity in a slightly different light. He was no more tempted to get a tattoo himself than he'd ever been, but he'd come to recognize that there was more artistry involved than he'd previously thought, which made him believe the tattooists probably thought of themselves as artists and not as mere technicians. Following that line of thinking made him wonder if the artists recognized one another's work. With everything else going against him, Jack thought it was another possible line of attack in the ID effort.

Tipping forward again, Jack sent the three images he'd taken of the tattoos with zero compression down to the printer in the front office. He wanted some high-resolution photos. Then he Googled tattoo establishments in lower Manhattan and found a highly rated one not that far away called Tattoo Art and Piercings. Checking their website, he learned they had three supposedly vaunted tattoo artists. It was on the West Side, but his Trek would get him there in a flash. Grabbing his bomber jacket, he left his office to head down to get the photos. As he waited for the elevator, he worried about running into Laurie, who had already warned him about not making any field trips. He was in no mood to get into another argument. Unfortunately, since it was lunchtime, the possibility of a confrontation wasn't a hypothetical concern. But he decided it was a risk he had to take, because for what he had in mind, he needed good pics.

Jack zipped into the front office and headed for the printer, with the idea of making it a very quick in-and-out visit. He waved a casual hello to Cheryl, who was on the phone, which he thought was auspicious because it precluded any conversation. But a moment later he noticed Laurie's door was ajar, forcing him to make a snap decision of whether to proceed or retreat. An instant later the decision became academic when Laurie caught sight of him through the open door and waved at him to come into her office.

Jack got the photos first. They were as clear as a bell, with good color. He then went into the inner sanctum and tried to gird himself. In retrospect, he did feel a bit guilty for having snuck out of the apartment that morning without so much as leaving a note.

"I'm glad to see you, and it's good timing," Laurie said. She was sitting at her desk with blueprint architectural plans spread out in front of her. "I have a few minutes before my next conference call. I missed you this morning." She spoke with a sincere and uncritical tone. Jack felt relieved, especially having been caught red-handed wearing his bomber jacket and advertising he was on his way out of the OCME. "I ended up oversleeping," Laurie added. "I suppose I was counting on you waking me up before you left, which isn't fair. It was my own fault. As usual, I stayed up much too late going over all that budget nonsense."

"It was too early when I left," Jack said. "The subway death had me awake before five. I was eager to get in here to find out why I hadn't been called about an ID, but the explanation turned out to be pretty simple. There'd been no ID because there had been zero calls from family or friends."

"That's strange," Laurie said. "Especially the way you described her. She certainly wasn't a homeless person." Laurie stood up from her desk, walked around Jack, and closed her office door for privacy. Then she stood on her tiptoes and gave him a peck on the cheek. Jack took it as a gesture of reconciliation and felt encouraged.

"It's more than strange," Jack said. "And it's driving me to distraction."

"And now that it has been more than twenty-four hours, it's beginning to remind me of my Japanese subway homicide, which took days to get an ID. You remember the case, don't you?"

"Absolutely, and I thought the exact same thing," Jack said. "And since 'imitation is the sincerest form of flattery,' I've been faithfully reenacting your efforts."

Laurie failed to suppress a laugh. "Isn't that ironic. I remember at the time you made fun of what I was doing and thought I was wasting my time."

"Guilty as charged," Jack confessed. "But in my defense, I haven't gone to the extent of getting transit videotapes. My victim certainly wasn't the victim of a homicide."

"Then how did you imitate me?"

"I called your nine-one-one supervisor friend, Cynthia Bellows, just like you did. By the way, she said hello and offered congrats for your becoming chief. Just like you did, I got the name and number of the person who made the nine-one-one call from the R train. Talking with her, I confirmed that the victim had appeared entirely normal when she boarded the train in Sunset Park, Brooklyn. I also learned she had a backpack and a phone, which obviously got stolen."

"Did you make the effort to talk with the assigned Missing Persons detective?"

"I did," Jack said. "But Detective Pauli Cosenza was no help at all. I had the feeling the lazy bum just pushed papers around his desk. Just to get ahold of him I had to let the phone ring almost forty times."

"My Missing Persons detective contact was also no help on the first call. I even remember his name: Detective Stedman. But the second time I called, he was like a different person. Maybe you should give your PD contact another chance."

"Maybe," Jack said. "But I'm far from optimistic. I did tell Sergeant Murphy to make sure the detective got all the information from here as it becomes available, like the fingerprints and these photos of the victim's tattoos." Jack handed the three photos to Laurie.

"I'm not a tattoo fan by any means," Laurie said as she studied each photo in turn. "But these are rather tasteful and interesting, and I guess she was a lesbian."

"That's the assumption, for whatever it's worth," Jack said.

"Well, the tattoos should help identify her," Laurie said. She handed the photos back to Jack. "What a fascinating case. I have to say, I'm jealous. Forensic pathology is so much more interesting than arguing with politicians and city employees about budgets and construction plans." She gestured dismissively over to her desk and the blueprints.

"You can always put in your resignation as the chief," Jack said. "As soon as they find someone else, you could come back and be one of us grunts."

Laurie sighed. "I've accepted this challenge, and I am going to see it through," she said. "I can't give up now. What about your virologist friend: Any more word from her?" When Jack had returned from playing basketball the previous evening, he'd told Laurie that all the rapid screens for the usual viruses that caused respiratory illness had been negative, not once but twice.

"Yes! I spoke with her around nine o'clock," Jack said. "She thinks she sees some early cytopathic changes in a human kidney cell culture that she inoculated yesterday. If it turns out to be true, then she believes some unknown pathogenic virus is involved. I'll be talking with her later today to confirm."

"Damn! That's not good." Laurie pressed her lips together and shook her head in dismay. "An unknown, rapidly lethal virus lurking on a New York City subway is a terrifying proposition."

"I couldn't agree more," Jack said, "which is why I still think we should alert the Commissioner of Health about what's potentially brewing."

"No!" Laurie said without hesitation. "I still feel the opposite. As I said yesterday, we are going to wait until we have a confirmed, verifiable diagnosis. In some respects, an unknown virus could cause more panic than a known one. What did your virologist friend suggest was the time-line for what she's doing?"

"She didn't say. She only commented that if a virus is present, then she'll have to try to identify it."

"Did she use the phrase 'try to identify it'?"

"I believe so, yes."

"Good grief! That's not very reassuring. Did she give you an idea of how she might go about trying to identify it and maybe an idea of how long it would take?"

"She didn't. I should have asked, but I didn't think of it. I'm not thinking right these days."

"It's a tough time for all of us. Don't be hard on yourself." Laurie walked over and sat on the couch. She patted the cushion next to her as a way of inviting Jack to join her.

"I did learn something else about the case that is surprising," Jack said as he came over and sat down. "John DeVries found no immunosup-pressant drugs on a toxicological screen that he ran overnight. I con-firmed with a nurse coordinator of the heart transplant team next door that that is totally unheard of, just like it is so strange that no one has seemingly missed this woman."

"Well, I have full confidence that you and Bart Arnold will figure it all out," Laurie said. "In the meantime, I wanted to tell you what I did this morning on the home front. I spoke with Caitlin about my mother."

"That's a start," Jack said.

"You're right that Caitlin is upset, and she's finding dealing with my mother difficult," Laurie said. "But you're wrong about her threatening to leave."

"She told me she was upset enough that she was thinking of leaving," Jack snapped. "I didn't make it up."

"Well, I just spoke with her this morning," Laurie said. "She admit-ted that my mother was hard for her to get along with, but she said she was dedicated to the children."

"Then she's telling you one thing and telling me something else entirely," Jack said. "Rather than debate who is getting the truth, I think the cause of her discontent has to be addressed. Did you talk with your mother this morning?"

"Of course I spoke with her."

"Did you talk about her giving us a break?"

"She's not all bad, Jack," Laurie countered. "She's getting JJ to interact with Emma. And she is spearheading getting a second opinion on Emma's diagnosis."

"But that doesn't require her to be living with us and tormenting both Caitlin and me. I feel guilty enough about Emma's autism and don't need her to continually blame the Stapleton genes. And if she mouths off about the MMR vaccine again, I'm going to scream. Why can't you just tell her we need some privacy? We have enough problems, especially if Caitlin were to leave."

"You know why I can't. It would devastate her, and she is already having a difficult time dealing with Emma's diagnosis and being eighty-three years old with some medical problems of her own. But I have thought of a possible solution."

"And what is that?"

"I'm going to talk with my father. Over the last few years, particularly after JJ's illness, I've been progressively able to talk with him about issues like this. He understands my mother better than anyone. Besides, he can't be happy she's been away for as long as she has."

"Fine," Jack said. "Talk to Sheldon. If you think he can help, that's great. We need some peace in our household so that we can deal with this new challenge."

A sudden knock on the office door diverted their attention.

"Come in!" Laurie called out.

The door opened. It was Cheryl. "Sorry to interrupt," she said. "But the conference call will be starting in just a few minutes."

"Okay, thank you," Laurie said.

Cheryl closed the door.

Both Laurie and Jack got to their feet. "I'll try to call my father after my conference call," Laurie said. "And I'll see when we might be able to get together."

"I hope it's as soon as possible," Jack said.

Laurie reached out and gave one of the lapels of Jack's bomber jacket a playful tug. "And *I* hope you're going out for a bite of lunch and not to cause trouble."

"I'll try to behave myself," Jack said with uncamouflaged sarcasm. He knew exactly what Laurie was referring to—namely, what she'd warned him about the day before. She didn't want him to become overly invested in the subway death case as a diversion from their domestic issues and create havoc for her as the OCME chief. And like the day before, Jack felt immediate irritation. He needed a diversion, and he wasn't going to be denied.

"Exactly where are you going?" Laurie demanded. Her tone had also changed. She was back to her role as the chief medical examiner, with all its attendant responsibilities.

"I'm going to a tattoo parlor," Jack snapped. "I realized it's a craze that had more or less passed me by. I want to rectify that. I used to think it was for drunken sailors and badasses, but I've changed my mind."

"I hope by this visit you're not hijacking Bart Arnold's job," Laurie said, refusing to take the bait that he might be interested in getting a tattoo himself. "I would prefer you don't go out in the field doing your own investigations. But if you must, Jack, please don't put me in a difficult situation. This job is already stressful enough."

"I'll try to keep that in mind," Jack said. He opened the office door and walked out with the tattoo photos clutched in his hand. He didn't say goodbye. He also avoided talking to or even looking at Cheryl. For the moment he thought it best to keep to himself.

12

Jack had seen tattoo parlors in the past, and it was his impression that they were always in the less-desirable parts of town and often appeared dark and uninviting, reflecting their old association with the underbelly of society, including criminality and gangs. He was mildly surprised that Tattoo Art and Piercing didn't fit that mold in the slightest. The neighborhood wasn't Fifth Avenue, but the commercial area was reasonably upscale, with a number of apparently successful businesses, just as the tattoo parlor appeared to be.

Walking in, Jack stopped just inside the front door. The interior of the shop was bright, clean, and cheerful, with a glossy, recently refinished blond hardwood floor. Glass-fronted and -surfaced display cases that also served as countertops extended down the length of the room. On the wall was a collection of carefully framed photos of men and women of a variety of ages and apparent social standing, all sporting a wide range of tattoos and piercings. The tattoos were literally on all parts of the body, whereas the piercings were mostly facial or on the ears, although several were on more intimate parts. A curtain separated the

front, public part of the shop from the back, where Jack assumed the tattooing and piercing was done in what he imagined were private rooms.

At the moment there were three customers, two men and one
woman, each being helped by a separate employee. All were looking at
catalog-like books and presumably trying to make up their minds. All
appeared to Jack to be in the twenty-five to forty-five age bracket. One of
the men wore a carefully pressed business suit and tie. The other man
and the woman were both more casually dressed in stylish jeans.

Almost immediately a fourth employee appeared. Like the other
employees, he was trendier in appearance than the customers. In particular, he had a fade haircut with the top portion dyed a light green color.
Tattoos covered the visible portions of both arms.

"Can I help you?" the man asked in a friendly voice. "My name is
Andre. Are you interested in a tattoo or a piercing?"

"Actually, I'm just looking for some information," Jack said. It tickled
him to think of Laurie's reaction if he did come back with an elaborate
tattoo someplace on his body. In some respects, he thought it would serve
her right. Then again, the fifteen-minute bike ride to the tattoo parlor
had helped clear his head, enough to make him embarrassed by his sensitivity and defensiveness when Laurie had called him out on his attitude
and behavior. He certainly didn't want to make her job any more difficult
than it already was and had no intention of doing so. But he was not
going to stay isolated in his office.

"What kind of information?" Andre asked. His tone audibly
changed.

Jack took out his medical examiner badge that looked for all the
world like a law enforcement badge. In the past he'd flashed it on occasion, as it invariably opened doors. Being in a tattoo parlor made Jack feel
slightly out of his comfort zone, and he wanted to get the conversation
off on the right foot. He flipped the wallet closed before Andre had a
chance to look closely at the badge's details. "I'm investigating an important death case," Jack explained. "The problem is we have no identifica-

tion, which we need. However, the deceased had three tattoos. I'd like to talk with one of your principal tattoo artists about them. Is that what they call themselves? Artists? I haven't spent much time in tattoo parlors."

"Absolutely they are artists," Andre said. "Some more than others. Just a minute. I'll be right back."

He disappeared behind the curtain. One of the other employees looked over at Jack briefly, having apparently overheard. He flashed a nervous smile before going back to his customer. Jack wondered what that meant, if anything. To pass the time, Jack looked into the display case. It contained a bewildering number and variety of piercing jewelry. On top of the display case was a large, heavy album of tattoo designs. Jack flipped through it rapidly. It was apparent to Jack that tattoo possibilities were truly mind-bogglingly legion.

A moment later, Andre reappeared with a youthful, slender, dark-complexioned, and swankily dressed woman in tow. She was as trendy as Andre and the others. She had long, luxurious, almost black hair with strikingly intense violet highlights, highly arched dark eyebrows, and numerous dainty nose piercings and jeweled nose rings. On her upper chest at the base of her neck, peeking between the lapels of a white coat, was an elaborate and intricate tattoo. She was wearing latex gloves, as if she had been in the middle of a procedure.

"Hello," the young woman said. "My name is Kristina Vega. I am the owner of this shop and also the chief tattoo artist. Who am I speaking with?"

"Dr. Jack Stapleton. I'm a medical examiner at the Office of the Chief Medical Examiner."

"This is not some unorthodox inspection of our facility, is it?" Kristina questioned.

"Not at all," Jack said reassuringly. He thought the question explained the other employee's nervous smile. With the invariable attendant medical problems associated with both tattooing and piercing, Jack imagined inspections were critical. "As I mentioned to Andre, I wanted to talk to you about some tattoos. I have photos right here." Jack unrolled the photos and spread them out on the surface of the display case. To keep them flat, he stuck the edges under the tattoo catalog.

Sensing she was going to be detained at least for a few minutes, Kristina pulled off her gloves. She asked Andre to go back and tell her customer she'd return shortly to finish up. Kristina then used her hands to smooth out the photos and studied them carefully. She took her time. Andre returned almost immediately and looked over her shoulder.

"Not bad," she said finally, straightening. "The Chinese character appears amateurish, but the puzzle piece and the palm are okay, with just minor blemishes and drifting of the pigments. I'd give the two a B-plus."

"Interesting," Jack said. He was impressed with this woman and wondered if she was older than she looked. Initially he thought she could be anywhere between twenty and thirty, but now he wasn't sure. She seemed remarkably mature. "But it's not grades I'm interested in hearing," he continued. "What I am interested in is how unique and recognizable this art is. You artists don't sign your work like other fine artists, for obvious reasons. But how distinctive do you feel it is? Presumably tattoo artists can recognize their own work. Is that fair to say?"

"It is, for sure," Kristina said. "Particularly custom designs. The more the tattoo is flash, the less recognizable it is, even if you did it yourself."

"I'm not sure I understand," Jack said.

"Tattoo flash are designs that exist out there in the world," Kristina said. "It comes from customers, tattoo artists, and even professional flash artists. It's out there. It's like this stuff on my walls or in this binder." Kristina patted the top of the tattoo catalog Jack had mindlessly flipped through. "It's generic stuff. You can buy it online with an outline, so it's easy to reproduce, and it can be reproduced over and over. Almost anybody can do it. But over the last number of years shops like mine have become custom shops. Everything is more or less stylized for the customer, which makes it unique and more recognizable."

"Okay, I get it now," Jack said. "What's your feeling about these three photos? Are these tattoos generic or recognizable?"

"The Chinese character is definitely generic. Totally! The puzzle piece is, too, since you can find all sorts of permutations of the idea online. The only unique thing is the name Helen."

"So this design is really common?" Jack said. Vinnie had confirmed as much during the autopsy, but Jack had hoped anyway that it could be a lead.

"Oh, yeah! It's common," Kristina said. She bared the volar surface of her own left wrist. On it was a tattooed outline of a puzzle piece containing the name Kate. "It's been common for a while for couples. But it's becoming particularly common now because it has been adopted for the autism awareness movement."

"What?" Jack demanded. He couldn't believe what he had just heard. It was as if Kristina had slapped him with a wet washrag.

"Yeah," Kristina continued, unaware of Jack's reaction. "I've done a few puzzle-piece tattoos myself on young couples with autistic kids. Not exactly like this but similar. It's something about the illness being a puzzle, but no one has told me specifically."

Jack struggled to regain his composure and reorient his mind. "What about the palm tree?" he asked.

"That is probably the most custom tattoo of these three," Kristina said. She bent over and studied it more. "Palm trees are quite popular because of their symbolic meaning. So whoever did this one probably just made it up as they went along. You don't really need an outline."

"When you look at a tattoo like that, do you have any idea what specific artist might have done it?" Jack asked.

"Not really," Kristina said. She bent back over to study the image again. "Although the way the fronds are drawn reminds me of a friend, but it would be pure speculation on my part."

"Is your friend here in the city?" Jack asked. It would be worth risking the time if the artist was accessible.

"No, she's in Detroit," Kristina said. "So it can't be her. But let me have my two other artists take a peek. Maybe they might have an idea. Are you thinking it was done here in the metropolitan area or maybe right here in Manhattan?"

"I don't have the faintest idea," Jack admitted.

The other two artists were both males and obvious devotees of their own craft. One of them also had an impressive collection of piercings on the helixes of his ears. Neither of them recognized any distinguishing characteristics of the palm tattoo that might suggest to them who the artist could have been. Kristina sent them back to their customers.

"Sorry we couldn't be more help," she said. "And I have to get back to my customer. Here's my card if you have any more questions."

Jack took the card, thanked the woman, and went out to get his bike. As he undid his locks, he felt decidedly discombobulated. Interacting with such a young, hip, and artsy crowd made him feel old and unfashionable, which he knew he was. But more important, Kristina had also managed to make him feel even more frustrated. Here he was, out running around to try to escape his unsolvable domestic pressures, yet through her they were managing to haunt him further. The idea that a tattoo on a corpse he was desperately trying to ID was similar to the tattoos adopted by the autism awareness movement seemed almost cruel in its coincidence.

13

By the time Jack pulled his bike up to the OCME unloading dock, he had been reenergized. Instead of addling him, the unexpected reference to Emma's diagnosis now only spurred him on to greater effort. Although he had struck out with the idea of a tattoo artist possibly identifying the subway death patient, he thought about using the tattoo as a way to get around the catch-22 described by the NYU heart transplant nurse coordinator. One of the things motivating him was the tattoo's location on the volar surface of the woman's arm, meaning it would have been right in the face of the anesthesiologist during the entire transplant procedure.

After stashing his bike in its usual location, Jack hastened to the back elevator. As he zipped past the mortuary office, Vinnie caught sight of him and called out a question. Jack didn't hear it, but he didn't care, either. Instead, he jumped on the elevator that happened to be waiting on the basement floor. The back elevator was the slowest of the lot, and Jack had learned over the years to nab it when it was available. Whatever Vinnie's question was, it could wait, and if it couldn't, Jack was certain he'd call now that he knew he was in the building.

Jack didn't even bother to hang up his bomber jacket when he dashed into his office but rather just tossed it onto his worktable. He sat down at his desk and frantically searched within the surface debris for Nancy Bergmeyer's mobile phone number. He remembered her giving it to him, and he remembered writing it down, but where? Being in a hurry, he didn't want to be forced to go back to using the institution's phone service, which he remembered being a lengthy process. Finally, he came across the scratch pad and there was the number.

Unfortunately, after several rings, he found himself switched to voicemail, forcing him to leave a message. As soon as he hung up, he also texted, to try to cover both bases. It worked. Before Jack even had a chance to hang up his jacket, his phone rang. It was Nancy Bergmeyer.

"Sorry to bother you again today," Jack began.

"No bother," Nancy said. "We have no case this week, and last week's patient is doing exceptionally well."

"I had an idea I wanted to run by you," Jack said. "The patient I autopsied yesterday had a very distinct and colorful puzzle-piece tattoo on the volar surface of her right wrist. It would have been hard to miss when she was a patient, especially for anesthesia. What if I were to ask if your transplant program had had such a patient? How would you respond? It's still a fishing expedition, but only for a very specific fish."

"That is an interesting question," Nancy replied. "I don't think I know the answer to it. I suppose I'd have to run it by the hospital attorneys. And just to be sure, the OCME has subpoena power, doesn't it?"

"Absolutely," Jack said. "There's no question of that."

"You know, it might work," Nancy admitted. "The more I think about it, the more I believe that if you just called up out of the blue and asked if we had transplanted during the last four months a young woman with a distinct puzzle-piece tattoo on the right wrist, I might have been willing to ask around and tell you straight off."

"That's what I want to hear," Jack said. "Okay, that clinches it. I'm going to call around at the various heart transplant centers here in the metropolitan area and pose that exact question. Who would you recommend I ask to speak with?"

"My counterpart," Nancy said. "As far as I know, all programs have a senior nurse coordinator who functions as a program director. We're the ones who have an overview."

"Thanks for your help. I really appreciate it."

"Good luck," Nancy said. "If I were you, I'd call Columbia-Presbyterian first. They do the most cases by far. I hope it works."

"Me too," Jack said. He disconnected, then moved over in front of his monitor. He Googled Maimonides Medical Center to find out if they did heart transplantation. If the subway death patient lived in Sunset Park, Brooklyn, Maimonides was the closest major hospital. To him that seemed a more important qualification than being the medical center that did the most cases. It was also true that somewhere in the back of his mind he recalled that the very first heart transplant done in the United States had been done at Maimonides. But he was in for a disappointment. Maimonides did not do heart transplantation, despite doing just about every other type of cardiac surgery.

Instead of going institution by institution, Jack Googled "heart transplantation in NYC metropolitan area" and then wrote down a list of the centers, along with the phone number of each program. He eliminated, for the time being, Westchester Medical Center, as it seemed just too far out in suburbia for someone who lived in town, and particularly in Brooklyn. That left seven centers that were possibilities, including two that were across the Hudson River in New Jersey. To be systematic, Jack started to the north, with Montefiore Medical Center.

Jack didn't know what to expect his reception would be, but he was pleasantly surprised. Since he had been involved in clinical medicine, a true sense of competition and customer service had replaced older, unpleasant hospital employee attitudes. It didn't take long for him to be speaking with Nancy Bergmeyer's equivalent. His name was Curtis

Freehold. He, too, was a certified nurse practitioner and the director of the Montefiore Heart Transplant Program.

After introducing himself as a medical examiner, Jack quickly explained why he was calling, giving all the necessary details about the victim, including a description of the puzzle-piece tattoo. He then asked if such a patient had been seen in the Montefiore program in the last four or five months.

"I personally don't remember such a patient," Curtis said thoughtfully. "But most of the day-shift nurse coordinators are here in the unit and I'd be happy to ask around. Our anesthesia team is available as well. I can ask them, too. Do you mind holding on? It won't take a moment."

"Not at all," Jack said. He was encouraged. Not only was Curtis pleasant and helpful, but he didn't mention HIPAA at all.

While he waited, he thought about calling Aretha back. He knew she said she would call him as soon as she knew something, but he was impatient. As Laurie had reminded him, getting a verifiable diagnosis of a specific virus was key, and probably significantly more critical than the ID. As Laurie had also reminded him, he couldn't be sure how Aretha intended to proceed if she determined a virus was indeed present from her tissue cultures. Would that take a day or a week or a month? Jack had no idea.

"Looks like I'm striking out," Curtis said, coming back on the line. "We even have a couple tattoo fans here in the unit, so I'm pretty certain the patient you're searching for didn't get her transplant here with us. I'm sure it would have been noticed. Sorry."

"Thanks for checking," Jack said.

"Leave me your number," Curtis suggested. "I'll put a note on the bulletin board, which we all look at every day. If someone has a different take, I'll give a shout."

Jack gave his mobile number and rang off. Going back to his list, he got the number of Columbia-Presbyterian and placed the call. The experience was similar to Jack's call to Montefiore. It was apparent to Jack that the programs were rivals on some level and coached in customer satisfaction. It was certainly a new age. Back when Jack was an ophthalmologist, just calling to schedule surgery at his hospital center had often been unpleasant because of hospital employee attitudes.

Once again, Jack got someone high up in the program's hierarchy on the line and posed his question. The response was just as helpful as at Montefiore, although in the end the director wasn't quite as definitive as Curtis had been. She openly said she doubted that a patient that fit the description had been treated, but she couldn't be certain. Also like Montefiore, she promised to get back to him if the situation changed.

While on hold with Mount Sinai Medical Center, the next hospital on his list, Jack thought again about Aretha and wondered anew what the tissue cultures were showing. The one thing that made him feel reasonably comfortable was that there had not been any similar deaths. He had told Bart he was to be notified immediately if there were. If this subway death was the index case of a new pandemic, it was at least taking its merry time getting going. Reluctantly, he couldn't help but wonder if Laurie was right after all in holding off on sounding an alarm.

"It doesn't seem like we've had any patients with memorable tattoos," Harriet Arnsdorf, the Mount Sinai heart transplant director, said when she got back on the line. "Everyone I've spoken with insists that they would have remembered what you described."

"I appreciate your asking around," Jack said, once more leaving his mobile number just in case.

After disconnecting, Jack sat back and rethought his approach. He was down to his last Manhattan-based heart transplant center, Manhattan General Hospital, before he would be trying the Beth Israel Medical Center in Newark, New Jersey. He couldn't help but feel a tad let down after the initial excitement of thinking that combining the heart transplant situation with the puzzle tattoo might lead to an ID breakthrough. Perhaps sending a photo of the puzzle tattoo would be more effective in jogging memories than a verbal description. With that thought in mind,

Jack took a pic with his phone of the puzzle-piece photo, with the idea of texting it to the rest of the program directors he spoke with.

As the call went through to the MGH Heart Transplant Program, which he noted was advertised as an integral part of the MGH Zhao Heart Center, Jack couldn't help but remember that MGH was certainly not his favorite hospital. The reason was that it was owned by AmeriCare, a large, publicly traded health insurance and provider organization that in the distant past had played a role in forcing him out of clinical ophthalmology and into forensic pathology. As a medical examiner, Jack did not have to bill health insurance companies, which he had learned to blame for ruining American medicine by turning it into a huge for-profit enterprise, to the detriment of patients and doctors alike.

Although it took somewhat longer than it had with the other three medical centers to get an appropriate person on the line, eventually Jack found himself talking with Bonnie Vanderway, MGH's Heart Transplant Program's clinical director. Jack immediately launched into his now practiced spiel, introducing himself professionally, describing the deceased in general terms, including a mention of the heart transplant three or four months ago, and emphasizing the pressing need for the OCME to make an identification. He didn't bother to explain why. As for the cause of death, he said it was yet to be determined.

"The one thing in our favor is that the body does have some unique identifying markings above and beyond its distinctive thoracotomy scar," Jack continued. "What I'm talking about are three widely separated tattoos. One of them is rather eye-catching. It's also on the underside of her right wrist, which would have been in plain sight with an IV. What I'm hoping is that you or one of your colleagues might remember this tattoo if this patient had had a transplant in your program. But rather than describe it, I'd like to send you a pic, provided you're willing to look at it. You've heard the phrase 'a picture is worth a thousand words.'"

"Of course, everyone has heard that expression," Bonnie said with a short laugh. "Sure. Send it on!" She gave Jack her mobile number, and

Jack responded by sending her the photo. A moment later her phone sounded, indicating an incoming message. "I'm opening it now," she said.

"Take your time," Jack said.

"Wow," Bonnie replied almost immediately. "This *is* colorful and eye-catching. And you know something? I think I remember it."

"Really?" Jack questioned casually. He didn't want to get his hopes up.

"I'm not entirely sure," Bonnie said. It was apparent to Jack that she was still studying the photo. "I think I remember seeing it in the CSR, or cardiac surgery recovery room, but just in passing. It was probably the colorful aspect that briefly caught my attention. When we're in the CSR we're pretty focused on our individual patients."

There was a pause as she gathered her thoughts. "I wish I remember distinctly, but I'm afraid I don't. But this I can tell you: It wasn't my patient. I'm also a nurse coordinator, so I have my own patients in addition to my supervisory functions. Let me ask around. Do you want to hold on, or should I call you back?"

"I'll hang on," Jack said. Sensing he might be close to success, he didn't want to let Bonnie figuratively out of his grasp. With the phone pressed up against his ear, he kicked back in his chair. Lifting his feet up and placing them next to his microscope, he tried to decide what he would do if he lucked out. The problem was that he had no idea how cooperative MGH would be. He'd dealt with the hospital on a few difficult cases in the past and had found them less than helpful and had subsequently gotten himself in hot water with Bingham. That was one of the field episodes Laurie was referring to yesterday. AmeriCare was an exceptionally profitable business, and their flagship hospital, Manhattan General, was run accordingly. Jack had had particular difficulty getting information out of the hospital, because bad news, which deaths usually involve, can impact the bottom line. As a consequence, Jack had gotten into a heated clash with the hospital's president. Making matters particularly dicey, the hospital president was politically tight with the NYC mayor, who was essentially the OCME's boss.

"Okay," Bonnie said without preamble when she came back on the line. "I was right. We did have a thirtyish female patient with a tattoo that looked like this pic you sent. I spoke with the nurse coordinator on the case, Tatiana Popov, and showed her the image, and she remembers the tattoo distinctly and thinks there's a good chance it could have been this individual."

"Is the time frame correct?" Jack asked.

"Gosh, that I didn't ask. Hold on!"

Jack could hear Bonnie yell in the background, asking how long ago the case was. He couldn't hear the muffled response, but Bonnie came back on the line immediately. "That seems to fit as well."

"Fantastic," Jack said. "If I give you my email, would you send me all the patient details?"

"Hmmm," Bonnie said. There was a pause. Then she added: "I don't think I can do that, not right away."

"Why not?" Jack questioned, even though he didn't want to hear.

"Well, we're specifically told by our executive director not to give out any patient information until we run all requests by the legal department, unless it is for immediate family. You know, with HIPAA and all, our hands are tied. The hospital admin is strict about this, and I don't want to get fired. Maybe I shouldn't have even told you about possibly recognizing this tattoo."

"As a medical examiner investigating a medical examiner case I have subpoena power," Jack said. Although it was true, Jack didn't want to be forced into that route as it would invariably take too much time. If the ID was going to have an effect on this subway death case, he needed the information now, not next week. There was nothing speedy about the legal route.

"I know that," Bonnie said. "Still, there are institutional rules that we have to follow. Besides, this wasn't what I would call a normal case."

"Oh?" Jack asked. "How do you mean?"

"It was a direct referral on the day of surgery from a hospital out in New Jersey that has an association with our Zhao Heart Center."

"A direct heart transplant referral?" Jack questioned. "That sounds unique. Is such a thing a frequent occurrence?"

"No, not to my knowledge," Bonnie said. "This was the first for me, and I've been here for almost two years and at a previous program for five years. But regardless of how she got here, it's tragic to hear she's passed away. And I'm sure all the people here associated with her case will feel the same, even though the patient was here for a much shorter time than usual. You can't help but get to know these people intimately. I know Tatiana couldn't believe it when I told her why I was asking about the tattoo. She reminded me the patient had done so well. She had been brought in here near death and four or five days later could have walked out if we hadn't made her use the wheelchair."

"Interesting," Jack said. He thought it was more than just interesting, but he didn't know quite what to say and was racking his brain to think of something. He didn't want Bonnie to hang up, which worried him as a distinct possibility with her sudden legal concerns. "What exactly do you mean by a 'direct' referral?"

"All the patients we operate on have to be accepted into our program and get on the OPTN, or Organ Procurement and Transplant Network, list for a heart. But that didn't happen in this case. She had been in the program of a New Jersey hospital that was in the process of obtaining its certification as a transplant center. I never knew the clinical details of this woman's case, like whether she had an implanted left ventricular assist device or not. As I said, she was not my patient. But what I remember hearing is that her clinical situation took a very sudden nosedive to the point that she needed an immediate transplant if she was going to live. And, like a miracle, the hospital where she was being followed came up with a targeted donation that was a good match. Since her hospital lacked certification, the patient and the cleared organ were airlifted here for the surgery."

"What's a targeted donation?" Jack asked.

"It is when the donor or, in this case, the donor family stipulates who the recipient is going to be. It is not very common with hearts, but it happens. It's usually in situations where the families are either related or know each other. I don't know what the circumstance was in this case. All I heard was that it was the result of a motorcycle accident. For those of us in the transplant business, motorcyclists are probably our most reliable resource."

"What you're saying is that the transplant was done at MGH but none of the preliminary work that's normally required was."

"That's right. All the pre-op preparation for both the patient and the organ, which had been harvested out in the New Jersey hospital, had been done in New Jersey. Everyone here was comfortable with that because their heart center and ours have an association, and their head heart surgeon had been recruited from our program. He'd been our number two heart surgeon. He even came in along with the patient and the heart and assisted during the procedure. He might have actually done it, for all I know."

"Now I understand why you described this as not a normal case," Jack said. "Well, if it's any consolation, it's not a normal case from our end, either. Not only do we not have an identification, which is extraordinarily rare for someone in her apparent social stratum, but Toxicology determined that there were no immunosuppressants in her system. Does that surprise you, knowing what you do?"

"That is pretty much impossible," Bonnie said. "All our cardiac transplants are on immunosuppressants. They have to be to avoid rejection, even with a good match."

"That's what I thought," Jack said. "It's just another point that makes this case not the normal run-of-the-mill, just like you said. To be truthful, I'm fascinated on multiple levels. I'm also convinced this case needs a bit more investigation before I can sign it out. I think a house call is in order. I can be over there in thirty minutes. Is it possible for you to still be there?"

"I was supposed to have left at three," Bonnie said. "Of course, I never do. I still have some odds and ends to attend to. On top of that, I don't know if I can tell you much more than I already have."

"I'll take my chances," Jack said. "And perhaps there are others who were directly involved with the case that I can chat with, such as the surgeon of record. I would imagine he would be interested in what was found at autopsy."

"That's a good point," Bonnie agreed. "I'm guessing it was Dr. Barton. I'll see if I can locate him. There's no doubt he'll want to talk with you."

"How will I find you?"

"Come to the Zhao Heart Center. The transplant program is on the fourth floor, north wing. Dr. Barton's office is down the hall from me, which will make that easy. I'll leave word for the heart center receptionists to page me when you get here."

"See you shortly." Jack was already on his feet. As he disconnected, he grabbed his leather bomber jacket. Then, as an afterthought, he grabbed one of the autopsy photos of the subway death, folded it in quarters, and stuck it in his back pocket on his way out the door.

14

As Jack cycled northward in the direction of Manhattan General Hospital, he was oblivious to the rush-hour traffic. Despite the frustrations he'd been experiencing to date with the subway death case, he now felt totally energized. Although he was well aware he needed proper identification only as an adjunct for potential epidemiological reasons if the causative agent turned out to be a virus capable of causing a pandemic, he now had a new and more personal stimulus for his interest in the case. His old nemesis, AmeriCare, and its sentinel hospital, MGH, were involved. And better still, the affair was beginning to feel as if it was not entirely kosher.

Like most doctors, Jack was cognizant of the seriousness associated with the distribution of organs for transplantation because of their shortage and the extent to which fairness was emphasized. Jack knew that at any given day about three thousand people in the USA alone were desperately waiting for hearts, with many patients dying before one can be found. He also knew that the distribution of the available hearts was carefully carried out by UNOS, the United Network for Organ Sharing. But from his conversation with Bonnie Vanderway, UNOS had not been involved with the patient he'd autopsied. Laughing at his own mixed metaphor, Jack thought he didn't have to be a rocket scientist to smell something fishy.

Jack began to whistle as he pedaled. He had needed a diversion, and now he had found one that filled the bill in spades, and one that was going to continue even if it turned out a virus was not involved. At the same time, he cautioned himself for Laurie's sake. The last time Jack had made a significant ruckus at Manhattan General Hospital over the results of a series of autopsies he'd done almost ten years ago, it had caused significant trouble for Laurie's predecessor. The fallout had almost gotten Jack fired. And now, on this occasion, especially after Laurie's specific warning, Jack knew he would have to be diplomatic, provided he was capable. Mainly, he would need to control his usual knee-jerk response of vociferously making it known to all parties involved when he confronted malfeasance or incompetence or a combination of both.

Reaching MGH, Jack found a street sign to lock up his Trek. He even locked up his helmet and bomber jacket with a separate wire lock that also secured the seat. He'd had a bad experience in the neighborhood and was intent on avoiding another.

For a moment he stood in the shadow of the soaring high-rise hospital. It had been a respected academic teaching hospital in its former life but had fallen on hard times in the early 1990s, when AmeriCare had been able to snap it up at a fire-sale price.

Inside, Jack took the elevators directly up to the fourth floor. He couldn't help but remember the episode years ago when he had exposed a supervisor in the hospital's laboratory who was purposefully spreading lethal infectious disease. The man had wanted to start an epidemic but luckily didn't understand the dynamics. He had mistakenly chosen microorganisms that didn't spread well person-to-person until he, too, had hit on the idea of influenza.

The moment Jack got off the elevator on the fourth floor, he was impressed. Although some portions of MGH had not been renovated after AmeriCare had taken over the facility, the Zhao Heart Center certainly had, and it had been done recently. It was the picture of modernity, and it appeared as if no expense had been spared. Jack imagined that patients couldn't help but be dazzled and inspired with confidence. Although, knowing AmeriCare as well as he did, he hoped that glitz was backed up by an equal attention to the equipment behind the scenes.

As the clinic day was winding down, there were only a moderate number of patients in the waiting area and none at the main desk. Jack was able to walk directly up to one of the two receptionists. As befitting the environment, she was smartly dressed, and she gave Jack a warm smile and her full attention. Even that was new for Jack. In the past he'd felt that the AmeriCare management style was deficient in small details related to customer service.

Jack gave his name and asked for Bonnie Vanderway, just as she had instructed.

"Yes, of course," the receptionist said. "We've been expecting you. I'll let her know you're here."

Jack looked around a bit more at the decor. It was truly noteworthy, and perhaps the best hospital clinic environment he'd ever seen. Turning back to the receptionist, he asked when the clinic had been redone.

"Almost three years ago," the receptionist said. "Do you like it, Doctor?"

"It would be hard not to like it," Jack said. "I bet patients like it as well."

"They love it," the receptionist said.

"I suppose it's named after a benefactor," Jack commented.

"It is," the receptionist agreed. "Mr. Wei Zhao."

"Mr. Zhao must have been a very thankful patient." Vaguely, he wondered how many millions it would take to have an entire heart center named after you in a private hospital.

"Mr. Zhao was not a patient," the receptionist said. "I was told he was a Chinese billionaire businessman. He's a member of our hospital board."

"Lucky AmeriCare," Jack said, and meant it.

"He is a very nice man," the receptionist said. "I met him."

At that moment Bonnie Vanderway appeared. She was a stocky woman with a broad face, and although younger than Jack had envisioned from her voice and her commanding manner of speaking, she exuded an air of assurance. Dressed in a long white coat over blue scrubs, she wore her moderate-length brunette hair neatly pulled back with a tortoiseshell barrette. After they had introduced themselves, Bonnie invited Jack back to her office. Despite the invitation, Jack felt she was mildly standoffish, which he didn't know what to make of, although he worried it had something to do with her recently expressed legal reservations.

"Can I offer you some coffee?" Bonnie questioned, once they were seated.

"I'm fine," Jack assured her.

"I managed to get ahold of Dr. Barton and he'll be stopping by momentarily," Bonnie said. "I also let the executive director know you had arrived. Her name is Katherine English, and she'll be stopping by as well."

"Excellent," Jack said, although he would have preferred some time with Bonnie alone. In his experience bigwigs tended to be less forthcoming in marginal situations, giving credence to the adage: Too many cooks in the kitchen can spoil the stew. "Sounds like we're going to have a regular party."

"Excuse me?" Bonnie said. She'd heard Jack's comment but didn't know how to interpret it.

"I brought you a photo of the patient, so we can possibly confirm the identity," Jack said, ignoring Bonnie's rhetorical question. As he unfolded the photo and smoothed it out on Bonnie's desktop, he silently scolded himself for already allowing a bit of his renowned sarcasm to emerge. He had to do better. For Laurie's sake, he was intent on behaving himself.

"Oh, wow," Bonnie said, looking at the photo. "That's not very flattering."

"Not likely to get her any modeling jobs," Jack said. "Autopsy photos make everyone look remarkably terrible. It's deliberate. They're taken so that every possible blemish and abnormality stands out in stark relief."

"Again, I wouldn't be able to be sure this is the same person we operated on here," Bonnie said. "Let me quickly show it to Tatiana. Do you mind if I leave you here for a moment? I think it would be helpful to be sure we are talking about the same person."

"I'll stay right here and mind my manners," Jack assured her.

While Bonnie was gone, Jack looked around the office. There was a whiteboard with a calendar, which Jack guessed showed all the upcoming cases for the month. It appeared that they did about two transplants a week, most likely dependent on the availability of organs. Another whiteboard appeared to be scheduling for the entire clinical team except physicians. It was a complicated schedule involving three shifts a day, seven days a week. As clinical director, Bonnie was a busy lady.

"Tatiana is willing to confirm this is the patient that she handled," Bonnie said, coming back into her office. "She would have come in person, but she's with a patient and his family." Bonnie tried to hand the photo back to Jack, but he waved it off, saying MGH could keep it for their files.

With a knock on the open office door to announce herself, a tall, aristocratic woman entered. Like Bonnie, she was wearing a long white coat, but underneath was a business suit instead of scrubs. Without any attempt at subterfuge, she gave Jack a once-over. Jack had stood when she arrived, and he stared back at her. Her straightforwardness reminded him of his grammar school principal back in South Bend, Indiana. It wasn't a wholly comfortable remembrance. Jack had been what the principal had described as a willful child, and she'd let him know on multiple occasions.

Bonnie formally introduced Jack to Katherine English, the executive director of the Heart Transplant Program.

"Bonnie filled me in on your earlier phone conversation," Kathrine said, dispensing with any small talk.

"There's been an update," Bonnie told her. "Dr. Stapleton brought in an autopsy photo, and Tatiana has confirmed it is a patient we operated on."

"I see," Katherine said. "That is obviously disappointing news for us.

We like to think that our patients all have long and healthy lives, thanks to our efforts."

"At this early stage, it's my impression that this woman's death was not immediately associated with her surgery," Jack said. "Actually, there was every indication your team did a great job. Grossly and microscopically, the heart appeared absolutely perfect, without a trace of inflammation."

"How did the patient die?" Katherine asked.

"Manner or cause?" Jack asked.

"Both, I guess," Katherine said.

"The manner was natural," Jack said. "The cause we don't know yet. The mechanism, I believe, was an overwhelming respiratory problem called cytokine storm, possibly of an infectious origin, which is why we are desperate for an ID. If it proves to be infectious, which we are attempting to do, we need to know her social contacts to either quarantine or monitor them."

"That makes total sense," Katherine said.

Another knock on the open office door heralded the arrival of another tall, aristocratic individual, making Jack wonder if AmeriCare was cloning these people. Jack struggled to rein in his instinctual cynicism. This new visitor was a particularly handsome male, about Jack's height, six-two, and about Jack's age. And like Jack, he appeared to be in excellent physical shape. Similar to Bonnie, he was dressed in a long white coat over scrubs. Unlike Bonnie, he had a stethoscope casually slung across his shoulders. A bit of ECG tape protruded from one of his pockets. A surgical mask dangled down over his chest.

"Hello, Dr. Barton," Bonnie said with obvious respect. She then formally introduced Jack to Dr. Chris Barton, cardiac surgeon.

"I understand you've brought me some bad news," Chris said to Jack. His tone was pleasant and his demeanor mild.

"I suppose you could say that," Jack said, struggling to behave himself. He was privy to what he called the "narcissistic cardiac surgeon personality," which saw everything from a personal vantage point.

"It has been confirmed it is one of your patients," Bonnie said.

"That's terrible," Chris said. "It's a tragedy, as the case went so smoothly, including the immediate post-op portion. I hate to see it mess up my stats."

Jack bit his tongue to keep from making an appropriate comment about the difference between someone's life and someone's stats. Instead, he said, "I thought you might be interested to hear that the heart looked fantastic. It was situated perfectly, and all the anastomoses were completely healed and fully patent. But I do have a question: I have been told it was a targeted donation. How common is that?"

"It's not common with the heart," Chris said. "Kidney and liver, yes, but heart, no. Yet it does happen."

"How was it that it happened in this case?" Jack asked. He decided to go for broke.

"To tell you the truth, I don't know the details," Chris said. "The patient and the heart came in together. I was just the plumber and hooked the thing up. It was a perfect donor heart and a good match, or so we were told. All the preparation in terms of matching and physiological testing was done at a sister institution."

"Any idea of where the heart came from?" Jack asked.

"I was told by the surgeon who came in with the heart, who happens to be a friend, that a motorcyclist with severe head trauma had arrived in the hospital's emergency room the same day the patient presented in cardiac extremis. Obviously, serendipity played a major role, because apart from the coincidental timing, both patients had the rare blood type of AB-negative."

"That is serendipitous," Jack agreed. "So this targeted donation occurred outside of UNOS."

"Of course," Chris said. "That's what a targeted donation is. It's from one person to another person. I don't know for sure, but I would imagine the families knew each other, or if they didn't, they do now. It was a gracious thing for the grieving family to do. A life was lost, but a life was saved. Well, at least for a few months."

"How does UNOS feel about such an arrangement?" Jack asked. Despite what he was hearing, his intuition was still ringing alarm bells. He couldn't help but feel there was something decidedly improper about this story. It was too coincidental, too pat. Besides, AmeriCare was somehow complicit.

"In this particular situation, UNOS had no jurisdiction," Chris explained. "But in all fairness, I was also told that the patient had been on UNOS's waiting list for a heart for over a year. AB-negative hearts are rarer than hen's teeth." He chuckled at his own joke.

"What about the other HLA antigens that should match between a donor organ and the recipient?" Jack questioned. "Were they a good match in this case?"

"Very good," Chris said. "I was told all twelve human leukocyte antigens matched, which is rare. I suppose that is why the patient did so well post-op. She was air-lifted out of here the day she got out of the cardiac surgery recovery room to continue her recovery at our sister institution. I couldn't have been more pleased with her course. I felt like a million bucks."

I'm sure you did, Jack thought but didn't say. Instead, he said, "Our Toxicology Department determined on a screen that the patient had no immunosuppressants on board. Does that surprise you?"

"It more than surprises me," Chris said. "In medicine, when you get an unexpected lab result, you do it again. I'd advise you to have your toxicologists do it a second time. The patient had to have immunosuppressants in her system. I know for certain, because we started them in surgery, kept them up while she was in the cardiac surgery recovery room, and sent them with her as part of her discharge packet."

Although Jack had more questions for the surgeon, another knock on the open office door caught his attention. Turning in its direction by reflex, he was in for a big shock. In walked the embodiment of everything Jack hated about AmeriCare, Charles Kelley, the hospital CEO and president. When Jack had entered medicine the previous century, the heads of hospitals were called administrators and were often doctors who had been willing to take MBA courses. The benefit was that the hospital continued to be oriented around their original, basic altruistic function of taking care of the sick. Now, at MGH, the chief was not a doctor but rather a trained businessman. It had been a necessary transition, because the main goal had changed from patient care to providing a handsome return on investment for faceless investors.

Charles Kelley was a striking figure. At six-eight, he towered over most everyone. Sandy-haired, continually tanned, impeccably dressed in silk suits, and commanding a multimillion-dollar salary, he seemed to have come directly from central casting. "Well, well," he said in a conde-scendingly acerbic tone, "if it isn't our favorite medical examiner."

Biting back equivalent sarcasm, Jack struggled to control himself. Previously, when he had first investigated and eventually outed the MGH microbiology terrorist who had been trying to start the epidemic for his advertising executive sister's benefit, Jack had had multiple run-ins with Charles. Charles had seen Jack as trouble from the word *go* and made significant attempts to have him fired. As Charles was politically con-nected, with close personal and professional ties to the mayor, he nearly succeeded. And now, since he was just as close with the new mayor and for the same reason—namely, significant campaign contributions—Jack knew he was on very thin ice. It was Laurie who would be in the cross-hairs now.

"I've heard you're here to bring us bad news," Charles continued.

"As a city employee I'm always striving to be of service," Jack said, and then inwardly lambasted himself for being unnecessarily provocative with such obvious sarcasm.

"I've got to do afternoon rounds," Chris said, interrupting the exchange between Jack and Charles. "So I'll be running along. Thanks for the info." He touched his forehead in a kind of half-assed salute. Jack watched him go with regret. He would have liked to ask more questions.

As Chris departed, Katherine spoke up: "It has been confirmed with a photograph that Dr. Stapleton brought that the person he autopsied is the individual we operated on for the Dover Valley Hospital."

"That's unfortunate," Charles commented. He stared daggers at Jack. "You certainly are a conveyer of distressing news. Tell me, do you rub everyone you meet the wrong way?"

"Just those people I don't respect," Jack said, and inwardly groaned at his lack of self-control. He was hopeless.

"I'll pretend I didn't hear that," Charles said. "Let's cut to the chase. I understand that you're looking to identify this unfortunate individual."

"It could be critical if it is determined she died of a potentially contagious disease," Jack said, hoping to move away from ad hominem retorts.

"I have spoken with our counsel. We cannot give you any medical details of our service without a proper subpoena. What I am willing to give you is her name."

"That's a start," Jack said. "I don't think details of her recent surgery will be critical. The name and permanent address and anything else you have will suffice for now."

"We don't have the permanent address," Charles admitted.

"Then the billing information will be adequate," Jack said.

"We don't have any billing information," Charles said. "The entire admission, including the surgery, was completely covered by our sister hospital, Dover Valley Hospital, whose heart center is associated with our heart center. It was their show. We were just being supportive to save a life."

"They paid you directly?" Jack said with amazement. This case certainly was unique on all fronts. One hospital paying another, even if they were associated, raised further red flags in his mind. Knowing Ameri-Care's penchant for maximizing return on investment, he couldn't help but wonder what kind of money was involved. His intuition was telling him millions, and Jack knew money talked.

"The Dover Valley Hospital was within weeks of getting their heart transplant certification," Charles explained. "If they could have waited, they would have. My understanding is that they had the insurance coverage all arranged, just like they had everything else arranged. It was the patient's condition that dictated a change in venue. All we had to do was have the patient sign our operative consent form and do the procedure."

"And the patient's name?" Jack asked.

"Carol Weston Stewart," Charles said. He handed Jack one of his business cards with the name hand-printed on the back. "I believe this satisfies the reason for your visit here to MGH. And now I would like you to leave. You helped us in the past, I'll give you that. But in the process, you were like the proverbial bull in the china shop, and I will sleep better tonight knowing you were escorted off the premises."

Charles turned and waved for several uniformed security men who had accompanied him to the heart center to come into Bonnie's office. As soon as they did, he directed them to escort Jack out onto the street.

"You mustn't make a fuss on my behalf," Jack said, trying to suppress a smile.

"Oh, but we insist," Charles said.

Jack made it a point to shake hands with Bonnie Vanderway, whom he credited for his progress of getting the sought-after name. Then he merely provocatively smiled and waved at Charles before he followed the security people out into the hall.

"Such a nice man," Jack said, as the group waited for the elevator.

Outside, as he unlocked his bike, Jack smiled anew. Not only had he managed to get the name of Carol Weston Stewart, but he had the satisfaction of possibly ruining Charles Kelley's day. But more important, he felt even more motivated about his diversion. The fact that Charles Kelley himself had felt compelled to become involved spoke volumes. It was like a neon sign proclaiming something weird was afoot.

15

Invigorated by his short-term success after so much effort, Jack made it back to the OCME in record time. Wondering when Laurie was planning on leaving for home, he headed directly up to the front office.

"Dr. Montgomery and her secretary left about twenty minutes ago," Carla Rossario said. Carla was Dr. Paul Plodget's secretary. Paul was the new deputy chief, since Calvin Washington had retired. "Dr. Montgomery wanted to get home early because company was expected. Then, right after she left, Cheryl took off."

Jack winced. He didn't like the sound of *company*. In his mind, it might have been the last thing they needed at the Stapleton-Montgomery household. For a brief moment he thought about calling Laurie to prepare himself for what he was going to be facing when he got home, but he decided against it. If there was a problem, he knew Laurie would have called or at least texted. Instead, Jack hurried up to his office. He wanted to see what he could find out about Carol Weston Stewart from social media. He knew he could have called Bart and have him do it, but he didn't want the MLI to have all the fun. He also wanted to check out Dover Valley Hospital.

Tossing his bomber jacket into the corner to avoid taking the time to hang it up, Jack sat down at his monitor with the idea of jumping onto the Internet. Instead, he found himself face-to-face with a Post-it Note from his old officemate Dr. Chet McGovern. It was a simple message to call Dr. Aretha Jefferson.

Hoping for more good news, Jack made the call. Aretha picked right up, as if she had been hovering over the phone.

"Hey, Jack!" she said, apparently able to tell it was he who was calling. "I've got some significant news for you. I'm ninety percent certain we're dealing with a seriously pathological virus. Currently the cytopathic effects are much more pronounced with the human kidney cells than they were just this morning. Now I'm just waiting for the titer to increase so I can start the identification process full-speed."

"Bravo," Jack said. "That's terrific news, even if it's also very scary. I don't like the idea of a seriously pathological virus being on the subway."

"You and me both," Aretha said.

"I've been making some progress as well," Jack said. "I now have a name to attach to the patient. I don't have any address yet or any other information, but that should come as a matter of course. I had a breakthrough by combining together a heart transplant and a relatively unique tattoo as my inquiry and just cold-calling the city's heart transplant centers. I hit pay dirt with my fourth call."

"You're the man," Aretha said. "Hey! It's after five. Are you going to run tonight?"

"Are you?"

"That's my intention," Aretha said. "I don't want my new friends to forget about me."

"I don't think you'll have to worry about that, with the way you played last night," Jack said. "Anyway, I imagine I'll see you. I think I'm going to need a run." Jack couldn't help but wonder exactly what Laurie had meant by *company*.

"Try to make it," Aretha said. "I have a little surprise to tell you."

"Why not tell me now?"

"I prefer to do it in person."

"Okay," Jack said. "See you then." He disconnected because he could see another call coming in. It was Detective Lou Soldano. As he switched over, he chided himself for not asking Aretha about the time frame for the identification process.

"I was hoping to hear from you sometime today," Lou said, after they exchanged the usual hellos. "Any info on those three cases we worked on yesterday morning?"

"Nothing yet," Jack said. "And to be truthful, I've kinda dropped the ball. I meant to check with Toxicology about the death-in-custody case, but it slipped my mind. And in respect to the gunshot case, I haven't even started the reconstruction. To be totally honest, that's going to be a while. I've been busy with that contagious case that I took after you left."

"Any change in your thinking about the suicide/homicide case?"

"No. I'm not going to change my mind about that one. I'm going to sign it out as a probable homicide. You better advise your friend Walter he needs legal representation."

"What's happening on the home front with you? Any change for the better?"

"I wish," Jack said. "Last night Laurie's mom was as irritating as ever. She'd found a family friend psychiatrist-cum-businessman who also subscribes to the discredited MMR vaccine theory of autism. Once again I allowed myself to get drawn into an argument of sorts just when Laurie showed up from work. She accused me of baiting her mother. I mean, talk about missing the point."

"Is the nanny still threatening to leave?"

"Laurie says she spoke with her this morning and claims everything is hunky-dory in that arena. I'll find out more tonight when I get to talk with Caitlin myself."

"I feel for you, buddy."

After hanging up with Lou, instead of going on the Internet as he'd planned, Jack put in yet another call. This time it was to Bart Arnold. He was hoping to catch the man before he left for the day, as it was now almost six. As Jack listened to the electronic sound of the phone ringing, he bemoaned how much he was being forced to be on the phone of late, despite how much he detested it. When all was said and done, Jack was a man of action, which was why he had chosen surgery as a specialty when he finished medical school.

"Hello, Dr. Stapleton," Bart managed between some heavy breathing, suggesting he had had to run for the phone. "You just caught me. A second later and I would have been in the elevator lobby and wouldn't have heard my desk phone."

"I'm glad I got you," Jack said. "I have some interesting news for you. I now have a name for the subway death. It's Carol Weston Stewart."

"Good work! How on earth did you manage? Hank Monroe and I have gotten zilch."

"A bit of luck was probably the most critical," Jack admitted. "Out of desperation, I just started calling all the city's heart transplant programs and described a thirtyish Caucasian female with a distinctive tattoo. I hit pay dirt at MGH, who did her surgery. I got confirmation with a photo."

"Simple but obviously effective," Bart said. "Is she from Brooklyn like we thought?"

"I don't know yet," Jack said. "All I know is the name. MGH claims they don't know any of the patient's details. Can you imagine? They did the surgery for a sister hospital in New Jersey called Dover Valley. Are you familiar with it?"

"I'm not familiar with that particular hospital," Bart said. "But I know where Dover is. I live in Jersey just across the GW Bridge. Dover's due west about thirty miles or so. It's a rural area but within commuting distance of the city."

"I was told the Dover hospital paid all the bills for the patient's surgery directly. Does that sound weird to you?"

"I haven't the faintest idea," Bart admitted. "With all the consolidation going on in healthcare, nothing surprises me anymore."

"It surprised me," Jack said. "It was the president of MGH who told me, and to be honest, I trust him about as far as I can throw him. He's the shameless-businessman hospital administrator type."

"Do you want me to follow up with this Dover Valley Hospital in the morning?" Bart asked.

"Thank you, but no," Jack said. "I just heard back a few minutes ago from the lab that it seems as if an unknown pathogenic virus is involved. Thank goodness we haven't seen any additional cases, but I'm still worried we will at some point. I'm going to look into the hospital myself. I don't want you MLI types having all the fun."

"Oh, yeah, of course," Bart joked. "Knock yourself out!"

"How long would you estimate it would take to drive out to Dover, New Jersey?"

"You are actually going to go all the way out there yourself?" Bart asked. As a matter of policy, he wasn't accustomed to the medical examiners doing their own field investigations.

"I don't think a phone call or two is going to be adequate," Jack said. "My intuition is telling me there is something about this case that is out of the ordinary. I think it's worth looking into above and beyond getting Carol Weston Stewart's details. When I know more, I'll fill you in."

"Drive time to Dover will depend on the traffic," Bart said. "I'd avoid rush hour if I were you. If you're driving from here, you'd use the Lincoln Tunnel. It's a pretty straight shot out Route Three. With no traffic, I'd guesstimate forty-five minutes."

"Thanks, Bart," Jack said. "I'll keep you informed."

"Wait! Hang on," Bart said. "I'm glad you called. I had tried to call you an hour earlier. I have some information for you. Hank Monroe and I have really put the pressure on the DNA people to get some stat results, which they've done. Hank has gone ahead and used it for CODIS and NamUs, which is all pending but now academic since you have a name.

But there was something about the results that the DNA people thought you'd like to know, and I promised to tell you ASAP. The CODIS results for the patient and the heart were exactly the same. They matched perfectly in all twenty loci."

"That can't be," Jack blurted out. Once again, the subway death case was playing with him, teasing him, or, more accurately, tormenting him. "Something got screwed up," he added. "It was a donor heart. I was told it was a good match, but it can't have the same DNA."

"That's what they said. So they went to Histology and got another piece of the heart and ran it again. The results were the same."

"I don't believe this," Jack said.

"Well, they didn't, either," Bart said. "In fact, Dr. Raymond Lynch, the head of the DNA lab, asked me if there was any chance you were running some kind of a covert personal test on their work. He felt that it couldn't have been a heart transplant unless it was from an identical twin."

"Good grief," Jack said. "It was definitely a heart transplant. I was told the donor had been in a motorcycle accident. I suppose it could have been an identical twin. No wonder it was a targeted donation."

"What's a targeted donation?"

"It's when a transplant organ is gifted to a specific individual outside the official sharing system."

"Well, now you know," Bart said. "I promised Dr. Lynch I'd tell you right away."

"Thanks, Bart," Jack said. He felt a bit shell-shocked.

After he'd hung up with Bart, Jack stared ahead for a few minutes with unseeing eyes. It seemed that nothing about this case was conventional. Could the donor truly have been an identical twin? What a bizarre coincidence.

Pulling himself over to his monitor, Jack went on the Dover Valley Hospital website. The first thing that confronted him was a number of photos, and he was impressed from the moment the page opened. He'd expected a small, generic community hospital with a bit of age. Instead, he was looking at pictures of a decidedly modern structure, considerably larger than he would have imagined, with carefully manicured grounds.

Selecting the "About Us" section and then the "Overview," he read that the hospital was private, nonprofit, and founded in the 1920s as a community hospital, but by the turn of the century had evolved to be more of a nursing facility. Threatened with bankruptcy, it had been bought by GeneRx, the largest local employer, with the goal of renovating it to serve the health needs of its employees. But then GeneRx, being the good neighbor it was, decided to return the hospital back to functioning as a community resource as well, so that all the inhabitants of Dover and the immediate towns would have access to superior healthcare and not be forced to travel to find it. With two hundred beds and ultramodern facilities, the hospital was now fully accredited by the Joint Commission as "a provider of high-quality, comprehensive, and humanistic care."

Moving on to the "Facts and Figures" section of the website, Jack read that it had been selected as a "Best Regional Hospital" according to a recent *U.S. News & World Report* with recognition of its 3T MRI machines, its hybrid operating rooms, its IVF, or in vitro fertilization, unit, and its certification as a transplant center that included heart transplants in addition to all the other more usual organs. He then read that the hospital was associated with the prestigious Manhattan General Hospital and many of its departments, although particularly through its own award-winning Zhao Heart Center.

Jack stopped reading and looked back at the mention of the Zhao Heart Center. "My word," he said aloud. "This Zhao guy gets around."

Going on to read the rest of the website, Jack found himself progressively more impressed, which considerably surprised him. Although he hadn't admitted it to himself, he had been prepared to have a negative feeling about the place. Yet the hospital sounded as if it was an island of healthcare excellence out in what he envisioned were the backwoods compared with NYC.

Jack's positive reaction to the Dover Valley Hospital stimulated a curiosity about the facility's owner, the company GeneRx. Jack had never heard of it, which wasn't terribly surprising, as he was not oriented toward business, particularly businesses relating to healthcare. GeneRx sounded as though it was definitely healthcare-oriented, and probably related to gene therapy, according to its name.

Typing "GeneRx" into his browser, Jack was in for yet another surprise. It wasn't in the same category as the donor heart and the recipient having the same CODIS result, but it was surprising nonetheless. GeneRx on its website was described as an up-and-coming biopharmaceutical company totally owned by a Chinese billionaire by the name of Wei Zhao, the same man Jack had just complimented as "getting around."

Reading on, Jack learned that although the company had only a few products on the market currently, it had almost a dozen in phase III trials, all of which were expected to be available within a year or two. Looking at photos, Jack could see it was a sprawling, modern facility that had most likely been designed by the same architects who had done the Dover Valley Hospital. Looking further, Jack could see that the complex included a farm, aptly called the Farm Institute, in the same architectural style. Jack knew enough about current bioscience to know that the cutting edge in drug development was proteins such as monoclonal antibodies. Although these proteins were originally made laboriously by cell culture, now they were often made in bulk by farm animals such as goats, sheep, pigs, and chickens. Using the latest methods of genetic manipulation, such as the gene-editing technique CRISPR/CAS9 to add genes or to remove them, these familiar barnyard animals were turned into transgenic, living bioreactors producing the desired drugs in their milk, eggs, or blood.

Fascinated, Jack next focused his search on Wei Zhao. In a fraction of a second there were millions of hits. Jack might not have heard of Wei Zhao, but a lot of other people obviously had. Most of the articles were about biotech and the pharmaceutical industry. A number were in Chinese. Glancing down the links, Jack found a promising Wikipedia article and clicked it open. There was more material than he wanted because he knew he needed to get home, so he skimmed it. Even the highlights were riveting.

Wei Zhao had been born in 1960 in Shanghai, China, to parents who were academics at Fudan University but also landowners. It was being landowners that was their downfall, as the family became targeted by students during the Chinese Cultural Revolution. Although only six years of age at the time, Wei was banished along with his parents to the countryside, where the parents were forced to work the land. All three almost starved. But as a resourceful teenager who was willing to accept the dogma and emulate the Red Guards, Wei ended up back in Shanghai, where he eventually managed to be admitted into the Shanghai Jiao Tong University. There he applied himself and studied biotechnology with a particular emphasis on pharmaceutical manufacturing. Seeing a future in generic drugs on the world stage, he founded his first company at age twenty-five and never looked back. He was a millionaire by thirty and a billionaire by thirty-five as he expanded into all aspects of the pharmaceutical industry. It was at that time that he expanded his operations into the United States and founded GeneRx in Dover, New Jersey.

Jack's mobile phone pulled his attention away from his reading. A quick glance confirmed the worst: It was Laurie, and he immediately felt guilty. Another glance informed him it was after six. He answered with a manufactured cheerful hello.

"Why aren't you home?" Laurie demanded. Jack could tell she was stressed, which he could have guessed would be the case. He wondered if it had to do with the "company" but resisted asking.

"Still at the grindstone," Jack said instead, trying to be cute. "I've made some progress on the subway case. I now have a name, even if I don't have a confirmed diagnosis."

"I need you here," Laurie said, not taking the bait.

"I'm on my way," Jack said. "I'll be home in twenty minutes or so."

"Don't take any unnecessary risks," Laurie cautioned. "I wish you'd use Uber or Lyft. I hate to think of you on that bike in traffic."

"It would be twice the time by car," Jack said, trying to help her see the bright side.

"At least you'd be in one piece."

After appropriate goodbyes, Jack grabbed his bomber jacket and headed for the back elevator.

16

Once again, there was a good turnout on the basketball court, Jack noted, as his route home brought him past the neighborhood park. It was obvious people intended to take advantage of the string of decent days the city had been experiencing. That day the high had been in the sixties, despite it being the beginning of November. Most important, Jack could see that Warren was already there. Jack had hoped his friend would be playing that evening, because Jack had a big favor to ask and wanted to do it in person.

After crossing the street, Jack carried his bike up his front stoop and deposited it in its usual location. Then he started up the main stairs. The closer he got to the apartment door, the more he wondered what he was going to find. Could Laurie have invited someone over who might get Dorothy to leave? Jack didn't know, but he thought it couldn't hurt to be optimistic.

Once inside the apartment, Jack paused to listen. He was pleased when he heard no TV sounds emanating from the guest room. He even noted that the guest room door was slightly ajar and the light was switched off. But then, as he started up the next flight of stairs, he began to hear the evening news coming from the family room TV. That was not a good sign, as he knew Laurie was not a network news fan, nor was Caitlin.

As Jack's line of vision crested the family room floor while he mounted the fifth flight of stairs, he caught sight of the people sitting on the gingham upholstered couch, and he slowed. To his horror, it was not only Dorothy but also her husband, Dr. Sheldon Montgomery, a retired Park Avenue cardiac surgeon. Both were glued to the television. It was apparent they had yet to see or hear him. As Jack reached the top of the stairs he could see that Dorothy was again in her bathrobe, meaning she was not going anyplace, and, equally distressing, Sheldon was similarly attired, but with the addition of a silk cravat.

Jack glanced over to the kitchen area and stared at Caitlin. In contrast to the Montgomerys, she was looking directly at him and rolled her eyes for his benefit. Turning his head, Jack looked into the playpen. Again, Emma was silently sitting in it with her beanbag toys lined up. Like she had the previous evening, she was constantly rolling her head and staring into space, seemingly locked in her own world.

Jack walked over to the playpen. As he did so, Dorothy caught sight of him and with a smile raised and briefly flapped the fingers of her right hand in a kind of constricted royal wave that Jack associated with Queen Elizabeth. Sheldon also nodded in Jack's direction. Then both Montgomerys redirected their attention back to the news, despite it currently running a commercial. Jack looked back at Caitlin, and out of the Montgomerys' line of sight, he hooked his thumb in their direction and flashed a questioning expression with arched eyebrows. Caitlin responded by closing her eyes and shrugging, suggesting she didn't quite know what was happening.

Jack spent a few minutes talking with Emma and stroking her. He got no response but didn't expect any. Then he continued down the hall toward the study that he shared with Laurie. He found Laurie and JJ at Laurie's desk. They were busy doing an art homework assignment.

"Hey, Tiger," Jack said as he tapped JJ's shoulder with his fist. Intent on his maneuvering with a pair of scissors, JJ didn't respond. Jack then bent over and gave Laurie a peck on the cheek.

"At least you got home safely," Laurie said. She reached up and gave Jack's arm an affectionate squeeze. "That's one thing less on my mind."

"Can I talk to you for a moment?" Jack asked.

"Talk away," Laurie said. She then put glue on the back of the star that JJ had just laboriously cut out.

"I mean out of earshot of this budding artist," Jack said. He tousled JJ's hair. JJ moved away from Jack's hand as he positioned the star to his liking in the diorama being fashioned from a cardboard box.

"I'll be right back," Laurie said to JJ. "Go ahead and cut a few more stars. It's coming along fantastic."

Jack walked over to the windows looking out onto 106th Street. He could see that a few more people had appeared on the playground in anticipation of playing basketball. When he sensed Laurie was behind him, he turned around.

"So you now have a name but still no diagnosis," Laurie said, assuming Jack wanted to talk about the case.

"No specific diagnosis," Jack said. "But we now have evidence with reasonable certainty that an unknown pathogenic virus is involved. But that's not what I wanted to talk about at the moment. What's with your parents? Why is your father here and in his bathrobe?"

"It's simple," Laurie said. "I called him today and explained about Mother. We both thought it would be best for her if he came over here. She's an entirely different person when he is around. She is not nearly so critical."

Jack stared at Laurie in disbelief. For a moment he was tongue-tied. Having both her parents camping out hardly seemed like a solution to their current struggles.

"He's going to talk to her about going home, but just not right away. I know you think her presence is disruptive but try to see the situation from her point of view. With both you and me away all day, she feels it is her duty to be here until Emma's status is determined and a plan of action is decided. She respects Caitlin but feels strongly that she is not family, and this is a quintessential family emergency. And on the plus side, she is very patient with Emma. Even Caitlin says so."

Jack could feel his blood boil, yet Laurie was making a certain amount of sense. Still, an overwhelming sense of frustration, helplessness, and guilt settled over him like a blasting mat. He found himself thanking his lucky stars he had the subway death case, with all its surprises and twists and turns, to fall back on to keep his sanity.

"Do me a favor!" Laurie said. "Go out there and try to be pleasant. My father likes and respects you. I know that for a fact. I'll be out as soon as I finish with JJ. You and I are a team, Jack. We'll get through this."

Jack was speechless. All he could do was nod in agreement, and he felt worse for it. He should have ranted and raged, but he didn't. He felt like such a milquetoast because two minutes later he was back out in the family room, pulling over a chair from the dining table so he could make nice with both Dorothy and Sheldon.

The timing was impeccable. The moment Jack settled into his chair the network news was over. As Dorothy switched the channel to PBS Thirteen, Sheldon turned to Jack.

"Evening, Doctor!" Sheldon said. He leaned forward, extended his hand, and gave Jack's a shake. "Was it a busy day?"

"It was busy, all right," Dorothy interjected. "But all his patients died." She laughed mirthlessly at her own joke, one she had used many times in the past.

"It was busy," Jack agreed. He wondered what they would have said if he'd described his visit to the tattoo parlor. Being a medical examiner was far different and more varied than most people imagined, even other doctors. As far as Dorothy's cutting remark was concerned, he ignored it, as he usually did. "And how was your day, sir?" Jack asked. He knew that Sheldon was essentially retired but still went into his group-practice Park Avenue office every day. What he did, Jack had no idea, since he had stopped doing surgery two years earlier. But as one of the founding members, he was able to call the shots.

"Dorothy mentioned you had unkind words to say about Hermann Cross," Sheldon said, ignoring the question. His tone was matter-of-fact and not accusatory.

"I was told he still adhered to the discredited role MMR vaccines played in causing autism," Jack explained. "For a doctor, I find that particularly unenlightened."

"He's trained in psychiatry," Sheldon said as an explanation. "And he is more of a businessman than a physician."

"I guessed as much," Jack said. He racked his brains for additional conversational subject matter until *PBS NewsHour* got under way. At that point, Sheldon's attention drifted back to the TV, and Jack was relieved momentarily of his hosting duties. For ten minutes he merely observed Laurie's parents and their slack faces as the news droned on. Emma was also in his visual field, and Jack found himself wondering how the brain function of the three people differed. The Montgomerys weren't rolling their heads, but their blank expressions matched Emma's.

With a sudden flurry of welcome laughter and activity, Laurie and JJ appeared. Laurie was chasing JJ, who was squealing as if terrified. For protection he ran into Sheldon's arms. It was a wonderful little normal interlude shattering the otherwise mausoleum-like atmosphere.

"Okay!" Laurie said with enthusiasm while clapping her hands. "What do you all say to the idea of a little dinner?"

"It's about time," Dorothy said. But to her credit, she got up off the couch with the intention of lending a hand.

Jack felt an irresistible urge to get out and do something, and the most accessible form of relief was basketball. With Sheldon still glued to the television and Dorothy finding things to do with Laurie, Jack went up to the bedroom and changed into his exercise gear. He knew Laurie would not be happy, but he felt it was a matter of self-preservation. He trusted she'd get over it if he didn't participate in the meal preparations.

Ten minutes later, as Jack was crossing 106th Street, he felt like a new man. When he arrived at the playground he could see that Warren was already playing, and as usual had managed to get himself on a solid team, suggesting that he'd probably be playing the entire evening. Unfortunately, Jack had arrived too late for Warren to choose him.

Intending to run in place and do some calisthenics after he figured out how he was going to get into the game, Jack joined the group of people standing on the sidelines. Quickly he found out that Flash, his other close basketball friend, had winners. When he found Flash, who was a large, bearded, and muscular African American man, he learned that there was a spot for him.

"We got a decent team," Flash remarked. "Well, except for you." He high-fived Jack to emphasize that he was kidding. "We also got David, Ron, and that new girl you brought around last night."

"You mean Aretha?" Jack asked. He went up on his tiptoes, trying to find her.

"You got it," Flash said. "She's hot."

"Where is she?" Jack asked.

"She's over at the sandbox, talking to my squeeze," Flash said, pointing.

Without a second's hesitation Jack jogged over to the sandbox. As he approached, Aretha saw him coming and stood.

"Sorry to interrupt, Charisse," Jack said. He had met Flash's newest girlfriend on several occasions.

"No problem," Charisse said. "We were just reminiscing about college days. You probably don't know, but I also went to the University of Connecticut. Of course, I didn't play basketball. I didn't even try. I'd never have made the team."

Jack looked at Aretha. She was dressed in the same well-fitting black top and matching black shorts she'd worn the previous evening. But tonight she had added a more colorful headband, wristband, and kicks. They were an electric yellow-green that elegantly set off the burnished mahogany color of her skin. It was a striking and fun fashion statement. "You look terrific," he said.

"Well, thank you, sir," Aretha said brightly. "It looks like you could use a little help in that department."

It was true. Jack's aged workout togs were a hopeless mismatch of boring dark colors. He wasn't even sure if his socks matched, and his sneakers looked worse for wear, with a visible hole on the outer side of the left one. When he'd been an ophthalmologist he'd cared about his clothes and shoes and even had several smart suits. But after the loss of his first family and after becoming a medical examiner and moving to New York City, he'd never given clothes much thought, especially when it came to exercise apparel. Seeing how put-together Aretha looked was a stimulus to make a little effort.

"This afternoon, just before you hung up, you enticed me to come out tonight by saying you had a surprise to tell me," Jack said. "Well, I'm here. So what is it?"

"It's about a piece of special equipment we have at the Public Health Laboratory. It's called the MPS machine. Have you heard of it?"

"Can't say I have," Jack said.

"It stands for Massive Parallel Sequencing. It's a technology that takes advantage of what is called high-throughput. It's also called second-generation DNA sequencing."

"You've lost me already," Jack said. "Why is this a supposed surprise for me?"

"Because not everyone has access to it, including me," Aretha said. "To use it, I had to put in a formal application, which I did yesterday. Today I learned I got permission."

"I still don't understand," Jack said.

"I can use the MPS machine to determine the unknown virus," Aretha explained. "In the past characterizing a new, unknown virus has been a laborious process. The MPS machine will do billions of short-segment DNA reads, which I can then run through BLAST."

"It's like you're speaking to me in a foreign language," Jack complained. "What the hell is BLAST?"

"Oh, sorry." Aretha laughed good-naturedly. "I forgot you went to school in the previous century. BLAST stands for Basic Local Alignment Search Tool. It's a bioinformatics software method for analyzing the billions of short segments of DNA produced by the MPS. It can search through an enormous database of known viral genomes for matches. That means that within days I could be able to identify our unknown virus. Without the MPS and BLAST, it could take literally weeks, even months."

"Okay!" Jack said. "Wow! Now I get it. Sounds great. Obviously, the sooner we have a virus nailed down, the better."

"That I am aware," Aretha said. "As a backup I sent off a couple samples to Connie Moran, who heads up the viral pathogen discovery team at the CDC."

"Uh-oh," Jack said. He made a face, as if he were suddenly pained. He explained: "My boss, the chief medical examiner, specifically ordered me not to involve the CDC at this stage of this case." He didn't mention his boss was also his wife.

"Why not?" Aretha asked. She was surprised. "This is right up the CDC's alley. They have a whole Department of Viral Diseases as well as a Respiratory Virus branch. This is what they do, and they are better at it than I."

"My boss is afraid of causing a disruptive and costly panic here in NYC until we have a firm diagnosis. And there is reason for her position. There's been so much worry and preparation and even agency-wide exercises for a new, deadly flu pandemic here in the city that she is afraid the response that was generated could not be controlled if it was a false alarm. So far, she has been correct. There hasn't been another case. Anyway, she has chosen not to let the Department of Health know about this case. Consequently, she doesn't want the CDC prematurely contacting the media or, worse yet, sending an army of CDC epidemiological investigators up here."

"Okay," Aretha said. "I understand. Well, I didn't provide any details. All I said was it was an unknown virus. Nothing else. I didn't even say the patient died."

"Good," Jack said. "That sounds innocuous enough. Hey, I think we are going to be on the same team tonight."

"Great," Aretha said, and she high-fived Jack.

Jack said he'd give her a yell when they were ready for her and headed back to the basketball court. His timing was near perfect. As Jack reached the court the final basket was made by Warren's team to win the game. Turing around, he yelled for Aretha to come over to the court on the double. She waved back to indicate she had heard.

As the disappointed losers slunk off the court, Jack, Flash, Ron, and David walked on. They were eager to take a few practice shots. But before he took any shots, Jack approached Warren and took him aside.

"I need to ask a favor, my friend," Jack said, talking quietly. "I'd like to borrow your wheels tomorrow. I need to drive out to Dover, New Jersey."

"Why Dover?" Warren questioned. Perspiration glistened on the well-defined muscles of his Greek-statue-like body, which always made Jack feel decidedly inadequate. "There's nothing out there but a bunch of little lakes and green mountains. Well, not really mountains. More like green hills."

"It's a complicated story. I want to visit a hospital, a pharmaceutical company, and a farm, which are all connected to a young woman I autopsied. She died yesterday morning on the subway with a flu-like illness."

"You're too much, Doc," Warren said. "You always have some weird shit happening. Sure! You can use my Escalade. It's on the south side of 106th Street, down near Columbus Ave. You'll need to gas it up. The thing is a thirsty mother."

17

It seemed strange to Jack to be driving to work. Actually, it seemed strange to be driving at all. Ever since coming to NYC to accept an associate medical examiner position at the OCME fifteen or so years ago, he could count on his hands the number of times he'd driven a motor vehicle. Back in Champaign, Illinois, when he'd been a practicing ophthalmologist, using a car was second nature, as he drove every day to and from his office and to and from the hospital. His Range Rover had been like an appendage. But when he arrived in New York he'd seen a car as a handicap and had adopted the bicycle. He wished more people would follow his lead. As far as he was concerned, the Dutch and the Danish urban dwellers had the right idea.

Despite a fine misty rain falling, Jack missed his morning ride and felt a bit claustrophobic confined inside a metal box, even a large metal box like the black Escalade he was driving. The car was a relatively new model, but the actual year Jack had no idea. Nor did he care. It was going to carry him out to Dover, New Jersey, that morning, and that was all that mattered.

Progress was slow, especially driving across town after using one of the traverses through Central Park. As he waited at most every traffic light in Midtown, Jack felt sorry for all the drivers, himself included. They all looked and acted angry, each trying to nose the others out of the way to gain an advantage measured in feet. It was an aggravating, dog-eat-dog world blanketed in exhaust fumes.

Like he did the day before, Jack felt a little guilty about rising early and sneaking out of the house, but not guilty enough not to have done it. After exhausting himself last night on the basketball court, he'd returned to the apartment, showered, and then tried to be social with Laurie's parents. But it hadn't worked. To keep the conversation neutral, Jack had tried to talk about his day and the trials and tribulations of making an identification on the subway death. Thinking Sheldon and Dorothy and Laurie, too, might find it interesting, Jack recounted his visit to the tattoo parlor. As an added piece of information, he described learning that the puzzle tattoo had been adopted by the autism awareness movement.

The mere reference to Emma's diagnosis forced the issue back into the open, and Sheldon's presence did little to ameliorate the controversies and emotional toll. Not only did the MMR issue resurface, to Jack's intense chagrin, but so did Laurie's failure to take maternity leave soon enough to prevent the developing embryo from having to deal with form-aldehyde and other preservatives and chemicals. Sheldon even brought up his lifelong disappointment in Laurie's choice of forensic pathology over thoracic surgery, which stimulated a comment from Dorothy that Laurie's choice had been an embarrassment for her with her fellow fund-raising friends. From Jack's perspective, the evening had turned into a disaster, and getting away that morning before facing anyone was an act of self-preservation.

Arriving in the area of the OCME, Jack drove directly to the 421 high-rise. There was little to no parking around 520 where his office was located, but plenty near 421. Next to 421 was a large open lot, which was to be the future home of the new morgue building. It was also the place that huge balloon tents would be raised if and when a 1918 influenza-like pandemic broke out. These tents were part of the elaborate emergency plans that had been drawn up to deal with such a disaster and would house additional autopsy space. Also, currently parked in this area were a fleet of large refrigerator trailers for body storage that would be delivered to all the metropolitan hospitals in a severe flu pandemic. They, too, were part of the extensive preparation and training the city had been doing in anticipation of a deadly pandemic. Jack was one of the people who knew that as many as five hundred deaths a day could be expected in such a circumstance, which was why the subway death scared him as much as it did.

Pulling into the lot through a gate in a temporary chain-link fence, he parked the Escalade. To avoid any problems, he left a note on the dash with his name and mobile number. He didn't expect any problems. He knew a lot of people in both 421 and 520 who took advantage of parking there.

Initially, Jack had every intention of hiking directly to 520, but since he was already in the shadow of 421, he thought he'd stop in and ask Janice Jaeger if she knew anything at all about Dover Valley Hospital. Janice had been the night-shift MLI for many, many years, and Jack had always been impressed with the range of her experience with local hospitals, even a few in New Jersey. It seemed that she had talked with all of them or visited them in the course of her investigative work. He found her at her desk, reading *The New York Times*. Once again, it had been a quiet night for her.

"What on earth are you doing here this early two days in a row?" Janice asked playfully when she looked up and saw Jack approach.

"You wouldn't want to know, trust me," Jack said. He then went on to ask her about the Dover Valley Hospital in New Jersey.

"That's a hospital I've never had any dealings with," Janice said. "Sorry. But I do know a little about the Morristown Medical Center, which is only about ten miles away. That whole area is familiar, if you want some general information. My parents had a home on Lake Hopatcong before they went to Florida. Hopatcong is just a bit beyond Dover."

"It's Dover Valley that I'm interested in," Jack said. "Thanks anyway."

"I hear you finally got an ID on that subway case," Janice said. "It is certainly strange it took so long."

"We didn't get an ID," Jack corrected. "So far all we've got is a name. That's the reason I'm interested in Dover Valley Hospital. I'm hoping to get a full informational ID from them."

"That's not what I heard," Janice said. "I heard people came in last night, IDed the body, and took it with them."

"What?" Jack practically yelled. "I hadn't heard that. Why wasn't I called? I thought there was a standing order for me to be called if that happened."

"When I came on duty I'd heard that order had been rescinded by Bart Arnold. Did you tell him you had a name?"

"I did," Jack said. "But only a name, as I said."

"Well, speak of the devil," Janice said. "Here comes Bart now."

Jack turned in time to see Bart come through the glass door leading out to the elevator lobby. With his extra weight mostly around his middle section, he moved with a particular rolling gait. As he approached his desk, he pulled off his hat from his mostly bald head and peeled his jacket off his shoulders. "You are in way too early, Dr. Stapleton," he called out. He dumped an armload of manila envelopes on his desk, then joined the others. "How was the night, Janice?"

"All quiet on the western front," Janice joked.

"Janice just told me that people came in, identified Carol Stewart, and then left with the body," Jack said challengingly. "Why wasn't I called?"

"You already had the name," Bart said defensively. "Consequently, I didn't think you'd want to be disturbed at home, so I told the MLIs not to have you called."

"But the name of the deceased was all I had," Jack complained.

"Well, now you have it all," Bart said. "I'm sure it's all in the computer. Pull it up, Janice! Let's show the gentleman."

A moment later, Janice had all the information on her monitor screen. Jack and Bart looked over her shoulder and read the details. The identification was made by Agnes Mitchel, whose own form of identification was a New Jersey driver's license. Her Denville, New Jersey, address was duly listed and her association with the deceased was described as neighbor and family friend, not next of kin, suggesting Carol Stewart was originally from that part of New Jersey. Also listed was Carol Stewart's current address in Sunset Park, Brooklyn, along with her Social Security number.

"Looks like just about everything you need," Bart said, straightening up. "And it's curious that this sudden identification and information gathering all happened just after you managed to get the name from Manhattan General Hospital. My guess would be that somebody from MGH called someone out in New Jersey about Carol's death, probably somebody at the Dover Valley Hospital."

"I'm sure you are right," Jack said. "God! This case never stops surprising me. And I'm shocked that the body was released with no next of kin involved."

"I can explain that," Bart said. "It was a bit out of the ordinary. I know because the forensic pathology resident who was covering last night called me about releasing the body, since the mortuary techs had asked him. There was no next of kin, but there was a representative from the Higgins Funeral Home in Dover who had accompanied Agnes Mitchel. This individual was in possession of two necessary important documents. First, he had an undertaker's license here in New York, as required, as well as one in New Jersey. And second, he had a legal release already signed by Carol Stewart's executor. Since the autopsy was done and there was no formal hold on the body, I said it could be released. Should I have not done that?"

"If they had a signed legal release from the executor of the estate, there wasn't much that could be done," Jack said. "They own the body once the autopsy has been completed. My concern is the potential infectious nature of the remains. Was the funeral director notified of that possibility when the body was handed over?"

"That I don't know," Bart said. "You'll have to ask the evening mortuary techs. But they are all sharp guys, so I imagine they brought up the possible contagion issue. Was the body in a sealed body bag?"

"Yes," Jack said.

"Well, there you go," Bart said. "That speaks for itself."

"For a thirtyish woman to have a standing executor of her estate is rather unique," Jack said. "But I suppose when you are facing a heart transplant, you are forced to think of such things."

"I imagine so," Bart said.

"When such a release is used, is it usually recorded?" Jack asked. As a busy medical examiner, the legal details didn't concern him. He let the legal people worry about such things.

"Of course." Bart bent over Janice's keyboard, tapped a few keys, and a moment later a legal release form appeared on the screen.

Not entirely sure why he wanted to read the document other than pure curiosity, Jack leaned forward and struggled with the tiny print. It was the usual lawyerly gobbledygook that bored him to tears, until the very end. It was then that he did a double take when he read the name of the executor at the very bottom of the page, because it was yet another major surprise. The executor of Carol's estate was none other than Wei Zhao. "I don't believe it," he blurted out. "What a damn coincidence. This guy seems to be all over the place."

"What guy?" Bart asked. He began to skim the release, clearly worrying that the night before there might have been some legal aberration.

"The executor," Jack said. He pointed at the name. "That's bizarre. Wei Zhao is a wealthy Chinese businessman who must be a local celebrity out there in northern New Jersey. He's the owner of a pharmaceutical company that's the area's largest employer. And he's quite a philanthropist. His company owns the Dover Valley Hospital, and MGH's heart center here in New York is named after him."

"Sounds very noble-minded," Bart said.

"We'll see," Jack said. "Why would this guy be this woman's executor? That doesn't make much sense to me. I tell you, this is by far the weirdest case I've ever been involved with as a medical examiner. I truly don't know what I'm going to find when I go out there."

"Are you still going to do a site visit? Even after we have all the identification information."

"I wouldn't miss it," Jack said. "There are too many oddities and unanswered questions."

"It doesn't bother you that you have no jurisdiction in New Jersey?"

"Details," Jack said flippantly. "Someone has to read the fine print on my ME badge to know it's from New York. I'm not going to lie."

"What about the address in Sunset Park, Brooklyn? Do you want me to send someone out there to check it out?"

"Hold off on that," Jack said. "Let's wait until we get a diagnosis of what killed her. Visiting the woman's apartment might require barrier precautions if some lethal virus is involved. Obviously, she lives alone. Otherwise, someone would have declared her missing."

"That's a good point," Bart said. "I'll wait for you to give us a green light."

Ten minutes later Jack was on his way, walking up to 520. If it had been a quiet night for Janice, chances were it had been a quiet night for the OCME in general. That was the usual pattern, even though it hadn't been the case the night before. Nonetheless, Jack was reasonably confident he'd be able to get a paper day to exempt him from any autopsies.

18

Emerging from the depths of the Lincoln Tunnel that runs under the Hudson River between Manhattan and New Jersey, Jack had to smile while thinking of New Jersey's nickname: the Garden State. The traffic was nightmarish, with trucks and buses, and there was hardly a tree, a shrub, or even a blade of grass in sight. It was all concrete or macadam and as densely built up as New York, just not as high.

Jack had been to the state perhaps a dozen times and thought of it as quintessentially suburban, with lots of single-family houses separated by green lawns. But those forays had always been over the George Washington Bridge. Where he was now, racing west on a sunken highway, it seemed decidedly dystopian. Yet the farther he drove, the more pleasant it became. He even began to progressively see trees clothed in autumnal splendor, as well as a few homes with white picket fences. After twenty minutes of rather frantic driving, it was apparent he was heading for the countryside.

The scenery was not the only thing that changed as Jack headed westward, away from the urban sprawl. His level of anxiety ratcheted down several notches, making him realize how tense he had been. He thanked his lucky stars for the subway death case having been dumped into his lap and wondered how he would have been coping had it not come his way. With Sheldon Montgomery now joining his wife in camping out in the apartment, Jack felt his living situation had gone from bad to worse, making it almost impossible for him to deal with the angst and guilt associated with Emma's circumstance. For Jack, who had a surgeon's mind-set, he felt totally frustrated that there was nothing he could do or fix about her disorder.

As a method of emotional defense, Jack consciously turned his mind away from his domestic problems and concentrated on the case at hand. First and foremost, he still didn't have a cause of death. He had a strong hunch plus probable laboratory confirmation it was a virus, but at almost forty-eight hours after the autopsy he didn't have a specific organism. He'd had cases of unknown viruses in the past, but all had been at least identified by this time. Second, the patient had had a heart transplant with a heart that matched her own DNA at the twenty CODIS loci. For that to happen by chance, it would have been somewhere around one in seventy trillion, meaning it could happen only if the donor was an identical twin. Yet had that been the case, Jack was sure it would have been all over the media. Third was the weird circumstance of a youthful, well-kept, and well-dressed woman who suddenly died and yet was not missed by friends or family and even now seemed devoid of kin. Fourth involved the strange circumstance of the victim having been operated on at one hospital with expenses paid by another. And last, how was it that the executor of the woman's estate, whatever it comprised, was a philanthropic billionaire Chinese businessman?

With some contemporary music playing in the background on the Escalade's radio, Jack mulled over all these unique issues and wondered how many of them he might be able to explain after his visit that day. He knew he wasn't going to learn anything about the virus. That was dependent on Aretha's efforts, perhaps with the help of the CDC. As for the others, he thought there was a chance he'd learn something, but he really didn't have a specific plan about how to go about doing so. Vaguely he thought he would just go to the Dover Valley Hospital and start asking questions. But before he did that, he wanted to stop by the Higgins Funeral Home to be a hundred percent sure they had gotten the message about the potential contagious nature of the remains.

Before he had set out, Jack had used Google Maps to locate the funeral home, as well as the hospital and GeneRx. It was a good move. Although the funeral home was in Dover itself, the hospital and the pharmaceutical company were situated a distance away in the direction of a federal property called Picatinny Arsenal. The site was north of Interstate 80, which Jack had used for about two-thirds of the drive from Manhattan. As he neared Dover, which was to the south, he exited the freeway and proceeded on side roads. He now could see what Warren meant about the area looking green. With the overcast sky and misty rain still falling, it reminded him of photos of Ireland.

The closer Jack got to his destination, the more revved up he became. His active intuition was again sending alarms that something about this strange case hinted that chicanery or worse was afoot, yet he had no idea whatsoever what it might involve. At the same time, he made himself a promise that he would make a Herculean effort at being as diplomatic as possible, meaning he would try to keep his reflexive sarcasm and self-righteousness to a minimum. The last thing he wanted was for complaints to get back to Laurie and make her job more difficult. There was also the issue Bart had raised that Jack had no official jurisdiction whatsoever in New Jersey, which could have legal repercussions.

Dover turned out to be a pleasant, modest rural town, with the tallest brick buildings only three or four stories tall. Google Maps had pegged the population at a bit more than eighteen thousand, and for Jack, coming directly from New York City, it appeared even smaller than that. Higgins Funeral Home was close to the center of town, and it was housed in a white, wood-framed Victorian building similar to a number of the funeral homes Jack had been forced to visit over the years. For

Jack, the experience was like living a cliché, including the decorum and appearance of the funeral director, Robert Higgins III. Gaunt and pale and dressed in a dark three-piece suit, he was perfectly cast.

Jack introduced himself without bothering to flash his NYC official badge and came right to the point. "I believe you have the body of Carol Stewart here in your facility, which was picked up last evening from the New York Chief Medical Examiner's Office."

"That's not correct," Robert said. He spoke slowly and precisely, his tone hushed, even though there were no visitors in evidence.

"What is not correct?" Jack asked. He tensed, wondering if he was in for another major surprise.

"The body was picked up by my younger brother," Robert agreed. "But it is not here."

"Has it already been cremated?" Jack asked. He couldn't think of any other reason the body wouldn't have been there.

"It has not," Robert said. "A second autopsy was formally requested by the executor of the estate. Early this morning the body was picked up by one of the Morris County medical examiners, who also has a small private office here in Dover."

"Is there no next of kin involved?" Jack asked.

"None," Robert said. "We have been dealing only with the executor."

"Interesting." That had become his stock phrase over the last couple days, adopted from Aretha. The request for a second autopsy by Wei Zhao was a surprise for Jack, although not nearly in the same category as the other surprises he'd been experiencing about the case. But this had a personal aspect, as it was a minor professional slap in the face, since there had been no attempt to contact him about the findings of the first autopsy. Jack felt strongly that a second autopsy was a total waste of time and resources.

"His name is Dr. Harvey Lauder," Robert offered. "And his office is only a few blocks away. Would you care for the address?"

"That would be helpful," Jack said. While Robert wrote down the address on the back of one of his business cards, Jack added: "The reason I stopped in here was to make sure you were told that the case may involve an unknown infectious virus and precautions need to be taken until it is ruled out."

"We understood that," Robert said. "And we communicated it to Dr. Lauder as well. We did not remove the body from the sealed body bag while it was in our possession in our cooler. When the body comes back we will treat it with the utmost care, whether it is to be cremated or embalmed, depending on the dispensation decided upon by the executor."

"That would be the prudent course," Jack said, unconsciously mimicking the funeral director's stilted language.

Once outside, Jack used Google Maps on this phone to locate the private office of the forensic pathologist. When he saw how close it was, he walked. It felt good to stretch his legs.

"I'm sorry, but Dr. Lauder is not here," an assistant-cum-secretary said. "He's at the Dover Valley Hospital for a case."

Jack left his card with his mobile number and asked if Dr. Lauder might give him a call. He thought there was a chance he might see the pathologist at the hospital, which was Jack's next destination, but in case he didn't, Jack wanted to find out exactly what was found at the second autopsy. He was also interested to learn why it was ordered.

Leaving Dover, Jack drove north, going under Interstate 80. Soon he was in even more rural environs. Now he understood even better Warren's laconic description of the area as "a bunch of little lakes and green hills." Especially in the direction of Picatinny Arsenal to the north, Jack was amazed at the extent of the virgin temperate forest, all in a blaze of color despite the cloud cover and lack of direct sunlight. It didn't seem possible to him that such an environment existed within a forty-minute drive of the concrete canyons of New York City.

Coming within sight of the Dover Valley Hospital and its neighboring GeneRx building, Jack could see that the photos he'd viewed online did not do it justice. Both buildings were larger and more impressively modern, with their sheathing of travertine marble and gold-tinted glass, as well as more carefully constructed than the pictures suggested. What had not been apparent also was the degree of physical security around GeneRx. Although it was partially concealed with elaborate plantings, a high razor-wire-topped fence faced the building and disappeared off into the forest on either side. Also partly hidden with evergreen trees was a manned gatehouse guarding the entrance drive.

The approach to the hospital was altogether different. Instead of the rather forbidding look surrounding GeneRx, it was inviting, with lawns, contoured shrubbery, and carefully attended flowerbeds bursting with mums and other fall flowers. What was not evident at either building was many people. As Jack parked and walked to the hospital entrance, only one other family emerged from the hospital and headed to their car. No ambulances came rushing with their sirens blazing, bound for the emergency room drop-off. The entire complex had a serene, futuristic atmosphere.

But inside the building it was different. As soon as Jack entered he felt immediately at home, as if he was back in Champaign, Illinois, in his former life, arriving at a more modern version of the hospital where he did his eye surgery. In contrast to the parking lot, there were plenty of people, and they were all in the usual outfits seen in a community hospital, including pink-smocked volunteer ladies manning an information booth. There was even a busy coffee shop and a sundries store.

Jack approached the information booth, deciding on a strategy on the spur of the moment. He had considered asking for Dr. Lauder, the fellow forensic pathologist, but decided he preferred to talk directly with someone who was part of the hospital organization and not a temporary hired hand. He ended up asking for the medical director of the Zhao Heart Center, with the idea of going for the jugular.

"That would be Dr. Theodore Markham," the volunteer said in response to his question. She motioned for Jack to pick up one of the red phones on the information booth's countertop. A moment later, Jack was talking to the man's secretary. When Jack asked for the doctor, the secretary asked who she could say was calling. Jack gave his full name and his official position in hopes that curiosity might get him a few minutes with the clinic director. The woman politely asked him to hold the line, promising she would be right back.

As Jack waited, he marveled at how much more civil people could be in contrast to how they were all too often in the city. But it turned out the secretary had been lying. She didn't come right back on the line as she'd promised. Instead, it was Dr. Theodore Markham himself.

"Is this really Dr. Jack Stapleton of the NYC OCME?" the doctor asked, as if he hadn't believed his secretary. His tone suggested true surprise, even glee.

"The one and only," Jack said, trying to tamp down his urge for sarcasm. He did not expect to be greeted with open arms after showing up uninvited at an institution that was possibly doing something not entirely kosher at best and immoral and illegal at worst.

"But this is an internal line," the medical director said.

"It is indeed," Jack responded. "I'm here at the information booth of your hospital."

"Well, isn't that terrific! I'll be right down."

Jack replaced the receiver with a sense of surprise. He'd been mildly concerned about how he'd be received, yet it seemed the man was truly delighted that Jack had unexpectedly dropped by. And this impression was confirmed when the doctor appeared. Although Jack had never met the man, he knew who he was the moment he got off the elevator. Of course, it helped that he waved as he rapidly approached, almost at a jog. He was of small to moderate stature and clean-shaven, sported a full head of dark, curly hair, and was smartly dressed with a crisp white shirt and fashionable tie. Most noticeable to Jack was that he moved with great energy, as though he'd had ten cups of coffee, such that his long white unbuttoned coat billowed behind him as if he were heading into a wind.

"Welcome!" the doctor said, enthusiastically pumping Jack's hand. "To what do we owe this pleasant surprise? Please call me Ted."

"I just had a few questions about a case," Jack said, nonplussed at his reception. In his role as the final arbiter of patient care or the lack thereof, Jack was accustomed to defensive posturing by physicians. Secretly he wondered what the man would say if Jack admitted that a large part of why he was there was the need for an engrossing diversion from emotionally problematic domestic issues.

"Well, we will do our best to answer them," Ted said. "Please, come up to my office." He gestured over his shoulder back toward the elevators.

"Sure," Jack said, following his exuberant host.

"It's quite a facility, isn't it?" Ted said as they boarded the elevator. He hit the button for the second floor of the four-story building.

"It's surprising," Jack said. "It's not what I think of when I think of a community hospital."

Ted laughed with genuine amusement. "It is actually unbelievable. This fabulous architectural wonder of a building is not even half of it. The medical equipment we have is astounding. And everything is essentially brand-new. Believe me, this place is going to be on the map big-time."

"How so?" Jack asked as the elevator door opened.

"Heart transplants, for one," Ted said. "That's going to be the main draw, although other organs will also be done. And our IVF clinic could rival the heart program. And gene therapy. And personalized cancer treatments. There are so many exciting things going on. I tell you, the sky is the limit. The secret is that we get to work directly with the hundreds of bioscientists across the lawn at GeneRx. That means we have a direct link from laboratory bench to hospital bedside. None of the usual town/gown divide. You've heard of the gene-editing marvel of CRISPR/CAS9, haven't you?"

"To a degree," Jack said as they walked down the hallway of a clinic that rivaled the Zhao Heart Center at MGH, which Jack had visited the day before.

"This little hospital stands to be the first out of the gate with the marvels CRISPR/CAS9 is going to bring to clinical medicine," Ted explained. He gestured for Jack to precede him into his attractive corner office. "GeneRx specializes in biologicals, meaning protein-based drugs made by living systems. In their case, it's mostly goats, sheep, pigs, and even chickens, and a few other animals, too."

Once inside and gazing out the window, Jack had a better view of the biopharmaceutical building, including the Farm behind it. The farm portion wasn't visible from the public road or from the hospital parking lot.

"Please, make yourself at home," Ted said, gesturing toward a group of Herman Miller chairs at a round table. "Can I get you anything?" he asked graciously. "Coffee, tea, water, or even a Coke if you'd like."

"A coffee would be nice," Jack said. While Ted went to ask his secretary to get the coffee, Jack looked around at Ted's many framed diplomas from big-name institutions, including the American Boards of Internal Medicine and Cardiology. Jack couldn't help but be impressed. Ted was an extremely well-trained academic cardiologist. Jack knew the type. They selflessly dedicated their lives to medicine as a true calling.

"I have a confession to make," Ted said when he returned and took one of the seats. "I took the liberty of calling our chief cardiac surgeon, Dr. Stephen Friedlander, right after you called me to say you were downstairs. I knew he'd want to come by to say hello and have an opportunity to thank you. We are all indebted to your efforts at identifying poor Carol Stewart."

"How exactly did you find out?" Jack asked.

"We got a call from Dr. Chris Barton right after you left MGH yesterday. He told us of your visit to the Zhao Heart Center and explained all the effort you had expended and what you had managed to accomplish, thanks to a tattoo. Of course, we were crushed to learn of her untimely death. She was a courageous woman who had struggled with cardiomyopathy for several years. She was well-known around here, truly admired, and liked. It was a real loss for all of us. But we needed to know because we need to find out why it happened, so it doesn't happen in the future. You did us a great service. Thank you so much."

"It's part of my job," Jack said.

"That may be true, but from Chris Barton's perspective you went way beyond what he would have expected," Ted said. "Anyway, thank you. So, what are your questions? I'll be happy to try to answer them, unless they involve details of surgical technique."

Jack had so many questions he didn't know what to ask first. At the same time, he wanted to try to be as tactful as possible and not squander his unexpectedly hospitable reception, which he was afraid might happen if he ventured too hastily into sensitive areas. Since one of the issues that both intrigued and bedeviled him the most was the apparent DNA match between Carol and the donor heart, he tried to think of the subtlest way to broach it. What popped into his mind on the spot was getting into a discussion about the motorcycle victim, as it would have had to have been an identical twin. Why such an extraordinary fact would have been kept a secret totally mystified Jack, but there had to have been a reason. Yet before he could put a guileful question together, the secretary returned with the coffee.

"Would you like cream or sugar?" Ted asked. He was solicitously holding both.

"Both, please," Jack said. Then as soon as the secretary had departed, and the cream and sugar had been stirred into his cup, which gave him a few extra moments to think, he said, "Dr. Barton told me about the coincidence of the fatal motorcycle accident happening on the same day that Carol Stewart's heart situation became critical. Was the victim related to Carol? Dr. Barton had told me it was a good match."

"It wasn't good, it was a fabulous match," Ted said enthusiastically. "The best I have ever seen, and with the rarest AB-negative serology, which is the reason we pushed for a targeted or direct donation. There was a twelve-out-of-twelve HLA match, zero reactive antigen, and a negative cross-match. It doesn't get any better than that."

"Was the motorcyclist related to Carol?" Jack asked, still skirting the issue.

"I believe he was a Stewart, but I'm not positive," Ted said. "Or he was related somehow. I personally don't get involved in that, as we have our own organ-donation team who deals with the grieving parents, to separate donor issues from recipient needs. All I knew was the heart matched extraordinarily well. The fact that the kinship issue wasn't stressed is because we have some hillbillies around here despite our proximity to the city. We might not have any families that are as hostile to each other as the McCoys and the Hatfields, but there are feuds, even within the same family."

The alarm bells that this case had set off in Jack's brain started ringing again. "So the motorcyclist was a male?" he asked, to be certain Ted hadn't had a slip of the tongue.

"Yes," Ted said. "Ninety percent of motorcycle driver deaths are men."

"True," Jack said. As a medical examiner, he was aware of the statistic. But that wasn't the source of the silent ringing he was hearing. If the motorcyclist was a male, there was no way he could have been an identical twin. Jack was back to square one.

"The reason it was such a serendipitous situation," Ted said, unaware of Jack's mental state, "was that Miss Stewart had been on the UNOS waiting list for a year. With AB-negative she clearly wasn't going to get an organ. Obviously, the motorcyclist's serology was also AB-negative."

"Dr. Barton mentioned that," Jack said.

"Other questions?" Ted asked.

"Yes." Jack struggled with what next to ask. "We were surprised when a toxicology screen revealed that Miss Stewart had no immunosuppressants in her system." Reluctant to go for broke, which would have happened had he stayed on the topic of how closely the donor heart matched, he'd changed the subject to the immunosuppressant issue. Now more than ever he was certain that something was amiss with this case, and the cynic in him began to wonder if the hospitality he was experiencing was to placate him.

"It was for good reason you found no immunosuppressants," Ted said. "She wasn't on them. She had been doing so admirably, even with her active immune system, which she had, by the way, that we were able to lower and eventually eliminate immunosuppressants. It was a function of how well she had accepted the donor heart, which thrilled us. You have no idea."

"Hello, hello," a voice called, as two figures bounded into the room. The first was tall but slightly stooped, with striking, prematurely white hair. In contrast, his face was boyish, with a lantern jaw and bright blue eyes. He was attired exactly as Dr. Chris Barton had been the day before at MGH, in a long white doctor's coat over scrubs, with a surgical mask dangling from his neck. The second man was similarly dressed but of Asian genealogy, with coal-black hair, small features, and a slight build. Both were smiling as if they had been laughing prior to coming into the room.

Jack and Ted stood as Ted introduced Dr. Stephen Friedlander and Dr. Han Lin to Jack, suggesting as he did so that they should all be on a first-name basis. Jack shook hands with both surgeons. At that point all four people took seats around the circular table.

Like a true surgeon, Stephen took control. He had a deep and commanding voice despite his boyish looks. "We are thrilled you surprised us by stopping by, Dr. Stapleton," he said. "As I'm sure Ted has told you, we heard the efforts you had gone through to identify our patient, Carol Stewart. As sad as the news was, I personally want to thank you very much for what you did. From what I understand, Carol's body might not have been identified until she missed her next follow-up visit here at our clinic and we reported it to Missing Persons. It is particularly sad, as I personally know she's been estranged from her family and had some setbacks in her own social life. I know because she told me not that long ago on her last follow-up visit, which, by the way, was perfect on all accounts. There was absolutely no sign of any coming catastrophe."

"As I told Ted," Jack said, "it is part of the job of the medical examiner to identify the dead. At OCME we learned that lesson the hard way after 9/11."

"At this point our goal needs to be finding out why she died," Stephen continued. "Whatever it was, we do not want it to happen again. Since we know you did an autopsy, we are interested to hear your findings."

"I have yet to sign the case out," Jack said. He appreciated finally being asked, but with Laurie's insistence on holding off on telling anyone, he wasn't sure how much he wanted to say, especially until he got confirmation from Aretha. "I'm waiting on some tests."

"We were concerned about a virus," Stephen said. "We sponsored a second autopsy here this morning."

"So I heard," Jack said. "And what was found?"

"We believe she died of a cytokine storm," Stephen said. "She had a strong immunological reaction to something in her system. Exactly what, we don't know. We thought about a virus, but that doesn't seem to be the case."

"Sounds familiar," Jack said. "I also suspected a virus—influenza, to be exact. But all the usual viruses have been ruled out with rapid screening tests, including influenza."

"We know it wasn't a virus," Stephen said with conviction. He sat back in his chair, his arms folded across his chest. "We know it for certain."

"And how is that?" Jack asked.

"We have access to electron microscopy, which is the benefit of having superb resources. We simply looked. Actually, Dr. Lin looked. Right now, he's our most experienced electron microscopist. There's no virus in her lung fluid. Case closed."

"Yes, I looked for virus," Dr. Lin said with a heavy accent. "No virus was present."

"That's curious," Jack said. "We began seeing cytopathic changes suggestive of virus in human kidney cell tissue cultures within twenty-four hours of inoculation. The plan is to search for an unknown virus." Although Jack tried to sound confident, he was shocked and dismayed to hear that no viruses were seen on microscopy. He wondered if Aretha had tried. He doubted it, as she surely would have told him. He didn't even know if the Public Health Lab had an electron microscope.

"Undoubtedly you were seeing the results of a viral contaminant," Stephen said confidently. "It happens all the time. If viruses had been present, they would have been seen on microscopy. Since there's no virus present, running viral searches is a waste of time and money. Our forensic pathologist thinks the case needs to be signed out as a therapeutic complication, despite her surgery being more than three months ago. We agree and think you should do the same. We can share with you our electron photomicrographs for your records for confirmation. What we will be doing going forward is an extensive study of the proteins in the patient's serum that must have come from the heart and keyed off the cytokine storm. We have that kind of capability. What we'll be willing to do, if you are interested, is keep you in the loop and let you know what we find. I'm sure we will publish the results, and we'd welcome you as an author."

"That's very good of you," Jack said, trying to keep his tone neutral. "I appreciate the gesture." Actually, it sounded to him as if they thought they could buy him off with nothing more than an authorship of a study that might get published and might not. Worse yet, from Stephen's body language, Jack sensed that the meeting was coming to an end despite his serious effort of being tactful and avoiding confronting them directly.

"Well," Stephen said, slapping his thighs in preparation of getting to his feet. "Consider it a standing offer."

Clearing his throat and deciding to go for the jugular, come what may, Jack leaned forward and said: "I think I should mention to you one test that was done in our lab whose results we already have in hand. We ran DNA analysis on both the patient and the heart to upload the profiles into CODIS in hopes of helping the identification process. A hit on either would have been helpful. To our shock both profiles were the same. Especially with twenty loci as the new standard, that is statistically impossible. Do you folks find that as surprising as we do?"

Both Stephen and Ted laughed, but it wasn't entirely sincere to Jack's ear. Stephen spoke up: "Of course we find that surprising, since we, too, know it is statistically impossible. Obviously, you should run the tests again. Surely there was a mix-up with the samples. I mean, we knew it was a great match, which we attributed to the possible kinship of the parties involved. I guess that's why we were able to wean her off immuno-suppressants so quickly."

"We ran it twice," Jack said. "And for the CODIS results to match, it would have had to have been identical twins. Obviously it wasn't identical twins, since they were of different sexes, as Ted confirmed. There have been cases of identical twins being separated at birth, but that could not have been the case in this instance. In theory we're facing a miracle here, but in reality it is more of an enigma that needs to be explained. The rapidity of Carol's death reminded me of the influenza pandemic of 1918. To be entirely honest, I'm worried about a new pandemic."

Jack sat back and watched the three people sitting at the table with him. Although Dr. Lin seemed unfazed, the other two were clearly dis-comfited, raising Jack's curiosity and reminding him of the Shakespear-ean quote, "Something is rotten in the state of Denmark."

"Could you excuse us for a moment?" Stephen asked.

Jack shrugged. "Of course."

Stephen and Ted both stood and left the room. It sounded as if they were arguing as the door closed behind them. Jack stared across the table at Dr. Lin, who smiled back at him. Jack tried to guess the man's age but couldn't. He looked particularly youthful, but Jack knew that couldn't be the case, as the man was already a surgeon. His face was seemingly devoid of facial hair of any sort. Judging from the man's accent, Jack assumed he was from China. To make conversation, Jack asked if that was the case.

"Yes, I am from China," Dr. Lin said. He smiled broadly. "I'm from Jiao Tong University School of Medicine."

"Are you in training?" Jack asked.

"Yes, I am training in cardiac surgery," Dr. Lin said. "My institution sends someone here to Dover every year for transplant work."

"Do you get good training here?"

"Oh, yes, the best," Dr. Lin said.

Jack looked up as Stephen and Ted returned. Whatever their disagreement had been, it seemed to have totally passed. Although they had clearly been uptight when they left, there had been a definite transformation. They were literally laughing as they retook their seats.

"Well, you are in for a treat, my friend," Stephen said, clapping his hands together with exuberance.

"That sounds encouraging," Jack said. "I've been in need of a treat for years."

"Ted and I both came to the conclusion simultaneously," Stephen continued. "We thought that to properly show our collective appreciation of your efforts, you should meet the boss, the brains of the whole operation, Dr. Wei Zhao. Of course, it depends on your interest. What I mean to say is that there is no compulsion involved. How does the idea strike you?"

"My dance card has some leeway," Jack said. Here was yet another surprise. Being offered the chance to meet the man of the hour was perhaps the last thing that Jack had expected on his visit.

"Perfect," Stephen said. "And I'm happy to report that we have already called our Han emperor, and he is delighted to meet you."

"I'm touched," Jack said. "When might this happen?"

"In about an hour," Stephen said. "Here's what Ted and I propose. We'll take you on a tour of our hospital or GeneRx. Your call. The meeting with Dr. Zhao will take place in our boss's home office, which is a short fifteen-minute drive. Are you game?"

"Absolutely," Jack said. "Sounds like a delightful afternoon."

19

The tour turned out to be far more interesting than Jack had imagined. Since he'd seen enough hospitals in his life, he chose to pass the time seeing GeneRx. As he had never visited a pharmaceutical company, much less one specializing in biopharmaceuticals, he didn't have anything to compare it to. But there was one thing for certain: He'd never seen quite so many biotech engineers all in the same place, and it seemed as if they were mostly Asian and not just Chinese. There were many Indians as well. And all appeared remarkably young, just like Dr. Lin. The only surprising thing during the tour was going through the gatehouse, which required everyone but Jack to show their ID badges. The process made Jack wonder how many pharmaceutical companies had equivalent security.

But even more impressive than the drug company was the Farm Institute, which was physically attached to GeneRx and in the same architectural style. Since it was the inhabiting transgenic goats, sheep, pigs, cows, and chickens who would be manufacturing all the enormously profitable drugs, they were being treated in high style by an army of caregivers and veterinarians. Some of the animals were in posh, completely sterile environments. Although Jack wasn't shown it, he was told the institute even had its own slaughterhouse, despite it sitting empty ninety-nine percent of the time, and also a miniature rendering plant to recycle the protein. The whole operation was entirely self-contained.

When the tour was over, they returned to the hospital parking lot, where it was quickly decided that two cars should be taken for the trip to Zhao's home. Stephen would drive his own, with the idea that Jack would be staying longer than the others. After a short discussion, it was determined that Ted would ride with Jack, and Han would go with Stephen.

With that decided, they were on their way, driving north on Lake Denmark Road. At first Jack tried to keep up with Stephen, but it quickly became obvious Stephen drove significantly faster on the curvy, rural road with his Porsche Panamera than Jack in Warren's top-heavy Escalade. And with Ted in the car for directions if needed, Jack was content to fall behind. There was no reason to hurry. The scenery was a bit of autumnal splendor similar to what Jack recalled from his childhood in Indiana. Except for Central Park, New York City was not a place to appreciate fall colors.

"This area is a lot less developed than I would have imagined," Jack said, looking out at the stretches of apparently virgin hardwood forest interspersed with rolling hills and small lakes that again recalled Warren's laconic description of the area.

"It's thanks to the Picatinny Arsenal," Ted said. "They have a lot of land. It's like a nature preserve."

Both men made it a point to avoid bringing up the subject of the strange CODIS profile match and kept the conversation light. Jack was thrilled with the idea of meeting the billionaire Wei Zhao and didn't want to put it in jeopardy by forcing the issue. He was confident there would be plenty of time.

For his part, Ted was happy to regale Jack with all the reasons working for Dover Valley Hospital was the best possible position for a doctor in any specialty, truly combining both clinical medicine and the latest high-powered evidence-based research. "Dr. Zhao is a true visionary, with the resources to back it up," Ted explained. "This place is the future of medicine with his leadership and commitment. You should think about coming out here. It's a great work environment and living style. We have access to the city for what it has to offer culturally."

"I can't imagine there's a lot of demand for a forensic pathologist like me," Jack said.

"I wouldn't be so sure," Ted responded.

"Is Dr. Zhao a medical doctor?" Jack questioned.

"No, he's a double Ph.D.," Ted said. "In both molecular biology and genetics."

"How old is he?" Jack asked, without even knowing why.

"I'm not sure exactly," Ted said. "If I had to guess, I'd say late sixties. But he doesn't look it." Then, pointing ahead, he added, "Slow down. It's the next left turn."

They turned off the main road, heading northwest on a road marked as private. Then, to Jack's surprise, they came to another security gate. Ahead, they could see Stephen's Porsche disappear around a bend, as it had already been cleared. As Jack pulled up to the gate and lowered his window, he wondered if Wei Zhao was a particularly paranoid individual. Such in-your-face security seemed a bit excessive.

After scrutinizing Ted's ID badge and then checking Jack's name against a list on a clipboard, the traffic gate rose. Pulling ahead, Jack's curiosity got the best of him and he said, "Why all the security around the man's house? I suppose I can understand it around GeneRx, with all the industrial competition in the drug industry, but out here it seems a bit excessive."

"It's been explained to us as having something to do with strained relations between Mr. Zhao and the People's Republic of China," Ted said. "He is a very wealthy man and prefers to live here in New Jersey even though his factories in China produce a host of brand-named drugs or ingredients for a large portion of the industry worldwide."

After a few twists and turns beneath a canopy of peach-colored oak foliage, the scene suddenly opened up to reveal an impressive house designed in a kind of contemporary Tudor style. With the modernity of the hospital and research building, Jack had expected something similar and more Asian in decor, with something like Japanese gardens. Instead, the house and the grounds had a decidedly English look, with a riot of flowers and shrubs. The roof was slate. Beyond the house was a small lake or pond surrounded by oak and maple trees.

Jack parked next to Stephen's car. Stephen and Han were waiting at the base of a walkway, which had a series of steps that led up to the house.

"It's a little different than Manhattan," Stephen said with a chuckle as the group filed upward. "As bucolic as it is, it's hard to believe it is only about thirty-eight miles as the crow flies to Times Square. Maybe you should think about moving out here. It's a wonderful lifestyle."

Jack didn't respond, but internally he smiled and joked to himself that these two doctors were sounding like they were members of the chamber of commerce, promoting the area.

When they arrived at the door there was no need to ring a bell or knock. It was opened by a slight Asian fellow a bit long in the tooth who obviously had been observing their progress as they approached. Stephen gestured for Jack to precede, and the others filed in after him.

The slender Asian shut the door behind the guests and then informed them that the boss was in the gym and that they should all follow him. As they did so, Jack had an opportunity to gaze around the home. The interior decor was pleasant but of an indeterminate style that, if pressed, Jack would have called nondescript American. Although everything was extraordinarily neat and of apparent high quality, there would have been no way for Jack to guess it was occupied by a billionaire Chinese business-man. The only exception was a large vitrine in the entrance hall filled with an extensive collection of jade objects. Somewhere in the back of his mind, Jack remembered Chinese people valued jade.

As they walked, Ted whispered to Jack, "The servant's name is Kang-Dae Ryang. He's been the boss's personal assistant for almost forty years. Interestingly enough, he's a defector from North Korea who swam across the Yalu River in the winter when he was young."

"I noticed all three of you have called Dr. Zhao 'the boss,'" Jack said. "Is that just a figure of speech or something more?"

Ted laughed. "It's something more. Bruce Springsteen is Dr. Zhao's favorite singer. Dr. Zhao loves American culture."

It was a rather long walk, as it was a big house. When they arrived, Jack was moderately surprised. He'd heard that they were going to the gym but didn't take it so literally. But it was a real gym, with every conceivable piece of workout machinery, and was nearly the size of the gym in Jack's old high school. And any preconceived notions Jack might have entertained before seeing Wei Zhao, he had to trash. With someone who was a reputed academic type, he'd expected a slight individual like pencil-thin Kang-Dae, probably nearsighted with glasses. The moment he saw Wei Zhao, he knew he'd been entertaining a foolish delusion. As the man stood from a weight machine he had been using, he seemed to keep rising. At six-two, Jack was usually as tall as or a bit taller than most people he encountered. Not so with Wei. Jack guessed Wei must have been six-four or even a bit taller. Even more surprising was the man's build. He had a narrow waist, with broad shoulders and bulging biceps.

While wiping perspiration off his face with a towel, Wei approached the group. His slight smile made his expression both welcoming and amused. He was wearing a tight-fitting black synthetic fiber V-neck top along with black sweats. He wasn't as muscular as Warren, but it looked as if he had been at some point in his life. He had straight black hair neatly trimmed and totally devoid of gray. His face was round, with wide cheekbones and small features. His eyes were as black as night and shined with penetrating intensity.

Stephen did the formal introductions, and Wei bowed during them. Jack bowed back, feeling mildly intimidated. Jack thought of himself as being in reasonably good shape, but here was a man obviously more than ten years his senior who appeared in peak physical condition. On top of that, he was superbly educated, with Ph.D.s in two subjects, not to mention that he'd amassed a literal fortune through his business ventures. In a competitive world it was a hard act to follow. Jack was thankful his self-esteem was reasonably secure despite what was going on at the home front.

"We owe you a good deal of thanks for your excellent and hard work," Wei said, echoing what Jack had already been told. "I heard you were remarkably persistent. Way to go!" His voice was almost accent-free and his syntax was unmistakably American.

"It is the role of the medical examiner to speak for the dead," Jack said. "For that to have meaning, the dead have to be identified."

"My sense is that there was more to your motivation than your job description," Wei said. "It was difficult for us to bear hearing the news, but necessary. We have to figure out what went wrong so it doesn't happen again. We are now a certified heart transplant center with plans to become one of the most active in the country. We cannot have mysterious and unexpected deaths. We appreciate your efforts."

"As I told the others, it is my job," Jack said.

"Humble as well as talented," Wei said. "You are the type of person we are constantly searching for to become part of the team. Would you be interested?"

"Thank you, but I'm very happy where I am, careerwise," Jack said.

"Who knows?" Wei questioned with a conspiratorial smile. "Maybe we can change your mind. To that end, I would like to invite you to have a bite of an early lunch with me, unless it's too early for you."

"That's very gracious," Jack said. "It's not too early for me and would be my pleasure." Once again, Jack was taken aback. He'd anticipated a short visit with the billionaire and had been wrestling with what to ask in the limited time he'd have. Now it seemed he'd have more than enough time over lunch.

"Well, in that case I think we should head on back to the hospital," Stephen said.

"I agree," Ted said.

Han merely smiled broadly in apparent enthusiastic agreement.

"If you have any more questions, don't hesitate to call or stop in," Ted said, handing one of his business cards over to Jack. Then the three doctors shook hands with Jack in turn, said goodbye, and trooped out of the gym behind Kang-Dae.

"Here's my suggestion as your host," Wei said. "I will send you up to the great room with Kang-Dae as soon as he returns, and he will provide whatever refreshment you would like. Or if you prefer, he could give you a tour of our grounds. It's up to you. Meanwhile, I will take a quick shower. Does that sound like an acceptable plan?"

"Sounds like a perfect plan," Jack said.

20

Jack's experience with luncheons was limited. He usually had no time, neither in his current life or in his past life, nor did he particularly like to sit around motionless in the middle of the day. Yet despite his lack of experience, he still thought this present lunch was strikingly unique. He was sitting with a Chinese billionaire catty-corner at a mahogany Chippendale table that sat sixteen, which was positioned in the center of a formal dining room with a huge chandelier. Large windows afforded a pleasant view out over the pond. Only Wei and himself were at the table. Earlier Jack had been introduced to Wei's wife, Pakpao, but she did not join them. Kang-Dae was in the room but not at the table. He was sitting motionlessly on a side chair near the door.

Wei had been true to his word when he said he would be taking a quick shower. Jack had no sooner gotten a glass of ice water from Kang-Dae and briefly looked at the framed photographs adorning the wall above the fieldstone fireplace in the great room when Wei reappeared. In contrast to his workout clothes, he was dressed in a dark, well-fitting suit, a white shirt, and a dark tie and looked like the businessman he was reputed to be.

As soon as Wei had appeared, Jack had to ask about the photos, as they were all of the same individual, Arnold Schwarzenegger. All of them showed Arnold posing with his over-the-top musculature in the many bodybuilding competitions he had won back in the 1970s.

"He was my idol back when I was a teenager," Wei had explained. "He's the one who got me interested in bodybuilding and probably saved my life. It gave me something to live for during a dark time in the midst of the Communist Cultural Revolution, when my parents and I were forced out into the countryside to work the land."

Although Jack hadn't had much time while Wei was showering, it had been enough time for him to again change his modus operandi. Earlier, when he'd thought his interview with Ted and Stephen was about to abruptly end, he'd decided to throw caution to the wind and put all his cards on the table. But now he had decided to reverse course, convinced that the confrontational style of going for broke would rather quickly put him out on the street and thereby end his sanity-saving diversion of investigating the conundrum of Carol Stewart's death. The fortuitous opportunity to meet the boss and establish a relationship put him in a good position to figure out what was going on from the top down, and his intuition was continuing to tell him loud and clear that something was definitely afoot beyond the possibility of a new pandemic. In Jack's mind, GeneRx and Dover Valley Hospital were in cahoots about something, and he meant to find out what it was.

"This is one of my favorite dishes," Wei said, as a young woman dressed in a traditional Chinese costume held a platter so Jack could help himself. "It's called Kung Pao chicken. It is a little spicy, but not as spicy as the Sichuan version. We Shanghainese cannot take the heat." He smiled at his own joke.

After both men had been served and the young woman departed, Jack was eager to start a conversation, but he held back, uncharacteristically unassertive. He was still a bit intimidated being in Wei Zhao's presence. Wei had no such hesitation: "Dr. Friedlander and Dr. Markham both mentioned that you were surprised to learn that we had ruled out virus contributing to Carol Stewart's death."

"That's true," Jack said. "A virologist at the Public Health Laboratory saw what she thought were virus-induced cytopathic effects on cultured human kidney cells."

"It had to have been artifact," Wei said. "It was one of our worries, too, until we saw there was no virus present with electron microscopy. What we are confident we'll be finding are some abnormal proteins released by the heart that apparently turned on an immune-inflammatory cascade, ultimately resulting in a cytokine storm. That's why we wanted a second autopsy, mostly to get samples of the donor heart and of the anastomoses with the large vessels. Something went terribly wrong, and we need to find out what it was. We've only been a certified heart transplant center for three months, and we will need to report this fatality, as we were responsible for the patient's post-operative care."

Jack nodded. There was no doubt Wei was clinically knowledgeable even though not trained as a medical doctor. The idea had entered Jack's mind that Stephen and Ted could be doing something behind the boss's back that the boss didn't know about. But that seemed far-fetched with the medical understanding Wei was revealing. Jack was certain that whatever was going on between Dover Valley Hospital and GeneRx, Wei knew about it and was intimately involved.

"I have ordered an entire team of molecular biologists to look into this case twenty-four/seven until it is solved," Wei continued. "It's a challenge. Carol's sudden death underlines our general ignorance about the complement system and the inflammasome."

"It is an area of physiology that needs a lot of study," Jack said, feeling pressure to respond.

"After your autopsy, what exactly did you think killed Carol Stewart?" Wei asked.

"I thought the mechanism of death was a cytokine storm," Jack said.

"We agree on that. But the cause, I'm not sure. Maybe an antigenic protein was involved, but there was no sign of inflammation in the heart. What worries me is the possible involvement of a new, lethal virus, whether associated with the transplant or not. The story of her getting on the subway in Brooklyn asymptomatic and then dying on reaching Manhattan is too much like a repeat nightmare of 1918."

"A virus worried us, too," Wei admitted. "We were relieved when we looked at the electron micrographs and saw no viruses whatsoever."

For a few minutes the two men ate in silence while Jack's mind was in a turmoil. He couldn't decide what to ask next. He wanted to bring up the matching DNA CODIS profiles but was contemplating how to do it diplomatically. Almost as if reading his mind, Wei did it for him.

"Dr. Friedlander and Dr. Markham also said that your DNA lab reported that the patient and the donor heart matched. We have extensive DNA sequencing ability. Our preliminary results show them to be close but nowhere near to being identical, so we wouldn't know what to make of your lab's results besides recommending they be repeated. But even that is unnecessary. We can send you full genome sequences in the near future for your records, because we are doing both."

Jack was about to argue that the tests had already been repeated when he decided to let the matter drop for the time being. He thought it best to talk to Dr. Lynch, head of the DNA laboratory, about the issue when he got back to the OCME. Jack was more interested in building bridges with Wei than in destroying them. He couldn't help but believe the closeness of the match between the donor heart and the recipient was critical to whatever weird thing was in progress, but pushing the issue could potentially be explosive.

"How is it you ended up here in New Jersey?" Jack asked, to keep the conversation away from testy subjects. "It is a long way from Shanghai."

"You mean here in New Jersey in particular or in the United States?"

"Both, I guess," Jack said. He really didn't care.

"I am fond of New York for business," Wei said. "But I needed space. New Jersey gives me access to both, as you can tell from this view from my dining room."

"Why the United States?" Jack asked. "My understanding is that you have done very well in China."

"I have done well in China, and it continues businesswise," Wei said. "I have been able to take good advantage of the Chinese economic miracle. But there are limits. Although pharma is expanding in China by replacing local remedies, prices are being controlled. Here in the United States that's not the case, because your politicians are dependent on pharma campaign donations. There is much more money to be made here in all aspects of healthcare, even if there are more problems with labor."

"The unreasonable price of healthcare is a rather sad state of affairs for us Americans," Jack said, although he didn't need to be reminded by Wei.

"And for me there is an even greater motivation," Wei said. "I'm fearful when I am in China today."

With a bit of surprise, Jack sat back and looked at his host, half expecting to see him smile to suggest he was being humorous. But Wei didn't smile. Instead he stared out the window at the pond, obviously in deep thought.

"What are you fearful about?" Jack asked. As a known billionaire, Jack would have imagined a life of extraordinary ease for him in China, with as much security and servants as he could possibly need.

"The government," Wei said nostalgically. "Things have changed over the last number of years, particularly with Xi Jinping's love for centralized power, both his own and the Communist Party's. Everything has become arbitrary for us successful businessmen. One day we are considered the darlings of the Politburo, the next an enemy. Xi has made it possible for businessmen to be snatched out of their offices or homes and declared corrupt at whim with no due process. It's a terrible way to live.

Several of my acquaintances have been arbitrarily jailed without access to lawyers, and no court dates."

"That's no way to live," Jack agreed.

Wei went on to tell several of the stories of his friends and the frustration he'd felt about not being able to help them.

"That is awful," Jack said, and meant it.

"I go back to my home in Shanghai as little as possible," Wei admitted. "Several years ago, I decided to completely pull out of the People's Republic of China, but the government has made moving capital progressively more difficult, particularly of late, with new restrictions by the PBOC, or People's Bank of China, and the State Administration of Foreign Exchange."

"You seem to be doing all right here in New Jersey," Jack said. "I was very impressed with my tour of GeneRx, the Farm Institute, and what I saw of the hospital. Also, I'd have to add the Zhao Heart Center at MGH in Manhattan. Very impressive and very generous of you."

"Thank you," Wei said. "We are proud of what we have been able to do. But it is not without effort and anxiety. Unfortunately, GeneRx has only two drugs on the market at present, although there are a slew in phase three trials. We need a breakout product or medical activity, of which we have a number in the wings. Presently I am dependent on the PBOC to allow adequate funds to keep everything afloat. But enough about me. What about Dr. Jack Stapleton? How is life for him?"

Jack straightened up by reflex. Wei's question took him aback. Although Wei had been talking in surprisingly personal terms, Jack had no inkling he'd ask for a response in kind.

"I know what your government salary is," Wei said, before Jack could respond. "You deserve more, a lot more. I'd suggest at least double, and we would be prepared to offer that. We need another pathologist of your stature."

"I like my job," Jack said, amazed that Wei was back to offering him a job, especially after just talking about financial insecurity.

"You have not had an easy life," Wei said. "Being forced out of clinical medicine must have been disappointing. And then to have your family killed after coming to visit you while you were retraining in pathology had to have been a life-shattering event. And now with your second child in your second family possibly having autism, I would think significantly raising your income might be a source of comfort. Autism treatment can be very expensive. Private industry pays significantly more than government jobs. It is something for you to consider."

For a few beats Jack didn't even breathe. He stared at Wei in total disbelief. As a habitually private person, he was shocked hearing his life story so casually thrown at him. He swallowed with some effort, as his mouth had gone suddenly dry while his emotions flipped back and forth between rage and incredulity. The only person Jack had confided in about Emma was Detective Lou Soldano, and Jack would have bet his life that Lou would never violate his confidence.

Controlling himself with some difficulty, Jack managed to say, "How exactly did you learn these things?"

"I asked my staff to construct a rapid dossier on you," Wei said. "With adequate resources it is not difficult. I was quite impressed with what you had been able to do in regard to Carol Stewart. What took me totally by surprise was that you would unexpectedly appear on our doorstep. To me that suggests that destiny is playing a role here, meaning that you will become part of the GeneRx team. Prior to the call from our Dr. Friedlander, I had expected we would need to approach you in the city, perhaps at your impressive home on 106th Street."

Jack forced a pinched half-smile as he continued to struggle with his volcanic emotions. Wei's in-depth knowledge of his life made him feel distinctly uncomfortable, off balance, and in marginal control. All at once, despite the additional questions he wanted to ask about the Carol Stewart case, Jack had to get out of Wei's house before he said or did something he'd regret.

21

Pulling off the rural road and onto the shoulder ten minutes later, Jack put the Escalade into park. He needed a moment to pull himself together. Although he'd managed to extricate himself from Wei Zhao's house without causing a scene, he knew that it had been precipitous, and that Wei had certainly noticed he was agitated. Still, the departure had been pleasant enough, with Wei presenting him with a business card and the encouragement to give him a call if Jack had any more questions about the Stewart case or if he had a change of heart about exploring employment opportunities.

The stretch of the two-lane road he was on was completely deserted and lined with dense oaks and maples past their prime in terms of color. There was no traffic in either direction, and the sun was peeking out through the clouds. Jack lowered the driver's-side window to allow some fresh air to waft into the cab. Along with it came the sound of birds. It was a perfect environment to catch his breath.

Jack knew that he had been a bit out of control over the past week or two and was fully aware he'd been using the Carol Stewart case as a diversion from everything going on at home. What he hadn't been aware of was his own fragility and instability. His excessive response to Wei's inappropriate lack of boundaries and violation of personal space scared him. For a brief moment his reptilian brain had almost taken over, and he had had to fight to keep himself from lashing out physically, which would have been a disaster on so many levels. Jack knew that he had a raging physicality that was the real reason he needed the almost nightly, exhaustive run on the b-ball court.

"You're pathetic," Jack yelled out the open window. Yet by even saying it, he felt it wasn't really true except for a fleeting moment in Wei's dining room. He was confident he was back in control and could now benefit from the incident by being prepared and not letting it happen again. After all, there was nothing that Wei had said that was any kind of secret that couldn't be found out by anyone who was truly interested. The question was: Why was Wei Zhao interested? The only explanation Jack could imagine was that it had to do with the wish to control him and stop his inquiries, which was why Jack thought he'd been offered a job, all of which made Jack more certain that something out of the ordinary was going on with GeneRx and Dover Valley Hospital.

With a sudden renewed sense of purpose, Jack struggled to get his mobile phone out of his pocket. He turned it on. He saw he had a few voice messages, but he ignored them. Instead, he quickly found Aretha's number and placed the call. With the phone against his ear, he thought of one of the key questions he'd not had a chance to ask Wei and lamented that he hadn't—namely, how and why Wei ended up as the executor of Carol Stewart's estate.

"I hope you are not calling to ask if I have had any luck with the MPS machine," Aretha said without even saying hello.

"If I thought it would help, I might," Jack admitted. "No, but I am calling about the same case. Did you by any chance look at the lung secretions with an electron microscope?" It felt good for Jack to talk to a normal, sane person. Ever since he'd walked into the Dover Valley Hospital and had been fawned over, he'd not had that sense.

"I've never met someone so single-minded about their work," Aretha said, and laughed. "No, I did not. We don't have an electron microscope here at the Public Health Laboratory. It would be nice, though. Perhaps you could put in a good word for us with the City Council."

"I'll do that next time I meet with them," Jack joked. "The reason I ask is that I was told someone else did out here in New Jersey. What they found was no viruses present. None. Does that surprise you?"

"Certainly it surprises me, especially with what I'm seeing with the human kidney cell tissue culture. There's virus in there, that I'm sure of."

"Could it be a contaminant?" Jack asked.

"I suppose it's possible," Aretha said. "But I have pretty good technique, or at least my professors thought so."

"What if we inoculate several more cultures," Jack asked. "Just to be certain."

"No problem," Aretha said. "Unless you or your mortuary techs were the source of the contamination when you did the collection."

"I hear you," Jack told her. "But if it were a contaminant, it would be some garden-variety virus."

"True, which we will be able to easily detect. I'll try to do that this afternoon."

"Thanks, Aretha."

"Are you going to run tonight again?" Aretha asked.

"I might have to," Jack said without elaborating.

After disconnecting, Jack checked his voicemail. There were two messages. One from Laurie and one from Hank Monroe, head of Identification. He was relieved there hadn't been one from Bart Arnold, as it meant that there had not been another subway death for forty-eight hours, certainly a good sign in respect to the pandemic threat. He then listened to Laurie's message. It was short and sweet, with a tone of mild irritation: "Give me a call!" It had come in two hours earlier. He shrugged. That couldn't be good news, as she was probably wondering where the hell he was. Thinking it might be best to put off responding until he got back to the OCME, he went to the second voicemail from Hank. It was more promising: "I have an address you might find useful. Give me a call!" Jack did just that.

"I've managed to get an address for Carol Stewart," Hank said, when he heard it was Jack calling.

"We already have an address," Jack said. "The person who came in last evening to identify her gave us her Brooklyn address."

"It's an old address of hers," Hank said. "I got it from her New Jersey driver's license. It's Fourteen Mercer Way in Denville, New Jersey. Since it's an old license, my thought was that she grew up there, meaning it's where her parents live. I checked it out. There is a Stewart family living there presently, Robert and Marge Stewart."

"Thanks," Jack said. "You're right. That may be useful information."

"I thought so. It makes one ask why they didn't come in to make the ID instead of Agnes Mitchel."

"You are absolutely right," Jack repeated. He again thanked Hank and disconnected. For another minute he sat there listening to the birds in the forest. Before heading back to the city, he had planned on going back to the local medical examiner's office to find out what the medical examiner had found on Carol's second autopsy and what he knew about the motorcycle victim, but with this new information, he changed his mind. Google Maps told him 14 Mercer Way was a short dash down Interstate 80, and he could be there in eleven minutes. Despite there being no guarantee that he would find anyone home in the middle of a weekday, he impulsively raised the driver's-side window, put the Escalade in gear, and set out for Denville.

By the time Jack found the correct house and parked, it was almost twenty minutes later. But on the plus side, he found both Stewarts at home. It was Marge Stewart who answered the door chime. She was a tall, severe-looking woman with her hair parted down the center of her head and pulled tight in a bun. She looked vaguely familiar to Jack in her white-collared dark-brown housedress, but he couldn't place her until she was joined by Robert Stewart. Jack then realized the two of them bore a striking and uncanny resemblance to the couple in Grant Wood's painting *American Gothic,* minus the pitchfork.

"Sorry to bother you folks," Jack said. As he gave his name, he flashed his NYC medical examiner badge without saying he was a medical examiner and from a different state. His hope was to speed up and encourage cooperation with the idea they might think of him as a law enforcement agent. He wanted it to be a short visit. "Are you the parents of Carol Weston Stewart?"

"We are," Robert said. He was as stern-looking as his wife and wearing a clerical collar. He had a tight, almost lipless mouth. "But that is all we are."

"Excuse me?" Jack questioned. He'd heard but didn't quite know how to interpret the comment.

"We have had nothing to do with her for years," Robert said. "So if you're here because she has caused trouble, it's not our responsibility."

"I see," Jack said. He was talking through a screen door, but it didn't seem as if the Stewarts were about to open it. "I can assure you that I'm only here for some information. Did you know your daughter had some serious health issues?"

"We had heard something to that effect," Robert said. "It was God's will. We know she had problems with her heart."

"Did you know she had had a heart transplant?"

"No, we did not."

"May I ask if the source of your estrangement was her sexual preference?" Jack asked, trying again to be as diplomatic as possible, even if it wasn't his nature. Even so, he knew he was pushing the limits of what he could ask these total strangers, even with the help of his medical examiner badge.

"Of course it was," Robert said bitterly. "Her behavior from age thirteen on was an affront to God. Homosexuality is an abomination and a violation of the Seventh Commandment. We could not have that in our house."

"I see," Jack said. He was going to ask if they were aware of her death, but he couldn't see any point. He thought it would only harden their self-righteous, narrow-minded indignation about her sexual orientation. "Thank you for your time."

As Jack climbed back into the SUV he felt a renewed sadness for Carol Stewart. Having to deal with her bigoted parents must have caused her significant pain as a teenager. Jack had a knee-jerk negative reaction to hyper-religious people, no matter what the religion. In his former life he'd been brought up in a Catholic family, but one that was less than perfect as far as following the dogma. By the time he'd gotten through college he'd become more of an agnostic, wanting to believe there was an organizing, moral force but unsure of what it was. Then, after the catastrophe with his first family, he'd become an avowed atheist, fully convinced a loving God wouldn't kill children or give them neuroblastoma or autism.

Meeting the Stewarts had only confirmed his feelings about religion. But the quick visit had not been a total waste of effort. He had gained more information about Carol. What he didn't know was what role it would play in the disaster that was about to unfold.

22

WEDNESDAY, 1:05 P.M.

"Yes, Dr. Lauder is here now," the secretary/assistant said in answer to Jack's query as she stood up from her desk. "What was your name again?"

"Dr. Jack Stapleton," Jack said. He was back at the very modest storefront private office of the medical examiner in the town of Dover. Jack was interested in finding out if anything at all had been learned at the second autopsy carried out at the Dover Valley Hospital. Other than providing samples of the heart, he couldn't imagine it had accomplished anything.

While he waited, Jack looked around the tiny, skimpy waiting area with Masonite walls, several molded plastic chairs, and some outdated magazines. Other than possible work relating to the Dover Valley Hospital and GeneRx, he couldn't imagine there would be much call for a medical examiner in such a small town. Jack thought it was a good thing the man did it part-time. He remembered from the Higgins funeral director that the ME also worked for the Morris County Medical Examiner's Office, apparently splitting his time. After the offers of employment by Wei Zhao, Jack tried to imagine himself living in the area. He couldn't. No matter how much they paid him, he thought he'd go mad.

"Dr. Lauder will see you now," the secretary/assistant said, reappearing from the inner office.

Jack retraced the woman's steps. The inner office had the same unrefined general appearance as the outer room. The furniture looked as if it had come from a secondhand store, and Dr. Harvey Lauder fit in perfectly. He was a short, stocky, pug-nosed man with thinning hair and a very obvious comb-over vainly attempting to cover a tonsure-like bald spot. His casual clothes had a baggy, lived-in look with a tear in his flannel shirt at the left elbow. As Jack entered, the ME got to his feet and extended his hand in a welcoming fashion. "Harvey Lauder," he said, giving Jack's hand a shake. He pointed to a single straight-backed chair and retook his aged, wooden desk chair.

"I got the card you left this morning, and I was meaning to give you a call," Harvey said. "I've just been up to here with work." He put his hand under his chin as he spoke, to indicate he'd been up to his neck. "So what can I do for you?"

"I wanted to find out how the second autopsy went on Carol Stewart," Jack said. "I was the one who did the first."

"So I heard," Harvey said. "It went fine. No problems at all."

Jack wondered exactly what he had done but decided not to make an issue of it.

"I haven't seen the slides yet," Harvey said. "They are not going to be available until tomorrow or Friday. But I don't expect any surprises. What exactly did you find on the first autopsy?"

"Extensive lung damage and edema consistent with a cytokine storm," Jack said. "The heart looked perfectly fine, without any trace of inflammation. However, we did find a mild inflammatory response in the spleen, gallbladder, and both kidneys. Toxicology was negative."

"Our toxicology is pending," Harvey said.

"It was a very rapid clinical course," Jack said. "She essentially died on a subway after having respiratory symptoms for about an hour."

"So I hear," Harvey said.

"How long have you been working with the Dover Valley Hospital?" Jack asked.

"About four years as part of my private practice," Harvey said. "I split my time between here and the Morris County Medical Examiner's Office."

"Meaning you must have been around when Carol Stewart got into trouble and acutely needed a transplant."

"Most definitely," Harvey said. "That was only a bit more than three months ago."

"I was told that the donor of the serendipitously well-matched heart had been in a motorcycle accident. Were you involved with that case as a Morris County medical examiner?"

"I most certainly was," Harvey said.

"Do you recall the name of the victim, by any chance?" Jack asked. "Was his family name Stewart?"

"No, it was Bannon," Harvey said. "James Bannon. He was a seventeen-year-old teenager, the poor kid."

"Dr. Ted Markham thought it might have been a Stewart, to explain why there was such a close match. But you are sure it was Bannon?"

"I'm absolutely sure. Maybe he was related to the Stewarts. There was a lot of inbreeding around here not that many years ago. Actually, it's still going on. Besides, he could have been adopted."

"Did you personally do the autopsy on James Bannon?"

"Why do you ask?"

"I'm curious about it and have some general questions," Jack said. "There are some things about the Carol Stewart case that intrigue me, including the source of the transplant organ."

"You know, not to be unfriendly, but I do want to remind you that you are in New Jersey, not New York. Maybe you should be asking your questions through the official channels."

"Yeah, I could do that, but you know what that's like," Jack said, trying to appeal to his sympathies as one ME to another. "As I'm sure you are aware, going through official channels takes forever, and I have to sign this case out in the next day or so."

"An autopsy wasn't done," Harvey said in a defensively forceful tone.

"Really?" Jack questioned. He was taken aback and disappointed. "In New York we autopsy all motor vehicle accidents."

"Generally, so do we," Harvey said. "But this one happened on a very busy weekend with multiple accidents and a double homicide, which is very rare for us. But the most important thing was that there wasn't any question as to the cause and manner of death. With no helmet involved, most of his brain had to be scooped up off Interstate Eighty. And then there was cardiac death after the ventilator was turned off in the hospital in conjunction with the harvesting of the heart. No mystery there, either."

"This all happened at the Dover Valley Hospital, I gather," Jack said.

"That's correct," Harvey said, regaining his composure. "It's the best-equipped hospital in the area. And the hospital did all the tests for alcohol and drugs, all of which were negative. It was one of those situations where an autopsy would not have added anything whatsoever and the family seriously objected to it. They were very vocal about it."

"Interesting," Jack said, falling back on his new favorite expression.

"I hope I have been of some service, but I do have to get back to work. If you'll excuse me . . ." Harvey stood and walked over to the flimsy door. He opened it and held it ajar as an unmistakable indication the meeting was over.

"Certainly," Jack said, getting to his feet and heading to the outer office. "I can imagine how swamped you are." As soon as the comment left his mouth, he regretted it. There was no reason to aggravate the man.

Harvey immediately shut his office door with demonstrative finality as soon as Jack had passed through. For a moment Jack stood where he was and looked back at the door questioningly, wondering why he'd gotten the bum's rush. He shrugged. Turning around, he gazed at the secretary. The room was small. She was only about four feet away, looking up at him expectantly.

"I was just chatting with Dr. Lauder about a case of his by the name of James Bannon," Jack said. "It was a Morris County Medical Examiner case that wasn't autopsied. Would you have the individual's home address?"

"I believe we do," the secretary said. Making use of the wheels on her desk chair, she scooted the few feet over to an upright file cabinet and pulled open the lowest file drawer. Jack wondered why she didn't use the monitor on her desk. As she searched, Jack could hear Harvey making a phone call through the paper-thin door of the inner office behind him. The sounds were muffled, but Jack plainly heard two names: his own and Dr. Wei Zhao's. He strained to hear what Harvey was saying but couldn't. The only other thing he managed to hear was a third name: James Bannon. Then he heard the phone being dropped into its cradle.

"Yes, here's the Bannon folder," the secretary said, pulling it out from the drawer. She opened it and then added: "The address is Five-ninety-one Spring Lane, Rockaway. Do you want me to write that down?"

"I think I can remember it," Jack said, tapping his head with his index finger. He thanked her and walked out of the office into the now sunny day.

After climbing into the car, Jack thought for several minutes what it could mean that the moment he'd left Harvey's inner office the man had called Wei Zhao, of all people. It was yet another curious fact that he added to the mountain of other facts he was amassing about the weirdness of the Carol Stewart case. He couldn't help but feel it suggested collusion, but collusion about what, he had no idea.

Although Jack was concerned about getting back to the OCME now that it was two, especially with Laurie's less-than-happy voicemail, he thought it would be a shame not to make one more house call while he was in New Jersey—especially since Google Maps informed him that Rockaway was only four miles away. He had hoped to get a copy of the autopsy report on the motorcycle victim who'd been the source of the heart for Carol Stewart. But now that he'd learned there had been no autopsy, he thought a visit with the family might be in order. There was something about this case, too, that nagged him, even though he didn't know quite what it was. At the same time, he wasn't looking forward to visiting the bereaved family. If they had not heard the news about Carol Stewart, Jack feared they'd be heartbroken anew to learn that their son's heart was no longer beating in the chest of the young woman. Jack understood that donating the heart certainly didn't bring their son back, but it must have been a source of some comfort.

Jack was about to put the Escalade in gear when his phone rang. Within the confines of the SUV the sound shocked him, and he answered in a mild panic without checking to see who was calling. That was a mistake. It was Laurie.

"Where in God's name are you?" she snapped. "No one has seen you all morning. And I didn't appreciate your sneaking out of our apartment this morning for the second day in a row. My father was clearly disappointed not to see you."

"I was heartsick not to see him, too, but duty called," Jack said, being intentionally provocative.

"I'm not going to respond to that," Laurie said.

"How has your day been?" Jack asked, to change the subject.

"To be honest, it's been a terrible day. I'm fed up with the City Council and all the politics involved. I'm getting nowhere on this budget problem."

"But you knew about the politics when you accepted the job," Jack said.

"To some degree, but I never thought it would be this frustrating. That aside, where the devil are you? Are you out in the field potentially causing trouble when I asked you not to?"

"It's so nice to be appreciated," Jack said. "Yes, I'm in the Garden State, smelling the roses."

"Don't tell me you went out and visited that Dover hospital you mentioned last night."

"I did indeed," Jack confessed. "But you'd be proud of me. I don't think I've made any enemies. In fact, I've managed to be so charming I've gotten multiple employment offers, so you better be nice to me."

"Are you joking?"

"I'm not," Jack said. "I've been treated like a hero. And strangely enough, during a rather formal luncheon that I was invited to, I was the one who got really bummed out and not my lunch companion. And even stranger still, I kept myself reasonably under control."

"Will wonders never cease," Laurie remarked. "I hope you haven't been using your medical examiner badge while in another state."

"Just a little," Jack admitted. "But I've flashed it so quickly there wasn't any chance of the people noticing it was for New York, not New Jersey."

"God help us!" Laurie said. "You realize, I hope, that you are taking a big risk. I wouldn't be at all surprised if showing your badge in another state is breaking the law. Think about it! It means you're posing as an official authority when you are clearly not. I don't know how to be more clear about this: Don't use it!"

"I'll keep that in mind," Jack said.

"And I must tell you that your field work isn't as benign as you seem to feel. I already heard from the mayor, who heard from Charles Kelley, the CEO of Manhattan General Hospital, that you were over there yesterday ruffling feathers."

"Guilty as charged," Jack said. "But it was only Kelley's feathers. And that is understandable. It's not possible to talk with that man without ruffling his feathers. But everyone else thought I was peaches and cream."

"All right, all right!" Laurie said, clearly losing patience. "This is my second call, wondering where the hell you are. The reason is that I have gotten two calls from the police commissioner, asking about the status of the police custody case. They want answers. Where are you on that case?"

"I need to get the toxicology report," Jack said.

"Well, get back here and do that!" Laurie snapped.

"Yes, dear," Jack said. He disconnected and turned the ringer off on his phone. It irked him to be clearly bossed around, even if it was her job to do so. The trouble was, he knew she was right. With the subway death case holding him in its thrall, he was letting everything else slide.

23

The Bannon homestead gave a totally different impression than the Stewarts'. Whereas the Stewart house was on the shabby side and in need of paint and attention to its gutters and downspouts, the Bannon dwelling appeared as if it had just undergone a major renovation, including a new roof. As Jack parked directly in front and looked at it, he wondered if the Bannons had recently won the lottery. There was even a new red Ford F-150 in the driveway, which made him optimistic that someone would be home.

Climbing out of the Escalade, Jack started for the house. Its architectural style was also different. It had an attractive gambrel roof with dormers. The Stewarts' had been the more typical and unimaginative ranch style. After just talking with Laurie and being reminded that using his ME badge in New Jersey was probably illegal, Jack reluctantly decided not to use it. Actually, he didn't really care. It just meant a bit more talking.

He pressed the doorbell and could hear it ring within. As he waited, he glanced around at the neighborhood. The Bannons' house was clearly the most well tended. On the house directly across the street, several of the shutters were hanging off precariously.

"Hi! Can I help you?"

Jack found himself facing a full-figured woman in yoga pants and a tank top. Her hair was piled on top of her head. In the background Jack could hear music that reminded him of the distant disco era. A bit of perspiration dotted her forehead. She appeared genuinely friendly, in contrast to the Stewarts.

"Hello," Jack said. "My name is Dr. Jack Stapleton. I'm a medical examiner from New York." He then pulled out his badge and held it up so the woman could plainly see it. At the last second, he'd changed his mind about using it, with the idea that by adding the New York part he was avoiding any illegality. He thought he needed the aura of authority, coming out of the blue and bringing up the sensitive issue of the lost son.

"I'm sorry to bother you, but I was hoping to talk with you and your husband for a brief moment about your late son, James."

"James?" she questioned. Her face clouded over. "Just a moment. Let me turn down the music."

A moment later the music stopped, and then the lady of the house reappeared. Also, in contrast to the Stewarts, she opened the screen door and motioned for Jack to come inside. With the Stewarts, Jack had been forced to have the entire conversation through the screen door.

"My husband, Clarence, is not here," she said. "He's at work at the Dover Valley Hospital. I'm Gertrude Bannon. Can I get you anything to drink? Water or a soda?"

"No, thank you," Jack said. Again, he was surprised. Somewhat similar to what had happened at the Dover Valley Hospital, he had not expected to be so well received. He'd even thought there was a chance the Bannons would refuse to talk with him at all.

"Would you like to sit?" Gertrude asked. She gestured to the living room.

"I'm not going to be here that long," Jack said, "but if you would be more comfortable, I don't mind."

"I think we will be more comfortable," Gertrude said. She led the way through an archway.

The room was modest in size and pleasant. But what caught Jack's eye was that all the furniture and the rug appeared to be new. Gertrude gestured for Jack to take the striped gingham couch. She sat in a faux leather La-Z-Boy recliner.

"First of all, I want to express my sincerest sympathies," Jack said. He was being truly sincere. He knew all too well what it was like to lose a child.

"Thank you," Gertrude said. "Are you sure you don't want anything to drink. Maybe a coffee?"

"No, I'm fine," Jack said. He looked at his host. She fidgeted. He was confused. She seemed to be nervous instead of saddened.

"You mentioned New York," Gertrude said. "Why are you here in New Jersey?"

"That's a good question," Jack said. "I'm here because of a death that happened in Manhattan. I don't know if you know this, but Carol Stewart, the young woman who benefited from your generosity by receiving your son's heart, has passed away."

"Oh." Gertrude drew in a breath. "I'm so sorry to hear that. What did she die of?"

"That is still to be determined," Jack said. "But it wasn't because of your son's heart. That was in perfect shape."

"I'm glad to hear," Gertrude said.

Jack studied the woman. She returned his stare and then modestly looked away. At first he was impressed by her stoicism, that she could deal with such information with such equanimity. But a second later he found himself feeling that her response was somehow inappropriate. She was still more nervous than distressed.

"Allowing your son's organs to save others was a very magnanimous gesture on your part and your husband's," Jack said. "I'm sure your generosity saved many lives, which must have been a source of some comfort. Nowadays almost everything can be used—lungs, liver, pancreas, even intestines. Have you had any contact with any of the people who were recipients of James's organs? I'm hoping that they can be a consolation to you, just as Carol Stewart was."

"No, we haven't," Gertrude said.

"Oh," Jack said simply. He was surprised but unwilling to make any kind of value judgment. It must have been the Bannons' wish to remain anonymous.

"What I have learned is that your son's heart was a perfect match for Carol Stewart," Jack said. "Are you and the Stewarts related somehow?"

"Not that I know of," Gertrude said. "We've never met the Stewarts."

"I see," Jack said. He scratched his head and then smoothed his hair. Every time he thought he had a grasp on the Carol Stewart story, he was proved wrong. Suddenly he had another idea. "Was James a biological child or was he adopted?"

"A biological child," Gertrude said without hesitation.

"Okay," Jack said, trying to maintain his own equanimity. "Out of curiosity, how long has your husband been working at the Dover Valley Hospital?"

"It's going on three months now," Gertrude said.

"Does he like it?"

"Very much," Gertrude said. "He thinks it is the best job he's ever had."

"Well, that's it," Jack said. "I don't have any more questions. Well . . . maybe I have one more. Were you and your husband paid to donate your son's organs?"

For a moment the question hung in the air like a ball of static electricity. Jack could hear the ticking of a clock somewhere in another room. Gertrude stared back at him with unblinking eyes, like a deer caught in headlights. Then, as if waking from a brief psychomotor seizure, she said, "No, we weren't paid."

"Then I have another question," Jack said. "Do you know what your son's blood type was?"

"I don't," Gertrude said.

"How about yours and your husband's?" Jack asked.

"Mine is O-negative, but I don't know what Clarence's is."

"Well, I want to thank you for your time," Jack said. He stood and headed for the front door, where he thanked her again and went out and got into his car. He was relatively sure the Bannons had been paid and Clarence had been given a job at the Dover Valley Hospital. The only problem was that he didn't know by whom and for what. Of course, the leading suspect was the boss, Wei Zhao.

For a few minutes Jack sat in the car, massaging his temples with his head down, staring into his lap. There were so many questions and so few answers. In some respects, his trip to New Jersey had been a success, and in some ways, it had been a disappointment. He now knew a bit more than he had that morning, and yet in other ways he knew less. Certainly, with the biggest conundrum, why the CODIS profiles matched, he had no clue, provided they did match. He felt like he wasn't sure of anything.

Sitting up straight, he looked back at the Bannon house, with its new paint job and new roof tiles, plus the new Ford F-150 in the driveway. It was obvious the Bannons had had a payday, and Jack could guess the source. With his suspicion that money had changed hands, he wondered if it was time to turn the whole caboodle over to law enforcement, such as the FBI. But as soon as the idea occurred to him he saw the negative side. The biggest negative was selfish. He needed the distraction and had nothing to take its place. With sudden resolve, he decided he'd hold off on letting the authorities in on what he suspected until he knew more.

With that thought in mind, Jack again consulted Google Maps. He knew he needed to get back to the OCME after having spoken to Laurie, but there was one more stop he wanted to make.

Jack started the SUV, put it in gear, and drove off. He wanted to make a quick stop at Carol Stewart's apartment in Sunset Park, Brooklyn, and try to figure out why no one had missed her when she died. Since there had been no subsequent sudden pulmonary deaths, he thought the exposure risk was small.

24

Visiting Brooklyn provided an additional layer of surprises in a day that had been full of them. First of all, Jack had had no idea Sunset Park was home to one of the largest Chinese American communities in the country. Most of the commercial signage was in Chinese.

The hardest part of the trip, which required going over the impressive Verrazzano-Narrows Bridge, was finding a parking place once he had arrived outside of Carol Stewart's building. With no other choice, he had to settle for a commercial spot and risk getting a parking ticket. It was another stimulus to make the visit as short as possible.

Carol's building was a relatively modern five-story brick structure. He was glad to see it was large enough for a live-in superintendent. His given name was Ho and his family name was Chang, but on the buzzer it was written CHANG HO in the Chinese order. Jack rang the buzzer while nervously looking over his shoulder at the SUV, half expecting a metermaid to appear spontaneously. Jack knew that Warren would not take kindly to getting a parking ticket. Warren felt strongly that the more you got, the more problems you had with the city.

Ho was a man of indeterminate age and slight habitus, in sharp contrast to Wei Zhao's muscular bulk. He also acted nervous and wary, which was equally as variant from Zhao's commanding assertiveness. Without saying anything, Jack held up his ME badge in front of the man's face and kept it there long enough for Ho to see it was a New York badge. It was immediately apparent that the badge had an unsettling effect on the super.

"What problem?" Ho asked with a heavy accent.

"You have a tenant by the name of Carol Stewart," Jack began. He had already seen her name next to the buzzer for apartment 2A, confirming the address. "Unfortunately, Miss Stewart has passed away."

"No, she still here," Ho said.

For a second Jack thought he was about to be confronted with another shocking revelation, until he realized that Ho had misinterpreted the meaning of the expression *passed away*. Jack rephrased it: "What I meant to say is that Miss Stewart has died. She is no longer with us."

"Ah, I see," Ho said. "Very sorry. She was a nice person."

"I'm sure she was," Jack said. "I would like to take a quick look in her apartment. Would you be able to open it for me?"

"Yes, I can open apartment," Ho said. He stepped aside so Jack could enter.

After one more reassuring glance over his shoulder at the Escalade, Jack stepped past Ho and started up the stairs. Ho followed close behind, getting out his keys in the process. At the top of the stairs, Ho pushed past Jack, who had paused, not knowing which direction to go.

A few minutes later, Jack entered a pleasant one-bedroom apartment that looked out onto 45th Street. Jack took the opportunity to glance yet again at the Escalade. So far, no metermaids.

Directing his attention back inside, Jack noticed that the furniture, although new, had a distinctively generic appearance, making him believe it was probably a rental. To Carol's credit, the apartment was neat and spanking clean. On the coffee table were a MacBook Pro and several copies of *Adweek,* a professional advertising magazine. A book titled *The Miseducation of Cameron Post* sat on a side table. There was no bric-a-brac.

"Did Miss Stewart live alone?" Jack asked, as he walked into the kitchen area. There were no dishes in the sink.

"Yes, she live alone," Ho said.

"How long was she a resident here?" Jack asked. He opened the refrigerator. It contained a moderate amount of food. Clearly, she was cooking for herself. There was also food in the pantry cabinet.

"Just a few months," Ho said.

"Did you notice if she had many visitors?" Jack asked, as he walked back into the connected living area.

Ho didn't answer immediately. Jack looked over at him. He seemed conflicted as to how much information he should reveal. "I'm not police," Jack assured him. "I'm a medical doctor trying to understand why she died."

"I see," Ho said. "She had visitors the first month. A man and a woman. They came at night and play music too loud. I have to tell Miss Stewart. But then the man and the woman didn't come back, so everything was good."

"Has there been any sickness in the building that you know of?" Jack asked.

"Last winter many people had the flu," Ho said. "This year so far okay."

"How about problems with pests, like mice or rats or insects?" Jack asked, just to cover all the bases.

"No trouble with pests," Ho said.

Jack walked into the bedroom. Ho followed at his heels. The bedroom was as neat as the living area. The queen-size bed was made. Jack opened the closet. There were a number of expensive-appearing dresses, blouses, and pants, all carefully hung up and appropriately grouped. There was an impressive collection of shoes both high heeled and flat and also a number of sneakers of varying colors. There were also boots. She obviously liked footwear.

Next Jack walked into the bathroom. It, too, was neat and clean, with the towels carefully hung and a bathmat folded over the edge of the bathtub.

"I guess she was a good tenant," Jack said, as he opened the medicine cabinet.

"Yes, a good tenant," Ho said. "Very nice person."

"Did she pay her rent on time?" Jack asked. He noticed there were no prescription medications in the medicine cabinet.

"No need for Miss Stewart to pay rent," Ho said.

"Oh," Jack voiced. He looked at Ho questioningly. "Why did she not pay rent?"

"The owner not require rent from Miss Stewart," Ho said. "She was special."

"Well, that was nice for Miss Stewart," Jack said, puzzled. "Do you know where Miss Stewart worked?"

"I don't think she worked, unless she work here with her computer," Ho said. "She didn't go out much."

"Did the owner come and visit her?" Jack asked.

"No, the owner never come here, even though he owns many buildings in the area."

"He must be a wealthy man," Jack said.

"Yes, very important man," Ho agreed.

"What is his name?" Jack asked, unsure of whether Ho would be willing to divulge it.

"His name is Zhao Wei," Ho said.

There it was, Jack thought. Somehow, he knew there was going to be a surprise if he visited Carol's apartment, and now he knew what it was. Wei Zhao was paying Carol's rent and possibly even paying her a salary, yet it most likely wasn't for romantic or sexual purposes. Not only was he the executor of her estate, but he was also her benefactor. *Why?*

Jack thanked the superintendent for his cooperation and left the building feeling even more perplexed than he had when he'd arrived. To make matters worse, there was a parking ticket under the windshield wiper of the car. With a sense of aggravation, Jack pulled it out and looked at it. It wasn't the amount involved that bothered him, it was having to tell Warren.

Once under way to OCME, Jack called Warren. The sooner he told him about the damn parking ticket, the easier it would be. To his surprise, Warren took it in stride.

"Don't worry about it," Warren said. "Check out the ticket carefully. A lot of times the metermaids make stupid little mistakes filling out the form. If they do, all you have to do is point it out to the authorities and they drop it. Are you running tonight?"

"I might have to," Jack said, echoing what he'd said earlier to Aretha. He had no idea what to expect when he got home that evening or even what he'd confront when he got back to work. It was obvious that Laurie was not thrilled with his behavior.

25

The drive from Sunset Park, Brooklyn, to the OCME was a relatively straight shot almost due north, using the Brooklyn-Battery Tunnel. The traffic was heavy but moving well, and Jack was able to relax to a degree. He was becoming accustomed to driving the Escalade, despite its size. At least he had good visibility, sitting as high as he was. He literally looked down on regular cars similar to the de rigueur Mercedes he had in his former life.

As he was trying to integrate Wei Zhao's apparent financial support for Carol Stewart with what he learned that day, he became so engrossed that when his phone rang it made him jump to the point of almost losing control of the car. With a bit of effort, he steadied the steering wheel and then guiltily looked out at the neighboring vehicles, wondering if anyone had noticed his sudden weave. One driver clearly had, because he gave Jack the finger. All Jack could do was mouth the word *sorry*.

Picking up the phone, he glanced at the caller ID. He expected it to be Laurie again, asking him why he wasn't back, but it wasn't Laurie. At least it wasn't her mobile number. Although he could tell it was an OCME number, he didn't know whose. Hoping it wasn't Laurie or her secretary, Jack answered. It wasn't Laurie. It was Bart Arnold, and he sounded stressed out.

"I'm so glad I got you. Are you still out in New Jersey?"

"No, I'm in Brooklyn, about to enter the Battery Tunnel. What's up?" Jack felt his own heart rate accelerate after he heard the urgency in Bart's voice.

"How soon do you think you will be here?" Bart asked.

"Fifteen to twenty minutes, unless FDR Drive is a parking lot. Why?"

"I think we have another one coming over from Bellevue as we speak. I just got off the phone with the ER."

"What do you mean by 'another one'?" Jack asked, but sensed he knew the answer.

"Another case just like Carol Stewart," Bart said excitedly, stumbling over his words.

"Another sudden respiratory death?"

"Yes, and uncannily similar in all respects but without the heart transplant," Bart said. "Young woman, apparently well dressed and not a druggie type. It even again happened on the subway, if you can believe it. This time it wasn't the R train from Brooklyn. It was the D train from Brooklyn. I mean, that's pretty fucking amazing."

Jack felt a bit of perspiration break out on his forehead as the implications of what he'd just been told occurred to him—namely, that Aretha's cytopathic effects were probably real and the lack of viruses on electron microscopy probably false. Jack shuddered. From the very moment he'd heard of the first case, he'd been terrified of a new lethal influenza virus running rampant in New York and spreading around the globe. Then, as time passed, first hours and then days, when there hadn't been another case and the influenza screen was negative, he'd progressively allowed his fears to abate to the point of becoming sidetracked by his stumbling onto a possible violation of the National Organ Transplant Act. As egregious as that might be, it wasn't nearly as critical as a possible new pandemic.

"What about an ID?" Jack asked. He hoped the case wasn't an exact replica.

"We are okay in that realm," Bart said. "We have a name: Helen VanDam, and an address in Bensonhurst. This time the victim was accompanied, and my understanding is that her companion will be in later for a formal identification."

"Helen?" Jack immediately questioned. In his mind's eye he immediately saw the name HELEN spelled out in Carol's tattoo. Could this be the same Helen?

If so, even that was scary by implying an infectious connection.

"I know what you are thinking," Bart said. "I had the same thought. But yes. It is definitely Helen."

"Do you know if Bellevue considered it a possible contagious case?"

"I reminded them," Bart said. "They insisted they had treated it as such from the outset, as did the EMS crew who got the victim off the train. This time it was the subway station at Thirty-fourth Street and Sixth Avenue."

"That's close to where Carol Stewart was picked up," Jack said.

"As I said, the cases are uncannily similar," Bart repeated.

"Thanks for the heads-up," Jack said.

"You should be arriving about the same time as the body," Bart said. "It's coming in a decontaminated body bag. Let me know what you find during the autopsy, and let me know if I can be of any help."

"Will do," Jack said. He disconnected. He then immediately pulled up Jennifer Hernandez's number and made the call. He felt guilty about paying so much attention to his phone while driving, especially after practically having an accident when it had rung. He glanced around at the other drivers. No one seemed to notice, although the highly tinted windows might have played a role in hiding his activities.

The conversation with Jennifer, the current on-call ME, was short and to the point. He merely informed her that another contagion case was coming in from the Bellevue ER that he would handle and do it immediately. She had yet to be informed from Communications but was glad not to have to think about what to do about it.

Next Jack put in a call to Vinnie, whose mobile phone number he also had in his contacts. Although Vinnie was officially off at three, he frequently stayed around, finding things to do and schmoozing with the other mortuary techs coming on for the night shift. Sometimes he stayed as late as five. Although he made it a point to act as if he didn't care, Vinnie was seriously dedicated to his job, especially after the tight bond had formed between him and Jack.

"Why do I dread getting a call from you when I'm officially off duty," Vinnie said without so much as a hello.

"I can't imagine," Jack said. "But what I can imagine is that you've had withdrawal symptoms, since I haven't been there all day to keep you in line."

"Oh, yeah, right," Vinnie scoffed.

"Listen, I'm going to make it up to you. I'm on my way in to 520 and will be there shortly. On its way in as we speak is another subway death just like the one we did on Monday. The name is Helen VanDam."

"Let me guess," Vinnie groused. "You want to do it right away. Shit! Why can't you be like everyone else around here? What's wrong with tomorrow morning?"

"I know you well enough to know you know why," Jack said.

"Okay, but I have to warn you, I'm still babysitting Carlos Sanchez, so you'll have to put up with both of us."

"I heard he wasn't working out too well," Jack said.

"The kid's a jerkoff, has zero initiative, and he's squeamish as hell. And he's a worse germaphobe than I am. Why the hell he thought he wanted to be a mortuary tech is a mystery to me. All he does is complain. He's not going to last."

"Have you said anything to the chief of staff?" Jack asked.

"Yes, I told Twyla Robinson, for all the good it did me. She thought I wasn't giving him a chance to prove himself. Personally, I think she doesn't want to admit she made a mistake in hiring him."

"If he's a germaphobe, this case, like the one on Monday, should turn him off enough to quit once we make sure he really understands what it is about. I mean, it terrifies me, and usually I'm relatively nonchalant around contagion."

"You have a point," Vinnie said. "He did not like the case you're talking about."

"I remember teasing him a bit about Ebola and influenza. We could lay it on a little thicker."

"It might work," Vinnie said. "He really hated the moon suit."

"Okay. With that decided, let's move on," Jack said. "I want to handle the case the same way we did the one on Monday. We'll use the decomposed room along with the moon suits. And take the X-ray and weigh the body without taking it out of the body bag like last time! We'll again do the photos and fingerprinting in the decomposed room after we get the body out of the body bag. And make sure we have enough viral sample bottles."

"Okay, boss," Vinnie said. "And don't let me down with Carlos."

"I'll do my best," Jack said. "Seems to me I remember you trying to protect him on Monday from my teasing him about losing mortuary techs to contagion from autopsies."

"Don't remind me," Vinnie said. "That was before I knew what a dick he was."

"Keep an eye out for the body to arrive so you can get right on it," Jack said. "It's on its way from Bellevue ER, so it should be there in minutes if it isn't already. And on my end, I'm happy to report the FDR Drive is moving along so I'll be there in a flash as well."

"Got it," Vinnie said. "See you soon."

After disconnecting with Vinnie, Jack made a final call to Aretha.

"Guess what?" he said when he got her on the line. His voice had an urgency that he didn't try to hide. "There's another subway death that sounds exactly like the first one."

"Wow! That increases the chances that we are dealing with a contagious virus," Aretha said, even before she heard the details.

"That's exactly my fear," Jack said. "I'm heading back to the OCME and will be handling the case immediately. So we'll have more samples. Will you be available?"

"I was planning on leaving at my normal time, but I'll stay. I'll inoculate more tissue cultures tonight. There go my chances for a game this evening."

"Sorry about that," Jack said. "But this is important."

"You don't have to tell me," Aretha said. "It's a bit terrifying."

"My thoughts exactly," Jack said.

"Oh, by the way," Aretha added. "In response to your question earlier. I ran another screen on the tissue culture and there is no garden-variety virus present. The cytopathic effects are being caused by a true unknown."

"Any results from the MPS?" Jack asked.

Aretha laughed. "Identifying an unknown virus is a time-intensive exercise, so no. But you'll be the first to know. Trust me!"

26

Originally Jack had planned to park where he'd parked that morning in the shadow of the 421 high-rise, but with time a factor, he drove directly to the 520 building. Although there was no place to park, Jack pulled into the unloading dock area and left the Escalade behind one of the OCME vans with a note on the dash. He also gave the keys to the security officer, whose office overlooked the dock.

After checking the decomposed room for activity and seeing it was still dark, Jack had taken the time to run up to the front office. He thought it best to let Laurie know that not only was he back, but he was doing another subway death autopsy. He also wanted to let her know that he had Warren's car and would be happy to give her a ride home after he finished the case. He'd known it was a risk that she'd be irritated with him for being gone all day, but he'd thought it a risk he needed to take, as it was important for her to know about the second respiratory death. As it turned out, she was again on one of her interminable conference calls with orders not to be disturbed.

After his quick visit to Laurie's office, he'd run into the ID room to touch base with Rebecca Marshall. He wanted to make sure she knew about the second death and ask her to call him when someone came in for the official identification. He'd told her he'd like to ask the individual a few questions himself, if at all possible.

Returning to the morgue on the basement level, Jack pushed into the locker room where the moon suits were stored. Carlos was already completely outfitted with his ventilator running, whereas Vinnie was in the final stages of prep, zipping up his suit. Like a rerun of Monday, Carlos had his arms stuck out from his sides at a forty-five-degree angle, as if he was afraid to move. Although Jack couldn't see his face, it was obvious the man was again clearly spooked. Jack was encouraged. He thought exacerbating the man's apprehensions, like he promised Vinnie, wouldn't be difficult, especially with Jack's own fears at the forefront, but for different reasons.

"Should we head into the decomposed room and start getting the body out of the body bag?" Vinnie asked as soon as he was ready to go. He was always thinking ahead, which was one of the many reasons Jack liked to work with him.

"Let's talk over the case before we start," Jack said while putting his legs into his suit as if he were donning a pair of coveralls. "This is a lot scarier than on Monday. Now we know we could be facing a real subway pandemic."

"True," Vinnie said, immediately taking Jack's lead. "Monday, we worried the case might be contagious, but now with a second case we know for sure."

"I want to get through this without one or all three of us coming down with the same illness," Jack said. "What makes it particularly scary is that it's an unknown virus."

"Oh, no," Vinnie said, feigning concern. "Don't tell me it's unknown."

"What difference does that make?" Carlos stuttered.

Jack had to take a deep breath to keep from laughing. For some reason it seemed that tagging a microorganism as an unknown did provide an extra aura of danger. "Unknown viruses are a lot easier to catch than known viruses," Jack said, now making an attempt at humor. For a moment he worried he'd overdone it, but Carlos quickly proved him wrong.

"Do you think you have to be on a subway to catch it?" Carlos asked.

"Now, there's a good question," Jack said. "If we take these two cases as indicative of the nature of the illness, we'd have to say yes."

"Then we should be okay," Carlos said. "I mean, as long as we don't go on the subway."

"Easier said than done," Vinnie said. "Besides, we might still be at risk. We're in the basement here at the OCME. It's kind of like the subway."

"Good point," Jack said. He inwardly smiled as he got his ventilator battery pack and hooked it up. He listened for the hum of the fan to be sure it was functioning normally. "This could be the start of something really big. The only other time people died this quickly on the subway was the 1918 flu pandemic. Back then at the height of the pandemic, New York City saw two to three hundred people dying each and every day."

"No shit," Carlos exclaimed.

"I kid you not," Jack said, as he got his head up into the moon suit. It made his voice sound slightly deeper. "All right, I'm ready. Let's do it."

As a group, they walked the short distance from the moon suit locker room to the decomposing room. Carlos lagged behind, using a shuffling gait that made him look like he was walking in wet pants. Once inside the small autopsy room, they first went to the X-ray view box, so Jack could view the film that Vinnie and Carlos had previously taken.

"Well, at least this one surely didn't have a heart transplant," Jack said. He didn't see anything abnormal, like old bone fractures or extensive dental work. "So now we know that having a heart transplant is not a requirement to come down with the subway pandemic."

Next they got the body out by folding the body bag over the sides of the autopsy table, just as they had done with Carol Stewart. It was obvious Carlos was an unwilling participant.

"I'd guess she's about the same age as Carol," Vinnie said. "And nice duds. She looks like she, too, had gotten dressed up for something."

"Very similar to Carol," Jack said. "To me it means she was feeling normal when she got on the subway. It's truly amazing how fast this subway pandemic kills. I hope you are not going on the subway tonight, Carlos."

"No, not tonight," he said nervously.

Jack took a series of photographs with the body clothed for identification purposes while Vinnie did the fingerprinting and uploaded the prints into the OCME database. Then Jack removed the woman's jewelry, which included a watch and a ring, both of which matched what was removed from Carol, further suggesting to him that it was not a coincidence her name was Helen. Although she had pierced ears like Carol, she wasn't wearing earrings. Jack then told the two mortuary techs to go ahead and start cutting off the clothes while he put the jewelry aside next to the specimen bottles.

Carlos was on the patient's right, and as soon as Carlos had the right arm exposed, Jack rolled it over to look at the volar surface. As he had anticipated, there was a duplicate of Carol's puzzle tattoo, with the only difference being the name. In this instance it was Carol.

"Shit!" Vinnie said, looking at the tattoo. "These two women must have been lovers."

"They might even have been married," Jack said. "I suspected that they might be a couple the moment Bart said this woman's given name was Helen."

"Do you think Helen caught this unknown virus from Carol?" Vinnie asked.

"That's my fear," Jack said. "Or maybe the other way around. One way or the other, it means it's contagious. That is for damn certain."

"I don't want to be in here," Carlos suddenly blurted.

"You're not having fun?" Jack questioned.

Carlos backed up from the autopsy table. He was still holding the bandage scissors in his gloved right hand. "You people are crazy. I don't need this." He tossed the scissors onto the countertop next to the sink as if he no longer wanted to touch them.

"If you are thinking of leaving the party, you have to disinfect yourself," Jack said, while he pointed to the side door that led into the connecting room designed for that purpose. "I trust you remember how it's done?"

Carlos didn't say another word before turning and barreling through the side door.

For a moment Jack and Vinnie paused and stared at each other, even though it was difficult to see their faces through the plastic face guards. When they suddenly heard the shower start in the other room, they high-fived.

"I think you accomplished your goal," Jack said. "Congratulations."

"Pardon the cliché, but let's not count our chickens before they hatch," Vinnie said. "Though it's looking positive. But it wasn't me, it was you."

"All right, enough fun and games," Jack said as he looked down at the partially exposed Helen VanDam with only her face and arms visible. "Let's get serious and knock this out. This could be the beginning of a major catastrophe."

27

Just as the clinical aspects of Carol Stewart and Helen VanDam corresponded, so did the autopsy results. Except for the heart transplant, the autopsies were mirror images of each other, down to the mild signs of inflammation with extravasation of blood in the gallbladder, spleen, and kidneys. Once again, Jack had been reminded of what was seen with hantavirus, even though he knew it wasn't hantavirus. But most important were the similarities of the extensive lung pathology, indicating that the victim had essentially drowned in her own body fluids and exudate. Both Jack and Vinnie had been impressed to the point of Vinnie joking that it wasn't a cytokine storm but rather a cytokine *cyclone*.

When the autopsy was over, Jack stayed and helped Vinnie clean up and disinfect all the sample bottles and the outside of the body bag with hypochlorite. With that done, Jack left Vinnie to deal with getting the body bag into the cooler and contacting janitorial services to clean the room itself. He also tasked Vinnie to get the viral samples over to Aretha at the Public Health Laboratory. In his mind there was no rush. He was about as sure as he could be that whatever the microorganism was, it was the same in both cases.

After hanging up his moon suit in the hazmat locker room and plugging the ventilator into the charger, Jack went into the main locker room to change back into his street clothes. But first he checked his mobile phone and saw there was a recent text message from Rebecca Marshall. It said that John Carver was on his way in to make a formal identification of Helen VanDam. Jack checked the time of the message. It was 5:11. Quickly he called Rebecca to find out the status. He learned that the man was there and had made the identification.

"Is he about to leave?" Jack asked. "As I said, I'd like to talk to him."

"Yes," Rebecca said. "We are all done, and I didn't think I was going to hear from you."

"Ask him to hold on," Jack said. "I'll be right up."

Instead of changing, Jack grabbed one of the white coats that were available for the MEs to use between cases and pulled it on over his scrubs. A minute later he was in the stairwell. The back elevator that served the basement took forever if the elevator car wasn't there waiting.

Jack was able to enter the ID area from the back through what used to be Communications before Communications was moved down to 421. The whole area had been greatly expanded over the previous fifteen years, particularly after the identification problems associated with the collapse of the World Trade Center. He found Rebecca Marshall in her cubicle and was told John Carver was waiting for him in the family ID room.

Walking into the family ID room, which was a modestly large space, Jack found the man sitting on a blue couch. He was the only person in the room, the furniture in which consisted of a large, round wooden table with eight wooden chairs in addition to the couch. On the walls were a number of framed posters of the 9/11 disaster with the phrase NEVER FORGET emblazoned across the bottom of each. Jack had wondered for years why the posters were still up. The only explanation he'd come up with was that they would remind grieving families that as bad as they felt, there had been worse times.

As Jack approached, John got to his feet. He was a slightly built, youthful man, probably in his late twenties, with a narrow and handsome face. He was impeccably dressed, wearing a tight-fitting and possibly one-size-too-small blazer. He had a shock of auburn hair with blond highlights that needed to be constantly pushed out of his face or snapped back with a sudden toss of his head. It was painfully apparent from the man's expression that he had been sorely rattled by the events of the afternoon.

Jack introduced himself and explained that he had done a postmortem examination of Helen VanDam and wanted to ask him a few questions. "I don't know what you have already told Mrs. Marshall," Jack added. "So I apologize if there is a certain amount of redundancy."

"That's okay," John said. His voice wavered. It was obvious that Jack had already added to the man's discomfiture.

Jack gestured toward the table and both men sat. Jack could see that John was trembling.

"I want to personally thank you for making the identification as you did."

"Thank you," John said. "I've never had to do this before."

"It's not easy," Jack said. "But it is extremely important."

"I can understand."

"I want to ask you if you knew Carol Stewart," Jack said.

"Of course," John said. "I recently got to know her quite well."

"Did you know that Carol Stewart had also recently passed away?" Jack asked.

"No, I didn't," John admitted with alarm. He took a deep breath and let it out. "When?"

"Monday," Jack said.

"What did she die of?"

"That's still to be determined," Jack said. "Whatever it was, the symptoms and signs were consistent with Helen's. We are concerned it might be a contagious disease. Strangely enough, both became stricken on the subway."

"Oh my God, it was terrible," John confessed. He closed his eyes for a moment and shook his head at the memory. "When we got on the subway, Helen was fine. She'd been fine. She hasn't been sick at all. We were having fun. We were coming into the city to shop. Then, before we crossed to Manhattan, she had a chill and soon started having trouble breathing. I didn't know what to do. Somebody called the conductor. It was awful."

Jack paused in his questioning for a moment, trying to figure out how to continue. "I'm sorry," he said empathetically. "I know this is not easy, but because it might involve a contagious disease, I need to ask some personal questions. From the matching tattoos on both women, I'm assuming they were romantically involved. Is that fair to say?"

"Yes, they were a couple," John said. "As far as I know, they had been living together for at least a year and at one point were thinking about getting married."

"What was your relationship with these women?"

"It's all rather complicated," John said.

"It might be important for us to know the details," Jack said.

"For the last three and a half months I've been roommates with Helen."

"And before that?" Jack asked.

"I had been living on and off with a girlfriend in SoHo but mostly off," John said. "But I've known Helen forever. We went to school together in Seattle, and from grammar school all the way through high school we'd been an item. We'd been in touch when we both found out we were here in the city. But then when Carol started getting really sick and was going to have her heart transplant, Helen more or less insisted I move in with her to keep her company and help her get through a diffi-cult period. She thought Carol was going to die."

"That was three and a half months ago?"

"That's right," John said. "I wasn't getting along all that well with my girlfriend, so I took Helen up on her offer. And then we kinda hit it off remembering old times."

"You mean you and Helen started an affair?"

"I guess you could say that," John said. "It was more a reawakening. She was needy, and I was needy, so there you have it. It surprised both of us."

"What happened when Carol came home?"

"Well, we ended up telling her what was happening. She seemed all right with it because she was limited in what she could do after her operation. Then, when she got better, she even tried to participate. She didn't want to lose Helen, and I was kind of a package deal by then. And she gave it a good go, but ultimately she told Helen she couldn't handle it. She actually got pretty angry about it all and moved out a couple months ago to an apartment in Sunset Park."

"Did you guys see her after she moved?"

"Yeah, for the first month. We made an effort. We hoped she'd change her mind, so we spent lots of evenings at her place. But it was clear it wasn't going to work."

"Do you mean neither you nor Helen saw Carol for about a month before she died?" Jack asked.

"That's right," John said. "We got into an argument the last evening we spent together. Helen and I got pissed. I mean, we didn't force her or anything. Carol was acting so bitchy and self-righteous, like she was better than us."

"To me it sounds like Carol decided she preferred a monogamous relationship," Jack said, treading carefully.

"Maybe, but I think it was more that by making the attempt, she only grew more sure she wasn't bisexual," John said. "I mean, she tried, and there's nothing wrong with being bi, but I don't think she liked it. She was a lesbian and just didn't get turned on by the opposite sex. That's what I think she realized. But you could be right that she wanted all or nothing with Helen."

"Okay," Jack said. "I appreciate your time, and I want to thank you for being so open. I know this has been a difficult day for you."

"The worst," John said without hesitation. "Now, let me ask you a question. If this is a contagious disease like you're saying, do I have to worry about catching it?"

"That is a very good question," Jack said. "The problem is, we just don't know. But we have your contact information, so we'll be in touch if we need to be."

"Is that it, then?" John asked. "Can I go?"

"One more question," Jack said. "If it is a contagious disease, we don't know who gave it to whom. As far as you know, did either woman travel recently outside the U.S.?"

"No. I mean, Helen didn't for sure. I suppose Carol could have, but I doubt it. She had been so sick and was always going back to see her doctor out in New Jersey someplace. And she wasn't excited about travel. She thought she'd gotten her heart condition on a business trip to South America."

"What about pets?"

"No pets," John said with an expression of disgust. "I won't live with animals, and both Helen and Carol felt the same way."

"What about pests, like mice around the apartment. Anything like that?"

"Yuck," John said. "No way."

"Thank you for your cooperation," Jack said. He pushed back from the table and stood. "If and when we discover what killed your friends and we think your health is at all at risk, we'll call you."

Leaving the family ID room, Jack intended to go back downstairs to change into his street clothes, but halfway to the stairwell he remembered his promise to Laurie to see to the police custody case. Instead of going to the basement, he beelined to the front elevators with the idea of heading up to the sixth floor to see if anyone was still in Toxicology.

As it turned out, Jack was lucky. Peter Letterman, the assistant director, who was an extraordinarily dedicated civil servant, was still in his tiny office despite the time. It was after six. Peter was more than happy to check on the case, and when he did, he reported to Jack that the blood cocaine level was 1.52 mg/l and the cocaine metabolite was 1.84 mg/l.

"These are high," Jack commented.

"Very high," Peter said.

"Dr. Montgomery is going to be happy," Jack said. "The police commissioner has been on her case in trying to prove forceful restraint was necessary. I think this does the trick."

"No doubt," Peter said. "The victim was clearly out of his mind and might have died of the cocaine without any help from the arresting police officer."

"Much obliged," Jack said. He was pleased to have something positive to give to Laurie to make up for her frustration at his being out in the field all day.

With the toxicology report in hand, Jack went to the back elevator to return to the basement. Before going to the front office to collect Laurie, he'd change into his civvies and check on Vinnie's progress. He was particularly interested in making sure the samples had gotten over to the Public Health Laboratory.

28

After Jack stepped out of his apartment building's front door, he paused on the stoop. From that vantage point he had a reasonably good view of the playground. As per usual, a basketball game was in progress, with the shirts against the skins sweeping up and down the court. Years ago, Jack had bought a bunch of oversized sleeveless red and blue jerseys to distinguish one team from the other, but no one would wear them, preferring the typical shirts-versus-skins, irrespective of the weather and temperature. At that moment it was in the mid- to upper forties.

As he stood there with the pleasant anticipation of rigorous physical activity with friends he cared about, Jack thought about his day. It had been one of the most unique that he could remember. From the cast of characters he'd met out in New Jersey, to the realization that some sort of skulduggery had gone on involving a heart transplantation, to the scary repeat of the subway cytokine death, he was hard put to think of any other day that came close.

The crowning event had been the drive home in the Escalade, with Laurie grousing in the passenger seat. Although she had been pleased to hear about the toxicology results on the police custody case, knowing the commissioner would be gratified, she was still unhappy with Jack's fieldwork in New Jersey, especially with his flashing his New York ME badge. After she had talked with Jack that afternoon while he was still in New Jersey, she'd asked counsel if his using his badge was legal. She'd been told under no uncertain terms that it was not. When she'd related this to Jack, his insistence that he was doing it just for efficiency and not to force testimony didn't assuage her irritation at his penchant for following his own rules.

Worse yet was that they had a marked difference of opinion about the second subway death and what to do about it in the short run. Jack had explained what he had found at autopsy and what he'd learned from John Carver. Although Laurie was in agreement with Jack that having another case did indeed point to a contagious origin, she was still unwaveringly adamant about not raising an alarm with any of the various authorities, such as the Commissioner of Health or the Commissioner of Emergency Management. For his part, Jack felt even more strongly that various agencies should be given some sort of notice in order to at least start the process of what would need to be done in the face of a major, lethal pandemic. He told Laurie that the speed these two patients had died from the time of their initial symptoms and the extent of the lung pathology were simply extraordinary.

"Do we have an actual diagnosis?" Laurie had demanded.

"No, not yet," Jack admitted. "But we have evidence in tissue culture that a virus pathological to human cells is involved."

He then went on to describe what he knew of Aretha's use of a Massive Parallel Sequencing machine and her belief she'd have a diagnosis soon.

"What's 'soon' mean?" Laurie had asked.

"I don't know for sure," Jack admitted. "To be honest, I'm not even entirely sure how the process works. It's based on bioinformatics and uses a database called BLAST."

"All right," Laurie said. "Tell me this: Are you one hundred and ten percent, absolutely, without any doubt whatsoever certain that these two women died of a pathological virus? From what you told me, they hadn't even seen each other for a month. That's one long incubation period for a viral respiratory disease."

As Jack remembered the conversation, he had to smile. He knew he'd made a mistake at that moment because he had paused long enough to make Laurie suspicious that there was something he'd not told her. When she'd forced the issue, he had to admit that people at the Dover Valley Hospital had seen no virus with electron microscopy in the lung exudate following a second autopsy.

"Well, there you go," Laurie had said. "We are not alerting anyone on such shaky grounds. No way."

"But that's like waiting to prepare for a hurricane when the wind has already started to blow," Jack complained.

But Laurie would hear none of it. Instead, she had subjected Jack to a prolonged lecture about what she had been learning in her role as the chief medical examiner about the realities of the political hierarchy and how it functioned or, in her estimation, malfunctioned. She was particularly concerned about the issue of emergency management.

"To tell you the honest truth," Laurie said, "I think they have over-prepared for a major influenza pandemic. Since 2004 they have had drill after drill and have set up a huge system with a hair trigger. There's even a computer algorithm called ED Syndromic Surveillance monitoring real-time emergency room pneumonia visits. The thing that scares me is that there are no checks and balances. The reason I know so much about it is that the OCME is part of it. That's why there are all those refrigerated trailers out in the lot by 421, which would be sent to all the hospitals in the city to try to deal with several hundred deaths a day."

"I think the authorities have a real reason to be worried," Jack retorted.

"Of course there is reason to be worried," Laurie said. "It's almost inevitable there will be an influenza pandemic with the way pigs and fowl are crammed together in the Far East, with their guts acting like virtual influenza incubators. My concern is the switch being thrown by a false alarm with no system in place to stop it. It will be like a bunch of dominoes lined up. Push the first one over and they all go over."

"I think you are being overly pessimistic," Jack responded. "I'm supposed to be the cynic, not you."

"You haven't had to endure the meetings I've had to endure," Laurie said. "And if you still think I am being unreasonably pessimistic, remember what happened in Hawaii in January 2018 with the incoming missile debacle. That's what I'm worried could happen here in New York about an influenza pandemic. It could happen so easily, and it would cause true panic."

Suddenly Jack's reverie was interrupted by his hearing his name called out. Looking in the direction of Columbus Avenue, he could see Warren and Flash standing beneath a streetlamp on the opposite side of the street near the entrance of the playground. Warren was carrying his basketball. He brought it every night and preferred it as the game ball, which no one questioned.

"Hey, Doc," Warren yelled. "You coming to run or are you going to stand there all night?"

Jack responded by quickly descending his front steps and jogging across the street. Warren and Flash waited for him, and they all fist-bumped.

"You were frozen there for so long, we thought you were changing your mind about running," Flash said.

"No way," Jack said. "I need a workout."

The three men commenced walking toward the basketball court, which was brightly illuminated with relatively new LED lighting that Jack had again paid to have installed. It was a far better system than the first one Jack had sponsored many years ago when he'd first come to the city. As they walked, Jack gave Warren back the keys to the Escalade and mentioned it was parked practically in the same spot it had been when he'd taken it. He thanked Warren profusely and told him that he'd gotten used to driving the behemoth and started to like it.

"It's a great set of wheels," Warren said. "Any time you need them and I don't, it's available, provided you pay that parking ticket. What did you think of Dover?"

"You described it perfectly," Jack said. "Lakes and green hills."

"Were you able to accomplish what you needed to do?" Warren asked. They entered the playground and passed the swings and sandbox. A couple of preteenagers were using the swings, even though that area was not lighted.

"To an extent," Jack said. "But not completely. It's complicated, which I won't bore you with. But I did have one rather strange experience. I ended up having a formal lunch with a Chinese billionaire businessman in his lavish private lakeside home. Strangely enough, even though the guy grew up in China, his role model was Arnold Schwarzenegger, and he's still lifting weights into his sixties."

Warren stopped short, grabbing Jack's arm in the process. "Come again?"

Jack repeated what he'd said, surprised at Warren's reaction. Warren was still holding on to his upper arm.

"That's a strange coincidence," Warren said. "Does your screwing around out in Dover have anything to do with investigating something shady?"

"That's a strange question," Jack replied noncommittally. "Why do you ask?"

"Two reasons," Warren said. "First and most important, the last time you were investigating a flu-like illness years ago, you attracted the Black Kings gang to our neighborhood, causing trouble. You remember that?"

"Of course I remember," Jack said. He had a chipped front tooth from being cold-cocked by the leader of the Black Kings as a lasting souvenir. Warren and a few of his friends had saved him from further bodily harm.

"And second of all, we have an Asian dude who's been suspiciously hanging around today since the middle of the afternoon," Warren said. He pointed up the street toward Central Park. "See that black Chevy Suburban about halfway up the block on the right side under the streetlight?"

Jack followed Warren's pointing finger and could clearly see the vehicle. He had learned over the years to take Warren's misgivings seriously. He knew that Warren, with the help of a bevy of youthful eyes, kept tabs on who was in the neighborhood since he didn't trust the police to do the same.

"What makes him stand out is that he ain't moved," Warren explained. "He's been just sitting in that truck for hours, which is suspicious, to our way of thinking. I mean, I don't know if he's Chinese or not, but just hanging around the neighborhood is weird, if you know what I'm saying?"

"I do," Jack said.

"You think his presence has anything to do with your bodybuilding Chinese lunch partner?" Warren asked. "Or whatever the hell you were doing out there in Jersey."

"I can't imagine," Jack said, but he wasn't entirely sure. He recalled Harvey Lauder phoning Wei Zhao after Jack's visit, which seemed strange at the time. But why have him followed, if that was what the Chevy Suburban was up to? Zhao already knew where he lived.

"Well, we'll keep eyes on him," Warren said. "I like you, Doc, but you do have a drift for causing trouble. I have to give you credit there."

The three men recommenced heading for the basketball court. Jack was silent. He couldn't contradict Warren, as he had caused neighborhood trouble over the years, and he couldn't help but ponder over the presence of an unfamiliar Asian driver lurking around his house and whether it had anything to do with him. Unfortunately, there was no way to know. It wasn't as if there was anyone he could call short of Wei Zhao himself, but Jack couldn't imagine doing that.

"What's with the home front?" Warren asked. "Is that why you were paralyzed on your front stoop?"

"Some ways it's worse and some ways it's better," Jack said. After the contentious drive home from the OCME, Jack had braced himself for the worst. But it had turned out to be not so bad. Both Dorothy and Sheldon were watching the network news when they'd arrived, and with Sheldon there, Dorothy didn't feel obligated to interact other than to say hello. Then the two turned to *PBS NewsHour*, giving Jack time to interact as best he could with Emma and then with JJ, who was still deeply involved with his school diorama project. At that point Jack had ducked out for b-ball.

"The couch is still available if you need it," Warren said.

"I appreciate it, my friend," Jack said.

When they reached the sidelines, Warren dealt with figuring out how the three of them were going to get into the game. As the most respected player, he could have gotten into the very next game, but he held out to play with Flash and Jack. Finally, it was determined that they would have to wait for two more game cycles.

Jack used the time to warm up by doing some running in place and other calisthenics and even shooting a few practice shots with Warren's ball when the playing teams were at the opposite end of the court. To his surprise and pleasure, he later noticed Aretha had showed up. This time her headband and wristbands were a hot pink, which were as dramatic as her yellow-green ones, especially the way they contrasted with her sneakers. He felt drab moving over and standing next to her.

"I'm glad you made it," Jack said. "I trust you got the new samples. At autopsy the cases were identical. The lung pathology was again off the charts."

"I got the samples," Aretha said. "Thank you, and I've already inoculated new tissue cultures."

"Great," Jack said. "Have you spoken with Warren about getting in the game tonight?"

"Yes, and I'm happy to say I'm playing with you guys."

"Perfect," Jack said. He passed her Warren's ball, but before she could step out onto the court to take a shot, the playing teams came in their direction. "And I guess there's no need to ask you if you have any results yet from the MPS machine."

"Correct," Aretha joked. "You'll be the first to know. I want to let it run another eight hours at least. The more time that passes, the higher the chances of success. I also spoke again with Connie Moran of the CDC."

Jack again made a pained expression, as he'd done the last time they were together when she'd told him she'd contacted the CDC.

"Don't worry," Aretha said. "I've not given her any more details, and she hasn't asked. For her it is just an unknown. But what I wanted to say is that she, too, is using the MPS machine, and they are far more experienced with it than I am. There's a good chance they can have a result way before me."

"If they do and come back with a weird virus, don't spill the beans about its origins. What I didn't tell you is that my boss at the OCME is also my wife."

"Really," Aretha said. "Wow. I'm impressed."

"Well, it raises the consequences if the CDC suddenly shows up and starts nosing around. I'll be in the doghouse big-time, domestically and professionally."

"Got it," Aretha said. The playing teams swept back toward the other basket as the ball changed hands. Aretha stepped onto the court and drilled a moderately long shot. Jack rebounded.

"What I also wanted to tell you is that the CDC also used the electron microscope on the sample," Aretha said. "And contrary to what the people in New Jersey told you, they did see virus."

"That's interesting," Jack said. Suddenly the thought occurred to him that Dr. Stephen Friedlander could have been lying. Prior to that moment, the idea had not entered his mind. Unfortunately, there was no way to know. It wasn't like he could call and ask.

"Connie said she was going to email me some of the photomicrographs," Aretha said. "I can forward them to you if you are interested."

"By all means," Jack said.

It took another half hour for Jack, Aretha, Warren, Flash, and Spit to get into the game, but once they did they functioned as a well-oiled machine. They won their first game so easily that they became overconfident and ended up being defeated in the second. Disgusted with themselves, they slunk off the court. No one person had been at fault. Everyone had missed baskets that they should have made.

"That's it for me," Jack said. Like the others, he was eager to atone for his poor performance, but he was feeling guiltier about having abandoned Laurie to deal with her parents alone than he was feeling embarrassed about his play.

"Ah, come on," Warren pleaded. "Let's not let these mothers feel they are better than us. One more game, that's all I ask. Look at the way they're strutting around like they are kings of the mountain. Shit!"

"Sorry," Jack said. "I'm on borrowed time as it is. If I don't go home now, I'll have to come and park on your couch. And ultimately, you don't want that."

"That's a hell of a lot better than letting these bastards think they're so great. One game. Be a sport!"

"Sorry," Jack said. Once he made up his mind, he was adamant. He said goodbye to Aretha and encouraged her to contact him the moment she had anything. He bumped fists with Flash and Spit and commiserated anew for their combined ignominy before starting out for home.

By now the rest of the playground was deserted. So were the sidewalks along the street. At the curb Jack waited for a yellow cab to pass before he started across, but he didn't get far. Off to his left he saw the lights in the Chevy Suburban that Warren had pointed out earlier suddenly switch on. Then the vehicle quickly swerved out into the street and lurched forward in Jack's direction with a screech of tires.

For the next second Jack debated whether he should dash forward to get to the other side or retreat to the curb behind him, but the delay cost him the opportunity to do either. The Suburban now screamed to a stop and the driver leaped from its cab. He was one of the tallest men Jack had ever seen, and he was armed. In his right hand he had an automatic pistol with an attached silencer. The suddenness of the episode had Jack momentarily paralyzed. It was as if he were watching the unfolding event on a screen rather than as a participant.

At the same instant the man was jumping out of the car, Jack was aware of a burst of activity from another parked SUV to his right and behind him. But he didn't turn to see what it was. He was hypnotized by the man in front of him who'd come around the front of his SUV and raised his silenced gun with both hands and pointed it at Jack.

The noise that followed was like someone striking a couch cushion with a baseball bat, not once but quickly several times in a row. They were the kind of sounds that were felt as much as heard. Jack started, expecting he'd been shot but confused as to why he didn't feel anything. Then, to his mounting shock, the man in front of him, who was no more than twenty feet away, fell over backward as if he'd been smacked in the face by an invisible hand.

The next thing Jack knew was that four men rushed by him, heading toward the downed individual. By now Jack had recovered enough to run ahead himself. He reached the group as three of the men hastened to hoist the stricken man off the pavement by his arms and his legs. The fourth man leaped into the Suburban, whose engine was still running. It was like a team executing a maneuver that they had practiced many times.

"What the hell is going on here?" Jack demanded. But the men, who Jack could see were all relatively young and of Asian descent, ignored him. Once they had the tall gunman off the ground, they wasted no time. They again went past Jack at a run, awkwardly carrying the stricken individual, who was not moving. At that moment the first Suburban laid a bit of rubber as it accelerated down 106th Street in the direction of Columbus Avenue.

From the direction of the playground Jack could hear someone yell his name, but he ignored it. Instead, he rushed after the mystery men lugging the wounded man. "Who are you people?" he shouted.

The busy men didn't bother answering or even to look at Jack. They concentrated on literally tossing the unconscious man into the backseat of the second black Suburban, then jumping in themselves. Jack tried to grab the arm of one of the men but received a vicious Karate-style blow to his chest for his effort, which caused him to stagger backward to retain his footing.

With yet another screech of tires, the second Suburban sped off in the direction of the first. At the same moment, a sizable contingent of fellow basketball players reached Jack's side, where he was standing dumbfounded in the street. Among them were Warren and Flash.

"You okay?" Flash demanded, grabbing Jack by his upper arms and looking directly into his eyes.

"I don't know," Jack admitted. He felt dazed. He detached himself from Flash's grasp and glanced down at the front of himself, as if looking for signs of blood. "I guess I'm okay."

"What the fuck was that all about?" Warren demanded.

"I don't know," Jack said. "I don't even know if I was involved or not. It all happened so fast."

"Were those gunshots we heard?" Flash demanded.

"I'm afraid so," Jack said. "But they weren't directed at me. The tall guy you said was hanging around the neighborhood seemed to get shot . . . unless the whole thing was staged." The idea occurred to him out of the blue. The entire episode seemed unreal.

Jack got his mobile phone out of the gym bag he always brought to the playground to carry a towel and extra wristbands. He turned on the flashlight app and walked back to where he thought the guy had been shot, if he had been shot.

Warren and a few others followed him. "What the hell are you looking for?" Warren asked.

"Blood," Jack said. "But I don't see any." He turned off the light.

"I saw what happened," Warren said. "Granted, I was back on the basketball court, but I saw the dude get shot. No question. What's going on, Doc? I need to know. I can't have this kind of shit happening around here. Sometimes I can't decide if having you in the neighborhood is an addition or a liability. These other dudes also looked possibly Chinese from where I was. Were they?"

"I'm not sure," Jack said. "They were Asian. That I'm sure of. And young, like college age. None of them spoke, or I don't think they did. It all happened so fast." Jack started to dial 911, but Warren grabbed his hand and stopped him.

"Who are you calling?" Warren asked.

"The police," Jack said.

"Why?" Warren asked.

"I can't believe you're even asking," Jack said. "Someone seems to have been shot. You even said so yourself."

"Yeah, but why call the police? What the fuck are they going to do at this point? You tell them you think someone got shot and was taken away in one of two black Suburbans. That's bullshit. You're just going to cause yourself and the neighborhood a lot of grief for nothing."

"The idea of not calling the police didn't even occur to me," Jack said.

"Well, I think you should give it some serious thought," Warren said. "For me, as a black man, I wouldn't call. There's no victim, and they sure ain't going to stop and search all one hundred thousand black Suburbans that are roaming around the city tonight, so there isn't going to be a victim. You're a medical examiner, and you know all that shit about corpus delicti. I tell you, the police are going to do zip except use it as an excuse to stop and harangue every black kid around here wearing a hoodie."

Jack pondered the situation because he truly respected Warren and cared about the neighborhood. He also again questioned if he'd been involved in the episode or somehow just caught up in it by accident. Yet he remembered the man pointing the gun at him, and Warren had said the man had been hanging around since midafternoon. Combining that with having met more Chinese people earlier today than he ever had made it hard to dismiss. Yet was it a coincidence? He had no idea.

"What about this Chinese billionaire you had lunch with?" Warren asked. "Did you guys leave on an okay note?"

"Not entirely," Jack admitted. "But I was the one who was bent out of shape. The man had me probed, personal life and all, and it provoked me enough to leave before I did something or said something I'd regret."

"What is it that you were investigating out there? You didn't answer my question earlier about whether it involves anything shady."

"There is possibly something shady," Jack said. "But certainly not something I would imagine could lead to murder."

"You're beating around the bush, Doc," Warren complained. "Tell me straight!"

"I was looking into some sort of irregularity in the way a transplant organ was obtained for a young woman who I autopsied on Monday," Jack began. "I don't know if you are aware, but there's a very elaborate system set up so that the allocation of available organs is fair. Unfortunately, there are episodes where the system is perverted, like for celebrities, because the supply doesn't come close to the demand, and it can be a life-threatening situation."

"That sounds pretty serious to me," Warren said. "Did any of the people you met act pissed you were out there asking questions?"

"Quite the contrary," Jack said. "They treated me like a hero, since it had taken me some effort to identify the woman I autopsied. They weren't aware that she'd died, and it was important for them to know, as they were responsible for her surgery. The Dover Valley Hospital is a recently certified transplant center, and they need to follow their cases closely."

"All right, Doc," Warren said. "What's it going to be? You going to call the cops or not? If you are, we're out of here. If you're not, we'll go back and run a few games."

"I don't know," Jack said as he continued to dither. Yet he was slowly calming down and able to think more clearly. What he realized was that he didn't know whether it was a crime not to report a crime. And if he was involved, whether he'd be considered an accessory after the fact.

"I think I have to call," Jack said.

"Okay," Warren said. "It's your decision. But I tell you what, I'll have some kids watching out for strange cars along your block. I'll let you know if those dudes or any of their friends come back."

"Thank you, Warren," Jack said as he fist-bumped his friend. Jack was appreciative of the offer. From past experience, Jack knew that when Warren said he'd keep an eye out, he meant it.

As Jack dialed 911 and put the phone to his ear, Warren herded all the other players together and announced that b-ball was over for the night. He specifically said he didn't want any witnesses to be available when the police arrived.

When the 911 operator came on the line, Jack described what had happened and gave his name and location. After making sure Jack felt safe, the operator told him to remain where he was and that police officers from the Twenty-fourth Precinct would be dispatched immediately.

"I still think you are making a mistake," Warren called out, as he and all the others, including Aretha, started home, with most heading in the direction of Columbus Avenue.

Jack waved to indicate he had heard, but didn't call out. Crossing the street, he went to his stoop and sat on the top step. A bit of light shown out through the door lights. It was a dark night, with isolated puddles of illumination under the widely spaced streetlamps. Even the lights on the basketball court had gone out with no one playing. His heart, which had been racing, began to slow.

Within minutes, Jack could hear the typical undulations of an approaching siren in the distance. As he waited for the police to arrive, he planned what he would say. Then, because of the unreality of the experience, his mind went back to the thought that the episode possibly had been elaborately staged. The main trouble with the idea was that there would have to have been a reason, and Jack couldn't think of one. Had he been caught in the situation by chance? He doubted it. According to Warren, the Suburban had been sitting there for hours, only to pull out into the street just at the exact moment he'd stepped off the curb. At the same time, thinking of the event as a true attempt on his life was equally as mystifying and confusing. Not only was he forced to explain why someone would want him dead, he'd have to explain why he'd been saved and by whom. It would mean there were two unknown groups: one that wanted him eliminated for an unknown reason and another that wanted to make sure he wasn't.

The undulating police siren eased off as the squad car made the turn from Central Park West onto 106th Street. It then drove toward Jack much faster than Jack thought reasonable. In the back of his mind he could hear Warren advising him not to call the police. Certainly, if there had been kids playing in the street, which they often did, they could have been in jeopardy.

The police car skidded to a stop and two uniformed officers leaped from the vehicle, donning their peaked hats in the process. With their hands on their holstered guns as if they thought they might have to use them, they scanned the area. It made Jack wonder what the message was that they had gotten. Both were Caucasian, with one decidedly older and heavier than the other. Simultaneously, they saw Jack as he got to his feet.

"Are you Jack Stapleton, who put in the call about gunplay in the street?" the older one called out.

"I am," Jack said as he passed between parked cars and walked out into the street to face the policemen. He squinted from a small LED flashlight held by the younger cop, who was shining it directly in Jack's face.

"An Asian man was shot by four other Asian men," Jack began. "Either that or the five men were a troupe and playacting very convincingly." Jack went on to describe what had happened as far as he could remember. He said on the spur of the moment that he thought the taller Asian man was aiming the gun at him, but he admitted that might not have been the case. Jack explained that the shooters were in a second Suburban behind Jack, essentially putting Jack in between them. "It all happened so fast, it's hard to remember the details," he added.

"Did you happen to catch any of the vehicles' tag numbers?" the older policeman asked. He eyed Jack's beat-up, drab workout clothes. Jack wondered if he thought he was homeless.

"No," Jack said. "It was dark and, as I said, it all went down so quickly. I wouldn't even be able to tell you what state the plates were from."

"Where exactly was the location that this individual was supposedly shot?" the younger officer asked. Jack could tell by his tone that he was skeptical of the whole story, which Jack understood was unique, since homicide perpetrators generally didn't make a habit of collecting their victims.

"Just about where your squad car is," Jack said.

The older officer directed the younger to back up the vehicle. When the younger emerged from behind the wheel, he now had a monstrous flashlight.

"Okay, where, exactly?" the older man asked.

Jack tried to remember how the Suburban was oriented and then how the tall man had come out of the car before pointing the gun in Jack's direction. "Somewhere around here," Jack said, indicating with his finger a circular area ten to twelve feet in diameter.

The younger officer used the light to illuminate the pavement in the indicated area. It was powerful enough to turn night into day. All three searched. There was no blood.

"Are you sure you didn't imagine this?" the older policeman said, looking askance at Jack.

"Were there any other witnesses?" the younger policeman asked.

Instead of lying and saying no to witnesses, Jack explained that he was a medical examiner at the OCME who had been playing basketball on the now darkened court. He pointed out the playground. He also pointed out his house, saying he was the landlord. This new information dramatically altered the atmosphere of the interrogation and increased the respect the two officers showed him.

"It is still a very strange story, sir," the older policeman added after a bit more discussion. "By the way, my name is Sergeant Bob Adams. This is Officer Stan Perkins."

"Nice to meet you both," Jack said. "I appreciate your responding to my nine-one-one call. But I'd like to ask, what exactly are you going to do about this episode?"

"We'll file a report and alert the detective division," Sergeant Adams said, tripping over his words. "I don't know what else we can do. Whether the detectives do any follow-up is up to them. I mean, without a body or some blood, there isn't much to go on. Is there something specific you would like us to do or think we ought to do? Would you like us to request some surveillance?"

"I guess not," Jack said. Although Jack wasn't terribly surprised that the policeman was essentially saying nothing would be done, once again he was impressed with Warren's street smarts. Warren had guessed the police would do little under the circumstances. Jack just hoped the second part of Warren's prediction wasn't correct—namely, that the cops would use the event as an excuse to harass black teenagers in the neighborhood. That had been a problem in the past and might happen again if police surveillance was instituted.

"We'll also let the duty desk know about the incident," Officer Perkins said. "They will alert any patrols tonight to look out for suspicious behavior involving Suburbans with Asian drivers."

"I think they're long gone," Jack said.

"I think you're right," Sergeant Adams said.

After the police had left, Jack wearily climbed the stairs up to the apartment. Although he hadn't played as much basketball as usual, he felt particularly exhausted. He wondered if it had to do with the scary and weird shooting or all the running around he'd done that day. The frustrating part about the day was that despite all the effort, he really wasn't any closer to a definitive cause of Carol Stewart's death, and now Helen VanDam's, nor to understanding the curious details surrounding Carol's lifesaving surgery.

Getting his keys out to open the apartment door, Jack took the opportunity to check the time. Inwardly he groaned when he saw it was almost 9:30. The guilt of having abandoned Laurie to her parents, which had kept him from playing a third basketball game, came back with a vengeance. He was certainly much later than he had intended.

Jack paused for a moment to think what he would say. He thought about using the shooting as an excuse but then quickly nixed the idea. If he'd been an integral part of the event, which was still a possibility, Laurie would insist he be more forthcoming about what he had been up to that day. He was reasonably sure that if Laurie heard the details, she'd demand he turn the whole affair over to the authorities. Since he was not willing to do that as of yet, he thought it might be best not to bring up the shooting. After all, he rationalized, he didn't know for sure it involved him.

As it turned out, Jack's reception was far better than he'd feared, even though he had ended up being gone for two hours. Apparently, the children had been uncommonly angelic, including Emma. Consequently, Laurie was in a fine mood and wasn't at all captious about his playing, and Sheldon proclaimed he was jealous of the exercise, wishing he was thirty years younger so he could have participated. Jack had smiled at this suggestion but inwardly was glad Sheldon was not thirty years younger. Not everybody could play street basketball, as it was more a contact sport than the uninitiated imagined. Dorothy was the only one who attempted to poison the atmosphere by making a point of complaining that Jack had not been available to help put the children to bed. To her credit, Laurie immediately came to Jack's aid by describing how easy it had been, even with Emma, who was often a struggle to get to nod off.

Despite the unexpected general bonhomie, the moment it was socially appropriate, Jack excused himself to take a quick shower. While he did so, Laurie was happy to warm up the pasta they had had for dinner.

29

With everything that had happened on Wednesday underscored by the bizarre and unnerving shooting episode, Jack had had trouble going to sleep and was still tossing and turning well after midnight. Also disturbing had been a call from Warren to inform him there was yet another Suburban parked on his block with an Asian driver. The only difference was that the driver was significantly younger than the previous, tall dude.

As a consequence, Jack was sound asleep when Laurie's mobile phone rang at 5:15 in the morning. Laurie was the night person, not Jack, but because she was a deep sleeper in the morning, she didn't stir. Although she had mocked people in the past who kept their phones close to them at night, now that she was the chief medical examiner, she always had hers hearby. Yet Jack always had to give her a couple nudges to bring her to a stage that she heard the phone's rather quiet ringtone. She'd chosen a tone called *Illuminate* that Jack was always trying to get her to change. It was a bit too pleasant. After the second gentle shoulder shake, she finally answered, and Jack buried his head under his pillow to try to screen out her conversation with the hope of possibly getting another half hour of sleep.

"Really?" Laurie questioned loud enough that Jack thought it capable of waking up JJ's gerbil a floor below. He could feel her sit up, partially pulling the covers off Jack's naked body. Instantly, any chance of him going back to sleep vanished. "Yes, of course," Laurie added at a more reasonable decibel level but with unmistakable urgency. "I understand and will see that it is implemented immediately."

Removing the pillow from his head, Jack looked at Laurie. She was rapidly scrolling through her contacts. "What's up?" he asked, but Laurie ignored him. In the half-light, with her moderately long mop of hair in disarray and her eyes thrown open to their fullest, she looked like a madwoman. A second later, having found what she was looking for, she placed a call. "Who are you calling?" Jack asked, but she still ignored him, even after he repeated his question.

"Paul, it's Laurie. Sorry to wake you so early, but I just got a call from the duty supervisor at the Department of Health, who'd gotten a call from the city's Emergency Operations Center. We are to initiate immediately the OCME Pandemic Influenza Surge Plan. No, it's not an exercise. It's the real thing. So get out your copy of the protocol. I'll be in the office as soon as I can, but since you're closer, make sure that the mortuary tents that will go in the parking lot next to 421 are retrieved from storage. And then start the process of dispatching the refrigerated body collection trailers to all the city hospitals. I'll see you as soon as I can."

The next thing Jack knew, Laurie leaped out of bed and dashed into the bathroom. She was so preoccupied it was as if he wasn't there, despite his calling out her name. He'd never seen her so animated in the morning. As long as he had known her, she'd been the antithesis of a morning person. Normally she dragged around with heavy-lidded eyes and a shuffling gait until she had a coffee.

Throwing back the covers, Jack followed her into the bathroom. Laurie was already in the shower and partially obscured by steam. The room was chilly, and she took showers hotter than Jack could stand.

Jack cracked the glass door to the shower and yelled over the sound of the water to ask her what was going on, although he had a pretty good idea from hearing her side of the conversation with Paul Plodget, the deputy chief medical examiner.

"New York City Emergency Management initiated the NYC Pandemic Influenza Preparedness and Response Plan that Bloomberg spearheaded in 2006."

"My God!" Jack exclaimed. "Do you know what caused them to do so?"

"The duty supervisor didn't know," Laurie said as she rapidly soaped herself. "It's not surprising. I'm assuming it had been a Case Load Hazard Trigger Point coming from city hospitals, which was set up a few years ago as an early-warning mechanism. My guess would be that there was a flood of really sick people yesterday and last night. It certainly wasn't from us at OCME. I would have heard for sure if there had been a surge of influenza deaths last night. My worry is that's what we're going to be seeing today."

"The timing is a bit ironic," Jack shouted. "I've been worrying about such a situation because of the two subway deaths. And now to have it happen . . . weird! I hope to God it's not a rash of cases like the two subway deaths."

"Let me finish showering!" Laurie yelled back.

Jack quickly shaved, and after Laurie got out of the shower, he got in. Ten minutes later they were both down in the kitchen to have a quick bite on the run.

"Should I turn on the TV?" Jack questioned.

"Don't bother," Laurie said. "We don't have time. Besides, let's not subject ourselves to media misinformation. We'll hear the true details soon enough."

While Jack rushed to make coffee, Laurie called the night medical-legal investigator, Janice Jaeger. She used speakerphone.

"Has there been a flood of influenza deaths?" Laurie asked, just to be sure. After she'd told Jack the trigger didn't come from the OCME, she wanted to be certain.

"There haven't been any," Janice assured her. "It's been a busy night, but no influenza deaths. Mostly overdoses but also a couple accidents and one homicide."

"Well, there's going to be a surge of influenza deaths if NYC Emergency Management is correct," Laurie said. "They've declared a Pandemic Influenza Emergency. So be sure to let Bart know the moment he arrives. Better still, try to get him on his mobile. Also call the mortuary techs and give them notice. Tell them I want everybody to be wearing personal protection gear, including N95 HEPA masks, with any presumed cases."

"Should I tell anyone else?"

"Yes. Call the duty ME and give the same message. We are probably looking at working twenty-four/seven for the foreseeable future. I'll be in my office in about a half hour."

After finishing her call, Laurie tossed down the coffee she had diluted with a dollop of fat-free milk. "It seems awfully early for an influenza outbreak to start," she said. "It's usually not until late December or early January."

"I agree," Jack said while quickly peeling a banana. "It must be a strain completely out of the ordinary, like the bird flu everyone has been worried about becoming transmissible from person to person instead of just from poultry to humans. That would be really bad. What would be the best-case scenario is that it's an influenza strain that this year's flu vaccine covers. Then the city could do a massive vaccination program to take care of it."

"Wouldn't that be lucky," Laurie said. "That could make all the difference in the world. But coming on this early makes me think it's got to be something out of the ordinary, as you said. Maybe it's something like SARS or MERS. Whatever it is, the prospect is really scary. I don't think there are nearly enough ventilators available citywide. Some scenarios have predicted up to a thousand hospital admissions a day in this kind of scenario. As you know, everybody in city government has been terrified of this happening for years. It's why there have been so many exercises and drills. Ever since I have been in the front office I've been concerned that all the Emergency Management people have been whipped up into a frenzy anticipating this."

"I understand," Jack said. "Should I call us a car?"

"By all means," Laurie said. "Are you coming with me?"

"I will." Jack took his phone out and opened a ride-hailing app. "The weather is hardly bike-riding weather, even for me." The wind was driving raindrops against the kitchen window hard enough to sound like rice. It was one of those particularly ugly November mornings.

"What are you people doing up so early?" Dorothy asked as she suddenly appeared, coming up the stairs. She was in her robe as usual. She was wearing what looked to Jack like a shower hat covering curlers in her hair.

"There has been a sudden, serious outbreak of influenza," Laurie said. "Apparently, it is a very dangerous strain. We have to get to work to prepare for"—Laurie paused, trying to think how best to complete her sentence—"for being busy."

"That's awful," Dorothy said, immediately understanding, despite Laurie's sanitized choice of words. "Especially since you have two young children to think of. For the life of me I don't understand why you didn't listen to me when I pleaded with you not to become a medical examiner. You could have been a pediatrician or a surgeon like your father."

Laurie rolled her eyes for Jack's benefit out of her mother's line of sight. "I'm going to wake Caitlin and tell her to keep the children home until we know more about what is going on with this influenza situation," she said, ignoring the irritatingly recurrent comment.

Jack finished summoning a car and slipped his smartphone into his pocket. He eyed Dorothy warily. He wished Sheldon had appeared with her. Despite Jack's initial misgivings, Sheldon was turning out to be a helpful moderating influence.

To Jack's relief, Laurie reappeared almost immediately. "Shall we go?" she asked him.

"By all means."

Downstairs, they each got umbrellas and then waited in the foyer until a car appeared and slowed. When it then stopped in the middle of the street abreast of their building, Laurie and Jack ran out into the rain and piled into it. It was a black Toyota Camry.

As they pulled away from the curb, Jack made it a point to glance out the car's back window. Although he wasn't totally surprised, a black Suburban that had been parked up near Central Park West pulled out behind them and followed at a distance. Facing forward, Jack wondered if the driver or drivers were Asian, and if they were, which group they might represent: the group that possibly wished him harm or the group that had seemingly protected him. Although he didn't know if he was guilty of wishful thinking, he had a sense it was the latter.

"I'm going to try to call the health commissioner," Laurie said.

"Good idea," Jack responded. As Laurie made her call, Jack again twisted around. As he expected, he could still see a black Suburban following at a distance.

30

From the backseat of the Toyota, both Jack and Laurie were appalled by the size of the crowd gathered in front of the OCME, and the line of TV trucks parked along the curb with their antennae extended. Jack tried to get the driver to go straight and stay on 30th Street so that he and Laurie could be dropped off at the receiving bay instead of the front door, but it was too late. The man had not understood the command and was already in the middle of the turn onto First Avenue.

With no room to stop in front of their destination because of the TV vehicles and the milling people, the driver was forced to pull ahead. As they passed the aged OCME building, it was clear to both Jack and Laurie that the throng were all journalists, a situation both had witnessed before, but not with quite so many people.

"My God," Jack commented as they passed. "What a horde. I've never seen anything like it."

"I'm not surprised," Laurie said. "The Pandemic Influenza Preparedness and Response Plan calls for an immediate information release to the Health Alert Network, and that's at least fifteen thousand subscribers. I'm telling you, as soon as the plan was initiated, all government agencies of the city, state, and federal government as well as most media outlets would have learned of it. I know because part of my indoctrination in becoming chief was to get up to speed by practically memorizing the OCME Pandemic Influenza Surge Plan, which is also automatically activated. It's our responsibility to coordinate with all the involved agencies. I've participated in several exercises and drills already in the short time I've been chief."

"All city agencies?" Jack asked. He swung around to keep the mob in view. He was wondering how difficult it was going to be to push through them to get to the OCME's front door. The only positive aspect was that at least the rain had temporarily stopped.

"All the important agencies from an emergency-management point of view," Laurie said. "Department of Health, Greater New York Hospital Association, fire department with EMS, police department, and of course Emergency Management. There's been so much coordination and so much planning and so much worry. It's why I didn't want to give anyone a heads-up when you were worried about the first subway death. A heads-up alone could have caused what we're seeing now. The whole system was like a tightly wound-up spring."

As soon as he could, the Uber driver pulled over to the curb, which was practically in front of the NYU Langone Medical Center. Jack and Laurie piled out to hurry south. Just beyond the entrance to the medical center's parking garage, they started to encounter the reporters, who were acting like a swarm of bees. The two medical examiners managed to get about halfway to the OCME front door before someone recognized Laurie. From the press briefings that she'd occasionally held in response to particularly newsworthy cases, Laurie was gradually becoming a known commodity.

"Dr. Montgomery," one of the reporters called out. "Can we have a statement about the pandemic?"

News of the presence of the chief medical examiner spread through the crowd like wildfire. Suddenly both Jack and Laurie were surrounded by pushy reporters, many with microphones or smartphones, all competing with one another to get theirs as close as possible to Laurie's face. Jack literally had to push several electronic devices out of the way. It was amazing how obnoxious reporters could be when competing for a scoop, almost as bad as paparazzi.

"I'm sorry, but I have no comment," Laurie called out over the crowd. "I will be briefed as soon as I get into my office and will schedule a news conference about the OCME's role in the current situation. It will be held within the hour in the auditorium at the OCME building, 421 First Avenue, not here at 520. Now please let us pass!"

Jack began acting as a point man to get Laurie through the crowd, at times yelling at insistent, pushy reporters with their microphones or cameras to give way. The going was slow.

"Please!" Laurie shouted from behind Jack. "Let us through! As I said, you'll have my statement within the hour. Before then, you people should be at Emergency Management out in Brooklyn or at the Department of Health, because they are calling the shots, most likely through the Department of Health's Incident Command System."

After Laurie's short but informative impromptu speech, the reporters opened up a path for her. But then someone shouted out to ask whether Jack was Dr. Jack Stapleton. Surprised by hearing his name, Jack stopped and tried to see who had asked.

"Over here!" someone shouted.

Jack saw a man wearing a New York Yankees baseball hat and waving his hand, about three rows back. "Are you Jack Stapleton?" he repeated. He didn't have to shout as loudly on this occasion, as the other journalists in the immediate area all fell silent.

"Yes, I am Jack Stapleton. Why do you ask?"

The pause in the crowd's murmuring vanished as everyone recommenced talking at once. Laurie was suddenly ignored as people pressed in on Jack, thrusting their electronic devices into his face. Now there was even more frenzy than before, as reporters battled with one another to get close. The questions came fast and furious, such as whether he had autopsied more than two victims, whether there was a specific diagnosis of this rapidly fatal subway disease, what exactly were the symptoms, was it a strain of influenza, how did it spread, was there any cure, should people leave New York if they could, and how did being on the subway cause it?

Jack stiffened. Suddenly it occurred to him that this whole hysteria and panic was possibly related to the two subway deaths, meaning that Laurie's fear of them stimulating a false alarm had come to pass. How or why, Jack had no idea.

In a mild panic himself, he turned and looked for Laurie. Now that she was being relatively ignored, she had skirted Jack and had made considerable forward progress. She was nearing the front entrance of 520, silhouetted against the building's blue-glazed brick façade.

Redirecting his attention to a woman reporter in front of him, Jack asked, "Why are people talking about the subway?" He had to shout to be heard.

"You don't know?" the reporter asked.

"Oh, come on, Dr. Stapleton," another reporter yelled. "Don't play dumb with us."

"Haven't you seen the *Daily News*?" the woman reporter questioned.

"I haven't," Jack admitted. Suddenly, one of the reporters shoved a copy of the tabloid into Jack's face. Its full-page headline read: SUBWAY PANDEMIC. It was surcharged over an image of an NYC subway car head-on. In slightly smaller print was: KILLS INDISCRIMINATELY. In even smaller print along the bottom was: *A wildly contagious pandemic as bad as the 1918 flu explodes in NYC subways on the R and D lines.* Jack snatched the paper and folded back the front page to read the first line of the obviously lurid article: *Anonymous, highly qualified, inside source from the Office of the Chief Medical Examiner confirms that senior NYC medical examiner*

Dr. Jack Stapleton has declared the city is facing a remarkably lethal pandemic of an as-yet-unknown virus that kills within an hour of first symptoms and will be possibly worse than the 1918 pandemic flu epidemic that killed 100 million people.

Thunderstruck, Jack crunched up the paper in his fist and held it in the air. He yelled out for everyone to hear: "Listen up! This article is untrue. I have not made such a declaration. There is no subway pandemic. Not yet!"

"What the hell does 'not yet' mean?" one of the reporters yelled disdainfully.

"Coverup," another yelled. "Come on, come clean!"

"How long will the subways be shut down?" another shouted.

"What about the schools?" another reporter yelled. "When will they reopen?"

"Listen!" Jack shouted in response to the rush of questions. "Dr. Montgomery already said she will be giving a news briefing at 421 First Avenue within the hour. I'm sure she'll address all these issues then and explain that this is most likely one big, unfortunate mistake."

From the response his outburst evoked, Jack could tell the crowd was in no mood to believe him or even listen. There was a sense of true panic in the air that was almost palpable. He was aware it was common knowledge among journalists and other informed people that health scientists all over the world had been fearing the appearance of a new, deadly global pandemic. It wasn't *whether* there would be such an outbreak but rather *when*, and there was a profusion of bad viral actors on the horizon capable of wreaking havoc, from bird flu to Ebola, or even something entirely new, like the World Health Organization's mysteriously labeled Disease X. In a very real sense, Jack knew that although everyone present had been panicked by the erroneous *Daily News* headline, probably no one had been surprised.

Clutching the newspaper he'd confiscated, Jack gave up trying to convince a crowd that had no intention of listening to him. He even felt a twinge of fear being at their mercy, so he recommenced heading for the OCME's front door. He was now determined and wasn't going to be denied. People plied him with questions, which he ignored. He even literally shoved a few people aside who tried to block his way, insistently thrusting microphones in his face and yelling out questions. When he got to the front door, he found it locked. Luckily, a few frantic knocks on the glass brought into view a member of the building's night security force, a reassuringly large uniformed African American man. He unlocked the door for Jack, and with commendable proficiency made sure none of the reporters came in with him.

Jack thanked the security person. For a few moments before the man had appeared, Jack feared he might be forced to turn around and fight the crowd again to get around to the receiving dock.

Once inside the building's reception area, which at this time of the morning was missing Marlene, the ageless receptionist, Jack sat on the faux-leather couch to quickly scan the *Daily News* article. As he assumed, it was an over-the-top example of yellow journalism. For sheer tabloid-style sensationalism, it even mentioned that he had claimed the subway pandemic would not only rival the 1918 Spanish flu but probably would be as bad as the Black Death that ravished Europe in the fourteenth century. To Jack's utter annoyance, he was quoted multiple times as the source of all the misinformation in the article, even the outlandish comparisons.

As Jack's anger mounted, he tried to imagine who was the supposed "anonymous, highly qualified inside source." It surely couldn't have been one of the other medical examiners. Although there were a couple lackluster M.D.s on the staff whose knowledge and judgment Jack openly questioned, he didn't think any of them were remotely capable of carrying off such travesty. He had the same thought concerning the medical-legal investigators. The consequences and turmoil of setting off the city's Pandemic Influenza Preparedness and Response Plan were much too serious. Jack imagined the city was probably almost in a lockdown mode. What he found particularly mystifying was the description of the anonymous source as an experienced employee of the OCME.

"Carlos!" Jack abruptly sputtered. Coming to him like a bolt out of the blue was the strong suspicion it had been Carlos who'd been the source for the article, despite Carlos hardly being a qualified or experienced employee of the OCME. With a burst of anger and indignation, Jack couldn't even remember the man's last name. But the more he thought about it, the more convinced he was and the more he regretted his decision to help Vinnie get the man to quit. Jack hadn't had a good feeling about the new hire from the start and hadn't been surprised when Vinnie described him as a jerk with zero initiative.

"Holy crap!" Jack yelled as he loudly swatted the paper and crumpled it in frustration. Then he guiltily looked around to see whom he might have offended with his outburst. Luckily, at that time in the morning no one else was in the room. Pulling out his mobile phone, he placed a call to Vinnie. At 6:25 A.M., he should have been on his way in to work. It took longer than usual for the call to go through, making him think the circuits were overloaded.

"Good morning, Doc," Vinnie said.

"Have you seen the *Daily News*?"

"Yeah, I've seen it," Vinnie said. "And I'm experiencing it."

"What do you mean?" Jack asked.

"No public transportation," Vinnie said. "I'm having to drive in to work. Is it all right to park at 421?"

"I suppose," Jack said. "But leave your keys in the car. It might have to be moved if they go ahead and erect the autopsy tents."

"Has there already been a flood of cases?" Vinnie asked. "I'll be there in twenty minutes, tops. There's zero traffic."

"There's been no cases as far as I know," Jack said. "I'm sure this whole thing is a huge mistake. There might be a subway pandemic in the near future, but there certainly isn't one right now to justify what's happening. My question to you is whether you think your charge, Carlos, could have been the source for the *Daily News* article."

"I hadn't thought about it," Vinnie said. "But yeah, he could have sold it. I certainly wouldn't put it past him. The guy is a dick, like I said."

"Did you see or talk to him after he walked out of the autopsy?"

"I didn't. Nor did I expect to. Nor do I think he is going to show up today."

"Okay," Jack said. "I'll see you soon."

Jack had the hunch that heads were going to roll because of the seriousness of the situation. He also had the nagging worry that some might think he was the source of the misinformation, as wound up as he'd been about the two subway deaths. With that thought in mind, it might be important to pin down the true source.

After uncrumpling the paper, Jack went back and read the *Daily News* article more carefully, in case there might have been subtle hints or suggestions of who the source was. But there weren't. What he realized with a more careful reading was how clever the article was in terms of scaring the bejesus out of the reader. It actually accurately described the clinical course of the two subway deaths and the autopsy findings. The article went on to say that the OCME had been contacted to confirm the details. Jack wondered who the reporter had spoken with, as it certainly wasn't him. He shuddered. Inwardly, he knew there was going to be hell to pay for this debacle.

31

With some trepidation, Jack entered the front office area. None of the secretaries had come in yet, and he wondered if they were going to have trouble running the reporter gauntlet. As he passed their desks he felt a little like he had in years past when he'd been summoned to Bingham's office, knowing full well he was going to be tongue-lashed for his out-of-office shenanigans. The difference was that back then he'd been guilty. This time he was innocent, so he didn't feel quite so vulnerable. Even more reassuring was that Laurie was now the chief. And in contrast to Bingham, he thought he could count on her recognizing his more positive personality attributes, even though at the moment he was hard put to think of any.

Laurie was sitting behind her desk. Dr. Paul Plodget, the deputy chief, was sitting directly across from her, taking advantage of the fact that Bingham's desk was a partner's desk. Both were on separate phones and both were mostly agreeing with whomever they were conversing. On the desk was a copy of the disturbing *Daily News*. Also in front of Laurie was a copy of the bulky OCME Pandemic Influenza Surge Plan and a notepad filled with her scribbling.

Jack walked over to the couch and sat down. It wasn't long before both Laurie and Paul were off their respective phones. They looked across the room at Jack. Both looked shell-shocked and not happy.

"What a mess," Laurie said. She shook her head. "This is a freaking disaster. The city has practically shut down. I can't believe it."

"I heard the subways and buses aren't running," Jack said.

"That's only half of it," Laurie said. "Just as I feared, it's been like dominoes, with one knocking over the next. Schools are closed. Most businesses are closed. All gatherings are canceled, including movies, plays, and concerts. Everybody who can is trying to get out of the city. All incoming flights are being diverted. It's craziness."

"Does anyone know how this disaster came to pass?" Jack asked. He knew Laurie's fear that something like this would happen, with all the preparedness efforts creating what she called a "wound-up spring." But how could a piece of yellow journalism have such an effect, especially in an era familiar with supposedly "fake news"?

"It was definitely this article," Laurie said, slapping the copy of the *Daily News.*

"I can understand that on a theoretical level," Jack said. "But it still challenges believability that a single tabloid article unleashed this kind of reaction."

"The proof is in the pudding," Laurie said. "What Paul and I already learned was that the scheduled supervisor for the NYC Emergency Management Watch Command in charge of the city's Emergency Operations Center had called in sick. In his stead was an underling who got ahold of the *Daily News* early this morning or had been informed of it, and he made one call here to the OCME to confirm there had been subway deaths as described. We still haven't found out whom he talked with, but it was enough for him to throw the switch. Here in NYC it was to HAN, or the Health Alert Network, but once that happened, the alert arborized to unleash the whole kit and caboodle of the Pandemic Influenza Preparedness and Response Plan."

"That's absurd," Jack said.

"Maybe so," Laurie agreed. "But it's what we have to deal with."

"Does NYC Emergency Management know that it is a false alarm?" Jack asked.

"They do now," Laurie said. "Paul and I made sure of it. So does the Department of Health. We talked with both commissioners at length, and we are all on the same page."

"So is the problem essentially over?" Jack asked, suddenly feeling a bit of encouragement.

"We wish it were that easy," Laurie said. "It's going to have to run itself out. Even FEMA was notified. The Department of Health Incident Command System took over mobilizing all the agencies under its jurisdiction, including both the NYPD and the NYFD, as well as all sixty-seven acute-care hospitals. Each one of those organizations are involved in their preplanned organizational strategies and have yet to be notified it's a false alarm. Also, now that the subway system was shut down, it will take days to reactivate. The bus system is a little easier in that regard, but even that will take more than twenty-four hours before it is up and running. It's all so much more complicated than one would imagine."

"No one even considered the possibility of a false alarm to prepare for it," Paul said. "Everyone is learning on the job."

"Which brings me to a question I have to ask you," Laurie said. "Did you have any contact at all with either the *Daily News* or the reporter who wrote this story?"

"I'm shocked you're even asking," Jack said, immediately taking offense.

"I was told I had to ask you by the Commissioner of Health," Laurie said in her own defense. "And she is my boss. Please answer the question so that I can honestly respond to her."

"Well, they only paid me fifty bucks," Jack said. "But I also got a free year's subscription."

"Please, Jack. This is no time for your acerbic humor. We've also learned that a CDC epidemic intelligence officer and team are already on their way here. We tried to say their presence wasn't needed, but we were told that they had already been involved, trying to identify an unknown virus from New York City, which I presume is from the initial subway death, and they want to look into that. Have you been in contact with the CDC when I asked you not to involve them?"

"The virologist from the Public Health Laboratory contacted them unbeknownst to me," Jack snapped. "She said she wanted them to help identify the organism since they were so good at it. It certainly wasn't my idea. And she said she gave them no details of the origin of the samples. If the CDC has associated them, that's their business."

"All right, back to the newspaper issue," Laurie said. "How did the *Daily News* get your name? I mean, yours is the only name in the article."

"Obviously, as it says in the article, they got it from the highly qualified, experienced inside source," Jack shot back. "Certainly that lets me off the hook."

"So you did not contact the *Daily News*," Laurie said. "Please, just tell me straight out so I can pass it on. Sometimes you can be such a child."

"I did not in any way, shape, or form contact the *Daily News*," Jack snapped. He stood up and started for the door. He'd had enough. He needed a moment by himself before he said something he'd regret.

"Where are you going?" Laurie demanded. She, too, was losing patience.

"I need to let you adults sort out this unpleasant fiasco," Jack said. "It's above my pay grade. Hopefully I can find some work to do being a medical examiner to keep myself on an even keel. If you have any more questions, don't hesitate to call."

Jack walked out of the front office, marveling at the irony. He'd started his mini-crusade to avoid obsessing over Emma's tentative diagnosis, which was responsible for turning his home life into an emotional trial. Now his crusade was turning his work life into something almost as bad.

32

THURSDAY, 6:56 A.M.

As Jack headed for the ID room, where all the OCME medical examiners started their day, he continued to fume about Laurie having the nerve to ask him if he had talked with the *Daily News*. Yet the more he thought about it, the more he could understand her position, if it was indeed true that the Commissioner of Health had gotten involved. Honestly, he didn't know if that part was true. Nevertheless, his comment that he needed to find some work to do to keep his mind occupied definitely was. That meant going through the cases that had come in overnight and finding a case to autopsy. He remembered Janice saying there had been a homicide. That might be interesting, as Lou Soldano would be involved on some level.

To avoid the reception area in case any of the press had managed to get in, Jack used the back route. Because she had been called earlier, Dr. Jennifer Hernandez was already at the desk, where the folders were stacked up of the cases that had come in overnight. Jack was also pleased to find Vinnie had made it in and was busy making coffee in the common coffeepot, which most people thought was possibly his most important responsibility.

"Have you heard that the pandemic influenza emergency has been called off?" Jack asked.

"I have," Jennifer said. "Thank goodness. The idea really terrified me."

"It is still a disaster par excellence," Jack said. "It is going to take days for the city to recover."

"True, but nothing like a real pandemic," Jennifer said.

"We could still have one with these subway deaths," Jack said. "There still isn't a specific diagnosis of the virus involved. At least it wouldn't be a pandemic spread by aerosol, meaning it wouldn't spread as rapidly."

"It still could be bad," Jennifer said. "Ebola and Marburg don't spread by aerosol, either."

"Good point," Jack said. "But with only two cases in three days, we certainly aren't dealing with the likes of Ebola." Then he called over to Vinnie: "Did you leave your car in the 421 lot?"

"I did. And I left the keys with security in 421."

"Did either of you guys have any trouble getting into the building with all the reporters outside?"

Both Jennifer and Vinnie said no simultaneously.

"We came in the back way," Jennifer added.

"Smart move," Jack said. "Vinnie, any sign of our friend Carlos?"

Vinnie laughed sardonically. "No. Nor do I expect to see him."

"I'd like to slap him around a bit if he was the source of the *Daily News* article," Jack said, and meant it.

"You'd have to wait in line," Vinnie said.

"Are you looking for a case to tackle?" Jennifer asked. She had already gotten to know Jack and his work habits fairly well.

Jack was about to answer in the affirmative and inquire about the homicide when he felt his mobile ring in his pocket. He motioned for Jennifer to hold on as he pulled out the phone. It was the night-shift MLI, Janice Jaeger.

"Dr. Stapleton, I'm glad I got you," Janice said. "Right after Dr. Montgomery phoned me this morning, I got a call on another case that was clinically similar to the two subway deaths but also slightly different. I assumed it was the first of many until I learned the pandemic influenza emergency had been canceled. Anyway, I know you asked to be notified when and if there were any more, so that's what I'm doing."

Jack moved a few steps away so he wouldn't bother Jennifer. "How do you mean 'clinically similar'?"

"It involved the rapid onset of respiratory distress in an otherwise healthy individual that very quickly resulted in death."

"And how was it different?" Jack asked.

"Well, first of all, it wasn't on a subway," Janice said. "It happened in someone's apartment. And second of all, it was a male in his late twenties, not a female."

"Was the case handled at the Bellevue ER?" Jack asked.

"Yes, and it was treated as potentially contagious, just like the other two," Janice said. "It is already in the morgue cooler in a sealed body bag."

"How about the identification situation?"

"Not a problem," Janice said. "The victim was accompanied by a friend, and I spoke with her at length. She's there at 520 as we speak, ready to make a formal identification as soon as photos are available. I thought you might like to talk with her."

"I would indeed," Jack said. "One more question: Was a transplant involved?"

"Not that I am aware of," Janice said. "Should I have asked?"

"No, we'll find out soon enough," Jack said. "Thanks for letting me know."

"You're welcome," Janice said. "I would have called sooner, but we really did think it was the beginning of a dreaded surge. We're so relieved we're not going to be overwhelmed."

"That we're not going to be overwhelmed with deaths is the good side," Jack said. "The bad side is that it is going to take the city days to recover." He disconnected, then stepped back over to Jennifer. "Is there a file on the case I was just talking with Janice about? A male with rapid onset respiratory distress, out of Bellevue?"

"There is." Jennifer handed the file to Jack. Jack opened it and read the name. He was shocked. It was John Carver. Could it possibly be the John Carver he'd interviewed yesterday after the man had made the identification of Helen VanDam? Jack thought it was possible, if not probable. After all, the John Carver he'd talked with had reputedly been intimate with both subway death victims.

"Vinnie!" Jack called.

"I'm right here," Vinnie said. "You don't have to yell."

Surprised to find Vinnie standing right behind him, Jack slapped him with the Carver file. "Let's get a jump on the day."

"It's only a quarter past seven," Vinnie whined. "I haven't finished my coffee or read the sports page. Have a heart!"

"This is another case just like the subway deaths," Jack said with mounting excitement. He needed something to take his mind off the morning's disaster, and this new case was perfect. "We'll do it in the same fashion we did the other two, meaning full moon suits in the decomposed room."

"If it is like the other two, I wouldn't be willing to do it any other way," Vinnie said. He could tell by Jack's tone that there was no way he was going to be talked out of getting right to work.

"Have one of the other skilled mortuary techs help you with weighing and X-raying," Jack said. "Then both of you suit up and take some photos for ID purposes and do the fingerprinting. When that's done, prepare for the autopsy. I should be down there by then. I'm going to go talk with the individual who came in to do the identification. It could be important. I'm starting to get a sense of the viral culprit we're dealing with."

Without waiting for Vinnie's inevitable further complaints about not having had enough coffee or gotten to check out the morning newspaper, Jack headed out to the family ID room. He passed the cubicles used by the identification clerks and walked into the room where he'd spoken with John Carver the day before. Sitting on the same blue couch was a woman Jack thought looked cut from a similar mold. She was about the same age, maybe a little younger, but also slender, well groomed, with blond-streaked hair and form-fitting contemporary clothes, and was rather attractive in a clean, well-scrubbed fashion.

Jack carried over one of the wooden chairs from the round table and sat down. He introduced himself and learned that the woman's name was Darlene Aaronson, originally from Orlando, Florida. She had a slight southern accent and appeared nervous, like a caged wild bird, crossing and uncrossing her legs and alternately chewing on her cuticles.

"I'd like to ask you a few questions about John Carver," Jack began. "I imagine this has been a difficult episode for you, and I hope talking about it isn't too upsetting. I've been told you are prepared to formally identify Mr. Carver when photos are available."

"Photos? Oh, thank goodness," Darlene said. She appeared to relax a degree. "I was afraid I'd have to look at the body, like they do in the movies."

"We use photos almost exclusively," Jack said. "Can you tell me if this was the John Carver who grew up in Seattle?"

"I suppose," Darlene said. "He did mention he'd gone to high school in Seattle, so I guess he grew up there."

"Does that mean you haven't known him for very long?" Jack asked.

"I just met him last night," Darlene said. "It was in my favorite Lower East Side bar. I had seen him before in that particular bar on several occasions."

"Were you introduced, or did you just start chatting?" Jack asked.

"He looked depressed and was nursing a drink by himself," Darlene said. "I went up to him and asked him what was wrong. He said someone he knew had died."

"He didn't say who had died or what they had died of?"

"No, and I didn't ask," Darlene said. "He didn't seem to want to talk about it. We talked mostly about music. We were both into music. After a few beers we ended up going back to my apartment to listen to some jazz."

Bad idea, Jack thought but didn't say.

"But tell me," Darlene continued. "What did John die of? No one would tell me at the emergency room. I asked several people. They just put me off."

"We're not sure," Jack said. "That's what we are trying to find out. How did his illness start?"

"What do you mean?"

"I'm assuming he was acting as if he was healthy when you met," Jack said.

Darlene gave a short, disparaging laugh. "I'll say. Very healthy."

"What I am asking is what were his first symptoms? A headache, or sore throat, or a cough?" Jack said, ignoring Darlene's last comment and its implications.

"A chill," Darlene said. "All of a sudden he was shivering for no reason."

"I see," Jack said. He considered that significant, as John had described Helen's episode as having started in the same way. Intuitively, Jack imagined the chill most likely heralded an acute viremia with virus particles suddenly bursting out into the bloodstream, and the idea brought a kind of revelation. For that to happen, the viruses had to be somehow isolated or locked away, and as far as he knew, there was only one way for that to happen. The virus had to be inside cells in a kind of dormant state.

All at once Jack thought he understood why Aretha had had so much trouble making a diagnosis. It wasn't a typical virus such as those that produced a cold, hemorrhagic fever, or even influenza. They were most likely dealing with an unknown retrovirus like HIV, which took two years to identify. And the moment the idea occurred to him, he wondered why he hadn't thought of it earlier. It explained why some people saw it with electron microscopy and others didn't.

"And the next thing I know is he was having trouble breathing,"

Darlene continued. "It got worse fast. Then he started turning blue, so I called nine-one-one. It was terrible."

"Excuse me," a voice called.

Jack turned and looked up into the face of one of the night-shift ID clerks, who was standing to the side and behind him. She was holding a number of recently printed photos. "If Ms. Aaronson would like to do the identification, we are ready," she said.

"May I see," Jack asked.

"Of course, Dr. Stapleton," the clerk said. She handed the entire stack to Jack.

Jack needed to look at only the top photo and immediately recognized that it was without doubt the John Carver he had spoken with the day before. For a moment Jack felt a tug on his heartstrings. He could remember the man asking if he had to worry about catching what had killed Helen and Carol. Jack hadn't known what to say, and now the man was dead. Whatever specific virus it was, Jack could now say with reasonable certitude that it was definitely contagious but with low infectivity and most likely spread by body fluids, similar to HIV. But what made it particularly worrisome was its ability to be far more rapidly fatal. HIV killed by gradually weakening the immune system, whereas this new, unknown disease apparently killed by suddenly unleashing the immune system in a totally uncontrolled fashion.

At that moment there was no doubt in Jack's mind that NYC was dealing with at least an outbreak of a new disease. Whether it would prove contagious enough to become an epidemic and then a pandemic, he had no way of knowing. Suddenly, he was no longer engaged in an undertaking merely as a way to deal with his daughter's affliction, but rather one that had a potentially grave public-health impact. For Jack it was a case that clearly demonstrated both the power and importance of forensic pathology, and it certainly justified his switch to the field.

But his work was far from being done. There was still one more major question he needed answered. Of the three victims, who was the index case? Who contracted this unknown disease and then spread it to the others? Carol was his guess, because she was first, but the order of the deaths might or might not be indicative of who got it first, as the illness apparently had a long latent period between contracting the virus and the appearance of the first symptoms. All at once he was pleased the CDC epidemic intelligence team was en route. Epidemiology was their baili-wick, and his crusade had morphed into an epidemiological mystery. One of the biggest questions was whether the disease had anything to do with Carol's heart transplant.

"Would you like to come back to my office, Ms. Aaronson?" the clerk asked, interrupting Jack's rapid musings. "We need to get your informa-tion and signature."

"Okay," Darlene said. "But I'd like to ask Dr. Stapleton a question, if I may."

"Of course," Jack said. He'd gotten to his feet. He was now eager to leave. He wanted to see if John's affliction was the same as Carol's and Helen's, just to be sure.

"Should I be worried about what has happened to John?" she ques-tioned. "I mean . . . you know . . . I spent time with him."

For a moment Jack was unable to speak, as his mind raced in circles in an attempt to come up with an appropriate answer. The question was essentially the same as the one John had asked him yesterday, and Jack felt he'd failed the man. Yet he truly didn't know what to say. There was no way to make a diagnosis of an unknown disease, nor was there any treatment. Clearly Darlene was at risk, especially if she'd been inti-mate with John, and Jack was probably correct about the illness spread-ing by body fluids, but there was no way to assay the risk or do anything about it.

"Well?" Darlene asked. She went back to chewing her cuticles. She had hoped for reassurance. Jack's silence was doing the opposite.

"To be totally honest, I don't know," Jack said, ultimately deciding truth was better than deception. "At this point, I'm concerned we might be witnessing the beginning of a new disease that potentially spreads by body fluids. You might have been exposed, but there is no way to know. Perhaps you should take that into consideration and avoid having intimate contact with anyone else for the time being. As soon as we know more we will be in touch with you. I can promise you that, since we'll have your contact information from the identification process. That's all I can say." It was essentially what he had told John, which didn't help the man. Yet on the spur of the moment he couldn't think of anything else.

33

Jack hit the button for the third floor in the back elevator of the Public Health Laboratory building. As he did so, he couldn't help noticing how beat-up the cab was. He knew it was the service elevator, which had to carry a huge assortment of freight over many years, but how that resulted in all the damage, he had no idea. There was not a single surface that wasn't scarified. As a civil servant himself, he wondered how it was that city property could look so worse for wear. Its battered state seemed fittingly emblematic of the disarray of his own life.

While he slowly ascended, he thought over the autopsy he'd just done on John Carver. It had been an unsettling experience, as there had been a moment at the very beginning that had made him pause. In all his twenty years as a forensic pathologist it had been the first time doing an autopsy that he'd had an emotional response, as it was also the first time he was called upon to eviscerate a person he'd so recently interacted with. He'd considered himself a professional hardened by repetition, but obviously it wasn't entirely true. The situation had made him realize he was more of a softy than he'd thought.

After that initial psychological bump in the road, the autopsy had proceeded apace. Once again, both he and Vinnie had done the procedure in full moon suits, even though Jack thought that the protection they used against HIV would have been adequate. Most important, the autopsy findings were exactly the same as Carol's and Helen's. The man's lungs were entirely filled with edema, exudate, and near liquefaction such that he had essentially drowned. It made Jack appreciate with striking clarity the human immune system's power to do harm as well as good.

After the autopsy was over and with Vinnie involved in cleaning up, Jack had taken it upon himself to deliver the lung fluid samples to Aretha, which was why he was currently in the Public Health Laboratory building's elevator. Yet playing delivery boy wasn't his only motivation. He also had been eager to hear if she'd made any progress on her identification efforts and to discuss with her his retrovirus idea. Getting there had been easier than he'd anticipated; the horde of reporters and TV trucks had abandoned their stakeout of the old OCME building.

Similar to his first visit on Monday, Aretha was waiting for him when the elevator doors opened on the third floor, just outside the level 3 biosafety laboratory. She was her typical lively self and was happy to relieve Jack of the new samples. Her cornrow hairstyle looked as if it had been recently redone. Jack imagined it took time to achieve, but the end result was a work of art.

"Have you recovered from that weird episode last night?" Aretha said straight off. "That was one strange scene. Did someone really get shot? That's so bizarre and scary."

"With everything that has happened today, I haven't even had time to think about it," Jack said. "I assume you heard about the pandemic influenza panic this morning."

"Oh, absolutely," Aretha said. "We were all called at the crack of dawn to get in here to prepare for what we thought was going to be a surge of samples. I can't tell you how relieved we were when it turned out to be a false alarm."

"Did you see the *Daily News* that started it all?"

"I haven't," Aretha said.

"You should take a peek at it. It's classic irresponsible journalism," Jack said. "How about your work? Have you made any progress on identifying the virus?"

"Not yet," Aretha told him. "But now that the influenza panic is over, I'm preparing to run my first BLAST search this morning with the nucleotide sequences the MPS machine has produced. So, fingers crossed. Let's think positively. I might have something interesting this afternoon. It's a little bit of a crapshoot. As I've said, you'll be the first to know."

"I've got my fingers crossed," Jack said. He held his hand up to prove it. He knew that the virus needed to be identified before a test could be created and a possible treatment decided on.

"I also spoke with Connie Moran at the CDC just a few minutes ago," Aretha said. "She's at the same point as I am but more experienced. So maybe she'll have something before I do. She's promised to call the moment she does, and I'll let you know."

"Terrific," Jack said. "There's one other thing I wanted to mention to you. I had a kind of revelation this morning. I'm thinking we are dealing with a retrovirus somewhat like HIV, but one that affects the immune system in an opposite fashion."

"Then we're on the same page," Aretha said. "I, too, have been thinking of a retrovirus. And so has Connie Moran, who I shared the clinical information with, including the autopsy findings this morning. I hope you don't mind. I thought it could help. The moment I did, she shared something amazing with me. She had been in contact with the European Centre for Disease Prevention and Control in Solna, Sweden. Are you familiar with that organization?"

"I'm not," Jack admitted.

"It's the European Union's equivalent of the CDC," Aretha explained. "She said she had been talking with them this morning and was told that they have had two cases of respiratory death that sounded just like yours.

Sudden onset and death within hours. One in London and one in Rome. They have an official alert out for any more."

"Really?" Jack questioned. "When did these deaths occur?"

"Both were yesterday," Aretha said. "I thought you might find it interesting, so I asked for the details. Both were Americans. The one in Rome was a twenty-six-year-old woman who died on a nonstop flight from New York, which caused the entire flight to be quarantined. A ghastly situation for those unlucky enough to be on the flight. The London case was a twenty-eight-year-old male New Yorker who had been in London for a week."

"Holy crap," Jack said. He was stunned.

"What the hell does *holy crap* mean?" Aretha teased. "You generation X's are too hung up on language. I think having two cases already showing up in Europe justifies at least a *holy shit*."

"You're right," Jack said, and laughed. He knew he was old-fashioned when it came to strong language, which good old Carlos had challenged on Monday. "This problem is already threatening to turn into a pandemic before it's even an epidemic. When you talk to Connie Moran again, see if she can get us the names and other details. The epidemic intelligence team that's on its way from the CDC will need to know, if they don't already."

"Do you want to see the electron photomicrographs from the CDC that I mentioned?" Aretha asked.

"I think I'll pass for now," Jack said. "I should be getting back to find out how my wife is doing handling the fallout from this morning's debacle."

"I could email them to you," Aretha said.

"Perfect," Jack said. "Good luck with BLAST!" He now held up both of his hands with his fingers crossed.

When Jack got to the corner of 26th Street and First Avenue, he glanced over toward the entrance of 421 that was set back behind a small patch of greenery. Milling about were a good portion of the horde of reporters who had earlier been camped out in front of 520. Their presence outside meant Laurie had yet to start the news briefing she had promised and was most likely still in her office. Accordingly, Jack headed north up First Avenue.

As he had noticed en route to the Public Health Laboratory, the traffic was still far lighter than normal. And only because he was looking at the traffic did he see a black Suburban moving slowly along the curb several blocks behind him. Could it have been the same vehicle he'd seen that morning? Jack had no idea, but it made him feel uneasy.

Since the reporters outside of the OCME had dispersed, the front door was unlocked and Marlene, the long-term receptionist, was sitting behind her raised countertop desk. It was always a pleasure for Jack to see her, and she greeted him with her signature warmth. There were a few other people in the lobby. Jack didn't know if they were reporters or grieving family members. He ignored them.

After being buzzed into the interior of the OCME by Marlene, Jack walked into the front office. Now both secretaries were at their respective desks. Laurie's private office door was closed, which Jack did not interpret as a positive sign. He stopped in front of Cheryl's desk. She was on the phone but quickly finished her call and hung up.

"What's the story?" Jack asked, gesturing toward Laurie's closed door.

"You're to go right in," Cheryl said.

"Fair enough," Jack said. He didn't know how to interpret such an order. What it suggested was that Laurie had anticipated his return. He didn't know if that was good news or bad. He opened the door, stepped in, and pulled the door closed behind him. Things hadn't changed since he'd left in a bit of a huff. Paul Plodget was still there, and he and Laurie were still sitting in the same positions as they had been earlier. There was obvious tension in the air.

"You people don't look very happy," Jack said.

"There's not a lot to be happy about," Laurie said.

"Is the city getting itself back to a semblance of normal?" Jack asked. Although Laurie was looking directly at him, Paul wasn't. Jack wondered why.

"Hardly," Laurie said. "Not with subways shut down and schools closed. But be that as it may, there is something I need to ask you."

"Well, here I am," Jack said, smiling in a cocky fashion while spreading his hands with his palms up. He knew it was a mildly provocative gesture that probably should have been avoided, but he couldn't help himself. Laurie's tone and Paul's avoidant behavior were suggestive that something unpleasant was coming along the lines of whether he had contacted the *Daily News*. Jack wasn't one to face adversity sitting down.

"What do you know of Carlos Sanchez?" Laurie demanded.

"Nice boy," Jack said. It was a quote from David Ben-Gurion, the founder of Israel, when asked about Ariel Sharon after Sharon had annihilated a Jordanian village as a reprisal. The quote had stayed in Jack's mind for the perfect situation. He thought this was it.

"Jack!" Laurie snapped. "Please be serious for a moment."

"I assume you are referring to one of our mortuary techs in training," Jack responded. "Am I getting close?"

"Yes," Laurie said with exasperation. "The police have learned that he was the source of the information that led to the *Daily News* headline and article. He made no attempt to deny it, nor the fact that he had been paid. He claims that you were the direct source of all the information. Is that true?"

"I had a sneaking suspicion that Mr. Sanchez had to be the one who'd spoken to the tabloid. Actually, I had forgotten his last name, so thank you for reminding me."

"You are avoiding my question," Laurie snapped. "Were you the one who gave this erroneous information to Mr. Sanchez, so he would call the *Daily News*?"

"Let's put it this way," Jack said. "I didn't say a word about the Black Death."

Laurie closed her eyes for a moment. Jack had the sense she was probably counting to ten, and he tried to convince himself to restrain the sarcasm. The problem was that accusing him of being the source via Carlos Sanchez wasn't that different from being accused of being the source who called the *Daily News*. He couldn't believe that Laurie could think he was capable.

"What in heaven's name did you say to this man?" Laurie demanded.

"All right," Jack said, now holding up his hands, palms out, as a calming gesture. "Let's put this all into context. Carlos Sanchez had been hired as a mortuary tech by our chief of staff. He was under Vinnie Ammendola's wing for training. Unfortunately, Vinnie quickly learned Carlos was not up to the job, something I sensed when we three worked together Monday on the first subway death, which, by the way, Carlos found very distasteful. As Vinnie said, the man was squeamish and a germaphobe. Anyway, Vinnie went to the chief of staff to get the man fired for being unsuitable as a mortuary tech, but Twyla wouldn't take Vinnie's word. Twyla ordered Vinnie to give the guy another chance."

"Please!" Laurie said, interrupting. "Please get to the point! What did you say to Mr. Sanchez?"

"To understand what I said, you have to understand the situation," Jack snapped back. "Do you want to hear or not?"

"I want to hear," Laurie said, struggling to control her impatience.

"When I called Vinnie to set up for the second subway death, he asked me if I could help dissuade Carlos from becoming a mortuary tech. Since we both knew his response to the first subway death autopsy, we thought we could emphasize what the second one suggested—namely, that the problem was contagious on some level. So that's what we did, and he decided being a mortuary tech was not in his future and stormed out."

"Did you use the term *subway pandemic*?" Laurie asked, losing patience.

"Yes," Jack finally admitted. "I said something like, 'Now we know we could be facing a real subway pandemic.' It was a little like those signs you see on Forty-seventh Street for 'genuine artificial diamonds.'"

"What about the 1918 flu pandemic?" Laurie asked. "Did you mention anything about that in relation to this possible 'subway pandemic'?"

"Yes, but again in a hypothetical context," Jack admitted.

Laurie looked at Paul. They both nodded as if in conspiratorial agreement. She then refocused on Jack. "Well, all this puts me in an unfortunate position. Paul and I have been on the phone with both the Commissioner of Health and the mayor practically since you walked out of here. And I have to tell you, the mayor is livid for fear this costly debacle will be blamed on him and his administration. Everyone knows what a big champion he's been of the Pandemic Influenza Preparedness and Response Plan to the extent of ordering almost yearly exercises and drills." Laurie cleared her throat before continuing. "I have been instructed by the Commissioner of Health and the mayor to put you on unpaid administrative leave while this entire episode is under official investigation and review. That means you have to surrender your official medical examiner badge. The mayor needs a scapegoat, and unfortunately you have been selected."

For a few moments, absolute silence reigned in the room. "I don't believe this," Jack finally snapped. "This is absurd. Especially since there very well might be a pandemic brewing that I need to continue investigating. I just autopsied a third case that was clinically the same as the first two. We're thinking it's some new retrovirus that spreads by body fluids."

"Has Virology identified an actual agent?" Laurie asked.

"No, but there's reason to believe they are close, not only here at the Public Health Laboratory but also at the Unknown Pathogens section of the CDC."

"Then it is appropriate for a CDC epidemiological team to be on its way," Laurie said. "I'm sorry, Jack. But these are my orders."

"I've just heard there have been two cases of the same illness in Europe involving two people from New York," Jack said, almost pleading.

"I'm certain the CDC people will be interested to hear," Laurie said. "May I have your badge?"

"Laurie, you can't do this!" Jack could hear the agitation rising in his voice. "What am I supposed to do?"

"Go home," Laurie said. "I'll try to expedite the investigation as much as I can and get you reinstated. Let me have your badge."

"I can't go home with your parents encamped in our guest room," Jack snapped. "I'll go crazy."

"I can't do anything about that now," Laurie said. "Maybe tonight. Right now, this problem that you must admit you are responsible for to some degree will be taking all my energy."

With sudden anger at himself and the world in general, including Laurie, Jack pulled out his NYC medical examiner badge in its leather holder and thumped it down on Laurie's desk. He found it hard to believe that Laurie couldn't have talked the mayor out of such a draconian consequence. To him it seemed unreasonably cruel to rob him of a large part of his identity, not to mention his defense mechanism against Emma's putative diagnosis and against the mental demons stemming from the demise of his first family. He needed to work. For Jack it was like being forced out of the house on a cold night with no clothes.

34

Continuing his juvenile acting out that began with how he'd surrendered his ME badge, Jack slammed the door to his office with such force that his kids' framed photos tipped over on top of the file cabinet. Without bothering to right them, he threw himself dejectedly into his office chair, leaned back, and stared up at the acoustical-tile ceiling. He had to fight against the urge to break something, but the only thing within reach was his microscope, and he wasn't that out of control. Since it had stopped raining, he wished he had his bike, but at the same time he acknowledged that even that might not have been a good idea in his current frame of mind.

After sitting there for some time, Jack wasn't even sure how long, his mobile rang. At first he just ignored it, since he didn't feel like talking with anyone, and it soon stopped. Yet in a couple of minutes it started again. And then yet again. Finally, when it rang again, its persistence got his attention. Arching his back, he managed to get it out of his pants pocket and looked at the caller ID. It was a number, not a name, meaning it wasn't anyone in his contacts. He was about to toss the phone onto his desk when he recognized the area code, 973. He knew that was New

Jersey. Partially as a diversion, Jack answered. To his surprise it was Harvey Lauder, the ME from Morris County who also had a private office in Dover.

"I'm glad I got you," Harvey Lauder said. "I've called a few times. I was determined. There's been a development out here that might interest you. Last night a young woman in her twenties came into the emergency room at the Dover Valley Hospital in serious respiratory distress of acute onset. It was just like the Carol Stewart case. Even though the patient got to the hospital quickly and was intubated and put on a respirator, she died. It all happened in just a little over an hour from the first symptoms."

"That does sound similar," Jack said. He straightened up. "Was it just the similar clinical course that made you think of Carol Stewart?"

"Not at all. Even more striking was that she also had had a heart transplant. It was done here at the Dover Valley Hospital as the very first case after the hospital received its certification. Everybody is heartbroken, as she had become a minor celebrity. She had been doing so well, just like Carol Stewart."

"That's extraordinary," Jack said. "Do you have a name for this new case?" He now sat bolt upright. His suspicion that Carol was the origin of the subway illness was now strengthened considerably with a second transplant recipient contracting it. Of course, there was always the possibility that this new victim was part of Carol and Helen's social circle. That would have to be ruled out.

"Certainly," Harvey said. "It's Margaret Sorenson. The reason I'm calling is to let you know that I'm going to do an autopsy in an hour or so at the Dover Valley Hospital. They have superb facilities, including the latest in personal protection equipment. I was speaking with Dr. Markham and Dr. Friedlander, and they were hoping you might like to come out and participate. They would be extremely interested to have your take on whether it's the same or different from Carol Stewart. They would also be more than willing to pay for your time. Are you in?"

"That might possibly work," Jack said, trying not to sound too eager. He felt suddenly energized. Under the circumstances, such an invitation unexpectedly being dropped into his lap seemed like a gift from above, even though he didn't believe in the "above." Shifting his mind from a paralyzing mixture of anger, depression, and self-pity to logistics, he wondered how difficult it might be to get ahold of Warren to see if he could again borrow the Escalade.

"They will be pleased if it works out," Harvey said. "They've offered a flat fee of five thousand dollars. Would that be agreeable to you? I know for a fact that it's on the high end of the spectrum. I was the one who suggested it, as they asked my opinion."

"That would be fine," Jack said. He certainly wasn't going to turn down being paid for something he wanted to do. Besides, the money would come in handy, since he had just been put on unpaid leave, which he wasn't about to reveal, for fear the offer might be rescinded.

"May I tell them that it's a go?" Harvey asked. "They're eager to move forward."

"I just have to figure out transportation," Jack said. "Let me get back to you."

"Maybe we can help in that regard," Harvey said. "The hospital has a service that runs back and forth between the Zhao Heart Center at MGH and our facility. Let me check. I'll call you right back. How would that be?"

"That would be very convenient," Jack agreed. He disconnected. He felt like clapping. A few minutes earlier he didn't know what the hell he was going to do with himself and was toxically angry. Now he was being offered an opportunity to jump back into the thick of the conundrum of the subway death, and best of all, Laurie wouldn't have a clue.

Picking his phone back up, Jack went into his contacts to pull up Warren's information. If the Dover Valley Hospital shuttle didn't work out, he wanted to have a backup. As he was waiting to see if Warren picked up, he thought about Harvey's having used the pronoun "our" in relation to the Dover Valley Hospital. It made him wonder if it was just a figure of speech or if Harvey Lauder had some proprietary interest in the hospital. The thought stemmed from a comment Wei Zhao had made. A second later his phone buzzed, indicating an incoming call. Jack terminated the call to Warren and answered. It was Harvey, already calling back.

"We're in luck," Harvey said. "We do have a vehicle in the city that can come and pick you up at 520 First Avenue. How soon would you be ready to go?"

"As soon as I cancel my lunch date with the Pope, I'll be ready," Jack said. He couldn't believe his luck that this was actually going to happen.

Harvey laughed. "I'm sure the Pope will be disappointed. We'll have one of our Suburbans at the front of your building in fifteen minutes. There will be a sign with your name on the passenger-side window. The driver will bring you directly here to the Dover Valley Hospital, and I'll meet you in the reception area. Any questions?"

"None that come to mind," Jack said. "See you soon."

For a few minutes Jack sat there staring ahead at nothing while his mind rekindled thoughts of his weird luncheon with Wei Zhao and how angry he'd become when it was apparent Wei had had him investigated. Jack's intuition was telling him that Wei and his sprawling organization were ultimately responsible for all that was happening, including his administrative leave of absence and the deaths of five people, maybe even six, if this new case did turn out to be the same as the others. Jack was aware he didn't have any real reason to believe this, but he did nonetheless, and under the circumstances he relished the opportunity to find out if he was correct.

35

THURSDAY, 10:05 A.M.

To avoid being seen by any of the higher-ups, Jack left the building from the receiving bay on the basement level. He certainly didn't want to run into Laurie or Paul and be questioned as to where he was going. He then walked west on 30th Street up to First Avenue. Traffic on the avenue was still extraordinarily light, indicating the city was still far from back to normal.

Just as Harvey had promised, a black Suburban was waiting at the curb directly in front of the OCME entrance. Although the city was full of black Chevy Suburbans, Jack couldn't help but wonder if this was the same SUV that had pulled out behind their Uber car that morning or the one that had been slowly trolling behind him when he'd returned from his visit to the Public Health Laboratory. Whether it was or not, it had a letter-size piece of paper with his name printed by hand in block letters taped to the inside of the tinted passenger window.

Jack walked directly up to the vehicle and opened the door with the intent of climbing in. He was surprised to find the seat already occupied by a youthful Asian man, who Jack guessed was in his mid-to-late twenties.

Before any words were spoken, the man leaped out the moment the door opened. He was well groomed, dressed casually but elegantly, and appeared fit, like a committed sportsman. "Are you Dr. Stapleton?" he asked with a heavy accent.

"I am," Jack said.

The man quickly opened the rear door and allowed Jack to climb in before he got back into the front seat. A moment later they were off. Because of the lack of traffic, they made good time heading across town on 31st Street.

The driver was also Asian and appeared to be close to the same age as the man in the passenger seat. He, too, was nicely dressed. Jack couldn't help but be moderately impressed with their clothes and grooming, considering how the current Generation Z seemed to prefer to present themselves.

After a few minutes of driving in total silence with even the men in the front seat not talking to each other, Jack thought he'd make an attempt at conversation. "Thanks for picking me up," he said as a potential opener.

Since they were at that moment stopped at a traffic light, the driver was able to turn around. "You are very welcome," he said. In contrast to the man in the passenger seat, he seemed to have no accent at all. He could have been an American, as far as Jack was concerned. But rather than initiating a conversation with Jack, the short exchange resulted in a seemingly heated discussion between the two men in what Jack thought might be Mandarin. It wasn't until they were about to enter the Lincoln Tunnel that they reached an apparent resolution, as both men fell silent.

"Is there a problem?" Jack asked. He felt like the odd man out yet somehow responsible for what sounded like a disagreement.

"No problem," the driver said, without any other explanation.

"Are you guys speaking Mandarin?" Jack asked out of curiosity.

"Yes," the driver said simply.

Jack shrugged. He didn't care one way or the other whether there was any talk. Instead of making an effort at chatting, he tried to think of how he was going to handle the visit to the Dover Valley Hospital with the invariable questions he'd face about his role in the snafu of the New York City shutdown. He knew they would have heard, as the news had undoubtedly gone around the world in seconds. But after thinking for just a few minutes, he decided he'd just have to wing it, mainly because he wasn't sure if they knew about his recent administrative leave. He knew the chances were good that the media would learn of it if the mayor was in as desperate need of a scapegoat as Laurie had suggested.

The next topic was how he was going to handle himself after the autopsy. The question in his mind was how forceful he should be with whom. He had many questions that needed answers, like whether the Bannons had been paid for their son's heart, or why Wei Zhao was the executor of Carol Stewart's estate, and how she and the donor heart could have matching CODIS results. He also wondered how he might finagle another interaction with "the emperor," Wei Zhao. Ultimately, Jack decided he really couldn't plan and would need to improvise depending on what he learned, starting with the autopsy of Margaret Sorenson.

Forty-five minutes later the two silent, statue-like men drove Jack directly up to the front door of the Dover Valley Hospital. But then, even before the car came to a complete halt, the man in the passenger-side front seat erupted in a flurry of activity and leaped out to open the rear door for Jack.

"Thank you, gentlemen," Jack said as he slid out of the Suburban. "It's been a memorable conversation."

Typical of the changeable weather in the Northeast, it had become a rather nice day with warm sun, in sharp contrast to what it was like when he and Laurie had gotten up that morning. As Jack walked toward the hospital's entrance he noticed considerably more activity than there had been yesterday, with people coming and going. Even an ambulance arrived, and with its siren trailing off, it raced around to the ER entrance.

Despite its futuristic architecture, it seemed like a normal, functioning community hospital.

Going through the revolving front door and expecting to have to head to the information desk, Jack was surprised to be immediately greeted by Harvey Lauder and Ted Markham. It was obvious that somehow they knew exactly when Jack would arrive. Seeing them together emphasized for Jack their differences. Although both were on the short side, with Harvey a bit shorter than Ted, they were opposite in body habitus; Harvey was stocky and phlegmatic, while Ted was slender and animated. Also, Harvey's pug nose and thinning hair contrasted dramatically with Ted's delicate features and his halo of dark curls.

"Welcome back," Ted said. He shook Jack's hand in an overly friendly fashion, gripping Jack's forearm in the process. "I hope you make this a habit. We're glad to see you again so soon. Thank you for coming."

"It's my pleasure," Jack said. He then felt obligated to shake hands with Harvey as well. As he did so he wondered what they would say if they knew the true extent of how much he appreciated the invitation. He also wondered what they would say if they knew he'd just been put on unpaid administrative leave from the NYC OCME.

"What would you like to do?" Ted asked. "Harvey has the autopsy ready to go in our autopsy room in our morgue, but if you'd like to rest and perhaps have a coffee, that's fine, too. It's up to you."

"I always think it best to get the work done first," Jack said. He was amazed they said nothing about the New York City shutdown. Could they somehow have been so busy at work and preoccupied with their own issues that they hadn't heard about it yet? Jack had no idea but wasn't about to broach the issue.

"I couldn't agree more about work before play," Harvey said, speaking up for the first time.

The group set off toward the elevators. Jack took note that both men were dressed in scrubs with long white coats over them. He wasn't surprised about Harvey, but he was about Ted. Somehow its casualness didn't jibe with his intellectual internal-medicine persona. "I notice you are wearing scrubs," Jack mentioned to Ted. "Does that mean you are going to participate in the autopsy?"

Ted laughed, more as an affectation than out of mirth. "I'm hardly going to participate," he said. "I'm going to observe. Margaret was our program's first heart transplant. We're as devastated to lose her as we were Carol, maybe even a tad more so."

Thanks to his high-energy state, Ted wasn't satisfied just hitting the elevator button once. He had to hit it a half-dozen times and then scan the board to see where all the elevators were.

"I do have a question," Jack said.

"Fire away," Ted said.

"Did Margaret know Carol?" Jack asked. "Were they friendly?"

"They certainly knew each other," Ted said. "They crossed paths here at the hospital on a few occasions. But as far as I know, that was about it."

"We deduced from her tattoo that Carol was a lesbian," Jack said. "Do you know if Margaret was as well?"

"I hardly think so," Ted said. "She was married to a local boy. Why do you ask?"

The elevator arrived, and the passengers filed out. Ted gestured for Jack to enter.

"I wanted to know if there was any chance they might have been intimate with each other," Jack said as he boarded.

"I can't imagine," Ted said. "Nor do I think it would matter." He got on the elevator behind Jack, and Harvey followed him.

Jack did think it mattered, even though it seemed as if Ted was uncomfortable with the line of questioning, so Jack let the issue drop. If Carol had gotten the illness that killed her from the donor of the heart, which Jack thought possible, the only way Margaret could have gotten it was from Carol. When he'd first heard about Margaret, he thought maybe she'd gotten the virus from having had a transplant, but the more he thought about the idea, the less probable it seemed. The chances of another donor carrying the same unknown virus were extraordinarily slim. Although such a situation had happened with HIV and organ transplantation in the 1980s, that was when HIV was much more significantly widespread.

"Dr. Friedlander and Dr. Lin will be joining us for the autopsy," Ted announced as the elevator descended.

"It's going to be a regular party," Jack said. It was one of his pet expressions.

"You do have a sense of humor," Ted said. He laughed again, in the same manner as when Jack had asked if he was going to participate in the autopsy.

"It comes with the territory, right, Harvey?" Jack said.

"A lot of forensic pathologists use humor to deal with the reality they face on a daily basis," Harvey said, essentially agreeing with Jack.

When they arrived at the morgue, Jack was blown away. Harvey had described it as superb, but in Jack's mind it was more than that. In comparison to what Jack was accustomed to at the NYC OCME, the autopsy room was akin to the difference between an operating room from the early twentieth century and a hybrid operating room of today. All the equipment was brand-new, including the latest stainless-steel autopsy table. The room itself was clad in a white composite material, including the ceiling. The floor was a white, spotted terrazzo that curved up at the edges to make cleaning easier. Jack could see that not only was standard X-ray available but also what was called 3-D virtual equipment.

"You weren't kidding about the facility," Jack said.

"Dr. Zhao allowed me to work with the architects," Harvey said proudly. "I was able to make a few suggestions. It is capable of biosafety three if needed."

"Impressive," Jack said. "Out of curiosity, do you have any proprietary interest with the hospital?"

"Yes, of course," Harvey said. "We all do. Dr. Zhao believes strongly that everyone feels part of the team. It's a corporation, and we all have been given a little stock."

"That's right," Ted chimed in.

"Interesting," Jack said, falling back on his newly adapted favored retort. He wasn't surprised. Wei had said as much yesterday.

"What level of personal safety would you feel comfortable with?" Harvey asked. "As I said, we can go all the way to biosafety three. But we believe that standard barrier precautions with face shields and latex gloves, not surgical gloves, et cetera, will be adequate."

"I'm comfortable with that," Jack said. He'd used a moon suit on the previous cases, but now that he was becoming progressively convinced a retrovirus like HIV was the culprit, he didn't think it was necessary.

At that moment Dr. Stephen Friedlander and his apparent sidekick, Dr. Han Lin, appeared. They were both dressed similarly to Ted and Harvey, with the addition of surgical caps and with surgical masks hanging down from their necks. It was apparent they'd been in surgery.

"Thank you for coming out here again today," Stephen said in his commanding voice. Han merely broadly smiled in apparent agreement. Stephen made a production out of shaking hands with Jack and didn't immediately let go. "We are pleased you could make it. We were all sorry to hear about that huge screwup in New York this morning that you got caught up in."

Jack inwardly cringed. *Here it comes,* he thought.

"That kind of ridiculousness is the reason I'm so happy to be out of there and here in the sticks," Stephen continued, still clutching Jack's hand. "We don't have the layers of bureaucracy you people have to put up with. One thing it does show is that under certain circumstances there can be too much planning and training. Is that your take?"

"That and the dangers of a disgruntled employee," Jack said. He started to relax. Stephen was immediately seeing Jack as the victim, not the cause, which was certainly how Jack viewed the event.

"Well, we're glad you haven't let the episode slow you down. We're

311

excited to have your help on our problem," Stephen said. He let go of Jack's hands before rubbing his own hands together in apparent anticipation of the upcoming autopsy. "Let me tell you exactly why we are thrilled you're here. Since you had the opportunity to see Carol Stewart's transplanted heart in situ, which we unfortunately were unable to do not being there with you, you'll be able to give us valuable information. From a technical point of view, we are interested in comparing Carol's heart with the transplanted heart in Margaret Sorenson, and you will be the only person who can do it from having seen both hearts in situ."

"Are you thinking from a surgical point of view?" Jack asked. He remembered being impressed with what he had seen.

"I'm talking about the totality of the situation," Stephen said. "The surgical technique being one of them, but also how the heart appears in its orientation in the chest and how the healing of the pericardium has progressed, along with the anastomoses with the great vessels. There were some technical differences in the two cases whose details I won't bore you with, but the unfortunate fact that these two patients passed away within months of their procedures offers us a rare opportunity to analyze their progress and decide which was best, Carol's or Margaret's. We'd like to try to get something positive out of these two tragedies. Am I making sense here?"

"I think I might be able to reasonably compare them," Jack said. In his mind's eye, he tried to remember exactly what he'd seen and what he'd thought when he'd first opened Carol's chest, and then later, when he'd removed the heart and lungs en bloc, and finally when he exposed the heart by cutting through the scarred pericardium. Most of it came back to him, so he thought he'd be able to make a comparison without too much trouble.

"All right, then," Stephen said, clapping his hands. "Dr. Lauder will take you into the locker room to change into scrubs. We'll meet you in the personal protective equipment room. Has Dr. Lauder asked you about your druthers regarding personal protection?"

"We went over that," Harvey said. "He's comfortable with standard precautions."

"Excellent," Stephen said. "So are we."

The locker room was as posh as the autopsy room was up-to-date. Harvey gave Jack scrub pants and a shirt. Jack used one of the lockers for his clothes. As he was pulling on the shirt, Harvey returned and asked if there were any special tools he required.

"That I require?" Jack questioned. "I thought I was observing, not performing."

"They want you to do the case," Harvey said. "I'll be assisting, if you need me. We'll also have two mortuary technicians to help us. Are you okay with that?"

"No problem," Jack said. Actually, he preferred to handle the case. Sometimes when he observed others, he got antsy that they were taking too long or being clumsy or, worse yet, incompetent. Jack's prior life as an eye surgeon had honed his hand-eye coordination and made him efficient with his time. He had no idea of Harvey's skill or lack thereof, but Jack had been mildly concerned Harvey might perform as haphazardly as he dressed. For Jack it was a comfort to know the scalpel and scissors and other instruments would be in his hands.

36

As far as Jack was concerned, the Dover Valley Hospital autopsy room was not only a joy to look at, it was a pleasure to use. There was even classical music piped in quietly in the background, reminiscent of how Jack had liked to perform eye surgery in his former life. Having it during an autopsy was a first for Jack. He hadn't even thought of piped music at the OCME, but now he considered making a suggestion to the design committee responsible for coming up with the plans for the new autopsy room.

There were seven people in the room, which included the two mortuary techs Harvey had mentioned and whom Jack had not formally met. Everyone was dressed in the same light green impervious gowns with full face shields. Jack was on the patient's right, which was his choice, along with Stephen. Directly across from Jack was Harvey, along with Ted. Dr. Han Lin was standing at the head of the table. The two mortuary techs floated. Jack had the instrument tray brought over to his side, as he preferred to pick up instruments himself rather than having them handed to him by Harvey. It was his strong belief that handing off instruments was a source of accidents, which Jack made a point to avoid.

Once he'd finished the external exam with Beethoven's Piano Concerto No. 3 playing almost subliminally in the background, Jack picked up the scalpel. After asking Stephen if it mattered to him if Jack cut through the woman's well-healed thoracotomy scar, Jack carried out a modified Y autopsy incision just as he had done on Carol Stewart.

Jack worked quickly and efficiently. Although he knew everyone present was interested exclusively in the heart, he followed his usual routine and first did the abdomen. Jack never varied the order he followed in his autopsies, to make sure he never forgot any step. He explained this to his audience, and they all said they understood. Stephen and Ted acted subdued as the case progressed, which was understandable, as autopsies were not part of their normal routine, and to the uninitiated they were brutal.

After checking the entire length of the digestive tract in situ, Jack removed the intestines and handed them off to one of the techs to wash out. He then inspected the rest of the abdominal contents. The only pathology he found were the signs of mild inflammation with extravasated blood in the gallbladder, spleen, and kidneys. He informed the group that Carol Stewart had the same findings, which he explained were later determined by microscopic section to have a mild amount of disseminated intravascular coagulation.

"Was it about the same amount of inflammation with Carol?" Ted asked, as Jack held up the cut surface of the kidney so it could be more clearly seen.

"I'd say nearly identical," Jack said. "When I first saw it, I thought of hantavirus, as it's a typical finding in those particular organs in fatal hantavirus pulmonary syndrome. But rapid tests for hantavirus were negative, as were tests for all the other respiratory viruses."

"Can we move along here?" Stephen said. "Han and I have a case on a live person pending at noon."

Jack didn't respond. He was already working significantly faster than he knew most prosectors functioned. In his current sensitive state, he couldn't help but be mildly annoyed at Stephen's increasingly impatient and condescending air, which was becoming progressively apparent and which hadn't been present yesterday.

Taking the heavy-duty wire cutters he'd requested at the outset of the case, Jack proceeded to cut through the wires holding Margaret's sternum together. They made a distinctive metallic snap as each one was cut. Harvey then participated by pulling each wire out with a pair of pliers. When the last wire was cut, the sternum split apart with an audible pop.

Using a couple of towels against the jagged cut surfaces of the sternum, Jack yanked them apart with a decisive cracking noise, which he knew was the sound of breaking ribs. The thorax was now completely exposed and mostly filled by the pale, swollen lungs. Shielded by its scarred pericardial cover, the heart was not yet in view. Jack left the towels in place to avoid anyone cutting themselves on the sharp edges of bone.

Stephen leaned over the open wound. "Do you mind if I palpate the pericardium?" he asked.

"Be my guest," Jack said. He was surprised the surgeon had asked. It seemed out of character with his controlling personality.

"Feels like a normal amount of scarring," Stephen said after running the balls of his fingers back and forth over the tissue a number of times. He then stopped and pointed. "This is where we closed the pericardium with a running suture." He then straightened up and withdrew his hand. "Do you think this is about the same degree of scarring you saw when you did Carol's post?"

Jack palpated the tissue between the lungs, imitating Stephen. He'd not done that with Carol until after he'd removed the lungs and the heart, so he couldn't compare exactly, but it seemed equivalent, and he said so.

"Did you open Carol's pericardium at this point?" Stephen asked.

"No," Jack said. "I didn't do that until I had removed the lungs and the heart en bloc. Do you want me to do the same here or would you like me to open the pericardium now, so you can see the heart in place?"

"I think he should use the same technique as he used with Carol," Ted said, speaking up for the first time. "That's the only way he will be able to truly compare the two."

Stephen agreed. "Go ahead and follow your usual modus operandi."

Using a pair of dissecting scissors rather than a scalpel, as he thought it safer, Jack proceeded to free up the lungs and the heart. He then lifted the entire mass up out of the thorax. He carried the weighty slab of flesh over to a nearby countertop and plopped it down on a scale.

"Is that heavier than usual?" Stephen asked, looking at the readout.

"Much heavier," Jack said. He then started to open the pericardium exactly as he had done with Carol, to expose the heart itself. "You can see there is considerable fibrotic scarring, but it is to be expected."

Both Stephen and Ted crowded in to take a look once the heart was fully exposed.

"My word, it looks entirely normal," Ted said. "Perfect orientation. I'm impressed even more than I expected to be. It looks like a very happy heart."

"I agree," Stephen said. "I don't mind saying so myself, but it was a perfect job."

"And a perfect donor heart," Ted added.

"How does it compare with Carol's?" Stephen said, turning to Jack. "If you were pressed to say which one you thought had been accepted the best, which one would you say?"

"It would be hard to say," Jack replied thoughtfully. "I'd say they were equivalent."

"Let's see the rest of the anastomoses," Stephen said. "The aorta looks fine, but there could be a difference with the others."

Jack pushed back the bloated right lung in an attempt to visualize the great veins called the superior and inferior vena cava. It was difficult because the lung was turgid with fluid.

"Why don't you go ahead and remove the lungs," Stephen said. "Just make sure the pulmonary anastomoses are proximal to the heart."

At first Jack wasn't sure what Stephen meant, but then he got it. Stephen wanted the connections he'd made when he'd done the transplant to be connected to the heart, not to the freed-up lung. Using the dissecting scissors again rather than the scalpel, Jack separated both lungs from the heart. The connections with the great vessels could all be seen. Jack stepped back to give Stephen and Ted more room. While they looked, Jack weighed each lung.

"They all look terrific to me," Stephen said. "I hate to blow my own horn, but they are all masterfully done."

"You're getting good in your old age," Ted teased. "But you're right. They all look terrific, well healed and without the inflammation we agonized about. I don't see any difference here with what we saw during Carol's second autopsy. It seems as if our experiment is a draw. What are your thoughts?"

"I have to agree with you," Stephen said. "How about you, Dr. Stapleton. Do you see any differences between Margaret's anastomoses and Carol's?"

"Not at all," Jack said. "They look comparable to me."

"So there we have it," Stephen said. "We didn't think there was going to be a difference, and there doesn't seem to be." He looked over at the institutional clock as if he was planning on leaving.

"I think you should see the inside of the lungs," Jack said. Without waiting for a response, he got one of the long-bladed knives used in autopsies and made some slices into the lungs' parenchyma, which under normal conditions were air-filled, light, and spongelike. As he made the cuts, the edema fluid burst forth, almost as if it had been under pressure. It was blood-tinged and mixed with exudate and bits of tissue.

"Whoa," Ted exclaimed. "That's rather dramatic. We didn't see that with Carol's lungs."

"That's because most of the fluid had drained out," Jack said. "It gives you a better appreciation of what the immune system can do when it's turned on to create a cytokine storm. It's not a mystery why these people died so quickly. This is a nasty virus."

"Are you still thinking this is caused by a virus?" Stephen asked. "We're continuing to look into the protein angle, thinking of something like a prion."

Jack started. The idea of a prion disease never occurred to him. But as soon as he considered it, he rejected it. "Prion disease only strikes neural tissue, not pulmonary tissue," he said. "No, this must be a virus, but I admit there are some aspects that don't make sense."

"And what are they?" Stephen asked patronizingly.

"This is the fourth case that I have seen," Jack said. "They are all exactly the same, which in my mind points to an infectious origin. If I had to guess, I'd say Carol Stewart is the index case, and she gave it to the others with whom she'd been intimate. For a number of reasons, I am thinking it is a retrovirus. Since she had just had a heart transplant and had never had any pulmonary problems, it is a reasonable guess she got it from the donor, who was carrying this unknown retrovirus that spreads via body fluids, like HIV."

"That's all very fanciful," Stephen said in the same tone of voice. "I have to give you credit for being creative. But you haven't told me what doesn't make sense."

"Margaret," Jack said. "I've been told that she knew Carol but wouldn't have been likely to share body fluids. That means that Margaret would have had to get it from her donor heart just like Carol, and unless this unknown retrovirus that's never been seen was widespread, which it can't be, the chances of that happening are infinitely small."

"I can see where that is a problem," Stephen said.

"How good a match was the donor heart that Margaret got?" Jack asked.

For a beat neither Stephen nor Ted responded. Finally, Ted spoke up. "It was an okay match, otherwise we wouldn't have done it."

"Where did it come from?" Jack asked. "Was it a local donation or from someplace far away?"

"That I'd have to look up," Ted said. "I don't remember offhand."

"Was Margaret on high doses of immunosuppressants, unlike Carol?" Jack asked.

"No," Ted said. "Just the normal amount."

"From the looks of the heart here, there seems to be no inflammation whatsoever. I don't have a lot of experience posting heart transplant recipients, but isn't there usually some rejection phenomena going on that's kept under control?"

"UNOS tries to make the best possible match to keep that at a minimum," Ted replied.

"Sorry to interrupt," Stephen said. "I want to thank you, Dr. Stapleton. This autopsy has been very enlightening, but I do have a transplant case starting in just a few minutes. If you'll excuse me." Without waiting for a response, he headed for the exit leading to the room to remove his protective gear. Wordlessly Dr. Han Lin followed.

"And I have a clinic full of patients to see," Ted said. "I also want to thank you for coming and helping us, Dr. Stapleton. You've provided us with important information. I hope we see you again real soon." Then he headed for the same exit Stephen had used and disappeared.

Jack, still holding the long-bladed knife he'd used on the lungs, felt suddenly abandoned. The exit of the three doctors had been so sudden and unexpected that he'd scarcely had time to react. It also seemed to contradict their previous warm hospitality. It was as if they had gotten what they wanted and that was it. They clearly hadn't been concerned with giving Jack an opportunity to ask any of his myriad questions. Now, as he looked across the room at Harvey, who had busied himself by supervising the removal of the skull cap to facilitate finishing the autopsy, Jack wondered if he might be able to provide any answers. Yet as Jack watched the man struggle with his current task, he wasn't optimistic. In comparison to Stephen and Ted, Harvey seemed like a dunce. Plus, Jack was wary of the man after hearing him place a call to Wei Zhao as soon as Jack had left his office yesterday afternoon. Whatever hanky-panky might be going on at the Dover Valley Hospital, he feared Harvey was probably involved. Whether that was true of Stephen and Ted, he had no idea.

"See any pathology in the brain?" Jack asked, as he returned to the autopsy table.

"None so far," Harvey said. "I hope you don't mind that I had the techs push ahead."

"Not in the slightest," Jack said, making up his mind that Harvey wasn't a good bet as a source. "In fact, I think I'm done here and would like to ask you to please finish up. I have a number of important questions for the doctors that I didn't get a chance to ask, and I'd like to catch them before they leave the morgue."

"But you're not done here," Harvey said with a whine.

"I beg to differ," Jack said. "All you have to do is check the brain and prepare some specimens for microscopic sections. That's not asking a lot with your capable hands. I've certainly accomplished what Dr. Fried-lander and Dr. Markham had in mind for me, and I assume this is a Morris County case."

"No, it was signed out to the Dover Valley Hospital," Harvey corrected. "And if you want to get paid, I want you to stay here and finish."

"I think I'll argue that point with the bursar instead of with you," Jack said, immediately taking offense. He'd suspected Harvey of being lazy and a laggard, but this seemed beyond the pale, as it would take him only ten minutes or so. He'd even given the man a questionably deserved compliment.

"Suit yourself," Harvey said morosely.

37

Knowing he was only in marginal control of his emotions after what the day had already wrought, Jack made an effort to keep himself on an even keel despite Harvey Lauder. Moving quickly, he pushed through the door into the side room, hoping at least to catch Ted. Unfortunately, he wasn't there. The room was designed to facilitate decontamination if the case had needed biosafety 3 protection. It was also where the latex gloves, the shoe covers, and the impervious gown were left for disposal and the face shield was left to be cleaned. Jack accomplished this on the run and then exited into the hallway. Picking up his pace, he power-walked down to the men's locker room. Going through the door, he practically bumped into Ted, who was already on his way out. Ted was dressed as he had been the day before, in a white shirt, conservative Ivy League tie, and a long, highly starched white coat.

"I beg your pardon," Jack said.

"Not at all," Ted said. "Wow! You already finished the autopsy? You are very efficient, I must say."

"I left the rest for Harvey," Jack said. "It was mostly done. I have some questions for you, if you don't mind."

"I'm afraid I do mind," Ted said. He pushed by Jack and opened the door to the hallway. "As I said in the autopsy room, I have a clinic full of patients that I ignored to observe the autopsy on Margaret. Thank you again for your help, but I really have to go."

Before Jack could even respond Ted was out the door and it began to close. Jack straight-armed the door and ran after Ted. In his usual hyper fashion, Ted was moving at a rapid clip.

Catching up to the man with some effort, Jack reached out, grabbed his left arm just above the elbow, and pulled him to a stop.

To Jack's shock, Ted responded by angrily yanking his arm from Jack's grasp. "Don't you dare lay a hand on me," he snarled.

Taken aback by this unexpected response in light of Ted's overly cordial behavior from their very first interaction, Jack raised his hands in a kind of surrender. "I'm sorry. I didn't mean to offend you."

"I don't like to be manhandled," Ted snapped as he smoothed the sleeve of his white doctor's coat. Without waiting for a response from Jack, he recommenced walking quickly to the elevators, where he hit the call button multiple times.

Jack caught up to him a second time. "I have more questions I need to ask," he said. His voice had an edge. He was both confused and put off by Ted's surprising behavior, but mostly the latter.

"It will have to be another time," Ted said. His eyes rose to see which elevator was going to arrive first.

"I visited the Bannons," Jack said. "It was their son who was the donor for Carol Stewart's heart. I got the impression that they might have been paid. Do you know anything about that?"

"Absolutely not," Ted said. He moved down to the second elevator, as the lights indicated it was on its way. "My role was with the recipient, as you already know. Like all centers, we keep a sharp separation between the recipient interests and those of the donor, to avoid even the appearance of unethical behavior."

The elevator arrived and the doors opened. Ted quickly boarded.

"How do you explain that Carol and the donor heart she was given matched with their CODIS profiles?" Jack asked. "We ran the test twice."

"I haven't a clue," Ted said. He hit the button for the second floor. The doors began to close.

Jack grabbed the edge of the elevator door and stopped it from closing. "How did it happen that Dr. Wei Zhao is the executor of Carol Stewart's estate?"

"I wouldn't know," Ted said. "Let go of the door or I will call security!"

Reluctantly, Jack let go of the elevator door. It responded by opening. "I need answers to these questions," he said. "I'm not going to give up until I get them."

"You're asking the wrong person," Ted said. "Ask Dr. Zhao. Maybe he can help you."

A moment later, Jack was staring at the blank, closed elevator doors. He felt a building rage compounded by the frustration of not understanding the sudden attitude change of Dr. Ted Markham. One minute he'd been warm and welcoming, the next cold and distant. Jack hadn't been as surprised by Stephen's sudden personality change. He'd never seemed particularly sincere to Jack.

As he walked back to the morgue locker room, Jack tried to remember what exactly he had said when both doctors suddenly morphed from being interested observers to wanting to leave. It had happened right after he'd posed the question of whether or not some evidence of rejection phenomena was expected to be seen with heart transplants. Jack had done only one other heart transplant autopsy prior to Carol Stewart. It had been way back during his training in Chicago, but he distinctly remembered seeing some signs of inflammation both in the pericardium and in the heart itself. And he remembered that case had been described as a fairly good match.

As Jack pulled on his chambray shirt and began to knot his knit tie, the required concentration calmed him down a degree. "What a day," he complained out loud. Intuitively he knew anger and acting out wouldn't help him get through the next five or six hours, as it never did. Instead he tried to think of what his options were. They seemed limited. He could go back to the city and try to participate in some way with the identification of the virus, but the moment he thought of the idea, he dismissed it. Bioinformatics was something he knew close to nothing about. When he thought about going home, he dismissed it out of hand. There was no way he would be willing to sit around and make small talk with Sheldon and Dorothy Montgomery. Of course, he could try to relate to Emma, but that might make him more depressed than he already was. He could spend some time with JJ, but JJ didn't get home from school until after 4:30.

Hooking an index finger under the tab of his bomber jacket, Jack slung it over his shoulder and walked out of the morgue locker room. As frustrating as his visit seemed to be becoming, he thought he wouldn't leave Dover Valley Hospital just yet. Going through his mind was Ted's suggestion. Maybe he should be directing his questions to Wei Zhao. The problem was how to do it. With the level of security the man insisted on, it wasn't as if Jack could walk up and ring his doorbell. Yesterday, it clearly had been Ted and Stephen who had gotten him the invite to the man's house. Maybe that could work again, and with Stephen in surgery, it left Ted.

Returning to the elevators, Jack took one up to the second floor. His destination was Ted's office, which he knew the exact location of, thanks to the man's hospitality yesterday. Jack didn't know what he was going to say after the unflattering brushoff the man had given him at the elevator, but he trusted something would come to mind. He was convinced one of his strengths was the ability to wing it in any given situation.

Walking through the Zhao Heart Center, Jack could see that Ted had not been exaggerating. The clinic was crowded with patients waiting to be seen. Jack passed the check-in counter, heading for Ted's private office. Jack thought it would be far more successful to talk with Ted's secretary, who had gotten Jack's coffee the day before, than with one of the clinic clerks.

As Jack neared his destination, he could see that Ted's office door was closed. He didn't know if that was a good sign or bad, as to whether Ted was there or down the hall seeing patients in the examination cubicles. Hoping to at least find out, he approached the secretary, who was typing on her monitor. She looked up when Jack made his presence known. Instantly, he could tell that she recognized him, but she made an effort to conceal it by merely asking if she could help him.

"I need to talk to the doctor," Jack said in a compelling tone.

"I will see if he's available. Who should I say is calling?"

"Dr. Denton Cooley," Jack said, coming up on the spur of the moment with the name of one of the most famous cardiac surgeons in America. He thought it was a name Ted would respond to in a positive fashion even though Cooley had recently passed away. Whether the secretary remembered Jack's real name, which he had given the day before, he couldn't tell. Without another word she disappeared inside the inner office.

Jack mentally ticked off the seconds she was gone from force of habit. He was glad he did. When she emerged just over ten seconds later she said, "I'm sorry, but he is not available. He has just stepped out."

"Interesting," Jack said, content to fall back on the same comment yet again. "Obviously you were just speaking with him, as it surely wouldn't have taken you so long to see he was not there. That means he's counting on me just going away. Please go back and tell him that I am not leaving until I talk with him, and I will be waiting right over there." Jack pointed to a modern couch off to the side. He then proceeded to walk to it and sit down. Placing his jacket next to him, he smiled back at the secretary.

For a moment the woman stood frozen in place, neither sitting back down at her desk nor returning inside the inner office. She had a confused and embarrassed look on her face, presumably from being caught in a flat-out lie. Eventually, she recovered, and she disappeared back into the inner sanctum for another ten seconds.

Picking up a magazine on hospital administration, as it was the only choice, Jack absently flipped through it. It was mostly advertisements. When the secretary reemerged, she made it a point to not even look at Jack, but rather went to her desk and recommenced her transcription efforts.

Jack looked at his watch. It was 12:48 P.M., which explained to him why he was hungry. He wished he'd taken the time to get some takeout from the coffee shop on his arrival, as his stomach was complaining. But he'd made up his mind. He wasn't going to move until Ted emerged.

Unfortunately—or fortunately, depending on how Jack looked at what ended up happening—Ted did not appear. Instead a group of four rather large, serious-looking, spiffily uniformed Asian security guards suddenly materialized. Jack had not seen them coming, as he was desperate enough to be actually reading an article about the economics of running an outpatient clinic. He became aware only after they had silently congregated in a semicircle in front of him. They were all youthful, trim of figure, and athletic-looking. All of them wore sunglasses. There were no smiles. It was a humorless, no-nonsense quartet.

In contrast to most hospital security personnel with whom Jack was familiar, these men were armed with holstered sidearms. As Jack was later to learn, they were part of the detail tasked with providing the security around GeneRx and the Farm, not part of the regular hospital security team.

"We would like you to come with us," the guard with three stripes on his epaulets said. He had no accent. His colleagues had either one or two stripes. He was clearly the leader.

"Sorry," Jack said. "I'm waiting to speak with Dr. Markham."

"That is not going to happen. Stand up!" the guard said. There was no inflection in his voice. It was clearly an order. "We are here to escort you."

"Escort me to where?" Jack said. He had the impression he was about to be forcibly deported back to New York City. With the sense of having been used vis-à-vis the autopsy and then summarily discarded, he felt his anger begin to rekindle.

"I was told to accompany you to Dr. Wei Zhao's home," the guard said.

"Oh, well, then. How apropos," Jack commented. Apparently, he wouldn't need Ted's help in getting to Zhao after all. He started to get up but then hesitated. All at once the guard's wording struck a chord. It sounded as if it had been an order, which evoked a reflexive pushback. Jack felt as if he'd been ordered around much too much of late, culminating in his administrative leave.

"If this is for another luncheon, I think I'll pass," Jack said superciliously. He reclaimed his seat and pretended to go back to his reading.

The guard barked a few orders in what again sounded to Jack like Mandarin. Jack was aware of a series of snapping noises, which he realized were the other three guards unsnapping the tabs holding their sidearms in their holsters. He then heard a jingling, and when he looked up the chief guard was clutching a pair of handcuffs. When Jack looked at the other three guards he saw they were all holding on to the butts of their holstered weapons. He got the message. These guys were not fooling around. Worse yet, facing these guards was bringing back last night's shooting episode in searing detail, a memory Jack was trying his best to avoid thinking about.

"Stand up!" the guard said. "Turn around and put your hands behind your back."

Jack nervously glanced at the eight unblinking eyes boring into him. He stood and did as he was told. If it had been one security person, he might not have been so amenable. But four was an overwhelming force. "This seems like a major overreaction," Jack said. He winced as the handcuffs were applied.

The guard then forcibly gripped Jack's left upper arm and urged him forward. One of the other guards picked up his jacket. As a group, they marched the length of the crowded clinic. Patients waiting to be seen glanced up at him. He wondered what they were thinking. He thought of some great comments—"This is what they do here if you don't pay your deductible on time"—but he didn't say anything. It was all rather embarrassing.

The final indignity was that they didn't use the regular elevator. They marched him down to the freight elevator, which they used to get to the basement and a freight dock at the rear of the building. There they had yet another black Suburban. Jack was put in the backseat between two of the lower-ranked guards. The chief guard got in the front passenger seat, and the fourth man drove. It was all very sober. No one spoke.

38

Somewhat reminiscent of the silent ride from Manhattan out to Dover, the first conversation didn't occur until the SUV stopped at the security gate on the driveway into Wei Zhao's home. It was between the driver and the guard in the gatehouse, who made visual contact with everyone in the car. Jack had no idea what was said, because it wasn't in English. He assumed it was Mandarin, just as he assumed his guard detail were all Chinese.

The same as yesterday, they parked at the foot of the flagstone walkway that led up to the house. Everyone piled out. It was a little difficult for Jack due to the handcuffs, but one of the guards who had been sitting next to him lent a hand. Once outside the car, the chief guard told Jack to turn around. When Jack did so, he removed the handcuffs.

"Handcuffing me certainly was unnecessary," Jack said as he rubbed his chafed wrists. It had not been a comfortable ride. The guard did not respond. Instead he handed Jack his jacket and merely pointed up toward the house. Jack got the message and started up the walkway. He sensed all four guards were following but didn't turn to look. Their heels clicked against the slate in a staccato fashion as if they were marching in step.

Once again, the door was opened the moment Jack approached. Kang-Dae bowed while Jack stepped within. When he turned around, he saw that the four guards were right behind him. They, too, entered the foyer.

"The boss is again in the gym," Kang-Dae said to Jack. Clearly, he had expected him. "I will show you." With another bow, he started off exactly as he had done yesterday.

For Jack it was a déjà vu experience that wasn't all that pleasant as he followed Kang-Dae. Since his last visit had been only the day before, his aggrieved mental state when he had left was all too poignant. He vowed to be in more control today, although things were hardly starting out on the right foot.

After only a few steps he realized the guards were not following, which was a relief. Their single-mindedness and silence made Jack distinctly uncomfortable. Jack relied heavily on the power of words and communication as the way to control circumstances.

As Jack entered the gym, he was again surprised at its size, despite it being less than twenty-four hours since he'd been there. It was so unexpected in a private house. He could see Wei in the distance using a piece of exercise equipment. Without saying a word, Kang-Dae stepped aside and gestured for Jack to proceed on his own while he took a seat at the door.

As Jack passed the line of exercise machines he wondered if there was a separate machine for every muscle in the human body. To him it all seemed excessive and unnatural. It was his opinion that a good workout on the basketball court was better, as it forced muscles to work together in tandem the way they had evolved to function. At the same time, he thought any exercise was vastly better than no exercise.

It was apparent to Jack that Wei had to have seen him coming, but the bodybuilder didn't stop what he was doing. As Jack got nearer he could hear the man speak with each repetition. Jack guessed he was counting in Mandarin.

The exercise that Wei was doing was for his back and gluteal muscles. With his hands clasped behind his head and holding a fifteen-pound weight, he was lying prone in an apparatus that supported his thighs and held his heels in place so that he could alternately bend at the waist and then raise his torso to the horizontal. Such effort seemed to Jack a poor substitute for the fun and camaraderie fostered by team sports. It even reminded him of the myth of Sisyphus.

While he waited, Jack had to admire once again the man's physique. He was dressed as he had been yesterday, in sweats and a V-neck black top, possibly with a bit of spandex, that showed off his muscles. Noticing the girth of his biceps made Jack wonder if Wei had ever been tempted to take anabolic steroids, despite their associated dangers.

After watching Wei complete fourteen repetitions—Jack counted by reflex—Jack felt his patience wearing thin, especially since his presence was a command performance via the chief guard. Despite his vow to keep himself under control, Jack felt his ire rising. Was Wei's ignoring him a way of putting him in his place? As if sensing these thoughts, Wei suddenly stopped and disentangled himself from the apparatus. He was breathing reasonably heavily and perspiring.

"Finished," Wei said. He used a towel to wipe his face. "That was my daily eighty reps on the Roman chair. Sorry to keep you waiting, but when I start I have to finish."

Jack didn't respond. He was sure that whatever he said would end up reflecting exactly the way he felt, which wouldn't be a good way to start the conversation.

"Have you ever used a Roman chair?" Wei asked. He took a drink from a plastic water bottle.

"Can't say that I have," Jack said. "It doesn't look much like a chair to me."

Wei laughed. "I have no idea why it is called that. It is a mystery. But thanks for coming back to see me."

"It seems that I didn't have much choice," Jack said, unable to control himself. As soon as the words left his mouth, he regretted it.

"Why don't we go into the lounge, so we can be more comfortable," Wei said, pointing the way. "There's also a selection of refreshments that I can offer you. I understand you haven't had any lunch."

"Whatever," Jack said. He was mildly surprised that Wei didn't pick up on his complaint of not having any choice for the visit, and even more surprised that Wei was also aware he'd not had anything to eat. The man seemed omniscient.

"I've heard that you felt there was no difference between Carol's and Margaret's hearts at autopsy," Wei said as they walked.

"They looked comparable," Jack said. "I was impressed with how well both donor hearts had been accepted. It was my impression that had the women not prematurely died, they would have led normal lives, at least from a cardiac standpoint."

"That's good to know," Wei said. "Thank you."

Jack again didn't respond. Wei Zhao had a peculiar way of making him feel off balance. He didn't know why he was being thanked.

The lounge was a sumptuous oasis of lounge chairs, a huge flat-screen TV, a small kitchen, a small round dining table with director's chairs, and windows that looked out onto the floor of the gym on one side and onto a large indoor pool on the other.

"How about a sandwich and a juice?" Wei proposed, heading into the kitchen. Silently, Kang-Dae appeared and now took up position in a straight-back chair next to the door to the gym.

A few minutes later Jack found himself feeling relatively relaxed, sitting at the dining table and eating a fresh mozzarella-and-tomato sandwich. His emotions felt as if they were following a sine-wave trajectory and were now on a pleasant upswing. Wei had gone back to being complimentary of Jack's medical curriculum vitae, including his extensive forensic pathology knowledge on top of his clinical experience of having been a practicing ophthalmologist. To cap off his eulogy, he surprised Jack by again offering him a position to head up the Pathology Department for Dover Valley Hospital, GeneRx, and the Farm Institute that would be half clinical and half research.

"Remember my original offer," Wei continued. "I will double your current salary. The position comes with some stock in our operation, but you will also have the option of buying more stock at about half the current value. My business philosophy rests on my employees feeling that they are, in effect, working for themselves."

"That's very generous," Jack said. "But as I mentioned yesterday, I'm happy with my current employment."

"I remember you saying that," Wei said. "But I also know that things have changed since yesterday."

"What exactly do you mean?" Jack questioned warily.

"Yesterday you weren't suffering an unpaid administrative leave of absence stemming from your central role in the mistaken pandemic flu scare that has crippled New York City. I would think that loss of income would have a devastating impact on your family, especially with a child tentatively diagnosed with autism."

With a new surge of anger, Jack stared back at his tormenter. The man was again seriously violating boundaries and personal space just as he had the day before. "How do you know this?" Jack managed, trying to keep his voice under control.

"I listened in on your wife's press conference at noon," Wei said. "It seems that some loose talk on your part with an unhappy employee was enough to cause a paralyzing disaster for the city. But as irresponsible as your actions were, I don't think they warranted your being put on leave. I certainly wouldn't have done it. Yet I can understand that your wife had little choice. At the same press conference, the mayor and the Commissioner of Health also spoke. It's clear to me that they both, particularly the mayor, felt the need for a scapegoat and you have been selected. If you ask me, your leave of absence is going to be lengthy, if not permanent, because of the political aspect. Shutting the city down like that even for a day is going to cost hundreds of millions of dollars."

Jack felt his face redden as he wrestled with his emotions.

"Consequently, this would be an excellent time to join our team," Wei continued. "We are in the perfect position to benefit mightily from the limitless promise of CRISPR/CAS9 in so many arenas, from bio-pharma to designer babies for the wealthy in our IVF clinics. This gene-editing tool will revolutionize medicine. From a business perspective it couldn't be more positive, and GeneRx and Dover Valley are poised on the cutting edge."

Jack forced himself to take the final bite of his sandwich and chew slowly, as if he was weighing everything Wei had said. Instead, he was concentrating on keeping himself in his seat and not flying off the handle.

"The dossier I had requested to be compiled on you described you as a very vocal person and noted that you always spoke your mind, come what may. Why are you being so silent now, when I am offering you the job opportunity of your life? I don't understand."

"That makes two of us," Jack said. "I don't understand, either. Why in God's name do you want me on your team?"

"I want you with us because of one of the key principles of business that I learned from my father," Wei said. "When I was a boy, and we had been sent out into the countryside during the cultural revolution to work the land, my father advised me always to make my smartest enemy into my friend. Following his advice, I made the leader of the Red Guards in our village into a friend. It worked. It was the reason I was sent back to Shanghai, which is how I got to the university. It is a principle I have fol-lowed ever since."

"So you see me as an enemy," Jack said.

"In a fashion," Wei admitted. "Yesterday I told you I had put an entire team of molecular biologists on solving the cause of Carol's death, which we all thought possibly had a proteinaceous origin. You thought it was a virus. We now know that you were right."

"You now believe Carol died of a virus?" Jack asked. He was shocked. It might have been the last thing he expected to hear from Wei.

"We know it was a virus for sure," Wei said. "And just today I heard you thought it was a retrovirus. Well, you were right again."

"Have your people identified it?" Jack asked, his amazement deepening.

"Yes, we have," Wei said proudly. "We've even sequenced it."

"It's amazing you could do it so quickly," Jack said. "A virologist at the Public Health Laboratory as well as one at the CDC whose specialty is unknown viruses haven't succeeded as of yet, as far as I know."

"I'm not surprised," Wei said. "This virus has never been seen as a human pathogen. We were able to identify it because we had an idea of what it was. And we have the best and latest equipment."

"What kind of virus is it?" Jack asked.

"It is a gammaretrovirus," Wei said.

"Interesting." Jack wondered how many more times he'd parrot the word before this case was over. In reality, he had no idea what a gammaretrovirus was. He didn't even think he had ever heard the term, which wasn't surprising. Like insects, new viruses were being discovered all the time. And the cynic in him made him question whether Wei was toying with him for sport. If Dover Valley Hospital and GeneRx were doing something shady as Jack suspected, there was no way Wei would be telling him truthful secrets.

"I'm sensing skepticism," Wei said, again surprising Jack with his apparent clairvoyance. "I think I should give you the big picture," he continued. "It might be the only way to sway you. Are you game?"

Unable to control himself, Jack raised his eyebrows and cracked a disbelieving, crooked half-smile. "I'm game. Why not? Fire away!" He had absolutely no idea what Wei Zhao had in mind.

39

THURSDAY, 1:42 P.M.

"Before I begin," Wei said. "Are you comfortable here?"

Jack glanced around at the lounge's decor, appreciating its sublimity and wondering how anyone could be more comfortable. They were in the most luxurious private home Jack had ever visited, sitting in canvas director's chairs at the small round dining table with views into a huge indoor pool on one side and an enormous private gym on the other. Jack had a half-full bottle of pomegranate juice in front of him and had just inhaled a freshly made, healthy vegetarian sandwich.

"We could go over to the great room, if you would prefer," Wei suggested.

"I'm fine right here," Jack said. "Let's hear the big picture."

"I'm assuming you remember what I told you yesterday about the Chinese government, particularly under Xi Jinping, and how it is restricting capital outflow from the People's Republic."

"I remember," Jack said. He fidgeted. He sensed this was going to be a long explanation, and business details weren't of much interest to him.

"Currently GeneRx and the Dover Valley Hospital are running slightly in the red, which I have been covering by drawing capital out of

China. With Xi Jinping in power, which looks like a long-term situation after he managed to have the Chinese Constitution amended, I need to find alternate capital sources. GeneRx has thirteen very promising drugs in phase three clinic trails. Any one of those could solve our near-term capital needs, but whether that happens or not depends on FDA approval, which can be frustratingly slow."

"I hate to interrupt," Jack said. "But could you speed this up? How about giving me the condensed version of the big picture?"

Wei paused and glared at Jack for a beat. "The dossier also said you could be tactless as well as vocal," he snapped, showing irritation for the first time. "I'm finding it unpleasantly accurate."

"I can be impatient," Jack admitted. "But remember that I am not here totally on my own volition."

"Do you feel you are not being treated with appropriate hospitality?" Wei challenged.

"Here, yes," Jack said. "But the ride to get here left something to be desired, as did my treatment at your hospital after I finished the autopsy."

For a moment Wei stared off into his gym, as if to get himself under control. He then got up and went to the refrigerator to get himself a pomegranate juice. After taking a healthy swig, he came back to the table and sat down. He cleared his throat and continued. "Dr. Markham informed me yesterday that he had told you about how the unique relationship between GeneRx and the Dover Valley Hospital was going to make it possible to bring the benefits of CRISPR/CAS9 to clinical medicine before anyplace else in the world. From a humanitarian and business perspective, it is a huge opportunity. It's going to change cancer therapy, gene therapy, organ transplantation, and what IVF can offer its clients like nothing else in the history of medicine. I am absolutely convinced, and so are a lot of other people."

"I'm happy for you," Jack said. "Sounds like a business bonanza. But how does all this relate to the deaths of Carol Stewart and Margaret Sorenson?"

Again, Wei stared off, this time into the pool area. As a billionaire businessman and active philanthropist, he was accustomed to fawning attention from his subordinates and just about everyone else. He was clearly finding Jack progressively more vexing, but after a second pause and a deep breath, he was able to continue. "Of all of the fabulous advances in clinical medicine that are coming thanks to CRISPR/CAS9, the first one to pay off right out of the gate is going to be organ transplantation. Do you know how many people die every day in America waiting for a transplant organ?"

"Not offhand," Jack said, rolling his eyes. "But I have the feeling you are about to treat me to the answer whether I care about it at this moment or not."

"You are a trying man," Wei said evenly, again taking offense at Jack's acerbic flippancy.

"I also find your sense of entitlement trying," Jack said. "I suppose you think it's entirely appropriate to have me shanghaied out of your hospital and brought here whether I wanted to come or not and then forced to listen to a lecture about your business problems. The irony is that I did want to come, but not under these circumstances. I'm interested in the deaths of two young women and the possibility of a new pandemic with a heretofore unknown virus."

"I'm getting to that," Wei retorted.

"You could have fooled me," Jack snapped back.

For a few beats the two men looked daggers at each other across the small table. The tension in the air was as palpable as static electricity. Jack in particular was struggling to rein in the churning emotions that had been honed to the breaking point. The helplessness he felt in the face of Emma's plight combined with the events of the past week—being forced out on leave, having to deal with his in-laws, being manhandled out of a community hospital, and possibly being shot at—had him on the edge of the precipice. Getting harangued by someone he was beginning to believe was probably a narcissistic megalomaniac was almost too much to bear.

"Maybe we should have beers instead of pomegranate juice," Wei said, breaking the tense silence. He got up, went to the refrigerator, and retrieved two bottles of Tsingtao. Returning to the table, he pushed one in front of Jack, then popped the top on his. Although Jack questioned the advisability of alcohol in his state, he went along. They both took long pulls.

"Okay," Wei said. "Back to how many people die every day in this country waiting for an organ. The answer is about twenty to twenty-two people. There are over a hundred thousand people on the UNOS waiting list, and almost one hundred fifty are added to the list every day. All of them are suffering. Why this is such a tragedy is that there is a solution to this problem. It is pig organs."

"Xenotransplantation?" Jack said. "It's been tried. The rejection phenomena make it prohibitive."

"That was before CRISPR/CAS9 was available," Wei told him. "This new gene tool is a game-changer."

Jack suddenly put his beer down on the table and eyed Wei. His jaw slowly dropped open. He was stunned. "Are you trying to tell me that Carol Stewart and Margaret Sorenson were transplanted with pig hearts?"

"No," Wei said. "They were transplanted with human hearts grown in pigs."

"Good God!" Jack exclaimed. He was aghast. "Did these women have any idea of what was happening to them? Did they know they were getting pig hearts?"

"Correction," Wei said. "As I already said, they were getting human hearts grown in pigs. There is a huge difference, and it is all thanks to CRISPR/CAS9. Essentially these were not only human hearts, but they were customized human hearts immunologically matched to the recipients."

"But did Carol and Margaret know where the hearts were grown?" Jack asked.

"Absolutely," Wei said. "We were totally up front with the women. They were both very smart and understood everything. They were scrupulously apprised of the work we have been doing for the last three to four years, including our extensive baboon experiments that started with appropriate-size pig hearts being transplanted into the baboons' abdomens as assist devices and then later into the chests as full cardiac transplants. We also were able to do some chimpanzee work in my Chinese institute, where we could still get away with it. As astounding as it may sound, we had no fatalities with either species over the entire period."

"I'm having trouble believing all this," Jack mumbled.

"Using pig organs for human transplantation is not some way-out idea," Wei said. "It's been touted in the scientific journals, and there are a number of companies here in the USA working on this technology at this very moment. Everyone knows it is going to happen. It's a horse race, and the spoils are going to go to the first company out of the gate. Knowing this, I committed our company to being the winner."

"So that I completely understand, both Carol Stewart and Margaret Sorenson agreed to be guinea pigs unbeknownst to anyone other than you and your people."

"That's correct," Wei said.

"This is insane," Jack said. "Why would they be willing to do this?"

"They believed in the evidence we were able to show them," Wei said. "They also knew that the chances of their getting a donor heart were small to none. Both had been on the UNOS waiting lists for over a year. With the rare blood types of AB-negative and A-negative, they knew their chances were nil, while we could engineer a perfect match."

"Why was Carol Stewart's transplant done under somewhat strange circumstances at Manhattan General Hospital?" Jack asked.

"That was an unfortunate timing issue. The reason was that her clinical condition deteriorated rapidly and necessitated she get her transplant prior to Dover Valley Hospital receiving its certification. We didn't have any choice if she was going to live."

"So the donor heart she got didn't come from James Bannon," Jack said.

"You are correct," Wei said. "Her new heart came from a cloned pig. We were forced to come up with an alternate story because the procedure was done at MGH, even though it was performed by our Dr. Stephen Friedlander. We were not prepared to announce our breakthrough until we could present both cases five or six months post-operatively."

"So the Bannon story was all an elaborate ruse to avoid a potential violation investigation by United Network for Organ Sharing," Jack said disdainfully.

"I suppose you could say that."

"Good grief!" Jack exclaimed. He ran a nervous hand through his hair. He was dumbfounded about what he was learning. His mind was struggling to comprehend it all while his emotions were like an over-stretched, taut piano wire. After a short pause he said, "I was brought out here today purportedly to make a comparison between Carol's and Margaret's donor hearts," he continued. "Dr. Friedlander said that there were technical differences between the two cases but didn't explain. Was that true, or was that another ruse merely to get me back here?"

"It was true," Wei said. "With the help of CRISPR/CAS9 we have developed two fundamentally different ways to produce human transplant organs in pigs. Our research has not proved one better than the other. Are you interested in the details? It requires a bit of technical genetic understanding. Would you like to hear? A few minutes ago, you were complaining your patience was waning."

"Let's give it a try," Jack said. He was interested and listening, but he was also getting concerned about being caught in the web of Wei's world.

"I'll try to make it brief," Wei began. "The basic idea in both approaches is to use CRISPR/CAS9 to alter the genetic makeup of pigs to create a customized organ. We started by using the same cloning techniques as were used with Dolly, the first cloned sheep. Once we had created an embryo, we used CRISPR/CAS9 to knock out all sixty-two known porcine retroviruses, called, appropriately enough, PERVs. From this embryo we created a line of pigs with no retroviruses, which we raised in a pathogen-free environment. Are you with me so far?"

"Keep going," Jack said.

"Now, the goal was to make a PERV-free pig that would produce a customized heart for a specific individual," Wei continued. "This required knocking out the pig genes responsible for creating the major histocompatibility complex, or MHC, along with the genes responsible for blood groups and then replacing them with the comparable genes from the patient who needs the heart. Again, this was accomplished with CRISPR/ CAS9. So far so good?"

"So far," Jack said.

"Now, here's where the two approaches differ," Wei said. "One involved creating only a transgenic pig, meaning a pig containing human genes. This included the genes I just mentioned, as well as the genes responsible for the creation of the heart itself. As it turned out, that was how Carol's donor heart was created. The decision was made by a coin toss, in which the women participated. Questions?"

"I'm okay," Jack said.

"Margaret's heart was created slightly differently," Wei said. "In her case it was the creation of a transgenic/chimeric pig. What we did was to make a pluripotent stem cell from one of her skin fibroblasts and add that to the developing PERV-free pig embryo containing her MHC and blood groups but without the genes required to make the heart. This information for forming the heart had to come from Margaret's stem cells, so once again it was a human heart but grown in a pig that was composed of both porcine and human cells, which is what is called a chimera. Are you clear on these two approaches? Obviously, they both worked, but the pure transgenic is easier and results in a higher percentage of piglets."

"What I'm clear about is your brazen presumption," Jack said. "I'm appalled that you were willing to do all this with no sanction from any regulatory organization like the FDA or even a legitimate Institutional Review Board."

"Knowing your reputation as someone who chooses not to suffer fools gladly, I'm surprised to hear you say that," Wei said with equal disdain. "I for one have little respect for such regulatory bodies. Biological science is moving much too quickly for bureaucrats to comprehend, much less regulate."

"The goal is patient safety and autonomy," Jack reminded him. "It's to prevent desperate people from being taken advantage of."

"We were absolutely convinced of the safety and the efficacy of what we were doing. We were not taking advantage of anyone."

"Oh, sure," Jack sneered. "I'm blown away to hear you say that after both patients died. This was a freakin' megalomaniacal experiment gone bad."

"Let's not be too quickly and falsely condemning." Wei bristled, clearly taking offense.

"How can it be falsely condemning when the patients died?" Jack demanded. "And not only did they die, they might have started a goddamn pandemic in the process."

"You are an opinionated, uninformed, self-righteous Western hypocrite," Wei snapped. "Instead of actually doing something, you're one of those people who just throw up their hands in the face of twenty-some people dying every day from the lack of transplant organs here in the USA alone and up to five hundred worldwide. And you do this with the solution right there, staring you in the face."

"But the two patients died!" Jack yelled. "How can you overlook this immutable fact?"

"They died, but their hearts were functioning superbly," Wei stated. "And both would have died months ago without the organs they received. You saw both hearts. They were perfectly accepted and functioning beautifully. Can't we have a civilized discussion here?"

"You are too much," Jack scoffed. "You want to have a civilized discussion over an uncivilized, unauthorized, unethical experiment that took advantage of two desperate young women. Even you said they died of a retrovirus, which they must have contracted from their pig hearts. That's the reality."

"The reality is that they were human hearts," Wei corrected. "And yes, they died apparently of porcine retrovirus, but not because of our protocol. What we didn't expect was sabotage."

Jack was about to shout back at Wei to give further vent to his self-righteous indignation when the meaning of the word *sabotage* penetrated his consciousness. It took some of the edge off his emotions. He stared at the billionaire, wondering if he had heard correctly.

"Just last night, or actually early this morning, we found something that we certainly didn't expect," Wei continued. "Both donor hearts contained a PERV, gammaretrovirus B, in very low titers that had been eliminated in our cloned line of pathogen-free pigs. After sequencing it and comparing it to the usual PERV, we found differences, meaning it had been artificially introduced. There is only one way such a situation could have happened. Someone planted the PERV deliberately to sabotage our experiment. And it wasn't a random choice. It happened to be one of the PERVs known to infect human cells."

"Why would someone sabotage your work?" Jack asked. He couldn't help but be skeptical. Was this some other strange ruse from this devious man?

"Obviously we do not know for sure," Wei said. "But we have suspicions. The Chinese government, which has an oversized presence in Chinese universities, as we all know, requires us to accept a large number of Chinese biotech graduate students as part of their training. Over the last number of years these millennials have been progressively imbued with a new Chinese nationalism that you have probably seen in the newspapers in relation to Chinese students at Western universities. Among this group, there is a growing intolerance to anything construed as negative propaganda directed at the new China. The Chinese government is behind it. I have been aware that some of these students who learned of my interest in getting my assets and myself out of China want me to fail.

I have no proof they were behind this sabotage event, but I believe so nonetheless."

"That's a rather facile and convenient excuse," Jack jeered. "I must give you credit for spontaneous creativity." His cynicism made him dismiss the idea out of hand despite having no idea why Wei Zhao was taking the time and effort to explain all this cutting-edge bioscience to him.

"Do you not believe what I'm telling you about this neonationalistic movement among Chinese millennials? Do you not believe what I told you yesterday about how arbitrary the Chinese Communist government has become in relation to some of us successful businessmen, and how they have restricted the flow of capital out of China to put in jeopardy our overseas investments that are not already self-sustaining?"

"I just can't relate it all to the deaths of these two young women," Jack sneered. "It is trying to justify something that is unjustifiable. Carol and Margaret paid with their lives. On top of that, there are four other young people who have also paid with their lives, with the potential of the start of a significant body-fluid-born pandemic here in New York City, London, and possibly Rome. That's already six people dead and counting."

"I'm not trying to justify sabotage," Wei snapped back. "What I am trying to explain is why it is akin to a terrorist attack on me and my company. When we find out who was responsible, believe me, they will be appropriately punished. As for the 'experiment,' as you term it, I think it was completely justified, and those women would be alive and well today had this terrorist act not taken place. Human organs grown in pigs is the future, and it is going to save countless lives. As for the potential pandemic, we have already made progress containing it, thanks again to CRISPR/CAS9."

"Progress how?" Jack demanded.

"In terms of detection and cure," Wei said. "With the help of CRISPR/CAS9, we have already developed both a rapid test to detect the virus in an asymptomatic patient and an ex-vivo method of eliminating it. The fact that the illness spreads by body fluids rather than by aerosol is a huge benefit, as it will be infinitely easier epidemiologically to determine who needs to be tested."

"Okay, okay," Jack said, trying to control his vacillating emotions. He nervously ran his hand through his hair while he tried to organize his thoughts. "Answer me this! Why are you taking the time and energy to explain all this to me? Why are you trying to convince me about something I obviously don't believe? It doesn't make sense to me."

"That is a good question," Wei said. "As I listen to you, I find myself asking the same question. Partly it is because I do see you as a potential enemy, and I would rather have you on our side. I want you to join our team."

"And why is that?" Jack asked superciliously. "Let me answer: I think you want me to stop investigating what happened out here in Dover."

"Why would I care at this point?" Wei questioned. "I've told you what happened. There is nothing more for you to investigate."

"I suppose that's true to an extent," Jack said contemptuously. "Maybe now you're more concerned with what I might do with the information, like give a call to the FDA's Office of Criminal Investigations."

"I suppose that is closer to the truth," Wei admitted.

"So you think by bribing me with double my current salary and some stock in your organization I would be willing to make a Faustian deal?"

"Hardly," Wei said, clearly struggling to contain his own emotions. "I thought I could appeal to your humanitarian instincts over bureaucratic requirements. Had the sabotage not taken place, within several months we would have been able to present our results with Carol and Margaret and thereby start our transplant program of human organs grown in pigs immediately. The public would have demanded it. Can you imagine how many lives we would be saving instead of waiting the five to ten years or more it will take going through the usual FDA approval process?"

"Tell me this!" Jack demanded. "Do Ted Markham and Stephen Friedlander have equity positions in your company?"

"Absolutely," Wei said. "As I said, I like all my employees to feel that they are working for a common goal. Everyone of consequence is a stock-holder and fully aware and supportive of what we are doing."

"Jesus H. Christ!" Jack exclaimed. "This is all worse than I could have imagined. Everyone is in collusion. Your entire institution's method of operating is a classic example of confusing means and ends. It's akin to the dubious ethical argument that it is justifiable to kill one person if you use the organs to save eight."

"Absolutely not," Wei retorted. "What we did has nothing at all to do with that simplistic, deontological Kantian argument. We are all more motivated by the consequentialism of ancient Chinese Mohism, as were Carol and Margaret. We were thinking of thousands upon thousands, not eight. Consequences matter. There's no question. And there is the issue of autonomy, which is equally important. The women were part of the decision. They weren't forced."

For a brief moment Jack buried his head in his hands to massage his scalp after hearing such word salad, the meaning of which he didn't even understand. He was outraged that he had allowed himself to get into a kind of philosophical argument with a paranoid, overzealous, megalo-maniacal narcissist who was all too willing to ignore rules in place to safeguard patients in experimental circumstances. But there was one thing that Jack had to give the man credit for: He was right about Jack having learned just about everything he wanted to know and more about the shady doings of GeneRx, the Farm Institute, and Dover Valley Hos-pital. Now the question was whom he would tell and whether he would have the opportunity to tell anyone, caught as he was in Wei's citadel. There was no doubt in his mind that the whole crazy affair would be fodder for the FDA, the CDC, and the FBI. After a moment of thought he decided that if he could, he would put it in Laurie's lap.

Suddenly emerging from the shelter of his hands, Jack abruptly stood up, startling Wei, who immediately followed suit.

"This has been a delightful party," Jack said with his signature sarcasm. "But I'm out of here." With that said, he took a step sideways around Wei toward the door to the gym. He had decided that his sole potential asset was surprise and intended to make a run for it.

With lightning speed Wei's hand shot out and grabbed Jack's arm in a viselike grip, yanking Jack to a stop. "Hold on!" he ordered. "You are not leaving until we have an understanding."

Jack stared into the man's broad face with its expression of absolute determination with narrow, unblinking eyes and compressed lips. Wei wasn't making a suggestion or an offer. It was clearly an order reinforced by his hold on Jack's arm.

For a few beats the two men stared into each other's eyes across the personality chasm that separated them. Then, slowly, Jack's eyes lowered to take in the hand gripping his left upper arm. There was a sense of foreboding in the air, as if a fuse had been lit on a powder keg.

What followed was an explosion of sudden cathartic action as Jack, in one motion, wrenched his arm from Wei's grasp and, with both hands on the man's chest, forcibly shoved him backward out of the way.

The burst of physical conflict surprised both men. Wei was shocked it had happened at all because invariably his Schwarzenegger-like size and muscles physically intimidated others. Jack was surprised because the man hardly moved despite Jack having given vent to his frustrations with what he thought was a mighty shove.

The next flurry of movement caught Jack off guard as Wei unleashed, more by reflex than thought, a martial-arts-style kick aimed at Jack's head. Thanks to Jack's superb physical condition, he not only saw the kick coming but was able to mostly duck under it. It also gave him an opportunity in the milliseconds that followed to rush the larger man. Jack had made an instantaneous decision that he wasn't going to stand off and be outclassed by exchanging blows with someone trained in martial arts.

In high school in Indiana, Jack had played defensive safety in football and had developed a forte for tackling, even players significantly larger than himself. As he plowed into the heavier Wei by leading with his right shoulder into the man's gut, Jack could hear the wind go out of the man's lungs. Jack lifted as he drove through the tackle, sending both men sprawling back onto the carpeted floor and colliding with director's chairs and lounge chairs. There was a tremendous clatter as furniture upended and shattered.

For a few minutes the two men rolled around on the floor, with neither gaining the advantage, although Wei was hampered by having to try to catch his breath at the same time. Both men were taken aback by the other's strength and athletic agility. Ultimately, the deciding factor was home court advantage. Both men had forgotten about Kang-Dae, who had gone for help the moment the confrontation developed. The scuffle had also been seen by security on closed-circuit television. Within minutes a group of five armed and uniformed security personnel rushed into the room and latched on to the struggling, entangled combatants, pulling them to their feet. As they wrenched the fighters apart, both Jack and Wei managed to get in a final punch. Both were a bit worse for wear and out of breath, Wei even a bit worse off than Jack, a fact that gave Jack a modicum of satisfaction.

40

Although the guards continued to restrain Jack, Wei was immediately released. Jack eyed the man, unsure of how Wei intended to take advantage of the circumstance. But once again Jack was surprised. Wei was far less angry than Jack reasonably expected, as the first words out of his mouth were, shockingly enough, complimentary. "I admire people in good physical condition," he said as he adjusted his V-neck, miracle-fabric workout shirt. It had become twisted around his torso. "Your physical fitness speaks well for your basketball playing and bike riding. Maybe I should look into both. You are certainly in far better shape than most Americans your age." He then retied the drawstring of his sweatpants.

Jack tried to shake off the two sizable men restraining him, but they responded by tightening their grip. Wei noticed and told his guards to let him go. Once free, Jack immediately rearranged his own clothes and straightened his tie, which had somehow remained in place through the tussle. While Jack made himself more presentable, Wei and Kang-Dae had an extended and animated conversation in Mandarin.

"I hate to interrupt," Jack said when it seemed Wei and Kang-Dae were going to talk interminably. Even some of the guards had begun to shift their weight out of apparent boredom. "As I said, this has been a delightful party, but all good things have to come to an end. I'll be heading off, if you can give me a hint how I might get back to civilization."

"That's not going to happen right at the moment," Wei said, interrupting his lengthy chat with Kang-Dae. "We are trying to decide what to do with you."

"I imagine the OCME will soon be curious as to my whereabouts," Jack said. "They'll be calling the Dover Valley Hospital before too long, since I haven't checked in like I was supposed to do."

"I doubt that very much," Wei scoffed. "It was one of the reasons we were intent on ferrying you out here after we heard you were put on leave. I think there is a good chance no one knows you are here." He sighed. "All this is so unnecessary. You could have made this much easier than you have."

"Sorry not to be more cooperative," Jack said mockingly, but under his bravado he felt a chill, as it was dawning on him that Wei had told him too much. It was true that no one, not even Warren, knew where he was, and his only connection at that point with the normal, sane world was his mobile phone in his pocket.

Wei shook his head in ostensible disappointment. "Your dossier specifically talked about your well-known aversion to bureaucratic incompetence and restrictive, inappropriate rules. I counted on it. In contrast to some others in our organization who thought of you as an existential risk, I thought otherwise. I believed you would relish the opportunity to push back against bureaucratic interference by helping us solve the problem of the shortage of organs for transplant. Thanks to CRISPR/CAS9, it is one of the first win-win opportunities in medicine today. But you have proved me wrong, Dr. Stapleton. So that's it! I'm done here."

Wei turned to the guards and, switching to Mandarin, barked out instructions to them that included drawing their attention to Jack's jacket draped over the back of one of the director's chairs.

"Wait," Jack yelled, as he realized what was happening. "Where am I going?"

"That is a problem," Wei said. "It is something we never thought about in planning our complex. The idea of needing a place for incarceration never occurred to us. We are going to have to improvise. I've instructed our guards to take you to the Farm Institute. We have some holding pens with which we'll have to make do. It will give you a chance to mull over all that we have talked about. Good day, Dr. Stapleton." With that said, Wei picked up his towel and headed in the direction of the indoor swimming pool.

Jack called after him, trying to suggest that they talk more, but Wei merely waved over his shoulder as the door closed behind him.

"Okay, Dr. Stapleton," one of the guards said with a heavy Chinese accent. He and his compatriots were dressed slightly differently from the guards who had brought Jack out to Wei's house. Although their uniforms were the same color, they were more elegant and made with a more refined fabric suitable for wear in a domestic rather than commercial environment. "Dr. Zhao asks that you hand over your mobile phone."

"I'm not in favor of that idea," Jack said with manufactured swagger. He was dismayed at the request coming out of the blue.

"I'm sorry, but Dr. Zhao was insistent," the man said. He had a name tag, but it was in Chinese characters.

"Sorry," Jack said. "I've been told by my parents never to give my phone to strangers."

In response to this feeble attempt at humor, the guard barked an order and two of the other guards immediately seized Jack for the second time, one holding each arm. The guard who had spoken with Jack then unceremoniously patted Jack's pants pockets until he located the phone. He then reached in and extracted it. A moment later it was in the guard's pocket.

He then motioned with his hand, and Jack was released. "Now we are going out to the vehicle," the man said. He tossed Jack his jacket. "We will go through the gym and exit directly outside. It is a short walk through the garden. Dr. Zhao suggested we not restrain you, but we will if you make it necessary."

"I get the picture," Jack said. He pulled on his jacket. He wasn't excited about returning to the Dover Valley Hospital with his hands cuffed behind his back. Besides, he liked the idea of an unencumbered walk through the garden. With his basketball playing and bike riding, he was confident he could outrun a good portion of the population. He also liked the idea that Wei's home was nestled along the border of the Picatinny Arsenal, which Ted Markham said was surrounded by an extensive virgin forest. What better place to lose himself, he thought. He wouldn't even mind getting picked up by the arsenal security, which he imagined would have to be a robust force, as large as the place purportedly was.

They traversed the gym in short order and exited outside. Although it was into the second week of November, the grounds were ablaze with fall flowers. There was also a Chinese gardener toiling in the flowerbeds, wearing what looked to Jack like a pair of blue pajamas. On his head was a flat conical hat Jack always associated with the Asian farmers and rice fields.

As they walked, Jack wondered if the property had a high chain-link fence around its periphery similar to what surrounded GeneRx and the Farm Institute. If it did, it could be a problem. Still, he thought it worth the gamble. He had no idea what to expect at the Farm Institute. The idea of being put in a pen as if he were livestock wasn't appealing in the slightest.

The break that Jack was looking for came as they exited the formal garden. Just beyond the flowerbeds was a short expanse of lawn bordered by woods on one side and driveway on the other. Jack's idea wasn't elaborate. He thought he had a good chance of outrunning these uniformed men handicapped by all their equipment festooned on their belts plus heavy-soled shoes. Jack, as usual, had on his black cross-trainers. He also had already pulled on his jacket and zipped it up.

Without warning, Jack bolted. He thought he'd made a clean get-away, as no one even tried to grab him. In the next second, he expected to plunge into the edge of the forest, but he never made it. Stunned in both senses of the word, physically and mentally, he was stopped in his tracks as his whole body seized up. It wasn't pain as much as shock—again, in both senses of the word. The very next moment he was on the moist ground, trying to recover his senses. He'd been Tased.

The guards gathered around. Two of them roughly hauled Jack to his feet. The one who had spoken earlier pulled Jack's limp arms behind his back and handcuffed them. When he was finished, the group half-carried Jack to their van. Jack was put in the backseat between two guards and the sliding door was closed.

By the time they passed through the security gate in Wei's winding driveway, Jack was back to normal, although again uncomfortable sitting against his cuffed hands. As they pulled out onto the county road, Jack tried to make conversation. "Sorry about that attempt to run away," he said, giving apology a try. "I didn't mean any disrespect to you fellows."

He got no response from anyone. The man who had done the talking was sitting in the front passenger seat. Besides the two men next to Jack, there was a fifth man in the third-row seat. It seemed unnatural that all these men were so silent. It was just the same as when Jack had been driven from the hospital to Wei Zhao's house with the GeneRx security people. Jack found it extraordinary. Verbal communication was as natural to Jack as breathing.

"You people seem preternaturally quiet," Jack said. "Is it me or are you always so silent?" There was no response.

Eventually even Jack gave up, and he, too, rode in silence until they turned into the entrance of Dr. Wei Zhao's commercial complex. As they were passing the turnoff to the hospital, Jack said, "I'd much rather go to Dover Valley, if you don't mind." As he expected, they ignored him.

A few minutes later they stopped at the gatehouse leading within the compound to GeneRx and the Farm Institute. As soon as the driver lowered the window, Jack shouted out that he was not a willing visitor and was being brought in against his will. "Help! Please call the local police," he yelled.

The people in the gatehouse ignored him, as did the other occupants of the vehicle. It was apparent everyone knew one another by sight. After the driver was given several keys, the van pulled ahead and the driver raised his window. Jack looked longingly at the GeneRx building as they passed. He felt he wanted to go anywhere but the Farm Institute. He was absolutely certain he didn't want to be put into an animal pen.

To Jack's surprise, the van did not stop at the Farm Institute's administration entrance, where Jack had entered on his brief tour the day before. Instead, they drove all the way along the front of the building and then rounded its end. Then they drove the length of one of the wings that stuck off the back and couldn't be seen from the front. Jack could now appreciate that there were three wings in total, such that the Farm Institute's footprint was a letter *E*.

The SUV came to a halt at the end of the wing where several semitrailers were parked off to the side. As the guards climbed out of the front of the van, Jack tried to figure out what part of the institute they had stopped at, but there was no signage whatsoever. There was a normal entrance door, as well as a receiving dock with a large overhead door. The only windows in that portion of the two-story wing were up high under the eaves.

The sliding door of the van opened, and Jack was helped out. "How about removing my handcuffs?" he suggested, once he was standing on the macadam of the driveway.

"When we have you in the pen, we will remove them," the guard said. The entire group walked to the door, where the driver used the key given to him at the gatehouse. Inside was a dark, windowless office. Everyone filed in after the light was turned on.

"Keep going," the guard said, as he pointed toward another door in the back of the room behind the desks.

The second room was cavernous and had a mildly disagreeable smell. It was filled with a significant amount of assembly-line-like machinery, with an overhead conveyor system whose function Jack did not immediately recognize. Although some natural light spilled in from the windows high on the walls, it wasn't enough to provide much ambient light down on the floor, and the machinery cast weird and grotesque shadows.

"This way," the guard said, pointing off toward the left in the direction of the main part of the institute. Jack followed several of the other guards who had gone ahead. After walking several hundred feet, they came upon a huge, heavy wire-mesh enclosure that extended off into the distance. A moment later they approached an embedded door made of the same material. Inside the cage, the floor was covered with what appeared to be sawdust.

"What is this building for?" Jack asked, unsure if he'd get an answer.

"It's the slaughterhouse," the guard said.

"Oh, wonderful," Jack said sarcastically. He'd been told about the slaughterhouse by Ted Markham and Stephen Friedlander back when they were acting as if they were trying to impress him. Now he was getting to see it much more intimately than he would have liked. It occurred to him that the hulking machinery they'd been passing was for processing and butchering animals.

The van driver used another key to open the mesh door. The hinges made an agonized creaking sound, as if they hadn't been opened in years.

"Turn around," the guard said.

As Jack turned around he noticed the man with the Taser had unsheathed his weapon, just in case. Jack had no intention of getting Tased a second time.

"Okay, inside!" the guard said after removing the cuffs and pointing into the interior of the huge coop.

Jack glanced through the door. The cage was about ten feet wide and ten feet high. To the right, it terminated after thirty feet or so, while to the left, it disappeared off into hazy darkness. It was hardly inviting, and as the understatement of the year, he was not inclined to go inside. "What is this cage for?" he asked, in an attempt to stall, even though he had a pretty good idea it was to hold animals before the slaughter.

"Inside," the guard said, giving him a shove to the small of the back.

Jack had to step up and duck down at the same time to enter. Behind him, he heard the hinges complain again prior to a loud mechanical click as the door shut and locked. Jack turned around. The guards were already leaving.

"Hey!" Jack called. "How long am I going to be here?" But the men didn't answer. They didn't even turn around. Eventually he heard the door to the office close. Then there was a heavy stillness.

Turning back around, Jack looked first to the right. Only ten to fifteen feet away he could see that the cage narrowed such that animals being herded in that direction would be forced into single file to facilitate them being killed and then hoisted up onto the conveyor system to be hacked into various cuts of meat. Turning again, he looked in the opposite direction. That way, the cage progressively widened before vanishing into a murky nothingness.

41

"You utter fool!" Jack was vaguely aware of voicing the words aloud as he berated himself for his lunatic behavior. He questioned how he could have been so stupid as to allow himself to be isolated in a fortified home and get into an actual physical brawl with its paranoid billionaire body-builder proprietor when he clearly knew there were shenanigans afoot. At the same time, he understood that his emotions had been stretched to the breaking point over the last few days, culminating in his having been put on administrative leave that morning. It had been his job and only his job that had been keeping him psychologically grounded.

The first thing that Jack did was look closely at the embedded door. He was able to immediately appreciate that the locking mechanism required a key on the inside as well as on the outside. There was no handle or latch of any sort. He hit the lock a few times with the base of his fist to sense how loose the latch bolt was within the strike plate. It wasn't loose at all. Next, he used a fingernail to feel how tightly the separation was between the lock's face plate and the strike plate. It was well engineered and tight, so there was no chance of using the old credit-card trick. Next, by embedding his fingers in the wire mesh, he tried to shake the door. It didn't budge. He imagined it had been built to withstand mistreatment by a two-thousand-pound bull, and he gave up on trying to get it open.

Turning around, he again glanced up and down the expansive animal cage and struggled with a sense of impotence. The chances of him being able to free himself from his current predicament were dimming rapidly from possible to probably not. Wei had said that Jack wasn't going to be heading back to the city at the moment, but what did that actually mean? How long might he have to wait? And why was he waiting at all?

Although Jack had been trying to avoid thinking about it by using denial, he was now forced to consider that maybe Wei was not thinking of letting him go at all. In his attempt to win Jack over, Wei had told him everything they had been doing to corner the market in providing custom-made human organs for transplant grown in pigs. In a very real sense, Jack now knew too much. Maybe the reason he'd been isolated so far out of sight was to see if there were any inquiries whatsoever as to his whereabouts. If there weren't, then they could do with him whatever they wanted.

With a shiver of fear, Jack recognized that there might have been a specific reason he had been put where he was. He remembered being told that the facility was not only a slaughterhouse but also a rendering plant, or what was known in the industry as an integrated facility. In such a place, an entire animal, composed of bones, teeth, fur, guts, hooves, fat, blood, and muscle, could be turned into useful products. Suddenly Jack could imagine himself becoming dog food and bars of soap. To make someone totally disappear, there was no better place.

With a sudden new sense of urgency, Jack began a rapid inspection tour of his lockup in hopes of finding a way out. He first walked to the left in relation to his entry point, knowing there had to be a good-size entrance for the livestock. He also thought there might be more doors similar to the one that had provided him access.

After only a short distance, Jack noticed the pen gradually had expanded in width until it was about twenty feet wide. And he did find more of the embedded wire-mesh doors every fifty feet or so, but they were all constructed with equivalent precision to the first. A quick check of each convinced him there was no chance any of them could be forcibly opened.

As he continued walking it became progressively darker, as there were no high windows in this portion of the cavernous surrounding building. Eventually he was moving forward more by feel than by vision, requiring him to have his hands extended out in front of him. After several hundred feet he collided with a wall. Since the light in this section of the cage was minimal, he was forced to use his hands rather than his eyes to inspect the wall. Rather quickly he was able to feel the outline of a pair of double doors that were devoid of any hardware. There weren't even any hinges, meaning the doors opened outward. He gathered these were the pearly gates for the animals heading for their doomsday.

In a moment of sudden, spontaneous panic, Jack pounded on the heavy doors. He yelled, "Help!" several times at the top of his lungs, but he only succeeded in causing a ringing in his ears. Quickly recognizing the futility of what he was doing, he gave up. He doubted there was anyone who could hear him, particularly anyone who might be inclined to help.

Turning around, Jack retraced his steps. At least he was heading back into the light. He again checked each of the embedded doors he passed, in hopes of having missed something, but he hadn't.

When Jack got back to the door through which he had entered, he kept going. Thanks to the daylight spilling down from the clerestory windows, he could now see all sorts of details, including that the cage narrowed to no more than five feet in width. He was even able to touch either side simultaneously. About twenty feet on, he came to a heavy grate that blocked further passage. Jack could see that the grate could be mechanically raised to allow individual animals an opportunity to proceed. Just beyond was the area where the animals were killed by being hoisted into the air onto the conveyor system via a hook behind their Achilles tendon and their throats being slit. The mild unpleasant odor Jack had noted when he'd first entered the huge, warehouse-like structure was the most intense where he was now standing.

Jack tried to raise the grate, but as he had assumed, it wouldn't budge. It was made of heavy steel bars. Turning around once again, Jack made his way back to the original entrance door. Reacting to a feeling of frustration and mounting terror, he gave it another shake, but wasn't any more successful than he had been on the first attempt.

With a feeling of utter dejection, Jack turned his back on the door and slumped down into a sitting position with his legs stretched out in front of him. He leaned back against the wire mesh. He was glad he had his jacket, as it was none too warm, and to take full advantage, he zipped it up and turned up the collar.

As he sat there, Jack found himself recalling having been in another somewhat similarly worrisome situation in which he'd been handcuffed to a drainpipe of a kitchen sink in a weekend mountain house in the Catskills by a wacky sister and brother. He'd been afraid for his life then, too, and had been ultimately rescued by his basketball buddy Warren. But the difference back then was that Warren had been involved to a degree, so his serving as the savior wasn't completely unexpected. In this situation, Warren only knew that Jack had gone out to Dover Valley Hospital to investigate some potentially shady doings. Would that be enough to bring Warren out to New Jersey to ask questions about Jack's whereabouts? Jack doubted it very much, unless Warren put together the shooting last night on 106th Street involving Asian men and Jack's having had lunch with a Chinese billionaire.

Being a realist at heart, Jack had to admit the chances Warren might come looking for him were essentially nil. That left Laurie. Would she think about having the Dover Valley Hospital checked when he didn't show up at home that evening? Jack shook his head. He could remember telling her that the powers-that-be at the Dover Valley Hospital had liked him enough to offer him a job. Now he could have kicked himself for not telling her more about his suspicions concerning the hospital.

Time passed agonizingly slowly. Jack heard absolutely nothing, making him feel as if he were being held on the back side of the moon. He wondered if the place was sound-insulated, as the slaughtering conveyor system would probably be extraordinarily noisy when in operation. Sound insulation to keep noise inside would also keep outside noise outside.

After several hours, Jack felt a progressive urge to urinate. Eventually he heaved himself to his feet and walked back fifty feet or so and peed through the wire mesh. When he was done he returned to the entry door. To get his circulation going, he ran in place for a few minutes and did some basic calisthenics. Even that slight amount of exercise made him feel a bit better. Eventually he sat back down in the same position he'd been in earlier.

By 4:30 the progressively meager light began to fade rapidly. By 5:00 it faded fast. By 5:30 it was dark and getting darker. Soon he couldn't even see his hand in front of his face. Deprived of visual input, his mind went back to finding fault with himself over the secrecy he'd maintained the last few days, choosing to share little with anyone, particularly with Laurie, because he was afraid she would have tried to curtail his activities. He was particularly sorry he'd elected not to tell her about the shooting episode, which he found himself mulling over anew.

After giving the episode a lot more thought, he had to admit to himself that the chances that he was intimately involved and not an innocent bystander outweighed any other explanation. But such an admission didn't get him anyplace. In fact, it seemed to raise more questions than provide answers. But it did remind him of one curious comment Wei had made toward the end of their conversation, when Wei contrasted himself with others in his organization who thought of Jack as an existential risk. Jack had not known what to make of the comment at the time, nor did he now, but it did suggest a difference of opinion resulting in two factions.

At some point, because of the lack of sensory input and despite his anxiety and fear, Jack actually fell asleep while sitting propped up against the wire-mesh door. He had no idea how long he'd been asleep when he was awakened by what he thought had been a noise in the oppressive silence. Straightening up, he strained to hear more, unsure if the noise had been a hallucination or real. But then there was the unmistakable sound of a distant door opening, suggesting the initial noise might have been a key being inserted into a lock.

Jack leaped to his feet. Hearing someone coming was both welcome and terrifying at the same time, evoking a schizophrenic response. He didn't know whether to hold his ground or flee into the dark depths of the cage. Then suddenly light entered the dark room in the form of dancing flashlight beams rather than the overhead lights being switched on. To Jack's wary mental state, flashlights seemed to auger something underhanded that needed to be feared. What he had been secretly fantasizing would happen was the general lights of the slaughterhouse suddenly coming on, and surprised workers discovering him. Someone coming in surreptitiously with flashlights was the opposite extreme, and it terrified him.

Desperately, Jack wanted to hide, but there was no place to go. Still, he spun around, and by running his hand along the wire mesh, he fled as fast as he could into the black depths of the cage, heading toward the sealed double doors at the very back.

Suddenly a voice with no accent broke the oppressive silence: "Dr. Stapleton! Where are you? We don't have much time."

Jack stopped and turned back. He could see it was two people rather than the five who had brought him. Both individuals had flashlights, which they were using to shine into the wire cage. The beams were sweeping rapidly around the interior, searching for him.

Taken aback by hearing his name, since neither group of security people that afternoon had used it, Jack was encouraged. He was even more encouraged about the lack of accent, combined with the comment of not having much time. He couldn't imagine someone saying that if they meant him harm, but he could if it were the opposite and they were under pressure. Hoping the rules of the game, whatever the game was, had changed, he called out, "I'm back here," and he began to quickly retrace his steps. As he got closer the two flashlights were directed at him, and he had to shield his eyes with his hands from the glare.

"Please, hurry!" the same accent-free voice urged. "As I said, we don't have much time. We need to get you out of here, and we need to do it immediately."

"That's music to my ears," Jack said. As he reached the embedded door, he was able to make out the man who was speaking to be significantly taller than the other, even a bit taller than Jack. The second, silent man was remarkably slender and a good deal shorter. The bigger man handed his flashlight to the other, which afforded Jack an even better chance to see him without the glare. Jack now could tell that he was a youthful-appearing Asian who spoke American English. He was dressed casually but smartly in an open-neck shirt, sport jacket, and jeans. Jack immediately saw that he was carrying a crowbar, which gave Jack pause with the concern it might be used as a weapon. But the man immediately put Jack's mind at ease by saying, "I want to pass you this crowbar under the door. It's best that it appears as if you found the crowbar and thereby managed to break out of here of your own accord. Understand?"

"Whatever," Jack said. It sounded good to him. He had no idea why it was necessary, but he thought he could worry about that later.

The man quickly bent down to slide the crowbar between the door and the floor, but there wasn't enough room. He stood back up, with his expression registering disappointment.

"There is a grate twenty to thirty feet down to my left," Jack said. He pointed. "It would be easy to pass it through the bars."

"Okay, perfect," the man said. In Mandarin he directed the other man to shine one of the lights in that direction. A moment later he and Jack met up at the heavy grate. The man passed the crowbar between the bars with ease, and Jack took it.

Without wasting any time, Jack hurried back to the embedded door. Using the straight end of the crowbar, he inserted the claw teeth between the door and the jamb, just above the strike plate. He had to use considerable force and wiggle the tool back and forth a few times to get the teeth to sink in deeply enough. Using the length of the crowbar as a lever arm, Jack was able to bend the door enough to pop the latch out of the strike plate. The door swung open, and in the next instant Jack was out of the cage.

"Drop the crowbar!" the man ordered. "The idea is that you found it in the cage and used it to break out."

Jack did as he was told, although he didn't drop it but rather put it on the composite floor to avoid the clatter it would have invariably made.

"All right, let's go!" the man urged. He took one of the flashlights from the slender fellow, and Jack got a quick glimpse at the second man's face. To his surprise, it was Kang-Dae, Wei's man Friday.

As a group they half walked, half ran back along the slaughterhouse floor to the office. Then, after quickly traversing the office, they held up at the door to the outside.

"Kang-Dae will go out and make sure we are good to go," the younger man said. "We'll wait here."

"Fine by me," Jack said, even though he wanted to get the hell out of the slaughterhouse as soon as possible.

The silent Kang-Dae turned off his flashlight, cracked the door, and slipped through. He moved like an apparition. One minute he was there, the next he was gone.

"I appreciate you coming to get me," Jack whispered. "Thank you."

"You are welcome," the man said.

"What is your name?" Jack asked.

"Call me David," the man said.

"David it is," Jack said.

A moment later there was a furtive knock on the door. David cracked it open. It was Kang-Dae. As usual, the man didn't speak but rather merely nodded to indicate the coast was clear. In response, David turned off his flashlight, pushed the door fully open, and gestured for Jack to exit.

Outside, there was a single light over the door. Otherwise it was intimidatingly dark as the Farm Institute was completely encompassed by forest and there was no moon visible. The three men ran a short distance across the macadam parking area to a black Range Rover parked alongside one of the semi-trailers.

While Kang-Dae climbed into the driver's seat, David went directly to the rear of the vehicle and opened the back. He motioned for Jack to climb into the storage area. "Sorry, but you have to ride back here until we get through security. It's not far."

Jack hesitated for a brief moment. Having been just sprung out of one situation of confinement, he wasn't joyous about climbing into another. But he understood the rationale. With some reluctance, he clambered in, rolling onto his back in the process. David activated the hatchback closing mechanism. A moment later, Jack again found himself in absolute darkness.

The car's motor started, and the vehicle backed up and then pulled forward. Jack sought something to hold on to in the darkness as he bounced around, but he couldn't find anything to grasp. Fortunately, it wasn't a big problem, since the roadway was reasonably smooth. It was only the turns that were mildly difficult to manage. Presently, Jack felt the SUV slow down and stop. There was some conversation in what he assumed was Mandarin, and a moment later they recommenced moving. They didn't go far before they stopped again. On this occasion, Jack could hear one of the vehicle's doors open. A moment later the hatchback lifted and the tailgate dropped down.

"Okay, Dr. Stapleton," David said. "My car is right here behind me. It's a black Lexus. I'd like you to get out of the Range Rover and get right in my car. The least amount of time you are exposed, the better it will be. I don't think anyone is watching us, but one never knows. Are you ready?"

"As ready as I'll ever be," Jack said. He then inched his way to the lip of the opened trunk, got to his feet, and then hurried to climb into the black coupe only a few feet from the Range Rover. In the short time he was outside, he could tell that they were parked off in the far end of the Dover Valley Hospital parking area. The brightly illuminated hospital looked like a jewel in the darkness.

A second later, David jumped into the driver's seat, pulled his door shut, and started the car. Outside, Jack noticed Kang-Dae had already begun driving away. Jack's escape had been pulled off with commendable efficiency.

"I assume you want to go back to the city," David said, putting his car in gear and heading after Kang-Dae.

"No, I'd rather go back to the slaughterhouse," Jack said, already recovered enough to indulge in a bit of sarcasm. "I was just getting comfortable."

David chuckled. "You are a trip, Dr. Stapleton. I have to say that much about you. Will we be going to your home or the OCME?"

"Home," Jack said, wondering how he was going to be received.

42

Jack turned to catch one more glimpse of GeneRx and then the Dover Valley Hospital before David pulled out onto the county road and gunned the Lexus. Ahead they could see Kang-Dae and the Range Rover. Both vehicles were heading north.

"Okay," Jack said, facing toward his liberator and beginning to calm down. "This has been one strange day. I suppose I shouldn't look a gift horse in the mouth, but I can't help it. I need to start by asking exactly who you are, David."

"That is entirely reasonable," David said. "My name is actually Zhao Daquan."

"Zhao, like Wei Zhao?" Jack asked.

"Exactly," David said. "Wei Zhao is my father."

"Interesting," Jack said. The catchword had never felt more appropriate. This whole affair, starting with the call from Bart Arnold about the first subway death, had been full of continual surprises. The idea that Jack had been rescued from a potentially calamitous situation by the son of his major antagonist seemed a kind of poetic justice.

"I suppose you want to know what is going on here," David said.

"Oh, no!" Jack responded. "I love being totally in the dark. It makes life so much more unpredictable."

David laughed again, this time with true hilarity. "I have to say, I like your humor, Dr. Stapleton. The background check my father had done on you characterized you as someone who liked to pun and use sarcasm. It certainly was on the mark."

"So you had access to my infamous dossier," Jack said. "That gives you an unfair advantage."

"I am happy to tell you whatever you would like to know about me," David said.

Ahead, Jack noticed that they were rapidly approaching the entrance to Interstate 80 East that would take them back to New York City, if that was their destination. Jack could see that the Range Rover had continued straight, going under the highway, presumably en route to Wei's home. For a few seconds Jack held his breath, but then at the appropriate moment David steered onto the entrance ramp. Jack secretly breathed a sigh of relief.

"Well?" David questioned. "What do you want to ask me?"

"Were you born here in the USA?"

"No, I was born in Shanghai," David said.

"You speak flawless American English," Jack said.

"Thank you for the compliment," David said. "I came here nine years ago to go to MIT to study biotechnology and microbiology. Now I am finishing my Ph.D. in genetics and bioinformatics at Columbia University's Systems Biology Center."

"So your plan is to follow in your father's footsteps?" Jack asked.

"In general, yes," David said. "In specific, no. My goal is to run my father's biotech and pharmaceutical companies in China, not here in the USA."

"From my conversation with your father, I get the feeling he's interested in pulling out of China and concentrating his efforts here."

"Unfortunately, that is the case," David said. "I am afraid my own father and his closest team members have become somewhat counter-revolutionaries. My father has always been a unique man, starting with his worshipping Arnold Schwarzenegger and becoming a bodybuilder and martial-arts devotee while studying biotechnology."

"I can attest to the martial-arts aspect," Jack said. "We were having a reasonably pleasant conversation when he unleashed one of those wild martial-arts kicks at my head. Of course, I started it by trying to shove him out of the way."

"You got into a physical fight with my father?" David questioned with obvious incredulity. "I can't believe you, Dr. Stapleton. And what surprises me, you came out of it without a scratch."

"I was saved by your father's security team," Jack said. "Who knows what would have happened if they hadn't shown up. And you can call me Jack. Rescuing me from the slaughterhouse entitles you to be on a first-name basis at an absolute minimum."

"Jack it is," David said. "I am currently heavier than my father and have also studied martial arts and done bodybuilding under my father's direction, but I would never challenge him to a fight, even though he is nearly seventy. You are very brave, Jack."

"Sometimes foolish but not brave," Jack said. "But let's get back to your story. You were calling your father and his peers counterrevolution-aries."

"That's correct," David said. "Especially of late. My generation feels much differently about China today than our parents did. China is ascendant. China is on its way to take its rightful place on the world stage."

"Are you suggesting there's a kind of new cultural revolution?" Jack questioned.

"In a fashion," David said. "China needed Mao to force a break from the stranglehold of the past to create a new mind-set for industrialization and pull China into the twentieth century. Now China needs a new incentive to break from the inferiority complex the country has suffered since the Colonial Period, as well as from the capitalist selfishness like my father exhibits. My father is a philanthropist, but he thinks of his billions of renminbi as completely his."

"There is an irony here," Jack said. "Your father admitted to me that he got his start as a Red Guard in the Mao Cultural Revolution. Now you are in a sense doing the same thing."

"I suppose that is true," David said. "But I want to be part of my Chinese heritage. I am proud of it, and I want to be part of the Chinese ascendency."

"You aren't afraid you have become too Americanized, having been living here for nine years?" Jack asked. "Will you find it hard to adapt to living back in China?"

"I don't think I will have any trouble at all," David said. "We Chinese university-age generation are all on the same page, whether we are in school in Wuhan, or Canberra, or Paris, or Boston. We are of the same mind-set to truly make China great again, pardon the hackneyed phrase. Whereas here in the USA there is depressing divisiveness and a kind of anti-immigrant neotribalism that is getting progressively worse, in China we millennials are coming together."

"I can't argue with you there," Jack said. "Let me ask you something more specific. How did you know that I was being held in the slaughter-house animal pen?"

"Kang-Dae called me in New York and told me," David said.

"And why would he do that?" Jack said. There still seemed to be more that Jack didn't know than what he did.

"It's a rather complicated story," David said. "Are you sure you want to hear it."

"There's nothing I want to hear more," Jack said. It didn't make any sense at all to him, as Ted Markham had told Jack that Kang-Dae had been Wei's personal assistant for almost forty years. And he acted as if he was totally devoted to the man.

"You have to understand exactly who Kang-Dae is," David said.

"I was told he originally was a defector from North Korea," Jack said. "And has been working for your father for practically a lifetime."

"That's correct," David said. "But the important thing is how he became my father's assistant. My father didn't hire him on his own accord. Kang-Dae was a Chinese government plant to keep tabs on my father that my father was compelled to hire, and Kang-Dae has continued in the same capacity to this day. It is all rather ironic in that my father has been aware of Kang-Dae's role practically since day one but never cared. Since Kang-Dae had no family, my father even let him live in a spare room in our house, despite knowing he was, in effect, a spy. I have known Kang-Dae my whole life. He's family without being family."

"But why would he go out of his way to tell you I was locked up in the slaughterhouse?" Jack asked. "Obviously your father thinks of me as a distinct liability, as he should. Kang-Dae witnessed our brawl."

"Because our goals coincide," David said. "The Chinese government doesn't want my father to succeed here in the United States, for fear he'll shut down his companies in China. Same with me and a large contingent of the Chinese interns that are here working in GeneRx."

"Your father thinks that these last two heart transplants with the pig-grown organs were sabotaged," Jack said. "Do you think that is true?"

"I know it is true," David said. "It was a regular old-fashioned conspiracy and a group decision. We thought the best way to delay the program was to reintroduce a pig retrovirus into the cloned retrovirus-free litter of pigs used to clone the customized pigs. I was the one who chose the B virus used, as it was known to infect human cells in culture. What none of us had any idea about was that it would be capable of eliciting a cytokine storm. That took us all by surprise. Actually, we counted on them finding the retrovirus well before the organs were harvested. The original protocol called for such a final check. We don't know why it wasn't done, although it is obvious it had something to do with the rapidity of Carol Stewart's clinical deterioration. It is tragic that the final check wasn't performed. Unfortunately it's something I'm afraid I am going to have to live with."

"Your father thinks that had this sabotage not happened, the two women involved would be alive and well today, ushering in a whole new era in transplant treatment. Do you agree?"

"My father has usually been right in such things," David said. "And he is probably right about this. It's why he is a billionaire and most of his colleagues are not. He knew from the moment he first heard about CRISPR/CAS9 that it was a breakthrough technology. He's absolutely certain it's going to change the face of clinical medicine. Revolutionizing the organ-transplant field is just the first of a host of amazing things it will be providing."

"You do understand that I will have to report all this," Jack said. "At a minimum, I'll be making sure the FDA's Office of Criminal Investigations will be alerted tomorrow morning." Although he understood everything David had said, in the final analysis it was the death of the two women that bothered Jack the most.

"I was hoping that would be the case," David said. "It's why I was intent on getting you out of where you were being held."

"Maybe I shouldn't be asking this," Jack said, "but if you hadn't shown up as a liberator, what do you think would have happened to me?"

"My father would have delegated your fate to one of his many underlings," David said. "He wouldn't have given it much thought. He is good at compartmentalizing."

"I was afraid of that," Jack said.

"You had impressed my father with the efforts you had made investigating Carol Stewart," David said. "Kang-Dae told me he was intent on convincing you to join the team. He thought that you would be a terrific asset in dealing with the problems that he expects he'll be facing from the usual regulatory agencies. I'm somewhat surprised you were able to resist, as he can be very convincing."

"I was never tempted," Jack said.

As they sped toward the city, Jack felt himself progressively relax the farther they got from the Farm Institute and its slaughterhouse. The traffic was light, even as they neared the George Washington Bridge, the world's busiest.

"Your father said something reassuring," Jack said, breaking the silence. "He said that thanks to CRISPR/CAS9, GeneRx engineers had already developed a rapid test for determining the presence of the new gammaretroviral disease and also how to cure it. Is that correct, as far as you know?"

"It is," David said. "It is another tribute to the power of this revolutionary gene-editing technology."

"That's terrific," Jack said. "That should make the elimination of the mini-pandemic this episode has caused rather easy."

"No doubt," David said.

Jack glanced around at the impressive interior of the sports car, with its sumptuous leather seats and swank-appearing dash. "Nice wheels," he said, trying to sound contemporary like Warren.

"It's not bad," David said offhandedly.

"It's the most impressive car I've been in," Jack said. "What model is it?"

"It's a Lexus LC 500 coupe," David said. "I'd asked for a Lamborghini but had to settle for this. As usual, my father didn't even ask for my opinion. That's the way it has always been."

Jack didn't respond. He guessed it would be difficult not to be spoiled growing up with a billionaire father. He felt immensely grateful for having been rescued from a potentially lethal predicament, even if it was due to a feud between an overindulged child and a megalomaniacal father. The real victims of the whole ordeal were those who had died and those who might still die from this new retroviral disease.

Once they had crossed the George Washington Bridge to Manhattan, David exited onto the West Side Highway, heading south.

"You seem to know where you are going," Jack commented. He hadn't given David the address.

"I've been living in the city for five years," David said. "I know my way around. And I know you live at Sixty-three West 106th Street. Kang-Dae sent me a copy of the dossier my father had ordered on you."

With some difficulty, Jack suppressed his knee-jerk irritation at the violation of his personal space that Wei Zhao's investigation represented, but the thought reminded him of the bizarre shooting incident the night before. He mentioned it to David and then questioned, "Is that something you know anything at all about?"

"I heard it was a close call," David said, suggesting he knew a great deal more than that.

"How so?" Jack asked, but it seemed as if his worst fears were being confirmed. If it was a close call, then Jack had been involved.

"Let me put it this way," David said. "Our group became aware of a possible plot to have you taken care of. We weren't entirely certain what that meant, so we decided it best to provide you with protection from a possible assassination attempt if that is what it meant. We were committed to not let anything to happen to you. We felt strongly that you were our best hope that my father and his minions wouldn't be able to sweep the current problems with Carol Stewart under the carpet. Unfortunately, it turned out that we were right, and it was a good thing we had some people there."

"I see," Jack said, trying to maintain his composure. It was now obvious he had come within a hairsbreadth of being shot.

"Come what may, my father fully intends to dominate what is going to turn out to be an extraordinarily lucrative porcine transplant business," David continued. "In that light, it might be wise for you to look to your own security over the next few days. Our group can continue to help, but realistically speaking, we are amateurs in comparison with what my father and his team are capable of marshaling. He's motivated. From his point of view, he thinks the societal good that will result in terms of lives saved and quality of life improved justifies everything he is doing."

A chill passed down Jack's spine and his pulse quickened as he began to truly contemplate the extent of the risks he had been so blithely assuming. He hadn't appreciated the extent that his actions and behavior had been propelled by a combination of his own inner demons and stresses both personal and domestic.

David turned off the West Side Highway at 96th Street. They rode in silence all the way to Central Park West and then onto 106th Street. Only when Jack's brownstone was in sight did Jack begin to truly relax.

David pulled over to the curb. Jack reached for the door handle, feeling extraordinarily lucky. He opened the door, got out, but then leaned back inside.

"I want to thank you for rescuing me," Jack said. "It truly was a rescue. I was in a hell of a lot more danger than I was willing to acknowledge. Thank you."

"You are welcome," David said. "And I want to thank you for your perseverance, as I think it will prove to be key in helping us thwart my father's exit from China."

"If that happens, it will be inadvertent," Jack admitted. "All my activities were in response to a combination of my own needs and a desire to speak for the dead, meaning Carol Stewart. That's what we forensic pathologists do."

"I understand," David said.

"I have one specific request," Jack said. "Would you personally see to it that the CDC gets the rapid test and the cure for the specific gamma-retrovirus first thing in the morning? I want that mini-pandemic to be a thing of the past."

"I will see to it personally," David promised.

Jack reached into the car and shook hands with the youthful Ph.D. student. "I hope your dreams come true in your life in China," he said, "and it all turns out as you hope."

"Thank you," David said. "Be safe!"

Jack closed the car door and waved as David laid a small strip of rubber on the pavement as a final statement. Jack watched the car's taillights quickly diminish in size and intensity before the car turned on Columbus Avenue and disappeared from sight. For a moment Jack stayed where he was, thinking about all that David had said. The main thing that Jack took from it all was that China was undoubtedly going to play a major role in his children's lives.

Turing toward his building and raising his eyes, Jack looked up at the façade. He was glad to see the warm, incandescent light streaming out of the window in the study on the fifth floor. It meant that Laurie was most likely working, and the image filled him with a renewed sense of appreciation and love.

THURSDAY, 10:25 P.M.

With a powerful sense of fatigue and an even stronger sense that he was lucky to be alive, Jack started up the stairs in his building. Still hearing David's warnings echoing in his ears, he seriously considered calling Detective Lou Soldano the moment he got in the apartment to find out if it might be possible to get a police detail to guard his house and family. Yet, as he rounded the first landing and started up the second flight, his mind switched to the idea of calling Warren. Jack had had the opportunity to see Warren and his boys in action on multiple occasions, and in terms of guarding the neighborhood and just knowing what was going on, no one could come close. By the time Jack got to the door to his apartment, he'd made up his mind. It was going to be Warren, not Lou, that he would count on.

Once he had his key out, Jack paused to buck up his courage. He expected Laurie to be rightfully annoyed with him for multiple reasons, including not having contacted her all day. If the tables had been reversed, he knew he would have been seeing red. Feeling appropriately penitent, he opened the door.

The first thing he noticed was a wonderful sense of calmness. There was no noise, and in particular there was no sound of TV. That had to mean that the in-laws were most likely in bed. Jack glanced over at the guestroom door. It was closed, and there was no line of light beneath it. He looked at Caitlin's door. It, too, was closed, but hers had a line of light, so she was obviously still awake. But since she was in her room, the children had to be in bed.

After hanging up his jacket and slipping out of his shoes, Jack climbed the next flight of stairs. As the kitchen and great room progressively came into view through the balustrade, he could see both rooms were vacant. There was only a single table lamp burning next to the couch. He'd not seen his home quite so peaceful in the evening for weeks. Before Sheldon had shown up, Dorothy would have the great room television on until all hours, sometimes watching *The Late Show with Stephen Colbert* and even *The Late Late Show with James Corden*.

In his stocking feet and as silent as a cat, Jack walked down the hall toward the study. The door was open, and a bit of light spilled out into the corridor. Both the children's doors were closed. When he got to the open office door, he could see Laurie bent over the desk, poring over construction blueprints. She was facing away from him. So as not to frighten her, he knocked softly on the open door. The ruse worked, as she twisted around calmly, probably expecting to see JJ. When she recognized it was Jack, her expression rapidly changed from relief to irritation.

"Where in heaven's name have you been," she demanded.

"Vacationing in the beautiful Garden State," Jack said, incapable of allowing an opportunity for a bit of sarcasm to pass. It was a reflex response almost beyond his control.

"Let's not make this worse than it already is," Laurie snapped. "Why haven't you called or responded to one of my blizzard of texts? Were you deliberately trying to terrify and antagonize me? What the hell were you thinking?"

"I wasn't doing a lot of thinking, I'm afraid," Jack said. "I was mostly reacting."

"What the hell does that mean?" Laurie said sharply, clearly losing whatever patience she was trying to maintain. "Why the hell didn't you contact me just to say you were okay?"

"All right, try to calm down," Jack said, keeping his tone as soothing as he could. "I'll explain everything."

"I have been worried sick about you," Laurie blurted. "And I've had to deal with that while trying to manage one of the absolutely worst days of my professional life, which you also bear a good deal of responsibility for causing."

"I'm sorry," Jack said, as sincerely as he could.

"Is that all you can say?" Laurie demanded.

"To be truthful, I haven't had one of my better days, either," Jack said.

"And what on earth do you mean you were mostly reacting and not thinking? And why New Jersey? What the hell were you doing in New Jersey all this time?"

"I was revisiting Dover Valley Hospital and GeneRx, and I have to say I have learned some astonishing things."

"It's after ten o'clock at night," Laurie said. "What have you been doing at Dover Valley Hospital until ten o'clock without so much as a call or, God forbid, a single text to say 'I'm still alive'?"

"It would have been difficult to call or text since my phone was confiscated," Jack said.

"Why?" Laurie demanded. "Who took your phone?"

"Listen!" Jack said, trying to sound more in control than he felt. "I'll tell you everything, and believe me, there is a lot to tell. But first I'd like to hear how you have fared here in the city with the flu pandemic false alarm."

"Luckily, things are getting back to a semblance of normal," Laurie said as Jack grabbed his own desk chair, pulled it over to Laurie's desk, and sat down. "The subways are mostly running again," she continued. "The buses are back in service. The airports are functioning relatively normally. The schools are also open—or will be tomorrow. Theaters are open. And the media has been extraordinarily helpful in getting out the message that there is no pandemic flu or any viral outbreak spread by aerosol."

"Thank God," Jack said. "But it is still being reported that there is a kind of mini-pandemic brewing. Correct?"

"Absolutely," Laurie said. "The media has made it clear that although most of the deaths have been here in the New York metropolitan area, there have also been similar deaths in London, Rome, Los Angeles, and San Francisco."

"I hadn't heard it's also popped up in California," Jack said. "Good lord, I don't know whether to be impressed or appalled. Considering the fluidity of the youth culture of today, I feel like a stodgy prude."

"There was a death in each of those California cities," Laurie said. "And I have to give the media credit for getting the general public to understand that the NYC subway played absolutely no role whatsoever."

"That's appropriate," Jack said. "Associating the outbreak with the subway as if it had something to do with its cause is an example of journalism at its worst."

"It's a tabloid tactic," Laurie said. "People harbor an atavistic fear of subways, like basements. Making the association probably sold more papers, which ultimately was the goal."

"Whatever," Jack scoffed. "It was irresponsible and certainly contributed to the panic, considering how many people rely on the subway."

"The regular media made up for tabloid irresponsibility," Laurie said. "They have gone out of their way to make it absolutely clear that the disease spreads by body fluids like HIV and not by the respiratory route. The initial fear that it was a rapidly fatal respiratory disease is what made this disastrous false alarm as bad as it was. All day today, while we have been struggling to control the situation, all of us, from the mayor on down, have marveled that no one seems to have anticipated this kind of false alarm could have happened. Even that bogus incoming-missile alert that happened in Hawaii in January 2018 didn't make anyone realize in retrospect that all the planning, drills, and exercises directed at the feared reoccurrence of a 1918 Spanish flu pandemic would have set the city up for a false alarm of this magnitude. The expense that this has caused is beyond belief, especially when the losses that businesses sustained are factored in."

"Has any solution been proposed?" Jack asked.

"Not specifically," Laurie said. "But in general, it is recognized that there has to be some sort of failsafe mechanism in place so this doesn't happen again. We can't have a single watch commander in the city's Emergency Operations Center sitting in front of a switch capable of unleashing the whole shebang."

"What about my administrative leave?" Jack asked. "Did that come up again?"

"No, and I didn't try," Laurie said. "Nor do I plan to, at least not for a few days. This has been a serious debacle and heads are going to roll, and it could be mine. Both the mayor and even the Commissioner of Health are looking at me. Particularly, the mayor sorely needs a scapegoat even bigger than you."

"I'm sorry," Jack said with true sincerity. "I've certainly learned my lesson about loose talk."

"I should hope so," Laurie said. "Anyway, I'm glad you're home."

"Thank you," Jack said. "What about the CDC? Did they show up even though it was a false alarm and not a flu-like respiratory problem?"

"They did for sure," Laurie said. "And they are centering their attention on the real outbreak. But tell me! Have you had anything to eat?"

"I haven't," Jack admitted.

"Are you hungry?"

"I should eat something, I suppose," Jack said.

"Caitlin made a pasta tonight," Laurie said. "There is some left over. Are you interested?"

"Sure," Jack said.

Together they walked out of the study and down the hall to the kitchen. While Laurie got the pasta out of the refrigerator and put it into the microwave, Jack sat at the countertop. He used her mobile to place a quick call to Warren.

"I have to make this very short," Jack said when he got Warren on the line. "I just got home after a harrowing day. The problem is that I'll be needing some serious protection for me and my family from a kind of Chinese Mafia. What happened last night out in the street wasn't an accident. The person who was shot was gunning for me. I'll call back later to give you the full story, but first I have to tell the story to Laurie. Can you supply the protection? It has to start now."

"I suppose," Warren said. "But I'm sure as shit going to need to hear why."

"I promise I'll give you all the details a bit later," Jack said before he disconnected.

"What was that about?" Laurie asked with concern. She had paused with her hand on the microwave door when she'd heard what Jack had said. "Why do we need protection?"

"I'll explain it all in a minute, as it needs a bit of background," Jack said. He put Laurie's phone down on the countertop. "First tell me what the CDC has done." He reasoned there was a grace period before the bad guys found out he'd managed to fly the coop and might have managed to get home.

Laurie eyed Jack for a moment, unsure if she were willing to let the protection issue wait. Jack assured her again he'd tell her everything but wanted to know what the CDC did.

"They did a lot, and I give them full credit for taking total command," Laurie said. As she spoke she got the pasta out of the microwave and put it in front of Jack. "They are incredibly organized and efficient. A full team arrived here this morning from Atlanta, headed by several Epidemic Intelligence Service Officers, and went to work immediately. They are all really incredible. Already they have made significant headway identifying all the possible contacts here in New York City. And two additional teams went out to the West Coast to do the same thing. And with their sister organization in Solna, Sweden, the European Centre for Disease Prevention and Control, the same thing was accomplished in London and Rome."

"Has the CDC identified the virus yet?" Jack asked. "Or has the Public Health Laboratory here in the city?"

"I don't believe so," Laurie said, "but I understand they think that they are on the brink."

"I already know what the virus is," Jack said. "So we can give them an important leg up. It's a type of gammaretrovirus B that has the ability to infect human cells."

Laurie's jaw went slack and slowly dropped open as she stared at Jack in disbelief. "How on earth do you know what kind of virus it is?" she questioned.

"My Jersey Boys told me," Jack said. "Kidding aside, researchers out at GeneRx in Dover, New Jersey, were able to identify the virus rather quickly because they had an idea what it was. And what's more, thanks to CRISPR/CAS9 and an entire team of molecular biologists working around the clock, they already have devised a rapid test to diagnosis it, as well as a cure to get rid of it. So we'll be able to give that to the CDC as well, which should go a long way to improving your standing vis-à-vis the mayor and the Commissioner of Health."

"Good Lord! It very well might," Laurie said. "A diagnostic test and a therapy! And so quickly. That's terrific! That will totally solve the outbreak problem. I've heard people extol the promise of CRISPR/CAS9, but this sounds extraordinary."

"As a gene-editing tool, there is no doubt that CRISPR/CAS9 is loaded with promise," Jack said. "Yet peril exists as well. In this instance it's rather fitting that CRISPR/CAS9 will be solving this outbreak, because it also caused it."

"You're talking in circles," Laurie said. "How on earth did CRISPR/CAS9 cause a fatal mini-pandemic of a heretofore innocuous retrovirus?"

"To answer your question, I need to tell you exactly what happened to me today, and, at the same time, I'll be able to explain why you, as the chief medical examiner, are going to be calling the Office of Criminal Investigations at the FDA in the morning. But first I have a confession I need to make."

"What kind of confession?"

"I'm afraid I have been selfish of late. Emma's tentative diagnosis really threw me into an egocentric tailspin. I understand that now. While trying to cope, I haven't been supportive of you and the stresses that you've been under, between being the new chief and your own struggles with Emma's situation. I'm truly sorry, and I'll try to be more understanding and helpful. I'm amazed you have the patience to deal with the politics while running the whole OCME. I'm really proud that you have been able to do it. I know I couldn't. No way."

Laurie blinked away a few threatening tears and took a deep breath. In her mind, Jack knew, she'd been an overly emotional type since her preteen years. "Thank you," she managed to say as she struggled to get herself under control in response to Jack's mini-confession. She had always considered her emotional lability as a handicap, especially as a professional. "It has been stressful for me for sure on all fronts, but I'm committed to do the best I can. Your support is enormously important to me."

"Well, I promise you will have it a hundred percent."

"I've been thinking, too," Laurie said. "And despite everything that happened today and maybe because of it, I found the nerve to tell my parents when I got home tonight that I thought it would be best if they returned to their apartment tomorrow. To my absolute surprise they took it in stride."

With some effort, Jack refrained from cheering aloud. Instead he said, "Thank you. I know that took guts, but it will be best for everyone. And thank you for putting up with me. I'm lucky to have found you. We might have our disagreements, but when push comes to shove, we really are soul mates." And while in his head he was doing cartwheels of joy, Laurie was none the wiser as he pulled her into his arms.

ACKNOWLEDGMENTS

I would like to acknowledge Dr. William Hurlbut, an adjunct professor of neurobiology at the Stanford Medical School in Stanford, California. Dr. Hurlbut was key in getting me invited to a conference at the University of California, Berkeley, to discuss the social dimensions of CRISPR. Participation in the conference opened my eyes to the promise of the gene-editing technology and to its perils, and was the origin of *Pandemic*.

ANNOTATED BIBLIOGRAPHY

Doudna, Jennifer A., and Samuel H. Sternberg. *A Crack in Creation: Gene Editing and the Unthinkable Power to Control Evolution.* New York: Houghton Mifflin Harcourt, 2017. In contrast to most books dealing with CRISPR/CAS9, this one is written for the general audience and is narrative in style and therefore highly understandable to those readers not conversant in the details of modern molecular genetics. It also deals equally with the promise and the perils of this new, powerful technology. I highly recommend reading the book, as CRISPR will undoubtedly affect all of us.